Copyright © **2021** by **Livia Halteh**

All rights reserved. No part of this text ı
downloaded, decompiled, reverse-engineered, or stored in, or introduced
into any information storage and retrieval system, in any form or by any
means, whether electronic or mechanical, now known, hereinafter
invented, without express written permission of the publisher. For
permission requests, write to the publisher, addressed "Attention:
Permissions Coordinator," at the address below.

Typewriter Pub, an imprint of Blvnp Incorporated
A Nevada Corporation
1887 Whitney Mesa DR #2002
Henderson, NV 89014
www.typewriterpub.com/info@typewriterpub.com

ISBN: 978-1-64434-165-0

DISCLAIMER

This book is a work of fiction. The characters, incidents, and dialogue are
drawn from the author's imagination and are not to be construed as real.
While references might be made to actual historical events or existing
locations, the names, characters, places, and incidents are either products
of the author's imagination or are used fictitiously, and any resemblance to
actual persons living or dead, business establishments, events or locales is
entirely coincidental.

CAFFEINE

LIVIA HALTEH

type
writer
pub

For my Mum, Dad, and Holly

Trigger Warning:
The following story contains profanities.
Reader discretion is advised.

PART ONE

CHAPTER ONE
Café Latte

"Morning, Aspen. Your usual?"

My tired eyes drifted up to the perky bartender, Vivienne. Her black hair was tied into a high ponytail as her pale fingers rested above the cash register. I gave a weary smile in return.

"You know me too well."

She flashed her pearly teeth at me, typing in the order and accepting my money, then returning my exact change. I made my drowsy way towards an empty table. While Café de Fleur was a gorgeous little café that made the best soy lattes in town, it wasn't the most popular, so finding a table was easy for me.

As I took my seat, I couldn't help but let my eyes drift over to the table beside me, hidden in the very furthest corner of the café. Isaac Hensick sat alone at his usual table, his long tanned fingers slid a graphite pencil across a small sketchpad, about the size of his palm, hidden from my sight.

Beside his muscular arm sat an untouched cup. His soft green eyes fluttered across the page, one step ahead of his hand as he marked the paper with his pencil.

Isaac is a classmate of mine, although he was barely seen in class. To be completely honest, my morning visits to the café were the most I had seen of him all day. He was a popular boy, well-liked—if not loved—across the entire school, but he was definitely not the studious type.

Every morning for the past two years he'd sit on that chair, too focused on his drawings to notice me, and too absorbed in his own world to even sip the coffee he always ordered.

Black coffee, three sugars.

"You're staring again, Aspen." Vivienne's booming voice woke me from my thoughts. "Here's your latte."

I looked up to see Vivienne in front of me, her arms extended with a takeout coffee cup in one hand and a small brown bag containing my usual biscotti in the other.

I flashed an embarrassed smile, taking my order from her hand.

"Thanks Viv," I mumbled gratefully, taking a long sip from my coffee. Almost instantly, my pounding headache was relieved. I let out a sigh in relief as the burning coffee slid down my throat and scalded my tongue.

I grinned up at Vivienne and she sent me a knowing smile.

"Have a good day at school," she said before returning to her counter, busying herself by tidying up the cake display.

"You take care," I replied, my eyes subconsciously moving back to Isaac.

He was in my French class, meaning he'd have to leave now to get there before the bell, but he made no effort to move from his seat. Instead, he stayed occupied with whatever he was drawing. His coffee remained untouched beside his scribbling hand, the steam long gone.

Turning away from him, I opened the door to exit the café and make my way to school. He could miss class as much as he wanted to, but I was going to turn up on time.

As I began my walk to school, I watched the people on the street with familiar faces of neighbors and classmates who probably didn't even know of my existence.

I guess I was what you'd call a wallflower. I was never involved with any school dramas or the subject of the grade's daily gossip. It's not like I minded it, though. It was always fun to observe, to not get caught up in all the drama, even if it made my life completely uneventful.

"Aspen, Aspen!"

At least I had my friends.

I turned to see my best friend Riley bounding through the hallway to reach me at my locker, her little blonde ponytail flying around the back of her head. For a such tiny person, she was always filled with nothing but energy, the exact opposite of me.

We've been friends since the fourth grade, when she stabbed Billy Johnson's hand with a pencil after he spent all lunch pestering me. She received a week's suspension and was forced to begrudgingly write an apology letter to Billy and his family. Ever since then, she was my closest and oldest friend.

"Good morning, Riley." I sighed, closing my locker and turning towards her with an exhausted, lopsided grin.

"Aspen, guess what!" she squealed, not even pausing for me to guess. "Arthur Andrews got a haircut!"

My grin turned into a sarcastic smile.

"Great."

"I know right!"

I chuckled at my best friend before turning to the sudden sound of a horde of teenage girls's squeals.

What do you know, Arthur Andrews really did get a haircut. Riley let out a sigh of admiration, leaning against my shoulder with a dreamy grin.

Her eyes followed Arthur Andrews in all his muscular, tanned glory; his cropped brown waves sitting neatly atop his head. He was the soccer team's captain, and Riley had been crushing on him for months.

"He's so cute. I'd love to go out with him."

I snorted at her, shoving her off my shoulder. "You and a hundred other girls."

"I can dream!"

A laugh spurt from my lips when a hand gently tapped my back. Turning, my eyes met with our other best friend, William.

William was a lanky boy with black hair that fell just above his brown eyes. We had become friends in our first year of high school, when Riley had dragged him out of his introverted bubble to sit with us at lunch.

"Aspen." He inhaled hard. He reached a thin arm out to loop around my shoulders.

"Ew, you're sweating!" I exclaimed, shoving his hand away as he panted frantically.

"I had to run for the bus," he explained, leaning against the lockers as he struggled to catch his breath. His face was all red, and a bead of sweat traced its way down from his forehead. He wiped it off, still wheezing.

"Yeesh, how far did you run for it?" Riley joked, nudging me with an amused look.

He gulped air down hungrily, his cheeks still flaming red.

"Well, I missed the bus," he continued, out of breath. "So I had to walk to school."

We stared at him in silence as I took a sip of my coffee. His story itself was tiring me out and I was already on the verge of collapsing from exhaustion. It had been a long week of minimal sleep, as most could probably tell from the purple bags lining my bloodshot eyes.

"But I saw Mitch on the way," William paused to turn to me, "that's my mom's dag of a boyfriend." He faced Riley again to continue, "So I went the long way behind Picasso's and since it's so long I had to run."

I stifled a giggle with a final sip of my coffee. I wrinkled my nose at the taste—it already turned cold from the short walk to school.

"You're an idiot," Riley scoffed, rolling her eyes at William. "You know, you're going to have to speak to him *sometime*."

"Over my dead body!" William spat, causing Riley and I to laugh in unison.

"William," I began, resting a hand on his arm. "It's not so bad. Give him a chance. I refused to talk to Sabrina's boyfriend for half a year, and now they're planning on getting engaged."

William's face contorted into an expression of horror.

"If my mother marries that buffoon . . ." He took a sharp breath through his nose. "I'm moving to Canada."

Riley found this hilarious, evident through her loud, high-pitched laugh. She squealed in short giggles, slapping William on his back. He fell forward, his lanky body no match for Riley's enthusiasm.

William smiled, clearly proud he had been able to make Riley laugh so hard, and I rolled my eyes at the pair. The warning bell soon rang throughout the hallway, alerting us to start making our way to our classes.

"I'm going to go work on that runaway plan," William muttered, turning to follow the trail of students trudging to their classrooms. "See you at lunch?"

I nodded, and Riley started walking with me towards our French class. William had chosen to take Spanish this year, claiming girls loved a Spanish speaking man which earned the silent treatment from Riley for a week for "betraying our friendship."

I took a step in the opposite direction, my shoes squeaking against the floor and causing her to pause in her tracks.

"I'll meet you there," I said to Riley, holding up my empty coffee cup.

She sent me a curt nod, turning to walk towards our class alone as I headed towards a nearby bin.

Before I knew it, the hallways were cleared, with me being the only person left as I made my way towards the closest rubbish bin. I quickly tossed the empty cardboard cup into the trash can before making my way back to Riley before Mrs. Dubois arrived.

My legs felt heavy as I dragged myself across the hallway. The sound of my shoes squeaking against the linoleum rang through my ears, contributing to the throbbing headache that had returned just behind my eyes.

I pressed my eyes shut, wishing I had gotten a second coffee to get me through first period. My body ached with fatigue, and my arms felt heavy by my side.

Six hours to go.

The sound of running footsteps snapped me out of my self-pitying daze. I peeled my eyes open a second too late when I collided with a sudden well-clothed wall, causing me to shout and trip backwards. Before I could fall, an arm snaked around my back to hold me back from the impact.

I squinted my eyes open, blinking through the confusion the collision caused, only to see the dazzling green eyes of none other than Isaac Hensick, who was studying my face with concern.

His hand gripped my waist tightly, his hair falling in messy locks over his forehead as he leaned forward to hold me. His brow furrowed as he watched me.

"Are you okay?" he asked, his voice raspy.

I nodded, speechless, stumbling out of his arms and on to my own two feet. His eyes sent shivers down my spine, preventing me from looking away. I felt locked, frozen in place, and quickly forgot about my fatigue and the pain coursing through my head.

How did he get to school so fast?

His perfectly pink lips parted once more, letting out that gorgeously raspy voice that I had only heard from a distance in Café de Fleur. His cheeks imprinted with those famous dimples as he spoke.

"Do I know you?"

My heart fluttered from nervousness. I never thought I'd see him this close before. I watched with fear as he narrowed his eyes, scanning my face, a hint of familiarity and confusion lingering behind them.

7

He was even more gorgeous up close.

Up close, I could see the brown lining in his eyes, blending with the green as it glittered beneath the fluorescents. I could also see the grooves of his dimples in the corners of his grin.

Silence settled between us. I swallowed thickly, my chest swelling with anxiety as I realised I had left an awkwardly long pause since he asked the question.

My throat felt tight and, unable to speak, I shook my head wildly, causing him to frown and wrinkle his brow at me. It felt so strange seeing him up close rather than our usual encounters at the café, if they could even be called that.

"Are you sure? I swear I've seen you before. Are you new here?"

I chewed on my bottom lip anxiously, shaking my head once more and clearing my throat.

How could he not recognise me? Despite being a wallflower, I expected him to at least be aware of my existence from the English class we share. Or the French class; or the art class; or literally from just walking around the same school for the past four years.

"No, I'm sure," I squeaked out, desperate for this awkward encounter to end and my heart to stop pounding so hard.

I clenched my fists, my nails biting into the skin of my palms.

He opened his mouth, ready to speak, when the final bell sounded. My heart began to race as I took the chance to escape.

"Well, that's the bell, better get going!" I rushed, stepping around him as I began to power walk towards my class. "Don't want to be late!"

Mrs. Dubois was way past retirement age, meaning she often turned up to class a little late, but I didn't want to be with Isaac for a moment longer.

I sent a thin-lipped smile and began taking long strides, sliding down the hallway as fast as possible.

His brows rose, and his mouth fell open—ready to speak, but with no words to voice. I kept walking, feeling incredibly awkward and watched as I moved through the halls, rushing to get to my French class nearby.

Nevertheless, I could feel his eyes on my back, tempting me to turn back.

Sending one last glance behind me, I noticed him still staring at me as I sped away from him just as I had suspected.

But I didn't expect his wide eyes to be swimming with one emotion.

Recognition.

CHAPTER TWO
Double Espresso

I stared blankly at the brown looking sludge on the tray in front of me.

If this is what the school considered a "healthy nutritious lunch" then I didn't want to see what they considered unhealthy.

"What's wrong Aspen?"

I turned to look at Riley's concerned face as she gingerly held her own tray of food with one hand, balancing it against her hip. William stood next to her, staring cluelessly between Riley and me.

"Nothing, I'm fine. Why do you ask?"

Riley turned to exchange a look with William, only to receive a confused stare in return. Rolling her eyes at William's usual obliviousness, she gestured to my hand which was grasping my tray, my fingers tapping furiously against it.

"You're tapping," she pointed out. "You only tap when there's something on your mind."

I looked down at my hand, my fingers freezing as I let out a sigh. I woke up with a headache again and struggled to retain any of the information that had been taught over the hours. I pressed my eyes shut, letting out a loud yawn.

"I'm just tired."

"You're always tired."

William released a chuckle at Riley's statement. "It's true. Do you ever get any sleep?"

I let out an airy laugh, turning my head away from them as I began to walk slowly towards the cafeteria exit—the noise of the students chattering only added to my headache. I woke up particularly late this morning after falling asleep just before sunrise, meaning I had to skip my coffee run and go straight to school. I was utterly exhausted.

My friends trailed behind me as we made our way towards the soccer oval. It wasn't a common place for people to sit for lunch, but it was mostly peaceful, despite the constant yelling of students playing soccer during the break. Besides, we sat at the edge, where we could lean against a tall tree and watch all the other students and their drama without being bothered.

I poked at the "beef stroganoff" on my tray for a minute or so, leaning my head against Riley's shoulder, when her voice pulled my attention away from my food.

"Ugh, it's her again."

I spun my head in the direction Riley looked at. Her face was scrunched in disgust as Lacey waltzed through the middle of a soccer game towards Sebastian Georges.

The players shouted complaints as Sebastian ruffled his long blond curls, holding a hand to his hip and the soccer ball under his foot. Hoots and shouts echoed across the field as Lacey came to a stop in the middle of the field, placing one hand on her hip.

"God, I hate her," Riley scoffed, watching as Lacey stared down the sweating soccer player in front of her.

"She's your sister," William spoke with a pointed look.

"*Step*sister," Riley muttered. "*Step.*"

Ignoring my friends, I watched as Lacey put her weight onto one hip, crossing her arms with a deep frown on her face. The group of soccer players surrounded her, whistling as they ogled her bare legs. I rolled my eyes at their idiocy.

11

"Where's Isaac?" Lacey screeched, earning a chorus of snickers from the soccer players surrounding her who were using this couple drama as a source of their own personal entertainment. "He didn't call me last night. Where is he?"

Sebastian tilted his head, smirking at his giggling friends. "Try his locker," he said smoothly. "Isaac forgot his phone there last night, maybe that's why."

Lacey stood quietly, pondering before breaking out into a wide smile.

"Thank you so much!" Lacey cried. "I knew he wouldn't forget to call me."

She squeezed Sebastian into a tight hug before turning and sprinting away from the oval towards the main school building. When she was out of sight, Sebastian spun to face his friends and let out a loud snort, earning high fives and slaps on the back.

I turned to catch William rolling his eyes, each of us knowing Isaac wouldn't be at his locker and this confrontation would be repeated again tomorrow.

"No offense, Riles, but your *step*sister is an idiot," William said, tapping his fingers against his knee as he sat cross-legged against the tree.

"Seriously, I've memorised that conversation by heart," I agreed, letting out a sigh and shaking my head. "I wish he'd just call her."

William and Riley let out a bitter laugh, nodding in agreement as I turned my head back to face the oval. They had restarted the game. I bit into my brown sludge, squeezing my eyes shut at the tangy taste and rough texture.

Suddenly, the sludge ended up on my face.

My arms flew up, my eyes widening in surprise as my tray flipped from being hit by a stray soccer ball. I let out a splutter, wiping the sludge from my face as Riley began to scream her head off at Sebastian Georges and his friends. Warm sludge dripped from my hair in chunks, dripping down my forehead and onto my top.

My heart stuttered to a stop. Oh God. People were staring now.

"YOU COME UP HERE RIGHT NOW AND APOLOGIZE!" Riley screamed, waving her arms.

"Or what?" Sebastian shouted playfully, nudging his friends with a wink.

Riley's face turned red and she released a threatening huff. I let out a breath, wiping the sludge off my clothes and on to the flipped tray. He really shouldn't have said that.

Riley's short legs began to move towards him, her fists clenched as she began to crack her knuckles, a menacing smile on her face. I shared a look of concern with William as he finally got the message and chased after Riley's quick steps. Before she could reach the bottom of the hill, William grabbed Riley under her arms, holding her up and carrying her back to the tree.

Riley swayed in the air, kicking her legs angrily as she fought against William's grip.

My anxiety instantly faded as everyone's attention was diverted to the tiny blonde kicking and swearing at Sebastian Georges and his friends. I picked sludge out of my hair, releasing a breath of relief.

"Let me *go!*" Riley screeched, flipping her ponytail in William's face. "He's asking for it!"

William chuckled. "Not for the sake of that poor boy's safety."

My gaze turned back to the field where Sebastian laughed at Riley's anger, his friends elbowing him and slapping his back as they joined his laughter. I rolled my eyes, turning back to the sludge covering my collarbones and shirt. With a sigh, I continued to wipe it off with napkins, praying the brown wouldn't stain.

At least no one was staring at me anymore. That was a perk of being a wallflower—you blended into the background. Nobody paid attention to me for longer than a minute. And that was how I preferred it.

"Hey!"

My eyes wandered towards Sebastian's voice as he stood at the edge of the oval pointing towards us.

"Pass me the ball, would ya?"

I sighed, standing from my seat and taking a step back. Swinging my foot, I kicked as hard as I could . . . only for the ball to go in the complete opposite direction, coming to a stop behind the old school building.

Great job, Aspen. Embarrass yourself in front of the whole school.

My cheeks began to flare up as I turn and jog towards the ball, the laughter of Sebastian and his friends echoing from behind me. As I reach the building, I hear Riley's voice snap at Sebastian, stopping the laughter immediately and making me smile.

I had to fight the rising nausea and the urge to run away and hide forever, feeling everyone's eyes on my back. I just wanted to get this over with and then never speak to any of Sebastian George's friends again.

Slowing my pace, the ball came into view. But I wasn't alone here.

My head turned as my eyes caught the sight of Isaac Hensick leaning against the wall, his eyes closed as his head leaned back, a lit cigarette held to his lips.

Beside him, a couple meters away, sat Arthur Andrews and an Asian girl with long black hair named Chloe Pepper. The pair leaned against the old brick wall, laughing and joking as Arthur traced patterns on her thigh.

The soccer ball sat just inches away from Isaac.

Taking in a deep breath, I began to walk towards the ball. My shoes crunched against the gravel, causing all three of them to turn and face me.

My heart raced as Arthur moved to stand, an angry look on his face. "Who the f*ck said you could come here?"

14

My eyes widened.

"I-I . . . the ball—"

"I did," Isaac interrupted smoothly, stepping away from the wall and facing his friend. "Is that a problem?"

Arthur swallowed, his eyes shifting to the floor. "No. No, sorry about that."

He turned away slowly, taking his seat and talking to Chloe in hushed whispers, sneaking looks at me every few seconds. I let out a shuddering breath, my heart racing at the thought of what they might be saying about me. I swallowed hard, clenching my fists and willing myself to calm down.

"Looking for this?"

When I turned back to Isaac, he had the soccer ball under his arm. He smirked, taking a slow drag from his cigarette. I nodded, my tongue suddenly feeling incredibly thick in my mouth.

He threw the ball to me and I held my hands out to catch it, only to miss it and let it hit me directly in the face, the ball sliding off and rolling back to Isaac's feet.

My cheeks turned red as I staggered back, not only from the impact but from embarrassment as Isaac let out an incredibly loud laugh. How many more times was this damn soccer ball going to hit me in the face today?

"Smooth," Isaac joked as he picked up the ball once more.

I blushed further at this, letting out a sigh. "Sorry."

"What for?" Isaac smiled. "Being so cute?"

My eyes widened. Did he just call me *cute?* My heart practically stopped as my breathing picked up the pace. I squeezed my fists tighter. Oh God, he had to go there.

"Sorry, too far?" Isaac asked.

I nodded furiously, avoiding eye contact with him. He laughed in response, striding towards me and handing the ball to me. I blushed and took it from his hands hurriedly, my fingers barely brushing his hand in the process.

I began to take steps back; the sound of Sebastian's complaining already beginning to sound from the oval. Isaac took another puff, letting a cloud of smoke roll over his lips and down his chin. His eyes casually scanned my body up and down.

"I knew I recognized you," he said with a grin. "I hear your voice at, uh, Café de Fleur every morning."

I stared at him quietly, not knowing how to respond, as he paused for another drag.

"Soy latte, no sugar and two biscotti." He grinned wildly, proud of the fact he managed to pinpoint where he recognized me from and for remembering my regular order.

What an idiot. A cute idiot, but still an idiot.

I stood in silence, practicing comebacks in my head, unable to think of a witty response, before he spoke again, obviously sensing my mental dilemma.

"So, what happened to you?" His eyes roamed over my body and I could feel my ears turning red beneath his curious stare, a half-smile pulling at the corner of his mouth.

"Excuse me?"

He stepped forward, a hand reaching to my face, causing me to flinch away. He scoffed at me, moving his hand back towards my face and running through my hair. My mind raced. How does one even react to this?

He stepped back with a smirk, presenting a chunk of beef between his fingers. I had never felt more embarrassed in my life.

"I-It— Sebastian kicked the ball, and I, you know, it's like beef stroganoff, and I was just sitting there! And Riley . . . I mean, you know, it hit me and . . ."

Isaac's deep laugh interrupted me, ringing through my heart.

"Hey, you don't need to explain." His eyes continued to scan my face, a smirk ever present, his dimples drilling holes into his cheeks. "It really brings out your eyes."

16

I let out an embarrassing snort at his lame joke, before curling inwards on myself, his eyes not moving from my face. I could just *melt* under his gaze.

Quiet murmuring caught my attention, and my eyes trailed over to Arthur. His face was riddled with confusion, brows furrowed as Chloe whispered into his ear, her eyes trained on us.

"I think your friends are waiting for you over there," I spoke, breaking the short silence between us.

Isaac turned, making eye contact with Arthur who raised his eyebrows questioningly. He turned back to me, but not before I had already made it halfway back to the oval, the ball in my hands.

I glanced back, Isaac's eyes watching me as I rounded the corner, when he suddenly yelled out at me through a boyish smile.

"See ya, *Aspirin!*"

CHAPTER THREE
Short Macchiato

"You spoke with *the* Isaac Hensick? And you ran away?"

Riley's hushed shouts drilled into my ear as we sat beside each other in English class. William sat across the room in his assigned seat, staring at us with a confused expression as he attempted to communicate with us using stupid facial expressions and exaggerated hand gestures.

I nodded silently in reply to Riley, trying to focus on the class work.

"Care to explain why?" Riley whispered. Her face was so scrunched up it looked like it was being sucked into the centre of her head.

"He's *Isaac Hensick*," I replied calmly, emphasising his name. "People like him don't associate themselves with people like me."

As I said his name, my eyes subconsciously drifted to his group of friends. The blond mop of curls belonging to Sebastian Georges sat beside the dark locks of Arthur Andrews—the seat beside them empty. As expected, Isaac didn't turn up in class.

Riley scoffed, shaking her head.

"Well, they clearly do."

"That doesn't help." I paused to scribble down some notes on *Emma* by Jane Austen. "I'm going to end up embarrassing myself."

It was true. Isaac Hensick was one of the *"It Boys"* of the school—the kind of person who only associated themselves with other *"It People"* of the school, like Arthur Andrews, *not* someone like me.

The whole school knew who he was, knew how he skipped school more than what was probably allowed, and how he messed around with any semi-attractive girl that crossed his path. He had a reputation to uphold.

Riley stayed silent for a moment.

"You're right. You will."

I narrowed my eyes at her, quirking a brow at her unusual response. "Thanks."

"But that doesn't mean you should avoid him!" Riley continued, ignoring my bitterness. "Aspen, this is your chance!"

I stared at her, confused at her sudden enthusiasm.

"My chance at what?"

"At a life outside of your bedroom," she whispered back. "Friends beside me and William. Maybe even a boyfriend."

"But I love you and William."

I glanced at William. His eyes narrowed as he twisted his hand in the universal "what" gesture. Ignoring his confusion, I caught him discreetly roll his eyes, making me laugh quietly.

"Not entirely sure William loves me, though," I joked, looking back at William to poke my tongue out at him.

He mimicked me, his tongue poking out between his lips right as Mr. Greene turned to ask him a question. Riley and I stifled our laughter as William got scolded in front of the entire class, his eyes glaring daggers into my head.

"Seriously, Aspen."

I faced Riley again. Her eyes had gone serious, although a gentle smile tugged at the corner of her lips.

"I've seen you watch him in the halls," she continued quietly. "Maybe this is your chance."

I didn't reply, hating the way my heart raced at her words. The way she gave me hope that maybe I could become friends with the boy I'd watched in our local café for months.

He was untouchable, especially by someone like me. I shouldn't get my hopes up.

I turned back to watch William as he pouted, Mr. Greene towering over him. Right as he was able to pull a detention slip from his desk, the lunch bell rang. I immediately grabbed my bag, packing my pens and tucking my chair in.

I strolled out the door, passing a glaring William on the way. Riley walked beside me, pulling a face at him as we left.

"You going to the library today?"

I nodded silently. It was normally this time of the week when my lack of sleep would catch up to me and I'd have to nap my lunch away in the school library. Riley has known me for so long, she knew my routine by now—my small telltale signs that the sleep deprivation had caught up with me.

It was one of the reasons I loved her so much. One of the reasons I liked to stick with my little group of friends instead of branching out. I didn't have to worry about my anxiety or appear weird to them. They understood me and accepted me for who I was.

"Okay, see you at history then." Riley grinned, back to her usual, eccentric self. She glimpsed at the class we just walked out of. "I'd better go see how William's doing after that."

I laughed. "Tell him I love him!"

She began to stroll back to the classroom, giggling as she walked. "Will do!"

I was at my locker in a flash, dumping my books inside before making my way towards the library with a yawn. I spent a lot of my lunchtimes napping in the library. It had become a sort of tradition for me to use the time to catch up on sleep, really.

It wasn't that I didn't enjoy the company of my friends—the library was just the most perfect napping area in the school, and I was the definition of tired.

I found it incredibly hard to sleep at night. My thoughts seemed to overwhelm me, not to mention that insomnia was a side effect of my medication. My mind would be flooded with thoughts; thoughts about the day, thoughts about the next day, worries about what I had said wrong, worries about what I might do wrong . . .

The only time I found myself able to sleep was when the fatigue hit me so hard, it overwhelmed any other factors stopping me from getting any shut eye.

And that was today.

As I stepped into the library, the warmth immediately enveloped me.

It was an ancient looking library. Creaky wooden floors covered in mysteriously stained rugs, shelves upon shelves of dusty old books that haven't been borrowed in what seemed like decades. Mismatched tables made from wood and steel were scattered around the library—a half-assed attempt at modernizing it by the principal before he inevitably gave up.

Not many people came to the library, especially at lunchtime. The room was so silent, the low buzz of the heater could be heard. It was comforting to me and, since the only teacher in the library was a seventy-year-old woman too busy reading to supervise; it was the perfect place for a quick nap between classes.

I slipped through the aisles of books around me, making my way towards my usual sleeping spot. It sat on an extended windowsill covered with pillows in the back corner of the library in a nonfiction section about reptiles.

It was a quiet nook in the corner of the quiet library—a corner that barely anyone roamed in compared to all the other corners of the library, or even the school. It was my private little haven.

"Ah, Aspirin!"

I stopped in my tracks as I reach my windowsill to see Isaac Hensick standing in my way, a book about blue-tongue lizards in his hand.

How did he even find this spot? Was he just coincidentally looking for reptile books?

I narrowed my eyes at him.

His hair laid messy against his forehead and his shirt was terribly wrinkled, diverging from his usual combed hair and ironed clothes. He must've had a bad night. Or a hangover. Maybe both.

"Aspirin?" I wondered out loud.

"Isn't that your name?"

I froze, not sure whether to laugh or to get angry. By the furrow in his brow, it was clear he wasn't joking. I let out a breath. "My name's Aspen."

"That's what I said." He stepped closer, shutting his book, a smirk appearing on his face. "Aspirin."

I bit my tongue, a blush creeping onto my cheeks. *Was he joking?* I suddenly wasn't so sure. His eyes pierced into mine, a smirk gently playing on his lips. I bit my cheek, unsure how to react to this whole situation. Isaac's voice saved me from my lack of words.

"What are you doing here?" he asked after a pause.

"I'm sleeping." I nodded nervously towards my windowsill, feeling jittery beneath his gaze.

Isaac's smirk grew into a toothy smile, his dimples appearing against his tanned cheeks. His eyes lit up with delight, and he stepped even closer, his voice dropping to a slick murmur.

"I can help with that."

My heart skipped a beat and my breath hitched somewhere in my throat. I tried to play it cool.

"I don't need anyone to tuck me in," I said smoothly, running a hand through my hair with a wavering smirk.

He didn't laugh. I shifted uncomfortably.

"I was joking," I clarified.

22

"Oh, so you do need someone to tuck you in?"

My cheeks flared up in embarrassment. I cringed at his booming voice, holding a finger to my lips and scanning the library in fear that someone may have heard us. His eyes flicked to my wrinkled brow and his lips stretched in a delicious smirk. He stepped closer.

"Oh, sorry." Isaac grinned cheekily, his voice growing louder. "Am I being too loud?"

My eyes widened, predicting what he was about to do. I turned on my heel, planning to quickly make my way out of the library before he further embarrassed me, but I was too late.

"What's wrong Aspirin? I thought we were going to sleep togeth—"

My hand was over his mouth before he could finish half-screaming his sentence.

"Was that really necessary?" I hissed in a whisper, my cheeks like fire.

My gaze darted across the library as I glanced through shelves, praying nobody heard us.

His eyes remained unmoving from my face. I could feel his smirk beneath the skin of my palm when suddenly it was accompanied with something wet and slimy. I tore my hand away from him.

"You licked me!" I screeched before covering my own mouth with my other hand, remembering I was in a library.

"Get used to it." Isaac winked, his lips shining and his eyes swimming with mischief.

My jaw dropped in shock. This boy, this insanely cute boy who couldn't even remember my name, was flirting with me.

I staggered backwards, my cheeks and ears turning red from embarrassment. My heart wouldn't stop battering within my chest.

"I—" My mouth was dry for words. "I've got to go."

I turned, beginning to make my way out of the library with a pout and a slimy hand. I was really looking forward to that nap too.

Suddenly, I felt wide awake, like I had chugged an entire jug of coffee. My heart was pounding in my chest, and every ounce of fatigue had vanished from my body.

My cheeks burned, matching my bloodshot eyes. It felt like I was walking with a sway, my head heavy and my heart still hammering in my chest.

How could one boy look so gorgeous? And how could this gorgeous boy be standing there flirting with me? I fought back a smile at the thought of it. *Flirting with me.* He seemed so different to the dazed boy sketching in the corner of a quiet café every morning; so distracted in his thoughts that his coffee turned cold before he'd even had a sip.

"Aspirin!" I heard Isaac say suddenly.

I stopped in my tracks, only a few feet away from him. I steadied my breathing, grounding myself before turning to glance back at him.

He stood in the same spot as before, holding his book against his chest as he grinned at me playfully. His eyes seemed amused, as if this was all a game for him.

"See you tomorrow."

CHAPTER FOUR
Cappuccino

See you tomorrow.

Those words haunted me for the rest of the day and all today. Isaac Hensick—the Isaac Hensick—intended to see me again today. And I was dreading it.

It wasn't that I didn't like him. I hadn't spent all this time watching him every morning in the café because I didn't like him. It was more that I didn't like myself when I was around him.

I was comfortable with Riley and William. It was like I didn't have to think around them. Everything felt natural. My heart seemed to quiet, my legs stopped jittering, and my mind fell still. I was comfortable with my two best friends, and watching Isaac Hensick from afar in the quiet café on Main Street.

I was comfortable being a wallflower, away from any kind of attention or drama.

I had spent forever curious about him, watching him sketch and drink his cold black coffee and bite his lip in confusion when he became so engrossed in his drawings that the world around him seemed to fade out of his focus. I didn't know how to actually interact with him.

I'd never even considered the idea that this day would come; that he'd actually speak to me, much less recognize me from the café.

I'd always thought I was watching him through a one-way mirror, staring at him from my own little bubble, but could it be possible he had been watching me too?

I almost laughed at the thought. It was impossible. He was always so engrossed in his thoughts and drawings. I have never even seen him speak to Vivienne, just a grunt of thanks whenever she topped up his coffee.

Around Isaac, I was something else. I was awkward and uncomfortable. My mouth turned dry and my heart hammered in my chest. I hated it, and I dreaded seeing him again.

My peaceful life as a wallflower was beginning to crumble.

So far, I haven't seen him at all today. I went to the café early, aiming to get in and out before he arrived. In fact, today was the least I've seen of him compared to other days.

Okay, maybe it was due to my amazing stealth skills, but it felt like I was just delaying the inevitable.

My heart raced as I made my way to my locker after chemistry class.

What was his deal anyway? I kicked a ball to his hangout spot and suddenly I see him everywhere. Was he teasing me? Was he trying to make me look like an idiot, anticipating his appearance all day only to not see him once? Was this his cruel version of revenge?

Maybe I was overthinking it.

"Aspen?"

I blinked, moving my eyes up to my locker to see my best friend's grinning face as she leaned against the locker beside mine. I let out a sigh and began to open my locker, shoving my chemistry books in and pulling out my modern history books.

"Hey Riles." I yawned. "How was . . ."

I paused, internally groaning as I tried to remember what class she told me she had.

"Biology was great, thanks," Riley joked, moving away from the locker. Her gaze fell to my fingers tapping on the door of

26

my locker. "You seem like you have something on your mind. What's up?"

I looked up to see her brow furrowed, eyes flickering between my own in confusion. I let out another sigh. I was probably just making a big deal out of nothing. There really was no reason to tell her what was on my mind.

I blinked my tiredness away, shaking my head, and sent her a sloppy grin to ease her worries.

"Just chemistry homework," I replied, partially telling the truth. "Where's William?"

"Cafeteria. It's pizza day. Got to get some before it runs out and we're stuck with mash." Riley smiled, accepting my excuse and moving the conversation along.

She heaved her bag higher up on her shoulder and nodded towards the cafeteria, her long blonde ponytail whipping the air. "Speaking of which, we'd better hurry too."

I shook my head with a gentle smile. "Not today, I'm headed to the library. Got less sleep than usual."

Riley chuckled. "Party animal."

"You wish."

We both let out a few giggles before Riley turned towards the cafeteria. "See you at history then?"

"Of course." I smiled before turning towards the library.

I began walking, letting out another yawn as I shuffle down the halls.

It was true. I've had the worst sleep in a long time. Paired with my usual nightmares and anxieties, my mind was crowded with Isaac and his sickening green eyes. It bothered me that he was suddenly speaking to me.

It was almost like a premonition of a bad event.

I pushed the heavy wooden doors of the library open, getting hit by a sudden gush of warm air. The smell of old books flooded me as I tread on the rough blue carpet, the wooden boards creaking under my weight. My eyes drifted to the teacher's desk where Mrs. Harvey lifted her withered eyes from her book to me as I sent her a curt nod.

She simply scowled and looked back to her ancient book, tattered at the edges, which caused me to roll my eyes and snake my way through the aisles of books towards my spot.

I read the spines of books on my way through the nonfiction aisles, passing books about Humpback Whales and 100 Facts about Tadpoles as I walked towards the reptile section.

As my window seat came into sight, I stopped in my tracks.

Sitting on the carpet in front of the windowsill I called my nap spot was none other than Isaac Hensick. His figure sat cross-legged, hair looking soft as it fell in short, wavy tufts over his forehead. Gripped within his tanned slender fingers was a slim book about Reptile Habitats.

Upside down.

That would explain the confused look on his face.

I stood ahead of him, speechless, jaw dropped, and eyebrows scrunched.

In my silence, Isaac seemed to notice my presence, raising his eyes and smiling at the sight of me. He closed the book tenderly.

"Ah, Aspirin!" Isaac gushed quietly. "I've been waiting for you."

I blinked, finally registering the situation. This gorgeous assh*le had planned to meet me here today after seeing me in this spot yesterday. He expected me to come back after I had missed my nap. I swallowed my anger and took a deep breath.

"Why are you here?" I asked, clenching my fist to stop my voice from shaking.

He held up the book he had been reading cockily. "I'm learning about reptiles."

I held a hand to my forehead, muttering a string of curse words under my breath. I seriously was not in the mood for this. All the nervousness in my body for him had just been thrown out of my mind, his gorgeous face and "out of my league"-ness being the last thing I was thinking about.

"Can you please—" I paused to suck in a shaky deep breath. "Can you please read that somewhere else?"

Isaac opened the book up again, giving me a slightly amused look, his eyes glistening with mischief and his cheeks dimpling with his arrogant smirk.

"I like this spot."

"Find another spot."

"Make me."

I met his eyes and he sent me a challenging grin. Tension swelled in the air as I swallowed thickly at the undertone of his voice.

I broke eye contact first, releasing a shaky breath.

Desperation washed over my body at his words. It was like the fatigue hit me all at once. I let out a loud sigh. I knew this fatigue wouldn't hit me again tonight; I'd have to spend another sleepless night suck in my thoughts.

A second later, he spoke up again.

"You can still nap here. I won't bother you."

I raise my eyebrows, staying silent as I search his eyes, considering his offer. His gaze remained steady on mine, his eyes hardened, and smirk gone. What was the catch? Why was he being so stubborn for this spot? Couldn't he just move and let me sleep in peace?

"I swear," he spoke, his voice grimly serious as if sensing my hesitance.

I stayed quiet, still staring at him as I weighed the pros and cons of this situation.

Pros: I'd be sleeping next to a super cute boy.

Cons: Well, anyone who's seen me sleeping before would know why this is a con.

"Are you going to stand there all day? Cause lunch is going to be over soon."

My eyes widened. He was right. My chest swelled. I had gotten a combined four hours of sleep over the past two days. I was desperate, and it seemed like the library in the middle of the day was the only place I was able to ever get a bit of continuous shut eye.

I took a step forward, causing Isaac to smile a lopsided, boyish grin.

"Just . . . just don't disturb me," I said finally, the defeat evident in my weary voice.

He nodded, his annoyingly cute smile plastered on his face. His eyes lit up with delight as I crossed my arms and marched towards my cushioned seat.

I curled on top of the windowsill, using my backpack to support my head. Isaac sat quietly at my feet on the coarse carpet, reading about crocodiles with a triumphant smile. I rolled my eyes, attempting to get comfortable—attempting to ignore that the Isaac Hensick was sitting beside me, and was so close that I could feel the heat radiating off of him.

I watched him for a moment, listening to the quiet turning of the page when he'd gotten enough of the Dwarf Crocodile and its taxonomy, until I was sure he was sufficiently distracted. I pursed my lips before closing my eyelids and taking a deep breath.

I was finally going to get some sleep.

I let my mind wander into random thoughts, trying to fall asleep, but something just didn't feel right.

I slowly peeled my eyes open to see Isaac's shining green eyes scanning my tired face, a wide schoolboy smile on his face, his dimples poking holes into his cheeks, and his shining teeth flashing from beneath his plump lips.

My cheeks turned fire-red while Isaac stayed grinning at me, not at all phased that he had been caught watching me sleep.

Or at least trying to sleep.

"And don't watch me while I sleep," I sputtered out, flustered. He flashed me a wink and turned back to his book.

I rolled my eyes, shutting them and attempting to fall asleep once more. I could feel the drowsiness begin to overtake me. Sleep began drawing me in, my mind turning silent and my heartbeat slowing, when I was suddenly brought back to the surface by Isaac's voice.

"Did you know that the Americas are home to more species of salamander than the entire rest of the world combined?"

My eyes flew open, my hand immediately wiping a spot of drool on the corner of my lip.

He smirked at me.

"You're cute when you sleep," he joked, pointing at his mouth to mirror where I had just wiped. "You drool. Did you know?"

I narrowed my eyes at him, embarrassment flooding my body, my cheeks turning a brighter red, creeping up to my ears.

"Don't disturb me," I grumbled through my teeth, closing my eyes once more.

I began to drift off to sleep again, the last image in my mind being the dark-haired boy reading about shingleback lizards sitting at my feet.

A shiver ran down my spine.

"And don't watch me while I sleep!"

He laughed.

Chapter Five
Americano

"Aspirin."

"Aspirin, wake up!"

My eyes slid open, Isaac's tanned face came into my blurred sight. His dark hair fell just over his eyes as he leaned over my face, shaking me gently.

Blinking, I realised exactly what was happening.

His fingers gripped around my arms, rocking me awake. I was vaguely aware of how strong his grip was and how close his face was to mine, his breath fanning over my face, the smell of smoke mingling with coffee.

I groaned, fighting a yawn, before noticing Isaac's smug expression.

I bolted upright, my cheeks bright red and drool covering half of my face. I wiped furiously at my skin, drying the drool with my sleeve and adding to the redness of my face as Isaac grinned at me mischievously.

Beside him sat a small pile of random books about reptiles. He had been reading here the entire time.

"The warning bell rang," he said simply as I swung my legs around to the floor.

"Thanks," I murmured, standing up from my spot and swinging my bag over my shoulder. I swayed slightly, still half asleep and dazed. Although, at this point, I wasn't sure if I was dazed from my nap or Isaac's cavernous dimples.

I walked a few steps, slowly and sluggishly, before noting he didn't walk with me. I spun to face him, only to see Isaac opening another book.

"Aren't you coming?"

He looked up from his book, his hair tumbling over his forehead as he stared at me. "Nah, you go. I'm not in the mood for class."

I nodded curtly, awkwardly staying in my spot as I continued to watch him read. It felt wrong letting him skip class. It almost felt like I had the responsibility to scold him and drag him by the ear to the classroom.

"Are you going go to class or are you just going stand there and stare at me all day?"

My cheeks immediately turned red as I began to stutter out a sentence. "I-I was just—"

"Relax, I'm joking." He smiled softly, before the corner of his lips tugged up in a cheeky smirk. "That is, unless you *want* to stare at me all day."

He flexed an arm at me, making me blush like a fool.

I rolled my eyes at him, my face turning red quickly, the heat rising to my ears. I turned on my heel, ignoring his laughter as I began to walk out of the aisle of books.

"Wait, wait, another joke, I swear!"

I ignored his voice this time, continuing to walk as I hear him hustle behind me. Suddenly, his arm was around my shoulders as we walked through the library.

A blush crept up my neck, but I fought to stare straight ahead and to keep my heart from racing. Thoughts began racing through my mind, but I shut them out, trying to ground myself.

His skin pressed into mine, and his fingers hung beside my face. I could smell his cologne mingling with the scent of coffee that seemed to follow him everywhere. His body clumsily knocked into mine every few steps and I could feel myself blushing furiously.

"So, what do you have now?" he asked cheerfully. We passed Mrs. Harvey at her desk, who simply glared at us, before pushing through the heavy double doors and into the fluorescent hallways.

I squinted against the light, my vision still blurring from my nap.

"English," I muttered, finally shoving his arm off my shoulder. "We both have English."

"You're in my English class?" Isaac asked in confusion, quirking a quizzical brow at me. "Wait, I'm in an English class?"

I stifled a laugh at his stupidity, rolling my eyes as he grinned at me, proud of the reaction he managed to get out of me. His cheeks dimpled with mischief as he watched me, and I felt a blush creep up my neck under his gaze.

It was strange having him watch me like this. Normally, I would watch him sketch in the café, blissfully unaware of my existence. Or maybe he was aware all this time.

As we sped down the hallway, our shoulders knocked into each other with each step, the second bell went off, making us late for our class. My heart skipped a beat. I've never been late to class before. I've never had *detention*!

Isaac didn't notice my wide eyes as I began to pick up my pace, him following behind me.

"Hey, why are you running all of a sudden?" he exclaimed, lengthening his stride to walk alongside me.

"We're late!" I cried, rounding a corner and reaching our classroom.

I pushed the door open, stepping into a quiet classroom where Mr. Greene sat at the front, marking attendance. His wrinkled face contorted into disgust, his lips curling in a spine-chilling grin.

He stood from his seat and walked ever so slowly to meet us at the door. I was a deer caught in headlights, my hands trembling and my heart racing.

"Ah, Miss Haste, Mr. Hensick." Mr. Greene smiled sadistically. "Nice of you to join us."

As I was about to go into my full-blown apology, Mr. Greene held up a finger to shush me.

"Detention. Both of you, today after school," Mr. Greene scolded, wagging a chewed pen at our faces.

"But—"

"No buts, Miss Haste. You were late. Maybe next time you should—" He paused to smile. "—Make more haste."

He snorted a pig-like grunt at his own joke, turning to grab detention slips from the corner of his desk.

I let out a defeated sigh, the feeling of crying began to wash over me. I felt queasy. Not only was I in trouble, I was in trouble in front of the entire class. I could feel the eyes of all the students on me and hear some whispers and snickers echoing from the back.

A lump rose in my throat. I clasped my shaking hands together, digging my nails into the flesh of my palms. I chewed on my lip, trying to ignore the muttering of the students, and the stares of Riley and William. It felt like too much all at once. My mouth quickly grew dry.

Beside me, Isaac threw a glance my way, his expression of nonchalance suddenly hardened as he stepped forward.

"I'm sorry Mr. Greene, but it's completely my fault that Aspirin was late. I was sleeping, and Aspirin took her time to wake me up and alert me that class was starting," Isaac lied smoothly. He set his jaw. "Please, sir, it wasn't her fault, she was only doing the right thing."

My face warmed. *Did he just call me Aspirin in front of the entire class?* I shrunk even further into myself.

Mr. Greene peeked over the set of small glasses perched on his nose. "Is this true, Miss Haste?"

35

I looked over at Isaac who sent me a slight nod and a wink. I blushed and swallowed the lump in my throat. *Was he really willing to take the fall for me?* I opened my mouth, torn between rejecting his lie and accepting his help.

He quirked a brow at my silence, nodding to Mr. Greene, his eyes wide as if telling me to go along with it.

Either way, I was desperate.

"Yes, sir."

Mr. Greene raised his eyebrows, wrinkles appearing on his forehead.

"You're aware that that is against school rules, Mr. Hensick? This will land you a week of afternoon detentions."

Isaac nodded proudly, the smirk wiped from his lips. "I understand, sir."

Mr. Greene turned back to his detention slips, signing one of them and handing it to Isaac. "Very well, take your seats."

Sighing in relief, I hurriedly walked over to my desk beside Riley, who immediately sent me a pointed look. I sat and pulled out my books, glancing at Isaac who sat at the end of the row behind me. His eyes remained trained on me and we made eye contact.

I mouthed a 'thank you' to him with a grateful smile. I couldn't believe he did that for me. He simply winked at me before turning back to his work.

"Did Isaac Hensick just *wink* at you?"

My smile fell at Riley's hushed voice. I bowed my head in a slow nod, avoiding eye contact.

"Care to explain *why?*" Riley whispered. "And why are you suddenly turning up to class late with cute boys? And why did he call you *Aspirin?*"

"It was *one* cute boy," I replied quietly, pulling my books open on my desk. "And it's like he said, I just saw him sleeping and I went to wake him up."

"That's bullsh*t!" Riley shouted, causing the class to turn to her.

I stifled a laugh as she muttered a sorry, allowing the class to return to Mr. Greene's incredibly boring lesson. I turned and made eye contact with Isaac who jokingly shook his head at me in a scolding manner.

William sat in front of him, staring at me with a furrowed eyebrow as he looked between me and Isaac.

I let out a sigh and quietly told Riley what really happened, causing her to reel back, her eyes ready to pop out of her head.

"He totally likes you!" Riley whispered.

"Shut up," I replied. "He's just teasing me. He's probably planning to embarrass me in front of the school just for kicks."

Riley stared at me with a thoughtful look. She pursed her lips and furrowed her brow, tapping her chin with her manicured finger. I rolled my eyes at her with a grin.

Her face broke out into a wide smile once more, her teeth gleaming at me. "Nope, he totally likes you! Oh, gosh!"

I giggled quietly at her exaggerations.

She was clearly joking, right? I've barely spoken to the guy. Besides, he was pretty much the polar opposite of what I looked for in a guy. He smoked, skipped class, would date pretty much every girl in the school, and lied.

But he lied for me.

I shook my head, ignoring my overthinking mind. I just needed to focus on my work for now; but I couldn't help it when my eyes drifted back over to Isaac.

He sat with his face buried in his arm, his back gently rising and falling as slept quietly on his desk.

I've never seen him in English class. It was somewhat comforting watching him at his desk, completely oblivious to the lesson and the trouble he'd get into if Mr. Greene caught him.

Yet he slept peacefully. His hair was messy and fell along his sleeved arm, his face hidden from my view. His book sat open under his arm with a pencil beside it. The paper had no writing on it, only drawings.

Drawings.

He was always drawing, and yet I've never seen any artwork by him. I glanced to the front of the classroom to see Mr. Greene enthralled in a Shakespeare sonnet before turning back to Isaac. Curiosity got the better of me and, before I knew it, I was squinting my eyes and leaning forward, attempting to see what he had drawn.

I made out the vague figure of a person before the bell rang, dismissing class.

How long had I been staring?

Isaac's head suddenly turned, his eyes meeting mine with a sly grin, causing me to turn as red as a tomato. My cheeks burned, all the way up to my ears.

God, how embarrassing. I avoided eye contact as I packed my bag, Riley rushed towards William to tell him the news I had just given her.

I slung my backpack over my shoulder and tucked my chair in before I began to walk towards the door. Isaac was beside me in a blink, looking straight ahead with a stupid smile on his face.

"Don't watch me while I sleep."

CHAPTER SIX
Black Coffee

The next morning, I woke up with a stale taste in my mouth and a killer headache.

My eyes were swollen and bloodshot from my lack of sleep. Dark circles stained the skin beneath my eyes, darker than ever. I let out a groan at the sensation of a massive headache drilling in the side of my head.

Could a day start off any worse?

I trudged through my usual morning routine of brushing my teeth, combing my hair and washing my face before applying a dab of concealer to cover my dark under eyes bruised with fatigue, praying they would become less noticeable after my coffee. I pulled on black jeans and a random shirt from my bedroom floor before walking out of my room, grabbing my school bag on the way.

I slipped into the kitchen, grabbing an oval-shaped pill and popping it into my mouth, washing it down with a glass of water.

My mother lied on the couch, her uniform from her night shift at the diner was still on as she had another shift in just half an hour. Her dark curls spilled over the sofa cushions.

"See you, Mom," I muttered, pressing a peck to her cheek on my way out.

She sent me a half-hearted smile, her tired eyes lighting up at the sight of me.

"Have a good day, baby," she whispered, her voice hoarse. I watched as she pressed her hands to her temple, her fingers rubbing gentle circles, and released a strained sigh.

"Mom," I uttered, pausing beside her. "Just stay home and rest. You look so tired."

She shook her head, her eyes squeezing shut. "No. No, I'm fine. Brina needs some new textbooks and—"

"And she'll pay for them just fine on her own," I paused, watching my mother lounging on the couch, purple bags lining beneath her eyes. "I can pick up some shifts at—"

Her eyes snapped open. "No. You focus on school. I'm the adult here. I've been doing this since your father left, I'll be completely fine. Now go on. You'll be late for school."

I pursed my lips, my mother's gaze unwavering as she stared me in the eye. I knew that look. It was the look she had given Sabrina when she said she'd attend community college. The same look she'd given me when I had tried to give her my coffee money for rent.

She was stubborn and I knew she wasn't going to budge.

So, I relented with a sigh.

Her expression immediately softened, and a small smile graced her chapped lips. She reached an arm out and I stepped forward into a small embrace. Her lips pressed against my hairline.

"I love you," she said.

"I love you more."

"Now go." She whacked my butt playfully and I sprung forward with a laugh. "Get to school, young lady. Or better yet, don't go. Have some fun, Aspen, while you're still young."

She gestured to herself, with a shake of her head and I laughed.

"I have fun at school," I muttered half-truthfully. Riley and William always provided a good laugh. I tried not to think about Isaac at her suggestion, or the skip in my heart when I thought about seeing him today.

40

I cleared my throat. "Besides, you're still young too."

She pulled a face at me and I chuckled before bidding her goodbye and waltzing out the door, clicking it shut behind me.

I shuffle out of the house and down the road towards Alum Creek Public. I was lucky to live close enough to the school to walk, but not close enough to enjoy it.

It was a cool morning. The breeze bit my cheeks as I made my way to Café de Fleur, just a few minutes from the school. My fingers were freezing and numb despite being buried deep in my pockets, and were shielded from the wind. I quickened my pace, my breath condensing in the cold air.

I entered the café with a sigh of relief as I was enveloped in warm air inside, the bell of the door rang to announce my entrance. Smiling at Vivienne, I walk towards the counter, excited for my latte to warm me up and rejuvenate me after a restless night.

I swung my bag off one shoulder, clutching it over my chest as I began to fish for my wallet.

Vivienne grinned at me wildly, her eyes full of smugness.

"So, when did you get a boyfriend?"

I paused to raise an eyebrow at her. "Well, I kissed Johnny Fedrago's cheek in kindergarten."

Vivienne let out a high-pitched laugh before nodding towards the far corner of the cosy café. "That cute boy's been waiting for you with your latte and biscotti."

My eyes widened as I turn, making eye contact with, of freaking course, Isaac Hensick. He offered me a smirk, raising his own cup to me before taking a sip from it. Unlike usual, his sketchpad was closed, his pencil sat beside his saucer.

I turned back to Vivienne who wiggled her eyebrows at me suggestively.

"Shut up," I said briefly before making my way towards Isaac, Vivienne's laughter echoing behind me.

My heart swelled in my chest as I approach Isaac. He looked handsome as usual, his cheekbones chiselled like a Greek

41

god, his dark hair pushed back to reveal his mischievous eyes and dimpled smirk.

"'Sup Aspirin," Isaac greeted as I reached his table. "Fancy seeing you here."

I rolled my eyes, crossing my arms over my racing chest. My fingers dug into my skin as I tried my best to seem nonchalant.

"Well . . ." He gestured to the empty chair in front of my untouched latte, a paper bag filled with biscotti sitting beside it. "Take a seat."

I narrowed my eyes at him, slowly scraping the chair back and sitting down across from him. He watched me as I held my still-hot coffee in my hands, the warmth rushing through my body. I peered up to see him watching me carefully, his eyes narrowed, making me raise an eyebrow in suspicion.

"Is it spiked?"

Isaac let out a dramatic gasp, holding a hand to his chest in shock. "Frankly, I'm offended you'd even suggest that, dear Aspirin."

I rolled my eyes again, sipping my coffee and letting out a delighted moan. Now *that's* what I needed.

I peered over the lip of the cup to see him watch me carefully. Immediately, my face warmed.

"Well, thanks for the coffee." I pushed my chair back, the wood scraping harshly against the tile floor. I gripped the takeaway cup and my school bag tightly. "But I'd better leave now before I'm late."

I stood up only for Isaac's tan fingers to grab my wrist gently as he slightly pulled me back with a faux pout. "Don't leave."

"I'll be late," I muttered, slightly annoyed at this boy, who I have never spoken to a week ago, and his constant pestering.

Besides, he was holding my wrist. He was asking me to *stay*. My heart pounded and I felt nauseous at the idea of making small talk with *Isaac Hensick*.

"Oh, sure, of course. Can't be late to school!" Isaac let out an exaggerated laugh, waving his hands in a condescending mimic of me. He quirked a brow, his cheek dimpling in a smirk. "Seriously, Aspirin, live a little. Sit down."

I paused. He was right. I was always living by the rules. *When was the last time I actually got into some trouble?* My mind drifted to my mother, her constant urging for me to live the life of a regular teenager.

I pursed my lips, putting my coffee and biscotti down as I took my seat again, earning a triumphant smile from Isaac.

I looked down at the table, noticing this was the first time I had seen him actually drink his coffee. His sketchpad was closed, the cover black with his name written in a messy white scrawl on the top corner.

I couldn't help but wonder what's inside.

"So, what's up?" I asked. My throat felt insanely dry, so I took a casual sip of my coffee, pretending my heart wasn't going into cardiac arrest.

Here I was, skipping class in a café with one of the cutest, most popular boys in school, making casual conversation over a free coffee. Riley would scream if she found out.

"Nothing much," Isaac replied. "What about you?"

"Nothing much." I shrugged uncomfortably. An awkward silence ensued, and I sipped my coffee. A second passed. "What about you?"

Isaac raised an eyebrow at me, a smirk playing on his lips.

"Nothing much," he said. "What about you?"

I blinked, not entirely sure what was going on.

"Nothing much . . ." I trailed off. "What about—"

"God, Aspirin," Isaac began laughing loudly, his eyes crinkling. "Is this the first time you've had a conversation with someone? Cause it's not going very well now, is it?"

I pursed my lips at his laughter and averted my eyes.

"No," I murmured quietly. My heart pounded in my chest. I could feel his piercing green eyes staring me down as he chuckled.

Isaac's laughter died down and he took a sip of his coffee, prompting me to do the same. I pushed a strand of my hair back behind my ear and looked around the café. This encounter was turning out to be incredibly awkward for the both of us.

When I turned back to face Isaac, I noticed he was staring at my rather lacking chest.

"Um." I brought his attention back to my face. "My eyes are up here."

He laughed at me, his chest vibrating. "Nice shirt."

My eyes widened as I looked down at my shirt, realising I had pulled on an incredibly stained pyjama shirt featuring the Sesame Street gang on it. My cheeks turned bright red and a lump rose in my throat.

Why didn't anyone say anything? My throat felt strangled, my head beginning to spin.

"Oh my gosh," I whispered, "I can't go to school like this!"

I stood from my seat abruptly, pushing the table and almost spilling our coffee in the process. I reached for my backpack, stumbling around the chair. Isaac quirked a brow at me.

"You're going all the way home to change your top?" Isaac asked, stopping me in my tracks.

"Obviously!" I exclaimed, my mind racing. "I can't show up like this! I'm already late for my first period; I don't want to bring even *more* unwanted attention to me. I'll be a laughingstock!"

I turned to leave only for Isaac to grab my hand once more, pulling me back roughly. I let out a quiet grunt at the sudden pull.

"I think it looks cute." Isaac smiled genuinely, letting go of my arm.

"I doubt anyone else will," I murmured, crossing my arms with a pointed look. "Now, if you'll excuse me, I have to run home now or else I'll miss first period completely."

"You'll miss it either way," Isaac replied, folding his arms.

"I live close," I shot back, my head spinning.

"Oh, yeah? How close?"

I paused, my mouth dry as the realisation hit me. He was right again. Even though my house was within walking distance, by the time I would reach home and back, I was sure to miss first period.

"Well, I can't go like this!" I practically shouted, despair washing over my voice as I threw my arms in the air dejectedly.

I stood there, the lump in my throat growing as I searched for a solution. My heart began to race, and I clutched my chest, suddenly finding it hard to breathe. The room around me began to spin, my palms shaking as I clung to my shirt.

I released a shaky breath and moved to look at Isaac.

He stayed quiet, his eyes soft as he watched me, fully taking in my panic. A second later, he began to take off his leather jacket.

"Here," he said, handing me the jacket.

I stared at it, struggling to speak as the ground shook beneath me. "Excuse me?"

"Here," he nudged it towards me. "To cover your shirt. If you leave for school now, you'll make it for first period, but if you go home, you won't be back until second."

I slowly took the jacket from him, my brow raised in suspicion. My heart began to slow, and I swallowed the lump in my throat, the room beginning to steady. The jacket was still warm in my hands, the leather smooth and dark, contrasting against my pale skin.

"Thanks," I dragged my croaky voice out, still unsure whether to trust him or not. He nodded nonchalantly, taking a sip from his coffee before gesturing me to put it on.

I pulled the jacket over my shoulder, zipping it up to cover my shirt.

The sleeves fell over my hands and the jacket sat too big on me. It smelled of him—coffee mixed with cigarettes and cologne. I inhaled it, the scent somewhat calming.

Tilting my head, I looked up at him to find him smiling down at me. I let out a weak chuckle, waving my hands with the too long sleeves flapping over my fingers.

"It's a bit big."

He laughed with me, grabbing my arm and carefully folding the sleeves for me so that it appeared to be the style of the jacket. I blushed at the kind gesture, the gentleness of his hands as his fingers brushed my wrists.

Surely, he was just being friendly. But the question was, why was he being so friendly to me? I barely knew him.

And his reputation was less than kind. I was a firsthand witness to the girls he played around with, Lacey being the latest subject of his games.

"What's wrong?" Isaac's voice made me realise he had been watching as I stared at his hands. "It seems like there's something on your mind."

I let out a quiet sigh, debating on whether I should voice my thoughts. He let go of my arm and sent me a smile. My heart fluttered, and my arms fell back beside my legs, my face warming.

"I was just wondering . . ." I began slowly before looking up to face him. "Why are you being so kind to me? I barely know you. Hell, I only know your name and your coffee order."

"You know my coffee order?" he cut me off.

My eyes widened, and my cheeks heated up at the realisation of what I had just revealed.

"Well," I stumbled for words. "You know mine."

He grinned cheekily. "Touché."

"Well?" I cleared my throat, my voice faltering with hesitance. "Answer the question."

He turned and took a final sip of his coffee, slinging his bag over his shoulder and collecting his notebook.

"You're . . ." He paused to smile at me, his eyes swimming with an unreadable emotion. "Interesting."

CHAPTER SEVEN
Mocha

Walking around school in Isaac's jacket made me think it would've been better in my Elmo shirt.

It was almost like his jacket was a magnet for attention. All around me, students were whispering and staring.

"Isn't that Hensick's jacket?"

"Why does she have it?"

"Who even is she?"

"Is she new here?"

I held my eyes to the ground, making my way towards my locker quietly, my heart pounding in my chest. I swallowed thickly, willing myself to stay calm despite the muttering mumble of voices that seemed to follow me through the fluorescent corridors.

By the time I reached my locker, Riley and William were already there. After four lessons without them, they were the only people I was looking forward to seeing.

"Hey, Aspen, how was—woah is that—"

I snapped my eyes up to Riley, cutting her off with a newfound fire.

"Yes, it's Isaac's jacket, whatever. Seriously, how are these people even realising its Isaac's? How popular *is* he?"

Riley stared, speechless while William nibbled on an apple, his head in some other place. She raised her brows at me in surprise.

I sighed and opened my locker, pushing my books in before hiking my bag higher on my shoulder and turning to face my friends.

"Sorry," I muttered finally. "I'm just sick of everyone whispering about it everywhere I go. It's just a jacket."

"Just a jacket? It's *Isaac Hensick's* jacket, actually," Riley pointed out. She quirked a knowing brow at me. "That makes it a big deal."

I pursed my lips, annoyed that she was right. Isaac was from a different world. Even his *clothes* were more popular around the school than me. I shook my head at the thought. It didn't matter. We weren't even friends.

I was overthinking it.

"So." Riley's enthusiasm began to return. She bounced on her toes, her blonde ponytail whipping the air behind her. "What happened? How'd you get his jacket?"

I opened my mouth to reply when she let out a loud gasp, her hands flying to her mouth.

"You didn't steal it, did you?"

I blinked, opening my mouth to explain what had happened at the café only for her to cut me off once more, her bright grin growing even wider, stretching over her cheeks. Her eyes glimmered with mischief.

"Oh, Aspen, you're *bad*! I'm finally rubbing off on you! What do you want to do next? Firecrackers in the gym? OH! Steal his," she lowered her voice and wiggled her eyebrows, "*underpants?*"

"Riley!" William shouted, spitting apple everywhere. "That's a great idea!"

"William!" I exclaimed, slapping a hand to my forehead. "God, even you?"

"Hey, what can I say? The boy's attractive." William shrugged.

"True that." Riley grinned, throwing an arm around William's shoulder.

I snorted at the pair, rolling my eyes as we began to make our way outside for lunch.

William's cheeks instantly turned red as Riley clung close to him. I smirked at them, trailing behind. He could fanboy over Isaac all he wanted, but he made it incredibly obvious that his heart belonged to Riley, even if she couldn't see it herself.

Riley chattered obliviously about something Lacey had done over the weekend while William continued to redden, his eyes wide with adoration as he watched Riley ramble. It was adorable.

We hiked around the grassy oval to reach our usual spot under the large shady tree, the breeze cooling our faces. I let out a sigh as I took my seat, unzipping my bag and pulling out the sandwich I had bought earlier from the cafeteria. Riley and William sat ahead of me, gossiping about Arthur Andrew's latest catch.

As they spoke, my eyes drifted past my friends towards the oval where Isaac's friends, Sebastian and Arthur, sat at the edge of the grass—Isaac strangely missing.

I turned to face the old school building where I had run into him the other day. *Would he be there again today?*

Suddenly, a furious looking Lacey ran from behind the old brick wall, tears streaming down her face as she let out cries of anger and loud sobs.

I stared at the building, no one else noticing the drama that had just occurred on the far end of the courtyard. Or maybe they were just ignoring it. *Was this a regular occurrence?*

"Aspen? Where are you going?"

I widened my eyes at William's voice, realising I had stood from my seat and begun walking towards the building. I looked down at the sandwich in my hand and looked back at them.

"Ah, cafeteria," I replied smoothly. "Wrong order."

"Okay." William shrugged, accepting my excuse before turning back to Riley and their little gossip session.

I sighed in relief and continued walking; my friends not even realising I was headed in the opposite direction of the cafeteria. As I reached the building, I took in a deep breath, the smell of cigarette smoke already evident in the air.

As I rounded the corner, Isaac came into view. He sat on the floor, his head leaning against the old brick wall. He wore a weary expression, his eyes closed, and his shoulders sagged in exhaustion. A lit cigarette sat between his lips. He almost looked peaceful.

Sucking in another deep breath, I clenched my fists and built my confidence, before walking over to him and sitting beside him, leaning my back against the wall. The gravel crunched beneath my feet, but Isaac paid no attention to it—probably expecting Lacey or one of his friends.

"You know, smoking is bad for you," I pointed out, alerting him of my presence.

His eyes snapped open and he looked at me in surprise. "Aspirin? What are you doing here?"

"I saw Lacey run out of here, wanted to make sure you were okay." I held up half of my sandwich. "Sandwich?"

He blinked, pausing slightly before saying, "Sure."

I allowed him to take half of the turkey sandwich, unwrapping my own half and taking a small bite out of it. I watched him take a puff of his cigarette, blowing out the smoke as the sandwich lay in his other hand. He reached the cigarette towards me.

"You want?" he asked, gesturing to the cigarette.

My heart raced, and I stumbled for words, "Uh, no. No, thank you. I-I don't like cigarettes."

He nodded slowly, putting out the cigarette on the wall and leaving the butt beside his leg on the floor.

"No, I—uh," I stuttered out. "I didn't mean you had to put it out. I don't mind, I mean—"

"Aspirin." He chuckled quietly, interrupting my rambling. "I'm not putting it out because of what you said. I'm putting it out, so I can eat your sandwich."

He held up the triangle of turkey on bread, unwrapping it and taking a bite from it.

"Oh." I laughed awkwardly, my ears turning hot, embarrassed at my misunderstanding.

He sent me an amused smirk and we sat in silence for a minute. I chewed my sandwich and stared at the ground, ignoring the growing blush on my cheeks and how quickly my heart raced. My mind raced as I tried desperately to think of things to say, when Isaac finally spoke.

"I smoke because of stress."

I quirked a brow at him in confusion. "Stress from school?"

Isaac laughed, looking at me with a gentle expression in his eyes. He shook his head, his tousled brown waves falling over his eyes as he stared at the sandwich wrapper in his hands. "Yeah, something like that."

I scrunched my brow, thinking of what he meant by that. What else could he be stressed about? "Lacey?"

Isaac was quiet for a while. "Sort of, I guess."

This only made me more confused. The two had been dating for just over a month—longer than any of his usual flings. And yet, there was constantly drama between the two.

"What do you mean? Do you not like her?" I paused to consider, my brows furrowing. "Why don't you ever call her?"

Isaac let out an awkward chuckle, rubbing a hand over the back of his neck. "Does everyone know about that?"

I nodded unsurely, feeling as though I had slightly offended him. "It's sort of like cable for lunchtime."

He laughed at my joke, lightening the mood and scrunching the empty sandwich wrapper into a ball. His laughter died off and we were left in silence once more. He threw the ball in front of him, landing among weeds and stray plants surrounded with litter and cigarette butts.

"It's a little more complicated than it sounds." He sighed, closing his eyes. His jaw set, and the air felt tense again, all at once.

I stayed quiet, allowing him to continue whenever he was comfortable. A moment passed and I picked at my nails, trying to ignore how my heart raced just from sitting beside him.

Finally, he said, "Don't get me wrong, I really like her."

My chest panged unconsciously at his words. I blinked. Maybe I was just feeling sorry for Lacey. He liked her, yet it seemed like he never showed it to her—at least from what I could tell from their daily lunchtime drama.

I suddenly felt like an intruder, invading in Isaac's business and personal dramas which I, along with half of the student body, watched most lunchtimes. I shifted uncomfortably in my place at the thought, but Isaac continued.

"We were just getting too . . ." He paused. "Err, close."

I watched him. His eyes were dark, his expression grim. His usual smirk was missing from his lips. It was strange seeing him so grim when he was usually a bubble of flirtatious mischief, relishing in my own discomfort.

In fact, it was strange enough seeing him so quiet. It was almost like I was back in the café, watching him so absorbed in his own thoughts, the dark expression on his face unwavering—watching him from afar.

I processed his words, not completely understanding his situation. "But you're dating, isn't that what's supposed to happen?"

"We're not dating." Isaac hesitated, his eyes drifting to the gravel ground.

I blinked. I wasn't the most experienced when it came to dating—in fact, I had no experience at all—but from what I had seen and heard around the school halls, it sure looked like Lacey thought they were.

Noticing my silence, Isaac released an awkward chuckle, running a hand through his hair. "I don't really date."

I laughed at this. "You've dated half the girls in the school."

"I didn't date them." His voice rose and grew defensive, almost cold, cutting my laughter off.

I swallowed, my laughter dying down. He sent me a sharp stare and a lump grew in my throat.

Right. He didn't date them, he just played around with them while waiting for the next girl to appear. I clenched my fists. I had somehow forgotten who I was speaking to.

He was Isaac Hensick.

I knew he was a player. He was infamous at Alum Creek Public for his reputation with girls, but he seemed different from the rumours when he spoke to me; when he watched over me as I slept, when he bought me a coffee, and gave me his leather jacket.

But he was always famous for his games, renowned for being the "*It Boy*" of the school—the boy every girl wanted. He was unattainable.

He had a reputation to uphold, after all, didn't he?

I clenched my teeth. I was just a wallflower. What was I expecting?

How could I have forgotten?

An uncomfortable silence settled between us, the sound of his friends playing on the oval in the background was the only thing that made any semblance of noise.

He glanced at me, his voice still cold when he said, "You should go, your friends are probably wondering where you are."

I looked at him, not really wanting to leave but the expression on his face showed he wanted to be alone. *Unattainable*, I reminded myself, and I stood.

"Thanks for the sandwich," Isaac said as I got to my feet, his eyes focused on the gravel floor. "And for checking on me."

I shrugged, my voice growing distant. "No worries."

I began to walk away, still processing the information that Isaac had just revealed to me. I should have known he wasn't serious about Lacey or about any of the girls he snuck around with.

I pulled his leather jacket tighter around me, inhaling his scent. *How many girls had he lent this to? Did he really just take me as another girl he could tease and play around with?*

I unclenched my fists, shaking my head as I reached the small hill Riley and William sat on. They fell silent, furrowing their brows as they watch me walk out from behind the old school building.

Riley's face broke out into a grin of realisation. "Let me guess, Isaac Hen—"

"I don't want to talk about it," I snapped, falling to sit beside William. I sighed, leaning my head on his shoulder. Riley's eyes widened, and she scooted closer to me.

"What happened, Asp?"

I pursed my lips. He was so kind this morning, offering me his leather jacket, that I forgot who he is—Isaac Hensick, the most popular asshole of the school. I was glad I realised it before I became too attached.

Yet, I still sank into the leather jacket, the smell of coffee staining the leather, and found myself missing him.

CHAPTER EIGHT
Flat White

The rest of lunch went by uneventfully. Riley and William took the hint and dropped the topic, moving on to chatter about some new movie or tv show I haven't heard of, their eyes occasionally roaming over to glance at me as I sat quiet, eyes trained on the sky.

The bell broke the awkwardness, and I found myself walking to my next period, visual arts.

Art was one of my favourite subjects. Ms. Laney, our teacher, was always super laid back, and even though I was severely lacking in any kind of artistic skill, I always managed to get good grades in her class.

I stepped into the classroom, beelining for my usual seat alone. Riley and William weren't in my class, instead opting to take physics, leaving me to my own company. Normally, I complained about having to spend an hour alone, but today I could use the silence.

They'd ask too many questions that I didn't have the answer to.

I clutched Isaac's leather jacket around me, settling into my desk and pulling out my pencils, when across the room, someone caught my eye.

Isaac sat there, his green eyes trained on me, his dark brown hair in a messy pile on his head. I turned, my cheeks turning red. He was staring.

When was the last time he actually turned up to art class? *Did he ever?*

I couldn't remember ever seeing him in our art class, but here he is—watching me. I blushed, feeling his heavy gaze on me.

We left off at lunch with an uncomfortable cloud hanging over us, and I was in no mood to talk to him. Yet, my heart pounded, and I found my eyes drawn back to him, his eyes still trained on me.

I look away quickly, my mind still racing with thoughts. Thoughts of how he was using Lacey and how he had denied that they were ever dating. Of his reputation. Of how different we were.

I wanted him to prove me wrong. I wanted him to be that nice, gorgeous, kind boy he was whenever he spoke to me. The one who bought me coffee, smirked at me, and lent me his jacket.

But the whole school knew about his reputation. The whole school knew how he had a new girl to toy with every other week, like they meant nothing.

I just chose to forget it.

I couldn't believe I'd thought . . . what? What had I thought? That we could be friends? That I could talk to him casually like I did with Riley and William? All because he, what? Noticed me for a few days?

I shook my head at myself.

I was an idiot if I believed someone like Isaac Hensick was living in the same world as I was.

"Alright, class," Miss Laney's voice broke my trance, and I turned to the front of the class to watch our eccentric middle-aged teacher waltz in, her arms full of notebooks. She laid them on her desk with a loud thud. "I have freshmen portfolios to mark today, so partner up, we'll be doing portraits."

I groaned. I was hoping for a theory lesson where I could get lost in my notes. Not only did I have no one to partner with in this class, I was terrible at drawing.

I was pulling out my sketchpad, trying to figure out who to partner with when a voice interrupted me.

"Aspirin?"

My breath got caught in my throat, and I found it hard to turn and meet those bright green eyes that made it across the classroom in seconds. My mouth felt dry for words, so instead I hummed in response.

His voice was a low drawl when he asked, "Will you be my partner?"

I gulped, finally turning to make eye contact. He stared at me, his face serious and his eyes hopeful. I quirked a brow at him, ignoring how heavy my tongue felt all of a sudden.

"What about your friend?"

Across the room, Sebastian Georges shook out his loose blond curls. Sebastian Georges was another one of the school's *'It Boys.'* It seemed like all the girls fell instantly for his curly locks and glistening smile. His bright blue eyes could melt the sturdiest of hearts.

But, like Isaac, he was unattainable. While Isaac preferred to play around with girls rather than date them, Sebastian avoided girls altogether, opting to focus on soccer instead. Which, of course, only attracted girls even more.

Even I had spent lunchtimes watching him kick a ball around the field. He moved gracefully across the grass with his face scrunched in concentration. It reminded me of Isaac, scribbling silently in the corner of Café de Fleur.

Beside him, Lacey sat with a girl whose name I didn't know. Lacey's eyes were swollen red, but a bright smile was plastered on her glossy lips.

"I'd rather be with you," Isaac muttered, stepping closer. His scent grew stronger, and I swallowed thickly. I felt like I was drowning in it.

"Okay," I squeaked, moving my things over to make room for him beside me.

Isaac fell into the chair next to me, pulling out his own notebook and immediately beginning to sketch. I was instantly transported back to the café at the sight of his long slender fingers clutching a graphite pencil, the sound of pencil on paper filling the air around me.

His eyes flickered up to my face and I blushed, moving to open my notebook and begin my portrait of him. There was a heavy silence between us, and we drew in this silence for about ten minutes, until Isaac finally spoke up.

"About what I said at lunch—"

"I don't agree with what you do," I interrupted, my eyes meeting his.

He paused, his pencil falling limp in his grip, and I continued, refusing to meet his eyes. I swallowed thickly once more, building my confidence.

I had to clear the air. Ever since lunch, the tension had become palpable between us. Even if it meant he never wanted to speak to me again, I needed to clear it. I straightened my spine, staring down at my paper as I spoke.

"You know, playing with all those girls's feelings. I know you think that it's fun to just mess around, but they have feelings too. You saw how devastated Lacey was. I mean, she's no Mother Teresa, but—"

"Aspirin," he cut me off, his voice loud. I paused, furrowing my brows at him. "I don't play around with them."

I blinked, my mouth open to speak, but no words came out.

"I don't date them," he began, sensing my confusion. "But I don't lead them on. Every girl I've messed around with came to me first, looking for a quick hookup. When they start getting too attached, that's when I end it."

"Like you did with Lacey . . ." I trailed off.

He nodded, moving back to his drawing. "I never play with their feelings. That's why I end it before they become too . . . clingy."

I blinked up at him. Clingy. *Was I becoming too clingy?* I shook the thought from my head, embarrassment quickly replacing my confusion.

I misunderstood him. I must have looked so naïve, asking him about Lacey and the girls he "dated.". Heat crept up my neck, turning my cheeks red.

"But your reputation?" I stuttered out, my brow furrowing as I spoke. "All those girls . . ."

He shrugged nonchalantly, a slight tinge of pink staining his cheeks.

"Sure, I've been around." I snorted at that. Talk about the understatement of the century.

He paused, giving me a knowing look and a smug smirk. "You can't believe everything you hear, Aspirin."

My cheeks only grew hotter. I opened my mouth to defend myself but all that came out was, "Oh."

He laughed, shaking his head, and continued, "But like I said, they were all just looking for a hookup."

I blinked. "Because you don't date."

"Right."

"You just—" I blushed. "Hookup."

"Exactly."

"Don't you want to fall in love?" I found myself asking before I could stop myself. I paused, instantly regretting asking it. He had just told me he didn't like it when girls were too clingy, and I asked him about falling in love.

I cringed at myself. This was it—the tragic moment where I embarrassed myself horribly in front of Isaac.

Isaac's eyes stayed trained on his paper, unfazed by the question, his fingers gliding across the notebook as he drew me.

I opened my mouth, frantic to take the words back and possibly also hide in my room for the rest of the week, but before I could take the question back, he spoke.

His voice was quiet and far away. "I never want to be in love again."

I stayed silent, processing his words. It was sad. I had never met someone who never wanted to be in love. Everyone in my life was desperate to fall in love; Riley, my sister, William. I gripped the edges of Isaac's leather jacket.

Even I wanted to fall in love, someday.

I narrowed my eyes, furrowing my brow. *Again.* Had he been in love before?

"Is that really what I look like?"

I snapped out of my thoughts to find Isaac leaning over to stare down at my drawing, his face too close to mine for comfort.

I reeled back, pulling the paper out of his sight. I tried my best, yet my drawing came out scratchy and disproportionate. Isaac's ears and nose were too big for his face, and his eyes were too small.

"As a matter of fact, you do," I teased, crossing my arms over my book and holding it tightly against my chest. I fought a smile, finally meeting his gaze.

He rolled his eyes, a smirk playing on his lips. "I'm about ten times sexier than that, dear Aspirin."

"I hate to break it to you, Isaac, but I'm really doing you a favour in this drawing."

He gasped dramatically, clutching a hand to his chest. I laughed, throwing my drawing onto the desk in defeat.

"I give up, I'm really hopeless at drawing."

"I can see that." He raised a brow at me, smirking at the butchered sketch.

"Oh please." I rolled my eyes at him. "Like you can do any better."

He smirked, tossing his notebook to land beside mine on the desk. On his paper, a small sketch of me sat . . .not me sitting in the classroom with a furrowed brow, but me sitting in Café de Fleur, a coffee in my hand and his leather jacket sitting heavy on my shoulders.

It was beautiful, especially considering the short amount of time he had been working on it.

"Isaac," I began, searching for the right words to express how fast my heart was racing. "You're really talented."

He shrugged. "I don't think I captured your rudeness in it, but we've still got time to work on that."

I laughed, smacking him harshly on his shoulder, earning an earnest chuckle in response.

"I forgot about your tendency for violence, too," he joked, pulling his arms up in defence as I moved to hit him again.

I stopped, our laughter dying down as I continued to admire the drawing.

He had drawn it so well. It was as if he copied it from a picture. From the way I clutched the cup with both hands, inhaling the bitter smell of coffee as the steam warmed my cheeks, to the way his jacket fell over my back. How the sleeves were too big for my arms and slouched at the shoulders. He captured it flawlessly.

My eyes trailed up to Isaac's face, his eyes trained on the picture, a small smile playing on his lips.

It was perfect.

CHAPTER NINE
Vienna

"Arthur Andrews is having a party!"

I sighed, closing my locker to find Riley's bobbing blonde ponytail beside me.

"That's great." I smiled, sarcasm dripping from my voice.

"I know!" she squealed, her tiny hands wrapping around my arm and squeezing tightly.

I yelped, whacking her hands off me and rubbing the sore spot she had left behind. "I don't know why you're so excited, it's not like you're invited."

"She's right." William appeared next to me, his shaggy black waves falling over his eyes as he shrugged at Riley.

"Wow, thanks for your support guys," Riley snapped, narrowing her eyes at us.

We sent her a shrug and she sighed, crossing her arms. Her lips pursed for a few seconds before a wide grin broke out on her face once more.

"I've got it!" she shouted, suddenly bouncing up and down again. She spun to me with a newfound sense of vigour. "Isaac Hensick!"

I blinked, my cheeks already beginning to heat at the sound of his name. "What about him?"

"You're practically best friends with him now, he can get us invited to Arthur Andrews's party!"

I shook my head with a snort. "No way. I am not asking him. I don't think I'd even call us *friends,* much less *'practically best friends.*"

William raised his own hands up, stepping closer beside me. "And I am not going to some trashy party full of drunk teenagers."

"Oh, come on!" Riley whined, her eyes turning large as she pleaded. "Arthur Andrews will be there. And he's so—"

"Dreamy," William interrupted, rolling his eyes. "We know."

"That doesn't mean I'm asking Isaac, though."

"Aspen!" she whinged, her voice nasally and drawn out.

"Riley!" I mimicked, screwing my eyes up to mock her.

She pouted at me, crossing her arms over her chest before sending a look to William, as if begging him to help her.

I turned, rolling my eyes and walking down the hallway. The other students already cleared the halls, desperate to get home for the day or already late for their club meetings. I was desperate to crawl into the warmth of my bed and binge watch The Office for the twentieth time.

"Aspen," Riley spoke again, her voice suddenly deadly serious. "If you do this one thing for me, I will never ask you for anything again in my entire life."

William snorted at this, causing Riley to send him a glare.

"Riles, do you really want to go that bad?" I asked, turning to face her as I walked.

She nodded eagerly, her eyes bright with hope. "I have never wanted anything more in my life."

I sighed. Her puppy-like enthusiasm was incredibly hard to turn down.

"Fine."

She screamed, her squeal piercing my ear and echoing down the hall as she bounced on her toes, pulling me into a tight hug. I peeled her off of me with a chuckle.

"That doesn't mean he'll say yes, though."

"Oh, he will." Riley grinned, throwing an arm around William's shoulder who turned bright red in response.

I rolled my eyes at his innocent love for Riley, shaking my head at the two. He made it so obvious. Every brush of her skin on his, he lit up like a Christmas tree. He was lucky Riley was denser than he was.

"So, movie night at mine?" I said, throwing my own arm around William's other shoulder.

He faced me with a grin. "Only if we're watching The Office."

"You guys know me so well."

*   *   *

I shouldn't have agreed to this.

I stood outside the café, my breath fogging up the glass as I stared inside. Vivienne sent me a strange look from the counter, but I was focused on someone else.

Isaac Hensick.

Isaac sat in his usual corner, his usual coffee by his hand, and his usual pencil scratching on paper. Despite becoming somewhat acquaintances over the past few weeks, we still rarely spoke at the café.

He was always too engrossed in whatever he scribbled into that little black book, and I was always too tired—or nervous—to even try.

I sighed, my hand moving to grip the door handle and pushing it open. The bell announced my arrival as I stepped inside, inhaling the warmth of the café and the bitter smell of coffee.

"Ah, Aspen." Vivienne smiled when I reached the counter. "I was wondering when you were going to come in."

65

I sent her a meek grin, pulling my bag to my chest to take out my wallet. "I just have some things on my mind."

"Some things, or someone?" Vivienne wiggled her brows at me, her eyes flickering between me and Isaac.

I scoffed at her. "I don't know what you mean."

"Your cheeks tell another story," she teased. I blushed even further at that, my ears turning red. Vivienne's smile grew wider, her eyes lighting up with delight.

I rolled my eyes at her. "You're lucky you're the best barista in town."

"Oh, you love me." She laughed, handing me my coffee in a warm takeaway cup and a paper bag of biscotti. "Have a good day, Aspen. I hope that something gets out of your mind and into your bed."

I sputtered, my eyes growing wide, causing her to howl in laughter.

"Thanks, Viv," I muttered, taking the cup and paper bag, handing her the exact change before turning to face Isaac.

Isaac didn't even notice that I walked in. His brow was furrowed as he sketched, his fingers wrapped so gently around the pencil, it was like it was floating across the paper.

We haven't spoken since our art class a few days ago. His leather jacket sat in my room all those days, waiting for me to build up the courage to approach him myself. And now it sat in my backpack.

I guess in a way, Riley was doing me a favour. She had given me that push I needed.

I pulled out his jacket from my backpack, clutching it so tightly in my hands, my knuckles turned white. I was nervous.

I sucked in a deep breath, straightening my back. Here goes nothing.

I walked over to Isaac's table, placing his jacket in front of him with a soft thud. His green eyes moved from his drawing to my face. I swallowed thickly and smiled at him.

"Hey, Isaac." My voice was shakier than I had anticipated. He had this uncanny effect on me where my throat grew tight and my heart pounded. It was like I didn't even need my coffee when I was around him—he woke me up just fine on his own.

A smirk appeared on his lips, and his voice came out in a husky drawl. "Aspirin. Fancy seeing you here."

It was a joke. I knew it, but I was too nervous to laugh. Instead, I made a choking sound that somewhat simulated laughter and he quirked a brow at me in response.

"Your jacket," I stammered out in an attempt at recovery, nodding to the leather pile of material that lay on the table. He made no move to take it. Heat crept up my neck.

"I see," he spoke simply, arching a playful brow at me. "I was wondering what you were doing with it."

"Well, I didn't know if I should wash it, or if it was dry clean only. I mean, I thought, maybe I should ask you or give it back straight away, but then I felt weird, but then I never asked so I never actually washed it, and—"

"Aspen," he interrupted me, shutting his notebook and grabbing his jacket. He pulled it on in one slick movement. "It's fine. Thanks for giving it back. I would have been fine with it if you kept it. I have a hundred like it."

"Oh," I said stupidly.

He smirked at my response, moving to lean on one hand. He looked stupidly sexy like that, and he clearly knew it by the smug look on his face. I shifted my weight to one hip and clenched my fists, swallowing thickly.

It was now or never.

"So, Arthur Andrews is having a party Saturday night since his parents are gone for the week."

I didn't even open my mouth to speak yet. He brought it up first. I stood there, speechless, and he spoke again.

"Do you want to come? You can be my guest."

"Yes!" I squeaked, almost cutting his sentence off.

67

He reeled back, his eyes wide, a playful grin on his lips. "I didn't know you liked parties so much."

"It's not that." I chuckled awkwardly. "Riley was desperate to go. It's actually one of the reasons I came up to you today."

He raised a brow at me. "So, it wasn't because you love my company?"

"Don't get cocky," I teased, rolling my eyes.

He smirked at me. "I'll show you cocky."

"Isaac!" I gasped, whacking his arm. I spun, scanning the café wildly to see if anyone had heard him. He laughed loudly at my reaction, a lazy grin drilling dimples into his tanned cheeks. He lifted a hand to catch mine on his arm, and he held it there.

"Your friends can come," he said, his voice almost as loud as my heart beating in my ears. "I'll see you there too though, right? Saturday night. I'll text you the details."

I fought to stop a blush from creeping up my neck. He wanted me there. His hand released mine and I found myself missing the feeling of his calloused palm resting over my fingers.

"Well?"

I blinked. His palm sat open in front of me.

"What?" I asked, furrowing my brow at him.

"Your phone. How else will I get your number?"

"Oh," I mumbled, fishing my phone out of my pocket. I unlocked it and dropped it in his hand.

He took the phone, quickly entering his details and sending himself a text message so that he could receive my phone number. He held it out to me, and I sheepishly took it back, our fingers brushing. A tight pressure grew in my chest and my skin tingled where we'd touched.

"Thanks." I smiled, gripping my phone.

"You'd better go, don't want to miss first period," he teased, smirking stupidly at me.

I nodded. "I'll see you, then."

"See you, Aspirin," he replied with a wide grin before turning back to his notebook, peeling the cover open and picking up the pencil again.

I sighed, turning to leave the café. I pushed the door open, the wind hitting me hard. I shivered and began walking, still processing what had just happened.

Isaac Hensick gave me his phone number.

My eyes widened at the realisation. *Isaac Hensick gave me his phone number.* I unlocked my phone, sliding through my apps to open the text message he had sent to his own phone.

To: Big Cock(y)
I'll see you on Saturday ;)

I blushed immediately, spinning back to look at Isaac through the window. He was already looking at me, his green eyes bright and his grin wide.

He sent me a wink, and my phone buzzed, alerting me of another text message.

From: Big Cock(y)
You love me.

I rolled my eyes, quickly changing his contact name and typing a message in reply.

To: Isaac
You wish.

I could hear his laugh from where I stood, so this time, I sent him a smirk and turned to walk to school.

CHAPTER TEN
Hot Chocolate

Parties were not my kind of thing.

I had been to my fair share of high school parties in the past, if by fair share you mean zero. I mean, I had been invited to a couple through Riley who seemed to know almost everyone in the school, but I never really had any reason to go.

Until today.

I tugged on my top, pulling it down in an attempt to hide a bit more of my midriff. Riley stepped closer, swatting at my hands and hitching the shirt even higher so that it rested right beneath my bra.

"Come on, Aspen," she scolded, smoothing out the top. "Live a little. You have a hot body. I'd kill for it."

I rolled my eyes at her. Riley came over early in the afternoon and immediately stuffed me in a pair of blue ripped skinny jeans and a black off-shoulder crop top with long sleeves. It wasn't anything too revealing, but it hugged my body tightly and showed off a good amount of my stomach.

I wrapped my arms around my exposed skin. I had never been too insecure of my body. I was lucky to be somewhat tall, and I had a nice waist to make up for my lack of cleavage. Riley on the other hand was all curves.

She wore a tight black dress with a deep, low-cut neckline. She had the chest and the hips to pull it off. She stood taller than usual in heels, looking to impress Arthur Andrews, while I wore my usual white sneakers.

"Shut up, Riley, you know you look hot," I teased, whacking her arm.

She grinned at me. "I know," she admitted, twirling her long, straightened hair around her finger. "But you needed the confidence boost."

I laughed, pulling her into a tight hug. "I love you, you know."

"You'd better, considering all the effort I put into getting you Isaac Hensick ready," she joked.

I snorted. She was right. She had pulled my usually messy brown locks into long neat waves and she had done my makeup so perfectly I looked like an Instagram model.

"You wouldn't even be invited to this party if it wasn't for me," I fired back.

"You're right, and I love you, Aspen," she spoke sweetly. Her smile turned into a mischievous smirk. "Which is why I'm going to be the best wingwoman ever and set you up with Isaac tonight."

I rolled my eyes, grabbing my phone and keys and shoving them into my pockets. "Riley, that's a pipe dream that's never going to happen."

She grinned, pulling her handbag over her shoulder and heading for the door. "Not if I have anything to do with it."

The twenty-minute ride to Arthur Andrews's house in the fancy uptown neighbourhoods from my place was mostly uneventful. Riley chattered on and on about how she was going to seduce Arthur through her witty personality and even better looks.

Meanwhile, I wrung my fingers together, nervous about the party.

My heart raced just standing beside Isaac, much less standing beside him in a dark loud room full of drunk teenagers.

That was if I'd even see him tonight.

71

The last text he had sent me was filled with the details of tonight's party. I replied with a thank you, and that was it. We were back to our usual routines.

Riley pulled up outside of Andrews's house. It was huge, with three stories and a lawn bigger than my house. Music blasted loudly, teenagers flooded in and out of the doors leaving red cups in their wake. Cars lined the streets and filled the driveway; we were lucky to get a spot nearby.

We jumped out of the car. Riley practically had to drag me to the front door.

"You'll love it, Aspen, I swear!" she shouted over the booming music.

I swallowed hard. I hope so. She clutched my hand, pulling me into the house. The party was well in motion. We walked straight to the main room where teenagers danced on top of each other, red cups filled with unknown liquids in their hands.

Riley grinned widely as I shrunk into myself. No wonder William opted not to come tonight. This was far from my usual scene.

"There's your boo!" Riley shouted directly into my ear. I turned to see her nod to our left.

There, across the room, Isaac leaned against the wall, girls on either side of him chatting excitedly into his ears.

He wasn't listening, though. His eyes were trained on us. I inhaled a sharp breath and heard Riley shout something incoherent over the music. She shook my shoulder, her voice raising louder, but I was too focused on Isaac.

All I could see were his piercing green eyes, trailing from my face, to my body, and back up. A smirk tugged at his lips, dimples drilling into his cheeks. A pressure grew in my chest. I felt frozen beneath his stare.

Riley's hand left my shoulder and I snapped back to reality. I turned to her, about to ask her to repeat what she said, only to find her gone.

My stomach flipped.

I spun, my eyes wide and scanning the room. It was dark and sweaty, where lights of all colours flashed across the room, making my head spin. My heart raced in my chest, and a lump rose in my throat.

Where was she?

Eventually, I spotted her in the kitchen with two beers her hands. She must've gone to get us drinks. She put one on the table, releasing a giggle and grabbing Arthur Andrews's bicep. He flexed, sending her a wink, and I turned away, wrinkling my nose.

At least *she* was having fun.

Turning back to the dance floor, I paused. Suddenly the thought of grinding on sweaty bodies and against grabbing hands seemed like too much. I blinked through the flashes of colourful lights, the loud music pumping and bass shaking the room. My ears rang with laughing and shouting and music and noise, noise, and noise.

My heart rose into my throat, and I found it difficult to breathe.

A body collided into my back and I stumbled forward, turning to see a drunk boy rampaging through the room.

So much noise.

So many people.

"Sorry," he slurred at me, a lopsided grin on his face. He took a sloppy step forward, his fingers finding themselves on my cheek. I felt queasy.

Ripping his fingers off of my clammy skin, I stormed away from the dance floor, sprinting up the staircase. My entire body trembled with electricity.

I needed a minute, just a minute, to calm down.

My mind raced as I walked. Riley was my ride home, and there was no way I'd ruin what she had been dreaming of the past year. She finally had her chance. I couldn't interrupt her. I needed to calm down.

I stumbled through the dark hallway. The floor spun under my feet. Blood pounded in my ears, and my fingernails dug painfully into my palms. My breathing sped up and I tried desperately to calm down. I had to get away.

I needed a minute.

Where the hell was the bathroom?

I swallowed breath after breath, testing every doorknob on the way until I finally made it to one unlocked room. The world seemed to sway beneath my feet.

I fell inside. The room was so dark I couldn't tell what else was in there, but I didn't care.

I slid to the floor, my fingers moving to clutch at my chest, my hair, the ground, the wall—everything. It was hard to breathe.

Really hard.

I wheezed, desperately pulling air into my lungs. Every gasping breath felt like a shard stabbing into my failing lungs. My body shook uncontrollably, my hands shaking so much that I couldn't grasp my phone. Instead, I grabbed my arms, hugging myself as I sucked in breath after breath.

Behind me, I was vaguely aware of the door opening and closing, and suddenly there was a hand rubbing my back as my breathing grew faster.

"It's okay."

It was Isaac's voice.

I let out a sob and fell into his chest, his hands rubbing my arms as he whispered into my ear.

"It's fine. It's okay. You're okay."

I didn't even realise I was crying until he moved his hand to my cheek, wiping tears from my skin. He held me, his arms tight around me as I trembled.

"Isaac," I cried, pulling my face into his chest, although my voice was strained and stuttering.

His chest vibrated as he spoke, "It's okay. You're okay."

I swallowed hard, closing my eyes. I knew what to do. I had to calm down. I had to breathe. I sucked in a deep breath, releasing it in a shaky sob, before taking another. My fingers grabbed at his shirt, squeezing into fists as I attempted to calm down.

I breathed in, counting in my head, and breathed out, still trembling.

I continued for what felt like hours until my breathing had slowed, and my heart rate was gradually returning to normal.

My hands were still trembling, and I brought shaky fingers to my eyes, wiping away stray tears.

I sighed, fatigue hitting me like a truck. I knew my eyes were swollen. I knew my makeup had probably smudged everywhere. I knew I'd have a headache in the morning.

And Isaac . . . embarrassment flooded my body.

"Isaac," I muttered, pulling out of his grip. My eyes had adjusted to the darkness and I could see his face, his eyes etched with worry as he stared down at me, his hands resting gently on my waist, rubbing circles against my skin.

He watched me for a moment, and I paused, swallowing the lump in my throat.

"I'm sorry," I said, embarrassed.

"Why are you sorry?" he asked, his voice quiet. "Are you okay? What was that?"

I wrung my fingers together, my eyes moving to the ground as I hiccupped. "It was a panic attack."

He stayed quiet. I could still feel his eyes on me. A heavy silence settled over us and I felt an overwhelming urge to fill it.

"I have them sometimes. Or had. I haven't had one in a month. I mean, I never go to parties, really. I thought I'd be fine. I thought I just needed a minute. But then I got here, and suddenly . . . suddenly . . . I thought my antidepressants were helping, and—"

"Aspen."

75

I had never heard him say my name before. My real name. I stopped rambling, finally looking up to meet his eyes. He stared at me softly. "It's okay. I get it."

A heavy silence fell between us. I didn't know what else to say. The only people who had witnessed me having a panic attack were my mother and my sister. Not even Riley or William had seen me break down like this, and now here I was, sobbing in front of Isaac Hensick.

His voice filled the silence, uneasy and testing the limits, "Why are you taking antidepressants?"

I pulled in a shaky breath. "I have anxiety."

My voice was quieter than I had intended, and a hiccup tagged onto the end of my sentence. Isaac grew stiff with realisation before it softened and he rubbed a calloused palm up and down my arm, warming me up.

I melted into his chest, the relief of the confession overriding my fatigue. He stayed quiet, rubbing my arms and back to comfort me.

Tears stained my cheeks, my makeup running and clinging to his shirt.

At this point, I was too tired to be embarrassed. I slumped over, my hands trembling but my arms sore and heavy as logs. My entire body felt drained—it was painful to move.

Isaac must have noticed this, because he stood up, reaching a hand to me.

"Come on, you look tired."

I blinked, tenderly taking his hand and pulling myself to my feet. He guided me to the middle of the room in the dark, where a large bed sat.

"Have some rest," he said.

I blinked down at the bed, unsure. "I don't know . . ."

"It's a guest room," he explained, flattening the sheets to have me sit. "Just rest here until you feel ready to leave."

I nodded, pulling my shoes off and settling into the blankets. Isaac stood over me, pulling the sheets up to my neck. I didn't want to think about how terrible I must have looked. Even lying down, my body felt sore and ached terribly.

"Will you stay?" I found myself asking, my voice quiet and weak.

He smiled at me. "Of course, get some rest."

I nodded again, leaning against the pillow. My fatigue was already taking over, pulling my eyes shut and tempting me to sleep.

Isaac slid to the floor beside the bed and rested his head against the mattress, his eyes trained on the door.

I smiled, remembering the first time he had guarded me as I slept in the library.

"Don't watch me while I sleep," I joked, my voice faltering as sleep enticed me.

I didn't see his reaction, my eyes already shut, but I felt his lips kiss my forehead, his hand stroke my hair. My mind turned silent at his touch and I fell asleep.

CHAPTER ELEVEN
Mochaccino

My head pounded and my eyes felt glued together. I groaned, turning and bringing my hands up to rub at my eyes.

My eyelids fluttered open and, for a moment, I felt disoriented. I sat in a large room with bare walls and a large bed that I didn't recognise. I blinked, confused, until my eyes landed on the tuft of brown hair at the edge of the mattress.

Then, the events of last night came flooding back.

Flashes of me hyperventilating and crying ripped through my mind—images of Isaac hugging me and tucking me into the bed.

My heart sank into my stomach and I bolted upright to find Isaac asleep, sitting slouched on the floor against the edge of the bed.

He had slept on the floor—he had really stayed with me all night.

His eyes remained shut, his neck tilted at an awkward angle against the mattress. His lips were slightly parted, and his chest gently rose and fell. His dark hair was tousled and fell over his brow messily.

How did he manage to look so perfect sleeping on the floor?

I turned, my heart thumping, to find my phone sitting on the bedside table. I quietly slid across the covers to grab my phone.

It was plugged in and charging. I smiled at the thought of Isaac charging it for me and moved to turn my phone on.

It came to life and immediately the screen was filled with notifications—texts and missed calls from Riley and William. I glanced at the time—seven in the morning—and sighed. I had fallen asleep all through the night and forgotten all about Riley.

I tapped onto our group chat, finding hundreds of texts ranging from *'Oh my Gosh, Arthur Andrews asked me out on a date!'* to *'Aspen, wya?'* to *'ASPEN WHERE ARE YOU'*.

Guilt washed over me, and I quickly shot them back a text message explaining I was safe, I was sorry, and I'd call them back later.

I swallowed, my mouth feeling extremely dry and my head pounding harder from the bright sunlight flooding the room. I had slept all night, yet I still felt exhausted. My body was sore and sluggish, and my throat felt dry. I opened my phone camera and switched it to the front facing camera, quickly cringing at my face.

My eyes were swollen and red. All of my mascara had been rubbed off, leaving dark smudges beneath my eyes. My hair had frizzed on end and the elegant waves had turned into knots.

With a sigh, I turned my phone off, sick of seeing my terrible reflection. I spotted my sneakers across the room beside the door. I had to leave. My mom would be home from her night shift soon. Unplugging my phone, I carefully pulled the sheets off me, trying to keep quiet and not wake Isaac.

I turned, quietly sliding off the bed, when the frame suddenly creaked loudly. I froze, my eyes darting to Isaac as he stirred.

He turned, his eyes fluttering open and his neck craning to face me.

"Aspen?" His voice was so croaky, I thought my heart would explode out of my chest. He was so cute.

"Morning," I squeaked.

He groaned, rubbing at his eyes. "What time is it?"

Before I could answer, he pulled his phone out of his pocket and glanced at the screen. His brow furrowed and he turned back to face me.

"How are you feeling, Aspen?"

My heart fluttered at the sound of my name—my real name—on his croaky morning voice. His eyes squinted through the morning light as he scanned me. I clung to the bed sheets.

"I'm good," I sputtered. "Uh, and you?"

The corner of his lips twitched up in a smirk. "Tired."

"Look, Isaac, I'm so sorry about last night," I began, my voice quiet and body stiff. "I just got so panicked and I really thought I just needed a minute, you know? And then . . . and then you slept on the floor all night, and I'm so embarrassed. Oh God, I'm so—"

"Aspen!"

I paused, turning to see Isaac's sharp stare focused on me. I melted under his gaze, suddenly insecure about my running makeup and messy hair.

"It's fine. I get it," he offered, smiling lazily.

He turned, stretching his back and cracking his neck, letting out a groan.

"Besides, I didn't sleep on the floor all night." He paused, turning to spot my wide eyes before letting out a nonchalant laugh. "Because I was awake most of the night. Party ended at three, then I stayed up a bit longer to make sure everyone left. Didn't want to leave you totally defenceless."

I narrowed my eyes at him, my brows drawing together.

"You stayed up all night?"

He nodded halfway through a yawn. "Well, I was going to wake you up, but you seemed totally out of it. I thought I'd just let you rest for a few hours and then before I knew it, I fell asleep too."

I fell quiet, my mind whirring. I embarrassed myself last night, had a panic attack for the first time in a month, cried in front

80

of the most popular boy at school, and yet he stayed up all night watching me sleep.

"I'm sorry," I said again. "Since I began taking my—" I paused, my eyes widening in realisation. "Sh*t. I need to go home."

Isaac furrowed his brow as I slid out of the bed, racing to pull my shoes on.

"What's wrong?"

"I'm supposed to take my medication every morning." I sighed while tying my laces. "I mean, it's not a huge deal if I miss it once, I guess, but it was just starting to work. I've never missed it before, and my mom will be home soon, and—"

I paused, my cheeks tingeing red in a blush. I glanced at him meekly to find him grinning teasingly at me. "Sorry," I muttered sheepishly. "I just need to go home."

He nodded, deep in thought, before standing from his seat and shaking his hair out. "Alright, we'd better get going then."

"What do you mean *we?*"

He raised a brow, pulling out a set of keys and twirling them around his finger. "Your ride left last night, didn't she?"

I sighed. Right. I left Riley without a word. I was supposed to be gone for only a minute, but instead ended up spending all night sleeping beside Isaac.

He slid past me with another yawn, pulling the door open. "You coming?"

I pursed my lips—it wasn't like I had a choice. I trailed after him, following him through the hallway and down the stairs. The floor was littered with all sorts of trash, from beer cans to red cups to—

I paused.

Was that underwear?

"Isaac!"

I bumped into Isaac's back as he came to a stop and I staggered back. He turned, a hand reaching out to grab my arm while his eyes drifted to the kitchen.

My stare followed his to find Arthur Andrews, Sebastian Georges, and three girls gathered around the kitchen holding trash bags. The girls somehow managed to look gorgeous despite having knotted hair and smudged makeup to match my own.

"Where'd you go last night, man?" Arthur Andrews asked, stepping forward. His eyes drifted to me, his brows furrowing in confusion. "Hi."

"Hey," I muttered awkwardly.

His eyes moved back to Isaac and he tilted his head inquisitively, as if to ask why I was there. Or more likely, why I was with him.

"Hey man, I'm just going to drop Aspirin home. I'll be back in a few minutes." Isaac avoided the question, smoothly falling back into my stupid nickname. He tugged me forward, moving towards the door.

I turned, watching Sebastian Georges's smirk and the girls's glares as we moved. I narrowed my eyes, noticing Chloe sitting amongst the girls, her eyes trained on Isaac's hand gripping my wrist. She scrunched her nose in distaste and I gulped, my stomach turning.

Isaac began leading me through the house.

"I think she hates me," I murmured, still thinking of Chloe's glare.

"Who?" Isaac asked, glancing back to see Chloe behind me, still shooting daggers into my back. He laughed lowly, shaking his head. "Chloe?"

I nodded and he pulled the front door open, dropping my arm.

"She doesn't hate you," he said, though I was unconvinced. His voice grew quieter as he stepped over the threshold. "She just doesn't want me to be hurt again."

I quirked a brow, opening my mouth to ask, '*Again?*' when he stepped forward, and unlocked his car. My mouth fell shut as I trailed after him.

82

The road was cleared of cars, leaving Isaac's own black sedan in the driveway. He gripped his keys, sliding into the driver's seat. I followed, slipping into the passenger seat and buckling my seat belt.

"So—" He started the engine. "Where do you live?"

I mumbled my address and he reversed out of the driveway. We were far uptown, meaning it'd take about twenty minutes before I'd arrive back home. That meant twenty minutes in a car sitting beside Isaac Hensick.

I stiffened.

His car was nice. Despite knowing nothing about cars, judging from the black leather interior and touch screen, I knew it was expensive.

"About last night," he started, and my heart began racing all over again.

Last night was the last thing I wanted to talk about. I still haven't gotten the embarrassment out of my system yet.

"What do you normally do? You know, if no one else is around?"

I blinked, turning to face him. It took me a second to realise he was talking about my panic attack. His face was crinkled with genuine interest.

"I just ride it out," I said, finally. "It always settles down eventually. Some last longer than others."

His eyes widened. "You mean longer than the one you had yesterday?"

I snorted. "I've had anxiety attacks that last an hour."

He released a breath at that, his face riddled with shock. It was true, though. I had been diagnosed with anxiety years ago following a trip to the emergency room when I had an hour-long panic attack. They gave me Valium to calm me down and, ever since then, this had become my life.

"My pills help, though," I continued. "I used to have them every other day, and we finally found something that works. I've been taking them daily for a month and haven't had a panic attack since. They're great. They mess with my sleep, but they're great."

He was quiet a second, the only sound being the hum of the car beneath us.

"Right," he said finally, his brow furrowed in thought. "I thought so. I mean, I googled it last night while you were sleeping, and it said that insomnia was a common side effect, and it made sense. You know? Because you nap in the library, and—"

"You googled it?" I interrupted.

He glanced at me, blushing slightly.

"I'm sorry, it's none of my business," he uttered. "I was just . . . I don't know much about anxiety. I've never seen anything like it before. I was so worried. I thought something happened to you—someone . . . did something to you."

I shook my head, my eyes wide at the idea that Isaac had tried to learn about my anxiety after seeing me panic like that. Instead of thinking I was weird, or pretending, he researched it. He tried to understand.

His hands gripped the steering wheel uncomfortably and I smiled, slightly amused that *he* was feeling awkward for once instead of me.

"No . . . no, I'm touched. I should be thanking you for calming me down," I spoke sincerely, my voice soft. "Besides, that was the best sleep I've had in a while."

He raised his eyebrows with a smirk, immediately reverting to his usual self. "I get that a lot."

"Isaac!" I gasped, whacking his arm.

He chuckled, his chest vibrating as he glanced at me. I giggled alongside him. He was great at lightening a conversation— at relieving my anxiety. I found my mind falling silent around him, like it did around Riley and William.

My heart glowed, and I bit my lip, turning to face the road.

"Isaac," I spoke, suddenly feeling confident. "Thank you."

I faced him, catching his eye as he glanced back at me.

"Seriously, thank you. For staying with me, for comforting me, for driving me home," I continued. "For watching me sleep."

He laughed at our stupid inside joke, and my smiled softened.

"Anytime, Aspirin."

He threw me a smirk and I grew warm.

Oh, God.

I was really falling for him.

CHAPTER TWELVE
Pumpkin Spice

I walked through the hallways, my shoes squeaking against the tiles and my head already pounding after an hour of writing notes about kidneys and nephrons. I sighed, rubbing my forehead with my cold fingers, my other hand clutching my books to my chest.

In my tired daze, I had grabbed the wrong books, meaning I'd have to stop by my locker before the next class to grab the correct textbooks.

Riley walked beside me, a bounce in her step, chattering on and on about how worried she had been at Arthur Andrews's party on Saturday, as if she hadn't already given me an earful all Saturday night and Sunday afternoon. William walked beside her, his eyes vacant as if he wasn't listening, but nodding haughtily nevertheless.

I pursed my lips, barely listening, when suddenly, she fell silent and came to a stop.

I paused beside her, blinking.

"What—"

I didn't have to finish my sentence. I dragged my eyes from the hallway floor to follow Riley's gaze. Beside my locker, Isaac Hensick stood. His normally tousled hair had been brushed back, exposing his glowing face under the fluorescent light. He sent me a boyish smirk as he leaned against the lockers, his arms crossed over his classic leather jacket.

"Aspirin."

"Isaac," I sputtered eventually, furrowing my brow. "What are you doing here?"

"Waiting for you," he answered simply with a shrug.

I opened my mouth to reply when Riley interrupted.

"We'll meet you later, Asp," she whispered, clutching onto William's arm and dragging him away. She sped down the hallway, glancing back at me to send me a wink and a squeal before bounding away. William was pulled after her, his brow furrowed in confusion. I ripped my gaze from their retreating backs to look back at the smirking boy in front of me.

Isaac's eyes remained focused on mine , studying me. The corner of his mouth twitched up in a half-smile and he lifted a brow at me. My face heated beneath his sharp stare, but I swallowed my nerves and continued facing him.

"I didn't see you at the café today," he said.

I blushed, my eyes moving to my locker. I pulled it open and he moved to stand upright, hovering over my shoulder as I dumped my books into my locker with a loud clatter—I was much too tired to be organised.

"I woke up late so I couldn't go." It wasn't a lie. Not entirely.

I had drifted to sleep close to sunrise and couldn't force myself out of bed in time to stop by the café. But I knew if I had woken up on time, I would've skipped it today anyway.

I just wasn't sure I was ready to face Isaac again after embarrassing myself in front of him.

He had seen me at my lowest—my hair matted and make-up runny. He had seen me panic after, what, a party? A normal, teenage party? It was a surprise he was even still talking to me.

"Lucky for you, I'm the greatest friend in the world." I turned to see him holding out a takeaway coffee cup, the logo of Café de Fleur printed on the front. "Soy latte, no sugar."

I didn't even notice him holding it. I took the cup from him, smiling meekly as our fingers brushed. My cheeks felt hot and his words echoed in my ears—he thought we were friends.

"Thanks," I muttered, slamming my locker shut with my other hand.

We were silent for a moment, me shifting on my feet and him oblivious to my discomfort, before he asked, "How are you feeling today?"

I swallowed a steaming sip of coffee, the heat instantly warming my body, eliciting a sigh from me. I looked up, meeting his eyes and sending him a grateful smile.

"I'm feeling a lot better," I began, searching for the right words. "Thanks, Isaac. I don't know what I would have done without you. Seriously."

And it was true. I've had anxiety attacks before—many times—although never in a dark crowded party at a stranger's house. And sometimes they led to me missing entire weeks of school trying to recover, to rebuild my confidence and calm my nerves.

If I had walked out of that room with tears streaking my makeup and someone noticed, I wasn't sure what I'd do. If I had been left to my own thoughts in that room, with my own overthinking—that would've taken me days to recover.

His smile grew at my words and he clapped a hand on my back. "Hey, no worries Aspirin. What are friends for?"

That words again. Friends. I never would have thought I'd be friends with the Isaac Hensick. He was the type of person I watched from afar—the type Riley wouldn't shut up about during lunch, no matter how many longing looks she received from William. He was decidedly not the type to buy me coffee and drive me home from parties.

At least, that's what I had thought.

Because apparently, he was the type to buy me coffee. He was the type to lend me his jacket and give me a stupid nickname. He was the type who stayed up until three in the morning, just watching me sleep because I had asked him to stay. He was the type to charge my phone as I slept, and research anxiety, and try to understand me.

And even before that, he was the type to hug me and comfort me, no questions asked, when I broke down in the middle of a party.

I looked up to realise we had fallen silent. He watched me carefully, his eyes soft. I swallowed thickly, searching for words to fill the pause, when he spoke first.

"So where are you headed now?" he asked.

I shuffled on my feet. "World History. You?"

He raised his brows. "Not sure. I've never gone to class at this time."

I sent him an incredulous look and he laughed.

"I'll walk you there," he said, shrugging nonchalantly.

He led the way, as if he knew where my World History class was. I followed, sipping delicately at the coffee he had bought me. We walked beside each other, our shoulders knocking and our shoes squeaking against the tiles.

The caffeine from my latte combined with the occasional brush of our hands sent my heart racing, and I felt more awake than I had felt in weeks.

The silence was heavy, and I felt the need to fill it with conversation. Isaac was way ahead of me.

"Did your friend enjoy the party?" he asked and then paused, his brow furrowing as if to think. "Rebecca?"

I sputtered out a laugh. "Riley loved the party."

It was true. She had spent the entire weekend chatting my ear off about how she had spent the entire night with Arthur

Andrews and even scored his phone number by the end of the party.

That is, when she wasn't scolding me for disappearing on her.

He sent me a charming smile that made my heart hiccup.

"That's great." His warmth spread to me and I found myself smiling up at him in response. "You know, I think I remember Arthur mentioning a girl named Riley."

I raised my brows. I had forgotten they were friends.

"And what did he say?"

Isaac smirked, raising a brow at me. "That, dear Aspirin, is confidential."

I gasped jokingly, holding a hand to my chest. "I thought we were friends."

He smiled at me, all dimpled and sincere. "We are."

I narrowed my eyes at him, ignoring the way my heart raced when he looked at me like that.

"So?"

"So—" He sent me a wink, a smug smirk tugging on his lips. "It's confidential."

I laughed, rolling my eyes. It was endearing that Isaac protected his friend like that, and honestly, it wouldn't feel right meddling in Riley's business like that.

We came to a stop outside of my classroom, and I tugged on the straps of my backpack. "Well, thanks for walking with me."

"No problem. I'll see you around?"

"Definitely." I grinned at the thought of seeing him again. The thought of him wanting to see me again.

He sent me a nod as a goodbye, pushing his hair back and turned to walk down the hallway. I stared after him, my heart still fluttering in my chest.

"So, what's happening between you two?"

I jumped at the sound of Riley's voice in my ear.

She snuck up right behind me, her eyes trained on Isaac's retreating back. I blushed, turning to enter the classroom, keeping my head down as I took my seat and the final bell rang.

"Nothing," I said, pulling out my books and pens.

Riley smirked, wiggling her brows at me, and I rolled my eyes.

"What's going on with you and Arthur Andrews? I didn't miss the way he was looking at you on Friday night. Did you end up texting him?"

It was Riley's turn to blush now. She turned away from me, tucking a strand of hair behind her ear. "There's nothing going on."

"Mhm." I smirked, narrowing my eyes at her.

"Seriously, it's nothing." She moved her focus to me, meeting my eyes with a stern look. "He's cute, but kind of stupid. He didn't get any of my jokes!"

I raised my brows, biting my tongue. I wanted to tell her that William always got her jokes. But she was still blushing, and I knew she was still thinking of the way Arthur Andrews stared down at her that Friday night.

Like how I kept thinking about Isaac and his stupid dimples and stupid green eyes.

I settled with, "That sucks."

She sighed, moving to flop down in the desk beside me as our teacher finally entered the classroom, apologising for being late as usual.

"I know," she groaned, screwing her face up in complaint. "At least I have your romance to vicariously live through."

"Romance?" I echoed. I blushed wildly, my ears turning pink. "I don't know what you're talking about."

She sent me an incredulous look but said nothing.

"Seriously!" I exclaimed with wide eyes. "There's no romance to be spoken of."

Riley smirked at me, turning to face the teacher, but I didn't miss her mutter to me smugly.

"You'd better tell that to Isaac then."

CHAPTER THIRTEEN
Ristretto

I felt like an idiot. I couldn't believe I thought things would be different after Isaac had called me his friend—after he said he'd see me around.

I mean, we did see each other around. We sent polite nods from across the café, but we never exchanged more than a quiet "hello." Sometimes we'd smile when we passed in the hallways; on the rare occasion that he bothered to show up at school. Our last text from before Arthur Andrews's party taunted me as I considered texting him each night, ultimately deciding against it every single time, only to reconsider the next.

Either Isaac's definition of a friend was very different from mine, or he only said it to be polite.

He was back to his old routine of skipping classes and disappearing from the school quad in the middle of lunch.

It had been nearly two weeks since I've had a proper conversation with him.

It was on me. I was the one who embarrassed myself in front of him. I was the one who told him to reconcile with Lacey. I was the one who encouraged him to go back to his world of popularity and relationships.

And I had to return to mine.

But I couldn't help missing him.

Maybe I was overthinking it.

"Stop staring," Riley scolded.

I turned to see her eyes riddled with concern, leaning against the tree beside William. William's gaze flickered between my face and the soccer field where Isaac and his friends were kicking a ball around lazily.

I sighed, thumbing my jeans. "I can't help it. You know he's going to disappear like he always does during lunch. I just—"

"Aspen," Riley interrupted. I turned my focus to her. She stared at me with eyebrows raised and a pointed smirk on her face. "Go talk to him."

"You think?"

"He said you're friends, right?"

I nodded.

"Then go. Friends talk to each other."

I swallowed. She was right. I needed to take matters into my own hands. If I wanted to talk to Isaac, I should just do it. What was I worrying about? William sent me a small smile of encouragement from beside Riley, and I stood, brushing my pants off from the grass.

"I'll see you guys later, then," I said, my voice quieter than I had hoped. I shouldered my backpack, shrugging it on before turning to the soccer field and sucking in a deep breath.

I shuffled down the hill, practicing what I was going to say in my head—rehearsing in an attempt to not make a fool of myself in front of him and his friends.

Hey Isaac, how have you been? Me? Oh, I'm good, just on my way to art early. Are you coming today? We should go together.

Isaac had left his friends and stood at the edge of the field, gulping down a bottle of water. I paused, taking in another deep breath and clenching my fists before approaching him.

"Hey Isaac," I began, pushing my voice to sound louder, more confident than I felt. Okay, it was going well so far. "How you been?"

Isaac turned, his brows rising in surprise to see me.

"Aspirin, hey!" His usual charming smile tugged at his lips and my heart fluttered. "Good, good. What about you?"

I mustered up my confidence and sent him a nonchalant smile. This was going well, definitely in my top ten social interactions so far. "Good! I'm just on my way to art early. Are you—"

"Isaac!"

I turned at the same time as Isaac to see a group of girls waltz up to him. They ignored my presence, flicking their pretty long hair over their shoulders and swaying their cute miniskirts. A girl with long black hair stood ahead of the group, calling Isaac's name.

It was Chloe Pepper.

And behind her was Lacey.

"Hey, Chlo," Isaac grinned, nodding at her. "Lace."

My heart sunk, suddenly feeling like I didn't belong here. This was Isaac's world. I didn't fit in with them, that much was clear by the way each person pointedly faced each other in a sort of circle, effectively cutting me out of the conversation. I shifted uncomfortably on my feet, turning my attention to the girls that had approached.

Lacey smiled at Isaac, a light blush tinting her cheeks. *When did they patch up their issues?* I haven't seen her crying lately, but I also haven't seen the usual lunchtime cable of Lacey shouting at Isaac in front of the entire school.

In fact, I hadn't seen them associate with each other at all.

"We're going to skip last period." Chloe gestured to her group of friends. "You want to come? We could use a ride."

I didn't miss the way she pointedly looked at Isaac, as if to show she was speaking to him and definitely not to me. I almost snorted, remembering Isaac's words the other day. *She doesn't hate you.*

I was entirely unconvinced.

Isaac laughed, his chest rising. "Is that all I am to you? A ride?"

He sent a wink to her and Chloe rolled her eyes, slapping him on the chest. Behind her, Lacey and the other girls giggled behind their hands. "Hurry up, let's go."

She turned and walked towards the main building, her group of friends trailing after her, their eyes still trained on Isaac. Lacey's gaze remained on him all the way to the building.

I wondered if she secretly used echolocation or something. It was impressive how she could walk all the way across the field without looking.

I turned back to Isaac; his eyes trained on Lacey. He watched her carefully, his eyes narrowed and mouth tilted. I paused for a moment, the silence slowly becoming too much for me to bear.

"Um," I said, finally, shifting uncomfortably on my feet.

Isaac's head snapped back to face me, and his eyes widened as if he just remembered I was still there. He rubbed the back of his neck awkwardly.

"Sorry about that. Hey, I'll see you around, okay?"

He was off jogging after Chloe before I could open my mouth to reply.

"Yeah, see you around," I muttered to myself, tugging on my backpack straps.

I was an idiot. Of course, he was just saying that to be nice. He meant he'd literally see me around in glances across the hall, not in conversations. Not hanging out together.

I knew that now. I had gotten my hopes up for nothing.

I sighed, the sound of the bell ringing in the background, and began walking to my art classroom.

I was used to being alone in art by now, so I took a seat in the corner, hoping no one would bother me. I really didn't feel like talking.

Ms. Laney entered soon after, clapping her hands together with a grin.

"Don't get settled yet, everyone! Today we'll be doing partner work!"

The class groaned, annoyed we'd be working in partners again. I chewed the inside of my cheek, praying she'd let me work alone.

"Come on, partner up. We'll be doing portraits of your partners in an abstract style," she announced, gesturing to the class to begin moving around.

Students chattered, turning to their friends and shifting their seats to partner up.

"Aspen," she said, snapping her fingers at me. "C'mon. Up up."

My stomach turned at being singled out, and I opened my mouth to tell her I had no one to partner with, when a person fell into the seat beside me.

"Want to be my partner?"

I turned, meeting the blue eyes of none other than Sebastian Georges. His shook out his blond curls and sent me a charming smile, his teeth a shining white against his tanned skin.

I opened my mouth, but no words came out. What was I supposed to say? It wasn't like I had a choice. I settled for a nod and he grinned wider, already opening his sketchpad.

"Are you any good at drawing?" he asked, quirking a brow at me.

I shook my head, my mouth feeling too dry to speak. Instead, I focused on opening my own sketchpad and beginning my drawing.

Sebastian Georges was speaking to me. But why? He never paid attention to me before this. He was always absorbed in his usual world of popular kids and soccer. He was another one of the "It Boys" that belonged in Isaac's world; a world completely different from mine.

Hell, the last time we'd spoken was when he kicked a soccer ball at my face and covered me in beef stroganoff.

"Me neither." He laughed, his pencil gliding across the paper. I thought of Isaac and how he could create artworks in minutes. "I normally partner up with my mates. We're all as bad as each other, but we were one odd today."

I nodded awkwardly, still focusing on my drawing. So that was why he was here, sitting with me. He had no choice either. I was a last resort. I couldn't blame him.

"At least today's theme is abstract," he flipped the page to show me the mangled drawing he'd begun. My head was an odd triangle, the rest of my body made up of rectangles and circles like a toddler had drawn it. "This could rival Picasso."

I laughed, my eyes finally moving to meet his and he sent me a proud grin, his chest puffed.

"Picasso was a cubist," I chided with a teasing smile.

"Ah, so she speaks after all." He smirked, tossing his sketchpad onto the table.

I rolled my eyes in jest, still grinning, and continued my artwork, not replying to his mischief. He pouted in response, batting his lashes at me.

"You were at Arthur's party, right?" he paused, waiting for an answer as I blushed awkwardly, thinking of how he'd seen me leave with Isaac in the morning. He shrugged at my silence, grinning.

"Back to the silence. That's okay, I can talk enough for the both of us."

I laughed. "I can see that."

"It's a talent."

"It's a curse."

"Wow! Insulting me and I don't even know your name." He placed a hand on my sketchpad, pushing it down to catch my eyes. "Which is?"

"Aspen. Haste." I met his eyes and couldn't help but smile. Like Riley, his enthusiasm was infectious. He grinned at me, his dimpled smile growing contagious.

"Aspen. My muse. It's been a pleasure."

I snorted and rolled my eyes. "That makes one of us."

He chuckled, leaning his chin on his hand against the table. "I think I preferred you when you didn't speak."

"Hey, you and me both," I retorted, and his laugh grew louder.

I smiled, forgetting how I entered the classroom upset and bitter. Sebastian's laughter was infectious. I felt better instantly.

Of course, Isaac still lingered in the back of my mind. But I can't lie, it was nice having some company.

CHAPTER FOURTEEN
French Press

"Wow, you're terrible."

I gasped, slapping Sebastian on the shoulder and earning a laugh in return. Giving up, I threw my sketchpad onto the desk, the awful surreal portrait of Sebastian scribbled onto the page. My pencil landed beside it with a clank and I sighed, crossing my arms—art really wasn't my forte.

Sebastian rubbed his shoulder jokingly with a pout. "Hey, don't hate the player, hate the game."

I rolled my eyes at him but couldn't help the wide grin that stretched across my lips.

It was the second day in a row Sebastian had partnered up with me in art. The second day in a row Isaac had skipped. Or maybe it was two weeks in a row? I had stopped keeping track.

If Isaac wanted to ruin his academic record, it was his problem. Besides, I had Sebastian to keep my company in class now.

I wondered if his friend was absent today too.

The bell sounded and I began packing my pens and books into my backpack. Today we had art before lunch, so I took my time, shoving my things into my bag.

Once done, I looked up, expecting to see Sebastian leaving with his friends, but instead he shrugged his backpack onto his shoulder and waited for me.

"You have lunch now?"

I blinked and he arched a brow at me.

"Yeah, you?" I asked, even though I knew he did. I'd watch him play soccer with Isaac and Arthur Andrews during lunch every day for these past few weeks.

"Yeah. I'm headed to the soccer field. Want to walk together?"

I smiled. I never would have thought I'd have a budding friendship with the school's hottest athlete, but here I was, walking to lunch with Sebastian Georges.

Today, the front of his usually messy blond curls was held back with a thin hair tie. His backpack hung off one shoulder and he walked with an air of confidence that I lacked. I felt so plain beside him, but for once, I didn't care.

Sebastian's smile was contagious, and I found myself smiling around him. He was like Riley—a bouncing ball of sunshine that infected everyone around them. And infect everyone, he did.

As we made our way through the halls, I didn't miss how students grinned at him and waved, calling out his name. He offered waves and nods in reply, his smile wide as I watched in awe.

We walked together, Sebastian greeting and slapping hands with half of the hallway until we reached the grass quad.

"Ms. Laney said next class we're finishing those portraits off," Sebastian mentioned as we exited the fluorescent halls.

I raised my brows. I hadn't heard her say that.

"No amount of work is going to improve that portrait of yours," I teased, smirking up at him.

He snorted. "Yeah, because it's already a masterpiece."

I laughed, shaking my head. "Really, where do you find all this confidence from?"

"Have you seen all this?" He gestured vaguely at his body, wiggling his brows at me.

I sputtered out a laugh, almost hunching over at his stupid expression.

"Aspirin."

I looked up to see Isaac standing in front of me. I blinked, looking around. *When had we reached the middle of the quad?* He watched me, his sparkling green eyes narrowed slightly, reflecting the grass of the quad. His dark hair was pushed back, as if he'd been running his fingers through it.

"Isaac!" Sebastian cheered, clapping him on the back.

Isaac's focus remained on me, his expression keeping neutral. A muscle in his jaw twitched. "What are you guys doing together?"

"We had art," I replied with a deadpan. "Which you'd know, if you weren't off skipping class."

His expression fell slightly, his brow furrowing. Sebastian grinned, nudging him roughly on the shoulder.

"Isaac was probably off with some girl," he teased. Isaac's eyes didn't move from mine and my heart panged. "I've seen Lacey eyeing you lately. I don't know how you do it, man. She hated you two weeks ago."

A blush rose to my cheeks under his gaze and I sucked in a shaky breath at the sound of Lacey's name. "Well, I'd better go."

"Wait! You should stay!" Sebastian grinned, bouncing on his toes. His curls bounced with him. "Play some soccer with us!"

My heart began to race. I was notoriously bad at saying no. I stepped back. "Oh, I can't. I'm really terrible."

"Oh, come on, Aspen! Have some fun!"

"Sorry, I don't think I should." I smiled awkwardly, taking another step back.

Isaac blinked, glancing between us, before his brows raised slightly in realisation.

"Yeah, Seb," he began playfully, shooting him a charming smile. "She's honestly terrible. She can't even catch a ball."

My face warmed at the memory of Isaac throwing a soccer ball at me only for it to smack me in the face, yet I was grateful. I met his eyes and he cut me a silent look that said he clearly knew I didn't want to play. I sent him a small smile in silent thanks.

Sebastian shook his head, nudging me. "Oh, come on. You don't have to be amazing or anything."

Isaac's head whipped back to his friend and his expression hardened. "Really, Sebastian, I don't think that's a good idea."

"Come on." Sebastian smirked at me. He paused, his smile growing, before raising his voice and quirking a brow at me. "As-pen! As-pen! As-pen!"

He began to chant and the pressure in my chest began to rise. Around us, students turned to look at the commotion he was causing.

Sebastian began to step back, clapping his hands together with a wide smile as he chanted.

"As-pen! As-pen! As-pen!"

My eyes grew wide, my breath beginning to speed up. *What was he doing?* I opened my mouth to say no, to stop him, but my mouth felt abruptly dry and the words refused to come out.

"As-pen! As-pen! As-pen!"

"Seb," Isaac muttered, stepping forward. "Drop it."

Sebastian ignored him, his grin only growing wider and his voice growing louder. My heart leapt, lodging firmly in my throat and taking any chance of me speaking with it.

I felt the gaze of students around me, watching me, staring at me, analyzing me. My palms began to sweat. I sunk my fingernails into my skin, willing myself to calm down, but my eyes flickered around the oval.

I turned, moving from student to student, each and every one of them staring at me. A few even joined in with the chanting, their voices sounding malicious and teasing to my anxious ears. I couldn't bear it.

103

I spun to see Sebastian, grinning, waving his arms in encouragement. Beside him, Isaac's eyes were trained on me, his expression hardened, his jaw clenching. He took another step towards Sebastian, grabbing his shoulder tightly.

"Sebastian, knock it off."

"As-pen! As-pen! As-pen!"

"Sebastian, seriously."

"As-pen! As-pen! As-pen!"

"Sebastian!"

My focus snapped to Isaac barrelling forward, grabbing Sebastian by the collar of his shirt. He fell quiet instantly, his eyes wide and his hands raised in surrender.

Isaac was fuming. His eyes were glaring holes into his head, his fist clenching Sebastian's collar as he breathed heavily down his neck.

His face was screwed up in anger, and he muttered some words to him. There was shouting, I think. The world spun beneath me, and there was shouting, and yelling, and gasps from somewhere behind me.

I vaguely heard Sebastian apologising, but I couldn't focus. All I could focus on was my breathing.

Breathe in. Breathe out. Calm down, it's fine. You're fine.

Suddenly, Isaac's fingers were wrapped around my wrist and I was being led back to the main building.

Breathe in.

We walked through the hallways without a word.

Breathe out.

He pushed through the library doors, storming through the aisles.

Breathe in.

We came to a stop in front of a windowsill. My windowsill. I fell onto the sill in a heap, my fingers digging into the cushions of the seat.

Breathe out.

My breathing slowly returned to normal and my heart began to slow. My trembling fingers fell still, and I sighed, relaxing against the cool glass of the window. I paused for a minute, shoving my fingers through my hair and attempting to ground myself.

After a moment, I lifted my eyes from the ground to meet Isaac's. He stared at me, concern written all over his face.

"I'm fine," I said before he could say anything. My voice was stronger than I had expected. "Thanks."

"Are you sure?"

"Yeah." I sighed, fatigue beginning to wrack through my body. "I'm okay. Thank you, Isaac. I feel like you're always saving me."

I managed a weak laugh, but he remained unconvinced. He narrowed his eyes, shaking his head.

"Sebastian's an assh*le. I should have done more. I should have . . ." he trailed off with his fists clenched.

Feeling brave, I lifted a hand and rest it on his arm. He turned to me, his expression instantly softened.

"He couldn't have known," I said. "He was just trying to have fun. He wanted me to have fun."

Isaac pursed his lips. "Still. He shouldn't have done that. He shouldn't have pressured you like that. In front of everyone."

"He didn't mean anything by it." I sent him a small smile. "I'm fine."

He clenched his jaw before nodding slightly. His eyes trailed down my body, scanning me, before moving back to my face.

"If you want to have a nap, go ahead."

I blinked, raising my brows.

"You look tired."

I laughed quietly, leaning my head against the window. I was like an open book under his gaze. "I haven't been getting much sleep lately. I guess that sudden shot of anxiety didn't help."

He smiled finally, and pushed a hand through his hair. He turned and sat in front of the windowsill, reminding me of the day I slept in here with him reading a stupid book about lizards by my feet.

"You're staying?"

"Of course," he replied nonchalantly, plucking a random book from a nearby shelf. "And don't worry. I won't watch you while you sleep."

I laughed at our inside joke, moving to lie against the windowsill. It felt natural. All of my earlier disappointment towards Isaac vanished, taking my anxiety with it. My mind went quiet around him. The racing thoughts of Sebastian and the crowd and art and soccer faded into silence.

All I could think about was the heat radiating off of him. The messy waves of his hair. How close he was sitting to me.

I rested on the seat with my eyes trained on the back of Isaac's head.

I looked at the broadness of his shoulders, how his hair crept down to the nape of his neck. He tensed, as if keenly aware of myself staring at him from behind.

I watched his muscles flex in his back, the bend of his shoulders, and the curve of his collar. I thought of how much I wished he'd hold me in those arms.

And I fell asleep.

CHAPTER FIFTEEN
Café au Lait

"Aspen?"

I turned, meeting the wide blue eyes of Sebastian Georges.

It had been two days since that humiliating incident on the soccer field. After I woke up in the library that day, Isaac had stayed behind, skipping class while I shuffled to English.

We quickly returned to our routine of not speaking to each other.

I was getting used to it.

That didn't stop me from staring longingly at him in the halls like an absolute creep. Could you blame me? He was like a Greek God, with his tousled dark hair and glowing tanned skin. His leather jacket reminded me of the smell of his cologne.

My heart raced at the mere thought of him.

I blinked, forcing myself to focus on the blond mess of curls in front of me. He stood over me as I sat in my usual corner of the art room. His brow slightly arched, and his lips pressed in an awkward, querying smile.

"Sebastian," I finally sputtered, eyes wide.

"I'm sorry," he gushed before I could say anything more. "I was stupid the other day. I shouldn't have pressured you like that in front of everyone. That's on me."

My expression softened into a small smile. He stared down at me, his eyes sorry and his mouth tugged into a frown.

I turned to face the ground.

"It's fine, really," I replied timidly. "Don't worry about it."

Sebastian's face broke into a grin of relief and he slid into the seat beside me.

"Thank God, I was scared you hated me now."

I laughed quietly and jokingly said, "Don't test me, though."

"Do you want to pair up again, today?" he asked with a grin, already opening his sketchbook as if expecting me to say yes.

It wasn't like I had a choice. I had no one else to partner up with in this class. I was always the odd one out.

I opened my mouth to reply when a voice interrupted me.

"She already agreed to pair with me."

I turned to meet the green eyes of none other than Isaac Hensick.

I didn't see him at lunch last period and definitely didn't expect him to turn up to class. I hated the way my heart hiccupped at his voice. He stood beside me, watching Sebastian with a clenched jaw and narrowed eyes.

Sebastian raised his brows. "When?"

"Does it matter?" Isaac spat, his gaze hardening.

Sebastian's eyes widened and he stood from his seat. "Sh*t, Isaac. Okay, fine."

His gaze turned to me and he sent me a lopsided grin. "See ya, Aspen."

He gathered his belongings and turned to leave, his friends quickly shouting after him on the other side of the classroom. I watched as Sebastian paired with another boy before returning my focus to Isaac.

Isaac's eyes trained on me as he sat beside me, pulling out his sketchpad as Ms. Laney blabbered on about our instructions for the day.

We were silent for a minute. Today's activity entailed sketching a still life, with each pair using a different prop. In front of us rested a basket of fake apples.

I focused on the apples, sketching circles on my page and shading in random places in an attempt to make it look less like a five-year-old child's shot at art.

Beside me, Isaac sketched slowly, his hands moving gracefully in smooth, calculated movements. Even though we were supposed to be sketching the still life, I couldn't help but peek over at Isaac every few minutes.

My eyes flickered to him for the dozenth time that lesson to find him smirking back at me.

I blushed, spinning to face the apples again.

"Surprised to see you back in class today," I stammered, trying to make it look like I was only trying to converse.

He held on to his smirk, seeing right through my bluff, and sent me a casual shrug.

"I just thought we haven't really been speaking much lately," he said.

I blinked. I had thought I was the only one who noticed—the only one who missed our conversations, even if they were short and most of the time awkward.

I realised he was staring at me and I hadn't replied.

"Well, I mean, you don't come to class—which is totally fine by the way—and you know, we both have our own friends and I guess responsibilities and commitments, so sometimes it can be hard, and it's not a big deal. We're talking now, anyway. Am I talking too much? I feel like I'm talking too much . . ." I found myself rambling.

Isaac smirked at me in reply.

"Aspirin," he said. "You always talk too much."

I blushed, fiddling with my sketch pencil. "I'm sorry."

He smiled wider in response. "I like it."

I could feel the warmth creep up my neck and stain my ears. He noticed too, his eyes trained on my face, our sketchpads long discarded, and sent me a smug grin.

I grew hot under his gaze, my heart speeding up. I thought of how he'd hugged me in his arms, of how he remembered my order and bought me coffee. I thought of how he'd lent me his jacket, how he whispered in my ears.

I thought of Lacey.

"So," I began after a moment, curiosity getting the better of me. "What's happening with you and Lacey?"

Isaac's face fell into a neutral expression and I momentarily regretted bringing her up. He shrugged.

"Nothing."

I sent him a pointed look and he laughed.

"Seriously, nothing is happening. We decided we're better as friends."

I had to stop myself from snorting. Friends. Lacey didn't stay friends with people for long—especially not with hot, tall, tanned, dimpled boys like Isaac.

I opened my mouth to debate him when the bell sounded. I blinked in disbelief. The lesson felt so short. I packed my sketchpad up alongside Isaac when he turned to me.

"Walk you to your locker?" he asked.

I fought the grin that stretched across my face, trying not to seem too eager. "Sure."

We walked out of the class side by side. His backpack was slung off one shoulder while I wore mine with both straps, my sketchbook clutched close to my chest.

We walked through the corridors, teasing each other about our artworks and knocking elbows.

The halls were full of students stopping by their lockers in the rush to get home. We passed them, students pausing and turning to watch us. Probably wondering why Isaac was lowering his standards from Lacey and Chloe to someone like me.

We reached my locker in seconds. William stood leaning beside my locker, his eyes growing wide when he noticed me walking with none other than Isaac Hensick.

"Aspen," William sputtered out, his wide eyes flickering between me and Isaac.

"Hey." I smiled, pausing to open my locker.

Beside me, Isaac came to a pause, leaning beside the locker and looking William up and down, his jaw set.

William practically trembled beside him. I had to stifle a laugh.

"What time do I go to yours again?" I asked, snapping him out of his daze.

Isaac raised his brows.

"Five," William replied. "Earlier if you can. Don't forget the KitKats and Skittles. She won't forgive you if you don't bring any."

I laughed, remembering the last time I had forgotten to bring them to a movie night. Riley had gone on a hunger strike, refusing to eat anything the entire night and refusing to speak to us until the next day when I bought her all the KitKats and Skittles she could want.

Granted, we were nine years old, but I never made that mistake again.

"Noted," I said, slamming my locker shut and shrugging my backpack on my shoulders to make it sit more comfortably.

Isaac leaned forward.

"You guys are meeting after school?"

I laughed. We've been meeting after school almost every other day since we met.

"Yeah, we're best friends," I said. "Besides, we're throwing a surprise party for Riley's birthday."

Isaac's shoulders sagged as if in relief.

"Oh, right," he said with a small chuckle. "Well happy birthday to her."

I smiled, opening my mouth to say goodbye when William spoke.

"You should come."

My eyes widened and I spun to face him, sending him a look that clearly said, "What the hell are you doing?"

William ignored my look.

"Really?" Isaac asked, quirking a brow, and William nodded frantically.

I clenched my jaw. There was no way Isaac would want to waste his Friday night hanging out with . . .us. I loved my friends, but we could get pretty weird when we were together.

We were an acquired taste.

Besides, I was sure Isaac had much more "cool guy" things to do on a Friday night than eat Skittles and watch rom-coms.

That's why I was so surprised when Isaac opened his mouth and said, "Sure."

I blinked in disbelief, my jaw turning slack.

"Great!" William grinned. He sent me a hopeful look and suddenly it all clicked together.

He didn't want to be a third wheel with me and Riley. He wanted me to be stuck with Isaac. He wanted Riley to himself.

I had to give it to him, it was smart. It was a great excuse for him to sit next to Riley all night and chat her ear off without her trying to include me.

"Great," I echoed finally, turning to smile at Isaac. "Well, I'm sure William will send you all the details. I have some Skittles to go buy."

I turned to walk down the hallway towards the exit, already beginning to overthink what will happen tonight, already overthinking how I was going to have to struggle to make conversation the entire night.

"Wait!" Isaac was beside me in seconds, his shoes squeaking next to mine. "Wait up, Aspirin."

"What?" I asked, not stopping. He walked next to me, quickly outpacing my steps with his long legs.

"Let me drive you."

"What?"

"Let me drive you. We're going to the same place anyway, right?"

I paused, blinking. "I guess . . ."

"So," he concluded with a smirk. "Let me drive you. As a thank you for the invitation."

I laughed, "William invited you. Maybe you should go hop in a car with him."

"Oh, right, see you then." He turned to walk away from me.

"Wait!" I shouted, spinning to stop him.

He stopped a smug smirk tugging on his lips. "Oh, so now you want a ride?"

I blushed and rolled my eyes, a small smile playing on my mouth.

"Let's go, Aspirin," he says as he stepped past me, striding nonchalantly towards the double door exits.

I swallowed my anxiety, taking a deep breath through my nose, and followed him.

Isaac slid into the driver's seat, starting the engine with a hum and immediately switching the radio on. I blushed, remembering the day he had driven me home after I had become a blubbering mess at Arthur Andrews's party.

I released a shaky breath and tugged on the handle of the passenger door. I quickly hopped in, buckling my seat belt and was instantly hit with the smell of Isaac's cologne.

113

"Alright," Isaac said, beginning to pull out of the parking lot. "Where to?"

I blinked, trying to ignore how close Isaac was to me. How his fingers gripped the steering wheel, how he placed his hand behind my seat while reversing.

"Well," I sputtered finally. "I need to buy some classic movie night snacks. Could we stop by Marty's on Hayes Street?"

Isaac nodded, taking a sharp right and driving towards the supermarket. He tapped his fingers against the steering wheel to the rap song playing on the radio. I felt so aware in my body beside him and desperately felt the need to fill the silence.

"Rap, huh?"

Isaac blinked, "What?"

"You like rap?"

He threw me a look. "Yeah, I guess."

"Cool."

I really made it more awkward, didn't I?

I cleared my throat, turning to watch the buildings pass by us outside the window, trying to stop myself from staring at Isaac as he drove. Hayes Street wasn't far from the school. It would be a ten-minute drive at most, with this after school traffic.

Besides, it was close to William's. I've worked there every summer since I was fourteen for some extra money to pay for my daily coffees. It really added up, even with Vivienne's student discounts.

"You guys do this often?"

I blinked, moving my focus back to Isaac. He glanced at me in the corner of his eye.

"You know, throw surprise birthdays for each other, have movie nights."

"Oh." My voice sounded croaky and strained. I coughed. "Yeah, always. I don't know if you've noticed, but I'm not much of the party type."

114

Isaac barked out a laugh. "Really? You had me fooled."

"I know, I just looked like the biggest party animal hiding in that bedroom hyperventilating," I teased back with an eyeroll. "I'm just multidimensional like that."

Isaac grinned at me, his cheeks dimpling as he glanced between me and the road.

The car began rolling to a stop as he turned into the parking lot at Marty's, and parked the car near the entrance. I tried to ignore the disappointment I felt at having arrived already. I wished it was a longer drive. I wanted to keep sitting here, joking like this.

Isaac slid out of the door as I unbuckled my seat belt. Before I knew it, he jogged around to my door and held it open with a grin and a dramatic gesture towards the supermarket.

"Miss Aspirin," he spoke with a posh British accent. "Welcome to Marty's Mini Mart."

CHAPTER SIXTEEN
Iced Coffee

Despite its name, Marty's Mini Mart is huge. It has over twenty aisles and a dozen checkouts filled with bored-looking cashiers.

The white tiles glared in the fluorescent lighting and the air conditioner blasted cold air at full strength. I shivered, wrapping my arms around me and rubbing the goose bumps from my skin.

Isaac came to a stop beside me. I tried not to think about how close he stood to me, how his heat radiated off his body, how he was so close I could smell his cologne. My body stiffened, feeling uncomfortably aware of myself next to him.

"So," Isaac began, looking around the mostly empty supermarket. "What are we getting?"

"Well, first things first," I said, rubbing my arms in an attempt to warm myself up. I turned, catching the sight of colourful packets of candy lining the aisles. "Skittles."

"Skittles?" Isaac sent me a look of confusion, quirking a brow at me. He followed my gaze, blinking.

"Skittles," I confirmed, moving towards the candy aisle.

He raised his brows, following me as I grabbed a basket and began the hunt for Skittles.

"Skittles aren't even that good," he said lightly, his voice amused and teasing. "You should try Warheads. They'll change your life."

"Trust me," I began, my voice grimly serious. I sent him a sour look, and he raised a brow. "You don't want to see Riley at a movie night without Skittles."

"What happens?" he asked, his voice piqued with curiosity.

"Two words," I said with low tone. "Hunger strike."

"Hunger strike?" he echoed.

I nodded firmly. "You should be glad you weren't there."

He narrowed his eyes at me, twinkling with mischief. "I'll take your word for it."

We made our way down the aisle, scanning the shelves for the familiar red packet of Skittles.

"Skittles," Isaac hummed, his head spinning left and right as he scanned the aisle. "Skittles . . . Skittles . . ."

Quiet piano music played over the speakers as I continued to look through the aisle. I forced myself to focus on the packets of candy on the shelves, and not on the cute boy beside me. I had to be cool. I had to stop thinking so much.

Oreos, Starbursts, Jolly Ranchers. I kept walking. *M&Ms, Twizzlers, Nerds . . .*

"Aspirin!"

My head snapped up to spot Isaac on the other end of the aisle with two middle-aged couples standing between us. I blushed as the strangers looked up to stare at the yelling boy with a packet of Skittles in his hands. He grinned at me, shaking the packet in the air, his eyes mischievous and playful

"Go long!"

My eyes immediately widened. I was torn between telling him to not even think about it and calmly walking away as if I didn't know him when the packet of candy came soaring through the sky.

I squealed, squeezing my eyes shut and holding my basket out. The Skittles landed with a thud in the basket.

"Goal!"

My cheeks grew hot under the gaze of the middle-aged couples, but before I could run away, Isaac jogged up to me and threw an arm around my shoulder, scanning the aisles thoughtfully. I wasn't sure if I was blushing from his arm around me or the embarrassment that was Isaac Hensick.

Either way, I was as red as the bag of Skittles resting in my basket.

"Okay, we got the Skittles, what's next?"

"Isaac!" I sputtered, my eyes wide and ears pink.

"Aspirin!" he mocked me, his voice high-pitched and nasally, a smug smirk on his lips.

I blinked, attempting to find the words. The couples had moved on, leaving the aisle with a glance and a glare in our direction. I sighed, fighting the chuckle that began to bubble out of my chest.

It was pretty funny.

And the way Isaac was staring at me, all smug and grinning, showed he knew it was funny and knew the internal battle I was going through. So, I settled my face into a deadpan and swallowed the laugh building in my throat, refusing to give him the satisfaction.

He raised a brow at me, smirking, and I held eye-contact, keeping my lips sealed shut.

"We need KitKats," I decided, turning to face the shelves.

He nodded, releasing me from his hold and turning to scan the aisles.

He leaned over, his lips pursed in thought and eyes narrowed at the shelves in scrutiny.

Behind him, I finally spotted the KitKats, grabbing a few packets of different flavors and tossing them into my basket. I was scanning the shelves for Riley's favourite flavor—matcha—when Isaac spoke right beside my ear.

"Wanna kiss?"

My eyes widened and I spun to face him, his breath sending a shiver down my spine. I met his stare, only to see Isaac grinning, a bag of Hershey's Kisses in his hand. I frowned, cutting him a sharp glare.

"What are you, twelve?" I shot back, rolling my eyes. "That joke's been around since middle school."

His lips twitched into a playful grin and I ignored how hot I suddenly felt and the prickle of goose bumps down my neck. I grabbed the bag of chocolate from his hand and shoved it into the basket, turning to walk past him.

"Hey, the offer still stands." He wiggled his brows.

A laugh finally burst from my lips at his stupid expression, and his grin widened, pleased with my reaction. I blinked, surprised at my own response, realising how comfortable I felt now. My mind had stopped overworking, overthinking everything. I fought a smile from forming on my lips as Isaac and I looked at each other, stupid expressions reflected on both our faces.

His eyes softened, and I had the feeling that he did it on purpose. He has been acting like an idiot to try and loosen me up. And it worked.

Warmth blossomed through me at the realisation. Still smiling, I turned, grabbing some Reese's Peanut Butter Cups and peanut M&Ms on the way down the aisle.

"You're not allergic to peanuts, are you?" I asked.

"Will you give me mouth to mouth if I am?"

I rolled my eyes. "I'd let you die a slow death."

"In that case—" He threw a bag of Doritos and some microwavable popcorn boxes into the basket. "I am not."

"That's unfortunate," I teased drily, nudging his arm. "Had my hopes up for a second."

119

He gasped jokingly, clutching at his chest. "Here I was, thinking we were friends, driving you around. Now I see it was all a lie."

I shoved his shoulder and he laughed loudly, trailing after me with a boyish grin.

We walked towards the cash registers and I emptied the basket onto the conveyer belt. The cashier muttered a "Hello, how are you?" and I ignored how my heart raced at such a simple social interaction.

"That will be $15.94," the cashier said, her voice dripping with false enthusiasm.

"Right," I muttered, reaching for my wallet and fumbling for cash.

Before I could find the correct change, Isaac stepped forward, passing his card to the cashier. "I've got it."

I blinked, opening my mouth to debate when he cut me off.

"I can't show up without a gift for the birthday girl," he explained, shrugging nonchalantly.

I swallowed my words, nodding, and stepped back. He was right, and if this would make him feel more comfortable being there, I'd let him do it. I mean, the cashier had already processed his payment anyway.

She shoved the receipt into one of the bags and handed Isaac's card back. He stepped forward and easily lifted the two bags of straight junk food into his hands, turning to exit the shop.

"Thank you for shopping at Marty's Mini Mart." The cashier smiled. "Come again soon."

"Thanks," I muttered, walking awkwardly after Isaac as he made his way to the car.

We crossed the parking lot, and, within seconds, we were back in his car, the engine roaring to life. I glanced at my phone. It was half past four. We had half an hour to get to William's house.

"So," Isaac said, beginning to pull out of his parking spot. "Which way is it to William's?"

"Actually," I said, pulling at my sleeves. "Can we stop by my place first? I need to pick up Riley's present."

"Sure," Isaac replied, driving out of the parking lot and beginning down the road.

I opened my mouth to direct him when he took the exact turn we needed, pulling easily onto my street. I raised my brows, ignoring the way my heart fluttered when he remembered where I lived.

He pulled up to my house in less than five minutes and rolled to a stop.

"I'll wait here," he said simply, nodding to the door.

"I'll be out in five seconds." I nodded, pushing the car door open and slipping out.

I rushed inside, stepping through the living room to grab the small gift bag sitting in my room. I was about to leave, turning back to the door before I paused, glancing at my reflection in the mirror.

My hair was tied up in a frizzy ponytail and I wore my usual blue jeans with a sweater tugged over the top. I pulled my sweater, scrunching my nose at the baggy material. Isaac had the unfortunate task of looking at me while I looked like this.

I sighed, thinking of Chloe Pepper's perfectly straightened hair and Lacey's expertly applied makeup. Thinking of their cute outfits that flawlessly fit their bodies that the boys spent their days staring at—including Isaac.

I pinched my cheeks. My skin was breaking out and I was greasy from a long day at school. I glanced at my alarm clock. I still had twenty minutes, and William's house was a five-minute drive from my place.

I grabbed at my hair tie, pulling it out and letting my hair out in loose waves over my shoulders. I combed my fingers through my scalp, trying to calm the frizz down and part it in the middle.

It was . . .almost decent.

I quickly shuffled into my bathroom, washing my face and putting on some moisturizer to refresh my blotchy skin. I grabbed some concealer, attempting to hide my dark bags and red spots before I curled my lashes, coating them in a generous layer of mascara and threw on some blush and light contour.

It wasn't much, but it was better than what I started with.

I glanced at the clock, hoping I hadn't left Isaac waiting too long, and jogged out of my house.

When I hopped back into his car, his eyes trailed over me, scanning my face.

I blushed beneath his gaze, self-consciously pushing my fingers through my hair as I buckled my seat belt. When I turned back to him, he was still watching me, a small grin tugging at the corner of his lips.

"Let's do this."

CHAPTER SEVENTEEN
Corretto

"Surprise!"

"Oh my God, guys! I had no idea!"

We all laughed as Riley fell to the floor in tears of joyful surprise. She held her hands to her mouth as she let out loud sobs. Meredith, one of Riley's close friends, wrapped her arms around her as Riley cried out "Thank yous" to everyone.

Beside me, Isaac stood awkwardly to the side.

"Is she always like this?" he whispered, his lips hovering so close to my ear. I could feel his breath fan down my neck.

I laughed loudly, chills running down my arms. "Pretty much."

Once Riley regained her composure, she closed the front door behind her and stepped fully into William's house. His mother was out on a romantic date with her "dag of a boyfriend" as William had put it, leaving the entire house to ourselves.

We kept it small. Just our usual trio, plus two of Riley's close friends Meredith and Peter. And of course, Isaac.

We all gathered around Riley, our gifts in hand. Riley held back a sob, wiping tears from her eyes, a glowing grin plastered on her face.

"Happy birthday, Riles," Meredith began with her quiet voice, passing a small blue gift bag to her.

Meredith was a mousy girl with long brown hair. Her dark skin contrasted with Peter's pale, freckled face, his blond hair short and spiked. Riley met them in middle school when she took cheer club with Meredith. They stood beside each other, grinning.

Riley took the gift bag with a smile. "Thanks Mer."

She reached into the bag, pulling out a small bottle of perfume. She grinned, pulling the cap off and smelling the floral scent with a sigh.

"It's so nice!"

"I'm glad you like it. It's from me and Peter." Meredith grinned, her cheeks tugging up as Peter pulled her to his side.

Meredith and Peter had been dating since middle school, and it was honestly no surprise they were still together. They were perfect for each other. Both were shy and quiet, and Peter seemed to just shower her with affection.

It was sickeningly adorable.

I stepped up next, handing Riley my gift bag. Isaac stood awkwardly behind me, empty-handed.

I smiled, grabbing his arm and tugging him to my side. "This is from me and Isaac."

Isaac's eyes widened, but he said nothing, only sending me a grateful smile. Riley raised an eyebrow at me suggestively and grinned before pulling out the branded hair straightener I had spent months saving up for.

"Aspen, I love it!" she squealed, hugging me with a grin. She looked up at Isaac and hugged him lightly. "Thank you, Isaac."

He sent her a gentle smile and rubbed a hand behind his neck. "It was nothing."

I chuckled and stepped back as she moved on to William's present.

William spent weeks coming up with the perfect gift idea, finally settling for a charm bracelet. Each charm signified a special event in their friendship. It was adorable. Riley must have loved it because she began squealing and tearing up all over again.

While she hugged William as a thank you, causing him to blush like a tomato, Isaac leaned closer to me.

"Thank you," he whispered.

"No worries," I muttered, a blush creeping up my neck.

"Let's watch a movie!" Riley squealed, traipsing into the living room and plopping down onto the couch.

"Well," I said, my cheeks turning pink at how close Isaac stood beside me. "Let's go."

I followed Riley into the lounge room. Peter and Meredith already made themselves comfortable, cuddling on one end in the dark. On the other end of the couch, William and Riley sat beside each other.

William's face was so red you could see him glowing in the dark, whereas Riley smiled obliviously at the movie. I stifled a laugh at the two, making my way to the air mattress William had left in front of the couch.

Isaac sat beside me, leaning against the couch as William started the movie.

We had movie nights at William's house all the time, mostly because his mother was the coolest mother on the planet. She wouldn't care if he got a girl pregnant, only fight over who it would be named after. I suppose it was because she felt guilty about William's hatred for her mother's new boyfriend.

Although, I knew William secretly just wanted his mom to be happy.

"What the hell is going on?" Isaac whispered to me. His brow furrowed in confusion at the movie. He leaned toward me, his shoulder knocking against mine.

I laughed quietly. "What do you mean?"

"Why is she angry at him?"

"Because he didn't kiss her."

125

"Why didn't he kiss her?"

"Because she's drunk."

"Why did she get drunk?"

I rolled my eyes and let out a loud sigh. "Isaac, just pay attention to the movie and you'll figure it out."

"But I can't pay attention with you next to me."

My cheeks turned bright red and I smacked him on the shoulder. I shook my head and turned back to the movie, trying desperately to pay attention, but all I could think about was his leg pressed against mine and our shoulders knocking with every tiny movement. Blushing, I sipped my glass of water only to realise it was empty.

I looked up at my friends. "Do you guys want anything from the kitchen?"

They all shook their heads wordlessly, occupied by the movie or, in William's case, by Riley's face. I laughed silently to myself and took my glass cup in hand, making my way towards the kitchen.

I stepped on the tiles, the cold floor making the hairs on my neck stand on end. I shivered, moving to refill my water before holding the cold glass to my cheeks.

I was burning. I haven't been able to pay attention to the movie at all. I was too focused on the way Isaac's shoulder rubbed against mine and the way his leg pressed against my thigh.

This was bad. How would I survive the rest of the night?

"Hey."

Speak of the Devil. I turned to see Isaac strolling into the kitchen, his hands stuffed into his pockets.

"Isaac?" I said, blinking. "What's up? I asked if you wanted anything from the kitchen?"

"I didn't." He shrugged. He paused, giving me a funny look. "I don't know what's going on in the movie anyway."

I laughed. "It's Riley's favourite."

We were quiet for a minute. Isaac leaned on the counter in front of me as I took a sip of my water.

"When's your birthday?" he finally said.

I rose my eyebrows. "What?"

"When's your birthday?" he repeated, leaning closer.

"What, are you going to throw me a surprise birthday too?" I teased with a snort.

His face remained serious. "Maybe I will."

I blushed under his gaze and moved to stare at the water in my glass. "October 24."

"Got it." He broke out in a smirk. "Though it's not much of a surprise if you already know, is it?"

I laughed, rolling my eyes. "What about you?"

"Me?"

"Yeah, what if I want to throw you a surprise party too?"

He chuckled at this, leaning his arm over the counter. "May 7."

"Got it," I mocked in a stupid low voice.

We laughed simultaneously and my heart hitched at the way he leaned forward, his dark hair falling over his eyes. Our laughter died down and we were silent for a minute before Isaac's eyes widened.

"Wait, October 24? That's in a few weeks." His eyes widened further, and he raised his brows. "Just before the Halloween Dance?"

I nodded, pursing my lips. The Halloween Dance. Every year, our school threw a Halloween Dance for the seniors. I hadn't been planning on attending. It wasn't like I had a date.

"Are you going with Lacey?" I asked before I could stop myself.

Isaac pursed his lips and shrugged nonchalantly. "I don't know. I haven't asked."

"Oh."

"What about you?"

I blinked. "Me?"

"Yeah." He stepped closer. "Are you going with anyone?"

I shook my head. "I'm not going at all."

"You're not?"

I snorted. "Remember? Not exactly the party type?"

He narrowed his eyes at me, staring me directly in the eye. I was suddenly keenly aware of how close he had become to me. His arm rested on the counter, almost touching mine. If I took one step forward, we'd be practically hugging.

"It's not a big deal." I shrugged, suddenly feeling extremely flustered. "I mean, you can have fun. With Lacey, you know? It's just- I don't really—"

"Aspen," he said, cutting me short.

My heart shuddered at the sound of my name.

"Did I tell you how pretty you looked today?"

I blushed, inhaling sharply. My stomach filled with butterflies.

"What?" I sputtered, finding it hard to tear my eyes away from his.

His hand reached out, a finger moving to tuck my hair behind my ear. The corner of his lips pulled up in a small smile. His eyes moved from mine to my lips.

"You look pretty today," he repeated, his voice low and quiet.

My eyes flickered his lips and back to his eyes, my ears growing hot. I swallowed thickly.

"I don't understand," I stammered, blinking in confusion.

He moved an inch closer. He was so close. I could feel his breath fanning over my lips. His eyelashes looked so long; his cheekbones so high. I felt tempted to just lean in.

"I really want to kiss you right now." His voice was low and raspy.

My heart raced. *Was I imagining this?*

His darkened eyes dragged slowly up my face to meet my eyes. His hand moved to cup my cheek; his hand warm against my face. His fingers brushed my hair from my cheek, and he leaned closer until his lips were less than an inch away from mine.

My eyes fluttered shut and I sucked in a deep breath through my nose. I could feel his breath fanning over my lips and over my neck. My heart was thundering in my chest.

"Isaac," I said, gently pulling away, only for him to hold me in place.

"Aspen," he whispered back. "Can I kiss you?"

I didn't hesitate. I answered for him, leaning in and pressing my lips against his.

My mind instantly fell silent.

I felt him smile into the kiss, his lips moving gently against mine in a slow kiss. I threw my arms around his neck, tangling my fingers in his hair. He tasted like coffee and popcorn all at once.

The only thing on my mind was, God, this boy can really kiss.

His hand fell from my cheek to my waist, pulling me closer against his body. He tilted his head, deepening the kiss. My own hands moved to rest my palms flat against his hard chest. I sighed, pressing my body against his.

Suddenly, Isaac pulled back, panting. His hair was messy from me running my fingers through it and his eyes flickered between both of my own.

I pressed a finger to my lips, in slight disbelief of what had just happened. He searched my eyes for a moment, unsure, and I tore them away from his gaze, embarrassed.

"I—" I cut myself off, not sure of what I planned to say. What was there to say?

Isaac seemed to know.

"I'm sorry," he said, blinking and stepping back. "I shouldn't have done that."

"What?" I sputtered, my brows drawing together.

He took another step back, his eyes wide and face flushed, before turning and rushing out the kitchen.

I blinked, my eyes trained on where he had just stood only moment ago, the touch of his lips and fingers still lingering on my skin.

What just happened?

CHAPTER EIGHTEEN
Turkish Coffee

"You can't avoid him forever."

"I can try."

Riley rolled her eyes at me as I peeked out from behind the wall. Isaac was nowhere to be seen. I sighed in relief, stepping out from my hiding spot with a wide yawn.

I've had a sleepless weekend. After Isaac stormed out of the kitchen, he left William's house, leaving me to overthink everything for the entire weekend.

I skipped the café this morning, not sure how I'd be able to face Isaac, not sure what I'd say.

Had I done something wrong? Was I that dreadful of a kisser that he had to leave in the middle of the movie?

It was so embarrassing. I could barely tell Riley and William about it—the words coming out like razors through gritted teeth. And coming to school today was like that multiplied by fifty. Every squeak of a shoe, flash of leather, scent of tobacco, and my heart rate was spiking all over again.

I was tired.

Riley rubbed my back as we walked towards my art class. I prayed Isaac would skip class today. Out of all the days he could skip class, today was the day I really wanted it.

"Told you so."

My eyes widened at Riley's teasing voice as we reached the classroom door. There, in my usual corner, sat Isaac Hensick.

His eyes reached mine, and I turned quickly to face Riley only to find she had disappeared, because of course she had. Because of course I had to choose a class with none of my friends in it, even though I hated art.

His eyes were still on me when I turned back. My cheeks burned. I took in a deep breath. My fingers tapped uneasily against my thigh.

I got this.

I exhaled, turning to walk into the classroom, completely avoiding eye contacting with Isaac.

Instead, I marched over to the opposite side of the classroom where Sebastian chatted jovially amongst his friends—he seemed to be friends with everyone.

I paused beside him, folding my arms over my chest.

"Sebastian."

They continued chatting as if I wasn't there. I cleared my throat, mustering up the confidence to try again before the adrenaline wore off.

"Sebastian. You're my partner today."

The group fell silent, their eyes moving to focus on me. I steadied myself, keeping my focus trained on Sebastian.

He raised his brows at me, a cheeky smile on his lips. "Am I now?"

I nodded, ignoring the way Isaac's eyes continued to burn into the back of my head.

Sebastian turned to the girls beside him. "You heard her. Move."

They didn't say a word as they grabbed their sketchpads and slid down a desk, making room for me to sit beside Sebastian.

Seconds later, Ms. Laney entered with the loud taps of her heels against the classroom tile.

"Settle down, everyone," she shouted, moving to the front of the class. "We'll be continuing our abstract portraits from our last class. Find your partners."

I couldn't help but glance at Isaac in the corner, wondering who he was planning to partner with. More accurately, wondering if he'd be partnering with Lacey. I dragged my eyes to his seat only to find him already staring directly at me.

I blushed, spinning to face my desk, pulling my book open. We had paired up in our last class and I had ended up with a terrible portrait of Isaac in my sketchbook. I stared down at it, feeling waves of longing and embarrassment rush through me.

It really was a mangled sketch of a portrait. Somehow, the eyes had ended up half the size of the nose, and the jawline . . . let's not even discuss that.

A smile pulled at my lips as I imagined what he might say about it. Probably something like, "Geeze, Aspirin. Maybe you should reconsider this subject."

"Did something happen between you two?"

I blinked, turning my attention to the curly-haired boy beside me. I raised a brow at Sebastian while he smirked back at me, leaning on his hand towards me. His eyes twinkled mischievously as he regarded me, and I warmed beneath his gaze.

"Why would you think that?"

"Aspen." He laughed. "You're as red as a tomato."

My hands flew to my burning cheeks.

"No, I'm not."

"Besides." He leaned closer, lowering his voice to a whisper as he stared over my shoulder. "He's staring at me like he wants to murder me."

I spun to find Isaac glaring at us, his jaw set, and fists clenched. He had partnered with a boy named Jack, though he wasn't being a very cooperative partner. Instead of drawing, his gaze flickered between Sebastian and me. I swallowed thickly and turned back to Sebastian.

"Well," I began slowly. "Maybe something happened between you and him."

Sebastian chuckled, shaking his head. "Fine, keep your secrets."

"I think I will." I quirked a brow at him, grabbed my pencil, and began to sketch lines onto the paper.

Sebastian barked a laugh at me, opening his own sketchpad to begin his portrait.

"Make sure you get my good side," he said, wiggling his brows at me.

I rolled my eyes, opening my mouth to insult him only for a loud yawn to cut me off. Sebastian furrowed his brow, scanning my face.

"Tired?"

"You have no idea."

"Oh." He paused, his eyes flickering to Isaac before widening. "Oh!"

"What?"

"I see now." He winked at me.

I stared at him for a second before my cheeks began to heat up. I whacked him on the arm.

"No!" I exclaimed, my heart pounding at the suggestion. "Nothing happened. Especially nothing like that."

He narrowed his eyes at me, a lopsided smirk tugging at the corner of his lips. "It's going to be hard to capture your bright red face in this portrait. Do you have a red pen?"

I laughed rolling my eyes, feeling my blush creep up to my ears. "Shut up."

Another laugh rumbled from his chest and he turned back to his portrait, scribbling across the page. I followed in suit, struggling to keep my eyes open. I had skipped my usual morning coffee—part of my master plan for avoiding Isaac—and with even less sleep than usual, it was hard to stay awake.

The rest of the lesson faded into a blur and before I knew it, the bell was ringing signalling lunchtime. I blinked, surprised with how fast the class had sped by, and found myself glancing to the corner.

Isaac was gone.

I raised my brows.

"He left halfway through the lesson." Sebastian leaned towards me, his eyes following my gaze.

I staggered back, eyes wide. "I don't know what you're talking about."

"Isaac." He smirked at me. "That's who you were looking for, right?"

I blushed, turning away and packing up my sketchpad and pencils. "No. I was just looking around."

Sebastian quirked a brow at me, following as I scraped my seat back and headed for the door. "Sure. See you around, Aspen. Tell Isaac I said hi."

"I'm not seeing him!" I sputtered out, but he only continued smirking at me.

He slipped around me, strolling out of the room and walking away. I rolled my eyes. As annoying as he could be, he was a great laugh for getting my mind off things. It was nice having a friend in art class.

I heaved my backpack over my shoulder and sped out of the classroom, heading straight for the library. I was desperate for a nap. Riley and William knew how tired I was after a sleepless weekend of overthinking about Isaac and probably expected me to spend the lunch period asleep in the library.

The library was warm and quiet when I stepped in. I sighed immediately, the warmth enveloping like a blanket, and shuffled towards my usual windowsill.

I sat on the sill, leaning back and closing my eyes. The warmth lulled me, wrapping around me, stroking at my skin. My exhaustion called to me, pulling at me until I couldn't open my eyes even if I wanted to. The world around me rang dull.

Sleep hit me abruptly, and just as quickly as it had come, it disappeared.

The school bell sounded, signalling the end of lunch, and I snapped awake.

I bolted upright, my eyes wide, and quickly wiped the drool pooling on the corner of my lips. How long had I been asleep? Somehow, I felt worse than before my nap.

I groaned, turning to the side and rubbing my eyes. I yawned, feeling incredibly groggy and drained. I stretched my arms up, blinking my eyes awake only to find Isaac Hensick sitting on the floor by my feet.

I raised my brows, my hands reflexively flying to my hair as I attempted to make myself look somewhat presentable.

"Isaac," I stuttered out. "I—"

I cut myself off, struggling to find the right words. What was there to say? We haven't spoken since . . . well, since Riley's birthday. Since he had left me in the kitchen, doubting everything I had done and said.

He turned to face me, his face neutral as he raised a hot takeaway cup to me, the logo of Café de Fleur clear across the cardboard.

I blinked.

"I noticed you were more tired than usual," he said simply, his expression remaining neutral.

I paused. He looked so handsome in this light. His dark hair swept just above his brow, his sharp jawline clenched, his lips plump and pink and—

136

"Thanks," I said, jumping up from my seat, my cheeks beginning to warm. I took the cup from his hand, ignoring how our fingers brushed in the process.

I turned, taking a sip of the coffee in the cup—soy latte, no sugar. I sighed, the hot liquid immediately warming me up, and began making my way to the library exit.

Isaac quickly fell in step beside me.

"Listen, Aspirin," he began, his eyes trained on me. "About the other night—"

"The other night?" I sputtered out, my heart racing at this sudden confrontation. I picked up the pace, taking larger steps towards my next class—this was exactly why I was avoiding him. I pushed the library door open, stepping out into the hallways.

His stare sharpened. "Aspirin, you know what I mean."

"Oh," I said. "That night."

Suddenly, he was in front of me. He swerved to step in front of my way, forcing me to come to a stop. I let out a shaky breath, keenly aware of how empty the hallways were around us.

"Look, I was just caught up in the moment," he began, searching my eyes frantically. "It was dark, and you were there and . . . can we please just forget about it?"

I furrowed my brows. He had kissed me. The cutest, hottest boy in the school—the boy I had been watching in the corner of the café for years, had kissed me—and now he was asking to pretend it never happened. I knew it was too good to be true.

I spent the entire weekend thinking of how he cupped my cheek, how he pressed his lips to mine. I replayed that moment over and over in my mind—and the way he sped out of the kitchen without so much of a glance in my direction.

He was right, it was better to forget it all.

"Forget about what?" I sent him a small smile. "Nothing happened."

He grinned at me, opening his mouth to say something, but I cut him off, sliding past him.

"Got to get to class," I said, making my way down the hall. "Thanks for the coffee!"

And I left him behind.

CHAPTER NINETEEN
Frappe

I leaned against the tree, adding a final piece of shading to the paper. My pencil scraped along the page, leaving a dark smudge in its wake.

"Finished?"

I turned. Riley and William both watched me carefully with half-eaten sandwiches clutched in her hands.

"I think so," I said, pursing my lips as I stared down at the drawing. It was definitely . . . not great. But hey, it was the best I could do, and I've been working on it all week. I was sick of drawing.

"Well—" William waved a hand at me, grinning widely in anticipation. "Show us."

I sent them a proud smile, holding up the paper towards them to reveal my artwork.

On it, Sebastian's gleaming face was sketched in an abstract style. It was decent, especially considering my previous artworks. I had spent the entire week sitting in the library with him, completing our art assignment that was due today.

I would spend hours just staring at his face, memorising every tiny detail. The slight dimple on his left cheek, the beauty mark at the corner of his lip, the faint scar below his hair line that he had gotten ten years ago in a bicycle accident, and then he would spend hours staring at mine.

All that was left was to turn it in.

"Nice." Riley smirked at me. She narrowed her eyes, furrowing her brow at the portrait. "Who is it?"

"I think it's Harry Styles." William squinted beside her.

"No, it's the other one," Riley teased, leaning closer. "Zayn Malik."

She glanced at me over the page, her eyes glittering mischievously, and I let out an exaggerated breath, rolling my eyes.

I flipped the page over, sliding it into a cover page and plastic slip to hide it from their view. "Shut up. It's not that bad."

"Well . . ."

I smacked Riley's shoulder and she hollered a laugh at me. "I'm only joking. You did great, Asp."

"Art is subjective," William piped in.

"That didn't sound like a compliment," I muttered, and he shrugged in reply, moving to take another bite from his sandwich.

Riley laughed, shaking her head. "It's great. One of your best."

"Thanks," I said, although it didn't mean much. I stared down at the drawing. The longer I looked at it, the worse it got, so I scrunched my nose and put it down.

"I just need to hand it in," I said, standing from my seat. I glanced down at the oval. Sebastian should be there, playing soccer as usual. I sighed, sending my friends a pointed look. "I'll be right back."

They nodded, waving their hands to gesture for me to leave. Holding the assignment close to my chest, I jogged down the hill, heading straight for the grassy oval.

In the oval, Arthur Andrews juggled a soccer ball on his knees, his friends guffawing like idiots around him.

Sebastian was nowhere to be seen.

I came to a stop beside Arthur Andrews, ignoring the way my heart pounded in my throat. The last time I stood here . . . I shook the thought from my mind. Swallowing thickly, I willed myself to be confident.

"Hey," I shouted, my voice steadier than expected. Arthur Andrews turned to me with a quirked brow, blinking as his friends grew quiet. I pressed my hands together, wringing my fingers. "Is Sebastian around?"

"Sebastian?" He glanced at me, then at my assignment clutched in my hands before nodding towards the school old building. "Try there."

"Thanks!" I smiled, relieved that I didn't make a fool of myself before turning and jogging towards the old school building.

The building was worn down, the red brick covered with graffiti and Sharpie drawings of explicit body parts. The smooth path quickly broke down into noisy gravel littered with old cigarette butts.

My heart hammered in my chest, and I thought of the conversations I had with Isaac there, leaning against the brick wall and sitting on the gravel. I haven't spoken to him much in the entire week since our conversation about the kiss.

While I wasn't avoiding him anymore, we were back to our old routine of polite hellos in the hallways. I've been busy with Sebastian and our art assignment, but I still missed the way Isaac would tease me—the way he'd call me Aspirin and remember my exact coffee order.

I stopped watching him sketch in the café corner during the mornings, trying to stop myself from pining over something impossible, and yet I couldn't stop thinking about him.

I rounded the corner, Sebastian immediately coming into sight.

And Isaac.

Isaac sat on the gravel floor, Chloe Pepper sitting beside him with her long black hair. Leaning against the wall, Sebastian stood with them, telling some sort of idiotic joke. His iconic wide smile was stretched across his face and his blond curls bounced with movement every time he spoke.

Chloe rolled her eyes at whatever he was saying, taking a drag of a cigarette. Meanwhile, Isaac watched him with a small smile, his green eyes lit up with enthusiasm and encouragement.

I forgot that Sebastian was friends with him.

I stepped forward, the gravel crunching beneath my shoes, and Isaac's gaze snapped up to meet me. He looked as handsome as ever, the sunlight making the green in his eyes match the green of the oval.

I buckled beneath his gaze, but clenched my fists, taking another noisy step forward.

He raised a brow at me, moving to stand. "Aspirin."

I hated the way I blushed at his nickname for me, the way my heart hitched at his voice. But I swallowed thickly, turning away from him.

"Actually," I stuttered out, avoiding eye contact with him. I met eyes with Sebastian who sent me a confused look, his brows drawn together. "I'm here for Sebastian."

Isaac paused, his eyes narrowing and brow furrowing. He clenched his jaw, turning to watch as Sebastian's face lit up.

I smiled awkwardly as Sebastian pranced towards me. He pushed his bouncy blond curls from his face, his blue eyes bright, the corners crinkling in a wide smile. Isaac stepped back, moving to sit again beside Chloe on the floor, who seemed indifferent to anything that was happening.

"Aspirin, hey." Sebastian grinned, pausing ahead of me. "What's up?"

At the sound of the nickname, I found myself glancing at Isaac, whose eyes had darkened significantly. I swallowed, his stare drilling into me, sending a shiver skittering down my spine.

I forced myself to focus on the blond boy in front of me. Clearing my throat, I held the assignment out.

"I finished my half. Are you ready to hand it in?"

"Yeah, sure," Sebastian said. He took the document from my hands and scanned the drawing in the slip, quirking a brow before smirking at me. His eyes filled with mischief. "Are you sure it's finished?"

I scoffed at him, not missing a beat.

"Actually, you're right. Your nose is way bigger than this. Give me a second."

He arched a brow at me, a wide grin on his face. "While you do that, let me colour my drawing in. It's missing that radiating redness from your cheeks."

"Shut up." I laughed, whacking him on the chest.

He chortled with me, his eyes brightening at his joke before settling down. "I'll go photocopy it and hand it in. Wait here."

"Oh, I can do—"

Sebastian turned and ran off before I could finish my sentence, leaving me standing around while Isaac and Chloe were muttering beside me.

I cleared my throat, awkwardly shifting my weight from one leg to another.

Isaac and Chloe ignored me, continuing to chat about something I couldn't hear. I didn't miss the way his leg was pressed against hers, or the way she laughed about something he said.

She was gorgeous. Her long dark hair fell neatly over her shoulders, her long lashes fluttering against her cheeks. She pressed a lit cigarette to her lips, drawing in a long, deep breath. Ashes fell from the end of the cigarette as it glowed a bright orange.

She exhaled, smoke flowing over her lips, before turning and offering the cigarette to Isaac.

Isaac glanced at it before raising a hand, waving it away and shaking his head. Though the tightness in his jaw and the tremble in his hand showed he secretly wanted to accept it.

I raised a brow at him. "You don't smoke anymore?"

The pair spun to face me and I immediately blushed. Had I said that out loud?

Isaac clenched his jaw, turning to face the gravel. "You don't like it, remember?"

My cheeks turned hot, my ears tinting a bright red. "So, you quit?"

He looked up then, meeting my eyes, and the silence between us grew heavy—unspoken words tainting the atmosphere. I could feel the tension press down on me, and I felt intensely uncomfortable in it, though neither of us made move to speak.

Instead, he scrutinised me from his seat, his fingers twitching against his leg. I wrung my own fingers together behind my back, trying desperately not to remember how his hair felt wrapped in my hands, or how his stubble felt pressed against my mouth.

Finally, he broke the silence.

"Yeah," he said eventually, his voice low—almost timid. "It's bad for you, remember?"

I sputtered out a laugh, bursting from my lips before I could stop it. Quickly, I clasped a hand over my lips, blushing from my sudden outburst. I didn't miss the way his lips twitched at my reaction, and suddenly all the tension melted away. I smiled widely at him, ignoring the blush that was most definitely growing on my cheeks now.

"Aspirin," he said quietly. It sounded so different on his voice. He paused and I waited for him to continue, but nothing came.

I stepped forward, the gravel crunching with the movement, and I opened my mouth to speak, when a voice echoed from behind me.

"It's done!" Sebastian hollered, sprinting over. "Ms. Laney said it was amazing, proper inspired work."

He paused to quirk a brow at me. "Oh, and she said yours was good too."

"Oh, shut up. You're just jealous that I'm clearly the better artist of us two." I giggled, rolling my eyes at him as he grinned widely at me.

"You're lucky it was an abstract assignment," he teased, quirking a brow. "Maybe you can scrape a pass."

"Oh, I'll be lucky if I can scrape a pass with you as a partner."

He laughed and continued chattering on about our assignment, cracking jokes about my artistic talents. I nodded, giggling along to his jokes, but I zoned out long ago.

Instead, my focus remained trained on the dark-haired boy with piercing green eyes. Chloe chattered on in his ear, occasionally puffing on the cigarette while Isaac nodded absentmindedly. His eyes were trained on the gravel, his fingers fiddling with each other, deep in thought. Somehow, the tension had flooded back, suffocating the air between us.

I found myself wishing it was him I was talking to instead.

CHAPTER TWENTY
Demi-Crème

I laid in bed; the glow of my phone bright on my face. My eyes strained against the dark. A YouTube video played quietly from the speakers, chattering on about some creepy conspiracy theory that I knew would only worsen my insomnia. I glanced at the time displayed at the top of the screen—four in the morning.

Another sleepless night.

I sighed, pausing the video in frustration, the sudden silence ringing through me. The room was dark, lit only by my phone screen and the moon, while the only sounds were my quiet breathing and occasional shuffle of pyjamas against skin.

I waited for a moment, closing my eyes to see if the fatigue would hit me—if, by some miracle, I'll be tugged into my dreams until daylight, but all I felt was the silence reverberating through my bones, my heart pounding in my ears.

The dreadful race of thoughts through my mind . . . never-ending.

I groaned, shifting in my bed sheets and moving to tap onto another YouTube video when a muffled thud echoed from my window.

I blinked, waiting, holding my breath. I was sure I had heard something.

I shifted, tilting my head towards the window, waiting—a second passed, then another, and nothing. I sighed, relaxing slightly into the mattress.

Did I imagine it? I ran a hand over my weary face. The lack sleep was really getting to me. I settled back into the mattress, trying to slow my heart rate again.

Thud.

I bolted upright, discarding my phone on my nightstand.

It was the middle of the night—no birds should be flying around at this time, and my neighbourhood was considered to be safe. At least in the seventeen years I've lived here, nothing of this sort happened.

What was that?

I slid out of the bed, my bare feet padding quietly against wooden floors as I made my way to the window.

I hesitated, sucking a breath in through clenched teeth. Then, I pushed the curtains apart only to be met with a face.

I screamed, staggering back and pulling the curtains shut.

"Aspirin!" a voice slurred, muffled behind the glass of the window. "Aspirin!"

I blinked slowly, my heart beginning to race in realisation.

Only one person ever called me that.

I shuffled forward, parting the curtains again to see Isaac's face staring at me through the window.

"Isaac?" I whispered, my jaw falling slack in shock.

He sent me a lopsided smile, leaning his forehead against the window. His hair was messy, strewn all over his sticky forehead, and his eyes were bloodshot. I didn't miss the way he gently swayed or the slur of his words.

"Are you drunk?"

He laughed, his cheeks dimpling as he grinned. "What! No!"

"You're drunk," I said in disbelief, mostly to myself. "Oh, my God, you're drunk. And . . . and you're here! What the hell am I going to do with you?"

I paused for a moment, watching him giggle to himself, before pulling myself together. I slid the window open and grabbed a fistful of his leather jacket, tugging him roughly into my room.

"Get in here."

He chuckled rolling through the window and landing on my bedroom floor with a hard thud, falling into a lump of giggles on the ground.

I shut the window behind him as he pulled himself to a sloppy stand.

"Aspirin," he slurred, swaying in his spot. "I missed you."

"Isaac," I said, grabbing his shoulders and forcing him to sit on the bed. He sat with no objections and I stood in front of him, crossing my arms over my chest. "It's literally four in the morning. What are you doing here?"

"I wanted to kiss you."

I raised my brows, my eyes wide. I was not expecting that answer. "W-what?"

"That night," he continued. His eyes dragged over my body and I suddenly became extremely conscious of the fact I was dressed in my pyjamas with no bra. I tugged on my shorts, pulling them lower.

His eyes flickered back to mine and his brow furrowed in thought. "At Rebebaba's."

I blinked. "Riley's?"

"Riley's!" He grinned. A hand reached forward and rested lightly on my waist. Immediately, I warmed beneath his calloused fingers, at the drunken way he gripped my waist over my pyjamas. He leaned forward to the point he was almost tumbling off the bed. "I wanted to kiss you so bad, but then Marcy . . ."

"Marcy?" I stammered. At the sudden sound of my voice, his fingers tightened, and my shirt rode up, his hand brushing the bare flesh beneath it. I shook my head, trying my best to ignore it. This was all too much. "Who's Marcy?"

Isaac groaned, his voice growing quiet and breathy. "Marcelina. I loved her. I don't want that. Not again."

I furrowed my brow at him. *Marcelina?* I ran through every Marcelina in my memory.

Marcelina . . . Marcelina . . . It wasn't a common name. The only Marcelina I knew . . . I blinked in realisation.

I vaguely remembered a Marcelina Pepper—Chloe's sister who had graduated last year. Was it that Marcelina?

I met Isaac's eyes to find him watching me carefully, his brows drawn together as he studied me. I blinked, self-consciously running my fingers through my messy, bed hair.

"Did you . . ." I trailed off, the words dying in my throat with a choking sound as Isaac's fingers suddenly pushed my white pyjama shirt up, resting his warm palm against the skin of my waist.

He gripped me tightly, pulling me forward so suddenly that I nearly fell on top of him. I rested my hand on his shoulder, steadying myself.

He gazed up at me, his eyes suddenly looking very sober and dark.

"I can't stand seeing you with Sebastian."

I blinked, trying to ignore the touch of his skin against mine. My brow furrowed. "Sebastian? We're just friends."

He grunted at this, scrunching his nose in distaste. We paused for a moment, the silence fell heavy between us, before he released my waist and fell back against the bed. The mattress squeaked loudly as he fell back, his head thumping against the blankets.

"Why are you awake?" he muttered. "It's late."

I shuffled on my feet awkwardly, towering over Isaac as he laid on the bed. I wasn't sure if it'd be strange to sit beside him, so I wrung my fingers and stared down over him.

"My insomnia," I replied slowly. My gaze moved to the ceiling. I had spent so many nights staring at it, waiting for sleep to hit me. "I can't sleep. I lie down and I just start thinking of all the terrible things that can happen. All the embarrassing things that have happened."

I paused, chortling out a stuttered laugh. "The antidepressants definitely don't help."

Isaac sat upright. He swayed on the spot. His hands braced on the bed to keep him steady. He sent me a lopsided smirk, his eyes falling half-shut in a lazy smile.

"So just think about me."

I snorted. "I do. All the time. That's the problem."

I blushed at the words that escaped my mouth, but Isaac's face remained neutral. I released a breath, shaking my head. At least he was drunk. There was no chance he'd remember this in the morning.

So, I continued, "You're all I think about."

His hand moved to my outer thigh, his fingers dancing on my skin as he gazed up at me, his face extremely serious. I leaned into his touch, moving forward until I was standing between his legs. He stared at his fingers, tracing patterns over my goose bump covered skin.

"You're all I think about too."

I laughed quietly at his meaningless, drunken words. "It's funny, though. When I'm around you it's like all my other worries just disappear. It's like . . ." I paused, meeting his eyes. "It's just me and you."

He grinned at me, a drunken lopsided grin.

"And," I continued, filling the silence when he didn't speak. "And, I feel awake. You know? Like . . . my heart races and my whole body feels like electricity is coursing through it. Like I've just chugged an entire jug of coffee. And . . ." I trailed off, my face warming at the burst of words. A small smiled pulled at my lips at the realisation. "I like it."

Isaac listened quietly, his fingers still skittering across my skin. He stared at his fingers intensely, watching where our skin met in silence. I followed his gaze, my stomach flipping at the feeling. It felt good to unleash all of my thoughts. To hear them out loud instead of playing them over and over in my mind, constantly wondering what they meant and how I felt.

I was glad he was drunk off his face. I was already burning in embarrassment from just thinking about it, much less saying it to his face.

His hand traced a path from my thigh to my hip before resting on my waist. He pulled me forward and I leaned down, my knee resting on the bed between his legs.

He tilted his face towards me, craning his neck until our faces were inches away. His breath fanned over my face, smelling strongly of alcohol as his hand moved to snake around my lower back.

Slowly, he pulled me forward and leaned back until he touched the mattress. I leaned over him, my hair falling over his face. My heart pounded in my ears, waiting. Always waiting for something.

"Aspen," he muttered. Silence enveloped us and my throat tightened at the thought of how close we were.

And then he kissed me.

His lips pressed against mine, softly at first. He was gentle, pulling me in for a simple, cautious kiss. I was stunned for a moment. He was drunk. He said he wanted to forget about our first kiss, but here we were, kissing on my bed at four in the morning.

And I kissed him back.

I tried not to think about how hard my heart was pounding, or how good of a kisser he was and how bad of a kisser I was. My mind was blank yet racing at the same time.

We broke apart, our eyes fluttering open and meeting each other's. Isaac smiled, his fingers dancing on my skin. His eyes were dark as he stared up at me, his breath hot on my skin.

"Sh*t, Aspen." He pulled me back in. This time, he moved fast. His lips worked against mine, his tongue sliding gently over my bottom lip. I sighed, my lips parting for his tongue to slip into my mouth.

His hand gripped my waist, his other moving to cup my cheek. Our teeth clashed as he grabbed me and flipped us so that he was hovering over me instead. His fingers moved to tangle in my hair, pulling at it gently to move my head and deepen the kiss further.

I sighed against his lips, my mind turning silent. Everything came naturally then. I knew where to put my hands. I knew how to tilt my head. His fingers dug into my waist, clinging onto me as if he was afraid that I'd disappear.

Isaac smiled into the kiss before drawing back slowly. His eyes glazed over as he scanned my face, his chest rising and falling as he breathed heavily.

"Aspen," he muttered. The mattress dipped and he stood from his spot over me. My body immediately grew cold at his lack of presence. "You should sleep."

I blinked, my mind still reeling, my heart still hammering. I didn't even notice the way his words had stopped slurring. My face burned, redness creeping up my neck and to my ears. "Only if you stay."

He paused, watching me carefully.

"Please," I murmured, not thinking. "Stay."

He nodded, slipping his shoes off and sliding onto the bed beside me. I pulled myself up to rest on my pillow, grabbing the sheets to hoist over us.

Isaac laid beside me, our faces inches apart. He smelled like beer and sweat, but I revelled in his presence. I leaned closer, and he rested a lazy arm over my waist.

"Goodnight, Aspen."

"Goodnight Isaac," I whispered, and I fell asleep to the sound of his chest rising and falling, the smell of alcohol still staining his skin.

CHAPTER TWENTY-ONE
Frappuccino

I woke up to light streaming through my window, hitting me directly in the eye. I blinked; my eyes blurry in the sunlight.

Why were my curtains drawn?

I paused, furrowing my brow and shifting slightly.

Why was my waist heavy?

I turned slowly, craning my neck to see Isaac Hensick lying beside me, his arm draped lazily over my waist. Sometime during the night, he had pulled his shirt off, exposing his bare chest. My eyes widened and I spun.

"Holy sh*t!" I shouted, rolling to the side and falling to the floor with a loud thud.

I groaned, rubbing my hip where it had hit the ground. Isaac Hensick was in my bed, and he was shirtless.

"Aspen?" Isaac grunted, his voice raspy and low. He groaned, pushing a hand to his forehead. "What time is it?"

I stood from the floor, grabbing my phone and checking the time. "Half past seven."

He sighed, burying his head into the pillow. His hair was matted and messy, flying in all sorts of directions.

I blushed at his bare back, his muscles flexing as he moved, and turned to face the wall.

"You . . . how are you feeling?" I managed, choking over my words.

Memories from last night—or rather, this morning—flooded my thoughts. His drunken slur, the way he stunk of alcohol, his lips . . . like I wasn't already red enough. I shook the thoughts from my head. He must have had a killer hangover.

Isaac flipped his head to meet my eyes. He narrowed his eyes against the bright morning light and sent me a grimace.

"I feel like sh*t," he groaned.

"Oh," I said, my eyes flickering between his face, his abs and the wall. "Do you . . . remember what happened last night?"

Do you remember my embarrassing monologue about how much I liked you? Do you remember kissing on my bed, even after you said to forget about our first kiss?

Isaac was quiet for a moment. I felt his stare on me, studying me, only causing my cheeks to darken even further. I swallowed thickly, trying my best to feign interest in my bedroom wall.

"No," he finally said, rolling so that his legs hung off the side of the bed. "How did I get here?"

I felt immediately relieved at not having to discuss our late night make out session in my bed. Yet, my heart sunk, slightly disappointed that he didn't remember what he said—what he did. I shook my head.

He'd probably just ask to forget about it anyway.

"Climbed through my window," I replied nonchalantly. "I nearly murdered you. Thought you were a local pervert, or something." I paused to glance at him and quirk a brow. "Although, maybe I wasn't wrong."

Isaac stood from his seat and I found it hard not to ogle his chest. He raised a brow at me, his cheeks dimpling in a smirk. "My eyes are up here, princess. Maybe you were the pervert all along."

I blushed deeply, my eyes flicking up to meet his. I opened my mouth to say something but found myself speechless. Isaac laughed at me, tugging a shirt over his head.

"God, I have a killer headache," he groaned, squinting his eyes at me. "Got an aspirin, Aspirin?" I rolled my eyes and he laughed at me. "Come on, that was a good one."

"Whatever," I said, though, I couldn't help the smile that pulled on my lips. I nodded towards my bedroom door. "I've got some in the kitchen."

I tugged the door open, my bare feet tapping against the ground as I walked towards the kitchen with him following after me. My house was small, nothing like William's fancy contemporary house. Mine was a little run-down and a bit snug, but the perfect size for a family of three—or two now that Sabrina was away at college.

I led Isaac to the kitchen where dirty dishes piled in the sink. Reaching up, I opened the medicine cabinet by the fridge and pulled out a bottle of painkillers. Isaac grinned widely, grabbing the bottle and dry swallowing two large pills.

I raised my brows at him. "You do this often?"

He winked at me in reply.

Isaac sighed, leaning against the kitchen counter and scanning the house. "Where's your parents?"

"My mom is at work," I replied. His expression remained neutral, not reacting to my intentional disregard of my father.

My dad had died when I was a baby, leaving my mom to take care of my older sister and I on her own—and despite the struggles, she did a damn good job at it, working long hours to put my sister through college.

I loved her.

Isaac suddenly widened his eyes at me. "She didn't find me in your room last night, did she?"

I laughed, imagining the chaos that would've ensued if that had happened.

"No, no," I reassured him. "She's been working all night. She'll probably be home soon though, so we'd better get going."

Isaac nodded, and I gestured to the kitchen.

"Help yourself to anything around here. I'm just going to quickly get ready for school." I paused. I've never had a boy sleep over before. What were the polite courtesies to offer in this situation? "Do you need anything? A . . . toothbrush?"

He quirked a smile at me. "Are you saying I have morning breath?"

"No—"

"Have you been kissing me in my sleep, Aspirin?"

My cheeks turned a bright red, my ears heating at the accusation. "No! Definitely not! I was just—"

"Relax." He laughed, stepping forward. "A toothbrush would be great."

I nodded, my cheeks still red, and led him to my bathroom. I reached into my cabinet, pulling out a spare toothbrush I kept in case Riley or William ever planned to sleepover. I handed it to Isaac, along with toothpaste, and he leaned in close to me until our elbows knocked against each other.

He smirked at the contact, watching in the mirror as my cheeks tinted red, and began brushing his teeth.

I watched for a minute, my mind whirring. *Isaac Hensick was in my bathroom brushing his teeth in the morning. What was happening?*

Isaac spat into the sink and quirked a brow at me. "Jealous of the toothbrush, Aspirin?"

I blinked. "What? No, I was just . . ." I paused before grabbing the toothpaste resting beside him. "I need to brush my teeth too."

I ignored the smug look he sent me and grabbed my own toothbrush, quickly brushing my teeth and washing my face. By the time we had both gotten ready and dressed, we had to leave for school.

We stepped out of my front door and I checked my phone. Almost 8:30. No time to stop at Café de Fleur.

"We have to go," I said, locking my door and speed walking towards the school. "First period starts in thirty minutes."

Isaac quickly fell in step beside me. "Oh, come on, who cares about first period? I have a hangover. I'd kill for a coffee."

I gripped my backpack straps, my eyes focused on the path ahead. "Well, go get your coffee then. I'm going to class."

"Ah." He smirked. "I'd forgotten what a goody two shoes you are."

I rolled my eyes, ignoring him. My house wasn't far from school, but if I wanted to stop by my locker before walking to my class on the other end of school, I'd have to be there early.

And with Isaac distracting me, I was cutting it close.

"Has it always been this bright in the morning?" Isaac groaned, squinting his eyes against the light.

I ignored him, speeding up my pace to get to school.

Isaac sped up to match me. "Woah. Slow down. Don't get too excited, it's just school. Happens every day, you see."

"Yes, and I'd like to be on time every day, you see," I shot back, lowering my voice to mock him.

"Feisty," Isaac muttered.

He silently fell in step beside me for a while until the gates of the school came into sight. I didn't miss the way he continued to walk with me as we passed Café de Fleur. I also didn't miss Vivienne's smirk at me as we strolled past the window together, arms knocking into each other as we stepped in sync.

"Finally," I sighed, walking through the school gates and slowly making my way to the main building. Isaac followed; his pace was lazy but quick due to his long legs. We pushed through the double doors, stepping into the hallway.

Almost immediately, the atmosphere grew heavy.

As the glass doors shut behind us, I felt as though every student in sight was staring at us—their gazes moving between Isaac's towering figure and me shifting uncomfortably beside him.

I winced, tugging on my backpack straps and walking to my locker in an attempt to ignore the whispers around us. Our footsteps squeaked on the linoleum floor, blending in with the echoes of whispers.

"Who's that with Hensick?"

"Why did they arrive together?"

"Is she new here?"

"She's not even pretty."

I clenched my fists, inhaling deeply. I felt the eyes of every student in the hallway digging into my back. My heart began to race, and my mouth felt uncomfortably dry.

I swallowed thickly, feeling a lump begin to rise in my throat.

"Aspirin, you good?" Isaac muttered from beside me.

I nodded, not finding the power in me to speak. Instead, I focused on controlling my breathing.

In and out.

In and out.

I focused on grounding myself and ignoring the whispers. I thought of how my shoes tapped against the hallway tiles, how my jacket clung to my arms, how my phone pressed against my thigh in my pocket.

In and out.

"Aspen," Isaac murmured. His voice was closer this time. "Are you okay?"

This time, I felt too weak to even nod, my head beginning to spin and the hallway beginning to cloud around me. My legs stopped moving and I swayed against the lockers for support.

Isaac stopped beside me, his arm wrapping around my shoulder as he leaned to whisper, his lips brushing against my ear.

"Aspen, calm down," he muttered. "Just take some deep breaths. I'm right here. You're completely fine."

His hand rubbed circles against my arm, and I took a deep breath, focusing on his hand on my skin.

"Good," he whispered. "Again. Breathe in and out. You've got this."

I nodded, the world beginning to clear again. I breathed in deeply, my eyes moving from the ground to his eyes. He stared at me, his brow arching in worry.

"You're okay," he muttered.

I nodded, his words swimming in my thoughts. I'm okay. I'm okay.

I breathed in, my chest rising and falling, the hallway steadying under my gaze. Most students had moved on, the whispering beginning to die down, the stares lessening.

I blinked, my heart slowing and the adrenaline still pumping through my body.

"You good?" Isaac asked gently.

I nodded, my mouth still dry.

"Yeah," I said, still regulating my breaths. "Yeah. Thanks Isaac."

He arched a brow at me, his lips frowning. "For what?"

"For being there . . . helping. I was panicking," I said, my cheeks heating up. "Thanks."

His face grew grim and his throat bobbed as he swallowed thickly. "I mean, it was my fault anyway."

"Hey!" I exclaimed, raising my brows. "Don't say that!"

"It's true." He removed his arm from my shoulder and stepped back, increasing the distance between us and beginning to walk slowly down the hall again. I followed suit. "They were staring because of me. It's dumb. I shouldn't have come in with you."

"Isaac," I said, meeting his eyes. "If I didn't want to come in with you, I wouldn't have."

We were silent for a moment. He watched me carefully, searching my eyes as I pursed my lips. I sucked in a deep breath, my stomach flipping beneath his gaze.

"I like having you around," I said, my voice quiet.

Isaac raised his brows at this. He paused before opening his mouth to say something, when—

"Aspen?"

I spun around, my eyes meeting with Riley and William leaning beside my locker. Their eyes moved between me and Isaac, a growing smile beginning to overtake half of Riley's face.

"I'd better go," Isaac stuttered out, his eyes wide. "I'll see you around."

I nodded wordlessly, my heart pounding in my chest. I practically confessed to him. My cheeks were turning red. I didn't have time to wallow in self-loathing.

Riley bounced towards me, tossing an arm across my shoulders.

"So, you and Hensick are coming to school together now?" She grinned. "What's next, going to bed together?"

I stayed silent, only blushing deeper at the memory of Isaac's arm slung around my waist. Riley's eyes doubled in size.

"You didn't."

"It wasn't like that!" I squealed. "He just . . ."

Riley quirked a smug brow at me. "Just?"

"Just . . ." I trailed off, searching for the right words. "Climbed through my bedroom window drunk at four in the morning?"

"Oh, my God!"

I cringed at Riley's voice echoing across the hallway, grabbing the attention of the students surrounding us. William chuckled at her enthusiasm as I spun to open my locker and fish out my books.

"And when were you planning on telling us?" Riley scolded.

"Riley." I turned to her, tilting my head. "It happened this morning."

"So?" Riley bounced on her toes. "You should've called us!"

"At four in the morning?"

"Yes!"

"I'll keep it in mind for next time." I rolled my eyes, a sarcastic smile on my face.

"Good." Riley crossed her arms over her chest, turning her nose up at me.

"So," William began, knocking my arm with his elbow. "What did you guys do together."

I closed my locker as we began to walk towards our first period together, my cheeks growing a deep red. My mind drifted to his lips on mine.

"Nothing!" I shook my head frantically. "Nothing happened."

William and Riley exchanged a look with each other.

"Well," Riley smiled, bouncing in front of me to cut me off. She nodded to a poster on the wall beside her. "Why don't you ask him to the Halloween Dance?"

I blinked, turning to the poster. It was covered with skulls and pumpkins and had large white bolded letters spelling out "Halloween Dance."

I had forgotten about it. I thought of how Isaac had talked about the Halloween Dance in William's kitchen minutes before he kissed me. I shook my head.

"No," I said. "I'm not going. He's probably going with Lacey, anyway."

"Ugh." Riley rolled her eyes at the mention of her wicked stepsister. "Don't get me started on her. She's been planning her costume all month."

I sputtered out a laugh at the annoyed expression on Riley's face. I could imagine Lacey screeching at all hours of the day planning her costume, complaining if anything was slightly different from her vision. Lacey was a perfectionist, and a loud one at that.

"It's not funny!" Riley moaned, frowning. "Besides, she's planning a group costume. You know what that means? She's going with a group. Not a partner!"

I pursed my lips, blinking. "Really?"

"Yeah." Riley grinned, her smile beaming and wide. "You should ask him."

I paused. If Lacey wasn't in the picture, maybe I had a chance. He had forgotten what happened last night, maybe it wouldn't be awkward. Maybe something would change between us. I could finally close that distance between me and Isaac.

Maybe this Halloween Dance was a good opportunity.

"Okay," I finally said, meeting Riley's eyes. "I'll think about it."

CHAPTER TWENTY-TWO
Vanilla Latte

"Here's your coffee, Aspen."

I smiled, taking the cup from Vivienne's elegant, long fingers. The warmth of the coffee cup immediately spread through my body and I sighed. The steam curled around my face, the smell of coffee already invigorating me.

Turning to the door, my gaze subconsciously drifted to the corner of the café—to Isaac.

He sat at his usual table, his untouched coffee resting by his hand as he sketched lazily into his book. His dark hair was combed back today, accentuating his high cheekbones and green eyes.

"Take a picture," Vivienne teased from beside me. "It'll last longer."

I blushed deeply, my face quickly becoming hot. I turned to face the barista, a meek smile playing on my lips.

"Am I that obvious?"

"The boy must be really dense if he hasn't noticed the way you look at him yet."

I groaned, my shoulders sagging in defeat. Ever since Riley had suggested it, I've been thinking nonstop of the Halloween Dance—more specifically, asking Isaac to the Halloween Dance.

I've been practicing in my head all week—the words I would say, the potential costumes. I was letting myself get carried away. Nevertheless, I wanted to ask him. I had to try.

I wouldn't be able to rest until I knew for sure.

"I'm going in," I muttered, taking a deep gulp of coffee.

Vivienne beamed at me as I stormed forward, crossing the café in seconds and pulling out the chair in front of Isaac with a loud scrape.

Isaac's eyes looked up, his sketch book immediately slamming shut and his hand moving to rest over it.

"Aspen!" he sputtered, blinking. "Hey."

"Hey," I said, my confidence beginning to fade beneath his stare. His eyes bore into mine and I found myself lost for words. "Hi."

He narrowed his eyes at me, pausing, before the corner of his lips twitched up into a smirk. He quirked a brow at me. "Hi."

I blinked. "Hi."

He paused, the corner of his lips tugging up in a half-smile, his eyes glittering mischievously. "We could do this all day."

I raised my brows, shaking my head slightly. "Right. Sorry. How are you?"

"Great," he said, his voice high with amusement. "And you?"

"Good," I replied curtly.

We were silent for a second, an awkward cloud settling over us. I was really bad at this. I clenched my hands into fists. I was going to do it. I had to try. I took a deep breath, building my courage, before blurting, "The Halloween Dance."

He tilted his head towards me, surprised that I had broken the silence and changed the topic.

"Right," he said, arching a brow. "It's next week, isn't it?"

I nodded slowly. "Right."

We paused briefly. Isaac's eyes looked down to the table, then back up to meet mine.

"Have you thought of anyone you want to go with?" he asked.

I cleared my throat, trying not to blush when I immediately thought of him as the answer to his question. "Yeah. I have."

"Really?" His eyes widened in genuine shock. "Who?"

"No one," I sputtered instinctively, my face heating. He raised a brow at me, and I glanced down at the table. "You don't know him."

I froze, groaning internally. I had woken up that morning and practically shoved my foot into my mouth. I cursed myself. *What was I doing? This was going all wrong.*

"Oh," Isaac said. He blinked, frowning for a moment, before saying, "Well, good luck, then."

"Thanks," I muttered, my heart heavy and eyes trained on my takeaway coffee cup. I tapped my fingers against it, my heart racing in sync with my tapping as I tried to regain my courage.

I was such an idiot. I had rehearsed it a million times in my head, but the second those green eyes were on me, my heart pounded, and my head felt light. I frowned, my leg shaking with anxiety. I had to try.

We fell silent again, a heavy pause settling over the conversation. My eyes roamed over the table in an attempt to avoid eye contact. I stared at his black coffee, still and cold in his mug, then glanced at his steady hands before my focus pulled to his closed sketchpad.

"What are you drawing?" I found myself asking, trying to lighten the atmosphere.

Plan B, I thought to myself. *Lighten the atmosphere. Get us joking. Ask him. If he rejects me, I'll play it off as a joke. It'll be a great laugh.*

Right.

I looked up from the sketchpad, beginning to gain confidence in my new plan. I met his eyes and sent a smile that I hoped seemed casual, and not at all prying.

Isaac froze, clearing his throat and slowly sliding it across the table towards himself. His fingers tapped against the cover. "Nothing much."

I narrowed my eyes at him. That didn't go well. The atmosphere felt tenser than before. My frown deepened and I decided to let it drop. "Oh. Okay."

"You'd better get going," he said abruptly, leaning back in his seat. His face lit up cheekily and he teased, though his mouth still twisted with tension. "Got to be in time for first period, right?"

I blinked—that failed spectacularly.

It was like I had figured out the worst possible way this could go and successfully achieved it. I told him I planned on asking someone he didn't know, and now he was practically telling me to leave him alone. Isaac looked up at me, still smirking playfully, oblivious to my shattered confidence.

I chuckled awkwardly, beginning to stand from my seat, ignoring the way my heart sank in disappointment. I didn't ask him at all, and he sent me an awkward look, the atmosphere tensing up all of a sudden.

This wasn't the right time.

So, I sighed and said, "Right."

I scraped my chair back, watching as he turned away from me to gaze out the shop front. I pursed my lips.

"See you, then."

He nodded, turning back to his coffee and sketchpad.

I sighed, sliding out from my seat and walking to the exit. I pushed the glass door open with a tinkling of a bell and began my woeful walk to school. I'd just have to ask him to the Halloween Dance another time.

I needed Riley and William's help, that was for sure. I was hopeless without them.

My mind drifted to him lying on my bed the other night, the moonlight shining on his cheekbones, his green eyes reflecting the stars in the dark. I thought of his slurred words, and what he had said the other night.

Marcelina.

Who was Marcelina? He had said that he loved her, didn't he? Then why was he with Lacey all the time? Why was he always moving from girl to girl? Was it a platonic kind of love?

By the time I arrived at school, I was only more confused. A blonde ray of sunshine bounced into sight in the corner of my eye. My shoulders fell in relief and I released a happy sigh.

"Riley," I sputtered. She spun at the sound of her name, her ponytail almost whipping my face as I came to a stop beside her locker.

"Aspen!" she squealed, her smile bright and gleaming.

I couldn't help but reflect her expression, a smile overtaking my lips. "Hey. I need to ask you something."

"Shoot."

"Do you know a Marcelina?"

She blinked, her face contorting in confusion. "Marcelina? Like Marcelina Pepper?"

"I thought so," I began. "Chloe Pepper's sister, right? What does she have to do with Isaac, though?"

Riley's eyes widened. "Did he mention her?"

I nodded. "Yeah, but he was drunk. Maybe he didn't know what he was saying, so—"

"No way," Riley interrupted, her brows drawn together in thought. "Lacey's spoken about her before. She has cried over her."

"What?"

Riley lowered her voice, glancing around the hallway.

"Why do you think Isaac's so close with Chloe? She's basically his only female friend," she paused, her eyes flicking up to meet mine. "Other than you, of course."

I shook my head, searching for answers. "Maybe Chloe's his childhood friend?"

"Yeah." Riley leaned forward. "They've been friends for years, especially after he began dating Marcelina."

I blinked, confusion flooding me at the revelation. "Isaac doesn't date."

"Not anymore," Riley corrected, sending her a pointed look. "He dated Marcelina Pepper for two years, they broke up when she went away to college. Total b*tch. She just wanted college guys, or something."

I furrowed my brow. Marcelina was a year older than us, so . . . "That was last year."

"Exactly," Riley said. "I thought he was over her, but Lacey's always crying about how he's still in love with her. I thought she was just full of sh*t."

My heart dropped. I had no words. Isaac was in love with Marcelina.

Suddenly, it all made sense. Isaac's vehement rule against dating, his playing around with Lacey, how he never wanted to fall in love again—he was still in love with Marcelina Pepper.

The girl who had broken his heart.

All of a sudden, I felt grateful that I didn't ask him to the Halloween Dance. I didn't think I could face rejection at the moment, not when he was still in love with the girl who had left him, and for what? College boys?

My heart ached for Isaac. I couldn't imagine dating someone for two years only to get dumped for college boys.

Riley's stare moved from my face to behind me, and I followed her gaze to see Chloe Pepper walking down the hall, her long black hair falling to her hips and swaying with each step.

"Guess I'm not the only one with a total b*tch of a sister," Riley muttered. She sighed, turning to meet my eyes. "It's an epidemic."

Her brow crinkled as she noticed my frown, and her eyes quickly widened. "But I'm sure Lacey's just being overdramatic. I mean, it's like you said, he was drunk! He didn't know what he was saying!"

I nodded, unconvinced but wanting to move the subject along. "Yeah. You're right."

Riley stayed silent, her usual beaming smile missing from her face. I sent her a small smile in reassurance.

"Well, we'd better get to first period."

CHAPTER TWENTY-THREE
White Chocolate Mocha

"Happy birthday!"

I groaned, pulling the phone away from my ear at the sound of Riley's screaming.

"Riley," I complained through a yawn. "It's too early for this."

"Early? It's nearly one in the afternoon! I've been up since eight, waiting for you to wake up," she chided. I could picture her beaming smile through the phone, shaking her head at me. "I'm just excited!"

I laughed at her enthusiasm. "Thanks, Riles. I love you."

"So," Riley began. "Do you want to hang out today? We can binge watch Harry Potter at mine?"

"Thanks Riley, but I kind of want to stay home today."

I haven't been able to sleep until the sun had already risen. I had spent all night overthinking about Marcelina, Isaac and Lacey and then worrying about my birthday and the Halloween Dance. I was way too tired to go out.

If anything, I wanted to go back to sleep.

Riley hummed in disappointment. "Okay, well, happy birthday, girl. I'll see you tomorrow at William's."

"Definitely." I smiled. "Bye."

The flat tone of the phone hanging up rang out of my speaker and I pulled the phone away from my ear. The screen shone at me, displaying my text messages. Beside the millions of texts from Riley and William, my sister had also left me a barrage of birthday wishes and a birthday card in the mail.

I smiled at the thought. Our family had always been small, and the house felt so much emptier with my sister away at college.

I flopped down onto my mattress, pulling the sheets over my face. My mother had already left for work hours ago, meaning I had the entire house to myself all day. I paused. The silence of the house rang through my bones, and I shuddered.

I rolled out of bed with a grunt, making my way to my bathroom to get ready for the day, before pulling out my laptop and opening Netflix. I planned to spend all day sitting in bed watching senseless episodes of Riverdale.

Cheesy, teenage cringe. The best way to spend a birthday.

I leaned into my pillows, my laptop wheezing as it pumped out scene after scene of trashy teenage drama.

I was just clicking onto my second episode of the day when a loud knock came from the door. I blinked. I just told Riley I didn't want to hang out.

I paused my screen, placing it delicately onto my bed and sliding out from beneath the sheets.

"Coming!" I called out, walking towards the door. My hand clasped the cold brass, and I tugged it open. "Riley, I said I don't—"

I pulled the door open, revealing none other than Isaac Hensick standing in front of me. He wore white t-shirt and sweatpants, his usual leather jacket missing.

"Hey." He smiled, pushing his dark hair off his forehead.

I paused, my jaw falling open, before slamming the door in his face.

Isaac Hensick was on my doorstep.

And I was in my pyjamas.

It wasn't a big deal. He'd seen me in my pyjamas before, but still . . . I pushed my hair back, straightening out the frizz around my forehead and combing through the matted nest of hair from lying in bed. I tugged at my shorts, pulling them lower, and pulled my shirt looser, wrapping my arms around my bra-less chest.

I cleared my throat, pulling the door open again.

"Oh, hey Isaac." I smiled as nonchalantly as possible.

He raised a brow at me, his eyes dancing with amusement. "Hey."

"What brings you here?"

His eyes dipped from my face to my body and I blushed, heat beginning to creep up my neck. He stepped forward, his hands moving from behind his back to present a small pink gift bag in his palms.

"Happy birthday, Aspen."

I raised my brows, blinking in surprise. "You remembered."

"Of course. How could I forget?" He stepped forward. "Are you alone?"

I moved back, opening the door to allow him into the living room. He stepped inside and I closed the door behind him with a shrug.

"Yeah. I'm not big on celebrating."

He spun to meet my eyes. "Where's your mom?"

"Work."

"Oh," he hummed, stepping towards me. His fingers wrapped around my wrist, pulling my hand up and placing the gift bag in my palm. "Well, happy birthday, Aspirin."

I smiled, opening the gift bag to find a small box inside. I pulled it out, slowly, before opening it to reveal a golden necklace, cursive letters spelling out 'Aspen' across it with a tiny golden leaf at the end of the word.

It was gorgeous.

I blinked, a lump beginning to rise in my throat. I didn't expect him to even remember my birthday, much less turn up at my house with the most perfect present. I was stunned.

"Did you know," Isaac began quietly, his voice low and close to my ear. "That the name Aspen means shaking poplar tree? In Greece, they say they're imbued with magic to protect the bearer from harm. That leaf at the end is the leaf of an aspen tree."

I released a laugh in disbelief, shaking my head. "No, I actually didn't."

He had done so much research, I couldn't help the warmth that spread through me. How long had he spent on this present?

"Some people use the leaves to treat fear and anxiety," he said, watching as I traced my fingers over the golden letters and leaf. "A leaf under the tongue will make you more eloquent."

"Ironic," I said, amused about how entirely ineloquent I usually am. I ran another finger over the leaf—maybe it'd work on me. I met his eyes to find him already watching me. I sent him a small smile. "Isaac. It's beautiful. Thank you so much."

He shrugged, rubbing the back of his neck timidly. "I hope you like it."

"Like it?" I sputtered out a laugh, my eyes flickering up to meet his. "I love it. I was beginning to think you didn't know my real name."

He chuckled, reaching to pluck the necklace from the box. "Do you want me to put it on for you?"

"Please."

I turned, moving my hair to the side as he wrapped his arms over my shoulders, placing the necklace delicately over my collarbones.

His breath fanned over my bare neck and I suddenly became aware of how close he stood next to me. I inhaled a sharp breath at the feeling of his mouth so close to my skin. His fingers

174

brushed my neck as she struggled with the clasp and I tried not to shudder beneath his touch. A click sounded and he stepped back.

"Done."

I smiled, my fingers drifting to rest on the necklace. "I love it. Really, thank you, Isaac. You shouldn't have."

He shrugged. "I wanted to."

I swayed on my toes for a minute, considering the thought for a bit, before nodding towards my room. "Do you want to binge watch some movies?"

He quirked a brow at me, his mouth tilting in a half-smile. "I thought you don't like celebrating."

"I don't mind." *If it's with you.*

He nodded. "Okay then. But only if we watch Harry Potter."

"Was there any other option, really?" I quipped with a smile.

He led the way, moving to my room and flopping down onto my bed. He picked my laptop up from the bed and moved it to his lap, quickly getting comfortable.

"Riverdale?" He laughed. "Really?"

"Hey," I scolded, standing beside the bed. "It's . . ." I trailed off. "Okay, yeah, it's pretty bad."

His eyes crinkled at the corners, his cheeks dimpling. "The first step to recovery is admitting there's a problem."

He closed the tab, searching instead for the first Harry Potter movie. After pulling it up, he turned to me, lifting a brow and patting the mattress beside him.

"Well?"

I blinked, realising I had paused at the door. I wrung my fingers. "Right."

I stepped forward, crawling onto the mattress beside him and he turned back nonchalantly to hit play on my laptop. I swallowed thickly, keenly aware of how our thighs pressed together, how our arms touched, and how close our hands rested beside each other.

I could feel the heat from his body spreading to mine.

"Harry Potter always makes me feel nostalgic."

I blinked, snapping out of my thoughts. I turned to see Isaac grinning at me. "What?"

"I always wanted to go to Hogwarts as a kid," he continued with a stupidly cute smile.

I turned back to the screen, watching as a tiny Daniel Radcliffe magically remove the glass pane at the zoo. "I never watched Harry Potter until this year."

Isaac was silent and I craned my neck to see him staring at me in astonishment. His eyes were wide, and his jaw had fallen slack.

"What?" I laughed, rolling my eyes. "It was too scary for me as a kid."

"You're—" he cut himself off, shaking his head in disbelief. "I don't know if we can be friends anymore, Aspirin."

"Honestly, Isaac," I teased, nudging his arm. "I have a name tag now."

He glanced down to my neck where his gift lay shining across my collarbones. His lips twitched up into a smile and his voice grew soft. "Yeah."

I blushed at the tone of his voice and the gentle look he gave me when he spoke. My own smile slowly fell, my eyes flickering to his lips. We were so close. I could feel his body heat radiating off of him, feel his legs pressed against mine.

Swallowing hard, I spun back to the movie – I had to pay attention before my mind drifted to dangerous ideas. I watched for a few more minutes, trying my best to focus as Harry Potter strolled through Diagon Alley.

But I couldn't help it when my gaze drifted from the movie to Isaac's hand, resting on his leg beside mine. I couldn't help it when I glanced at his thigh pressed against mine, or when my eyes drifted to his eyes, already watching me. I blushed, my eyes turning back to the movie.

I needed to pay attention before I get carried away.

Yet, despite the movie playing noisily from my laptop speakers, and Isaac's distractingly cute expression as he stared at the Hogwarts Great Hall with amazement, my mind drifted to Marcelina.

I still haven't asked Isaac to the Halloween Dance, and now that Riley told me about his history with Marcelina Pepper, I wasn't so sure I wanted to.

He'd probably reject me, after all.

I couldn't believe that it didn't click when he mentioned her all those nights ago. She was only a grade above us, and despite never having seen Isaac hang around with her at school—or Isaac at school in general—I've heard rumors and whispers about them. Rumors about Isaac Hensick having a crush on someone, rejecting all girls who begged for a single date until he eventually wound up with Marcelina Pepper.

But that was ages ago, and apparently, they'd broken up last year.

All those years of Isaac chasing after her, and she broke up with him on the off chance that she'd meet a cute boy in college to replace him with. I frowned at the idea.

How long had he been in love with her? Was he still in love with her? Did he even like me? What was our relationship like? We were friends, right? But I didn't make out with Riley or William. Could we even be called friends?

My mind raced with questions and I struggled to pay any attention to the movie. Instead, I chewed my bottom lips, my brow furrowed.

The movie faded into a blur and then the second one, and before I knew it, the sound of jingling keys grabbed my attention.

I bolted upright, my eyes darting to my open bedroom door, my heart pounding in my chest. Isaac's eyes widened as he sat up to watch me.

Before he could say anything, I blurted out, "My mom's home."

CHAPTER TWENTY-FOUR
Cold Brew

"So, Isaac . . ." My mom smiled from across the table. "I hope you enjoyed the food. It's Aspen's favourite."

Isaac's smile sweetened and he picked a final piece of chicken off his plate. "It's incredible, Mrs. Haste. You're an amazing cook."

"Oh, stop it," my mother cooed.

"Yes, stop it." I gagged.

My mom rolled her eyes at me from across the table. "Thank you, Isaac. Appreciation is hard to come by in this household."

I laughed at my mom's teasing voice, deciding to play along. I sent her a wide-eyed smile, smiling sweetly from across the table. "Mom, thank you for making this delicious meal."

"That's more like it." She winked with a grin. She paused, her brows shooting up. "Oh, wait, before we clean up . . ." she paused for dramatic effect and her grin widened, "I have a surprise."

Her cutlery clattered down onto the table and she stood from her seat with a scraping of the chair.

She still wore her waitress uniform—a blue dress that flared at the waist where a white apron was tied. Her short dark hair was pulled up into a ponytail away from her tired face. Dark circles sat beneath her eyes, the corners crinkling with her grin. She turned, moving into the kitchen to retrieve a small box.

"Happy birthday to you," she sang, opening the box to reveal a cupcake. A candle sat in the middle surrounded by a sea of pink frosting. With one hand, she held a lighter, quickly lighting the candle before setting it in the middle of the table.

Across from me, Isaac sent me a smug smirk, remembering that I hated celebrating my birthday—and surprises. I rolled my eyes at his smug look and turned back to my mother.

"Happy birthday dear Aspen," my mom continued to sing. "Happy birthday to you!"

I pursed my lips. *Why was it always so awkward when people sang happy birthday to you? I just never knew what to do, or how to react.*

"Hip, hip!" Isaac shouted smugly, his eyes trained on my uncomfortable reaction.

"Hooray!"

I laughed awkwardly. "Thanks guys."

"Make a wish!" my mom squealed.

I raised a brow at her. "I wish we'd stop celebrating my birthday."

"Aspen!" my mom scolded.

"Sorry." I chuckled. "Sorry. I do love it, mom."

She raised a brow at me in a gesture that meant hurry up and I paused. A wish. What would I even wish for?

I wish Isaac . . . I shook my head, refusing to finish that thought. I cleared my throat.

"I wish for good grades." And I blew out the candle quickly.

"Okay." My mom clapped her hands together. "Well, I'd better get going. I left work early for this, so I'd better get to my next shift on time."

I smiled, standing from my seat and pressing a kiss against my mom's cheek. "Thank you, Mom. I love you."

"Oh." My mom sighed through a tight-lipped smile. She rubbed my arms with her hands. "My baby's seventeen."

She squeezed my cheeks and I winced, catching Isaac's smirk in the corner of my eye. I swatted her hands away, blushing deeply in embarrassment.

"Okay, okay." My mom laughed. "I'm leaving."

She turned to Isaac and his smirk shifted to a glowing smile. His eyes lit up and she pulled him into a polite hug.

"It was so nice to meet you, Isaac." She grinned mischievously, lowering her voice. "Take good care of my daughter, okay?"

"Mom!" My face burned in embarrassment.

"Okay, okay!" she gave in, but sent him a mischievous look. He raised his hands, smiling. "Bye kids."

"Bye, Mrs Haste," Isaac called out, as she reached the front door, his voice dripping with politeness. "Your dinner was lovely."

The door shut with a click and I whacked Isaac's chest with a hefty thump.

"Ow." He smirked, clutching the spot I'd hit him. "What was that for?"

"For sucking up to my mother," I said, grabbing the empty plates and beginning to load the dish washer.

"She really loves you," Isaac said, following suit.

I blushed, a small smile pulling at my lips. "I know."

I closed the dishwasher with a thud and met Isaac's eyes. It really was extremely strange to see Isaac standing in my home. If someone told me a year before that the Isaac Hensick would be eating dinner in my kitchen on my birthday, I'd probably faint from laughing too hard. He watched me curiously, a small smile playing on his lips.

"Sorry about that," I said. "I wasn't expecting her to be home so early."

He shrugged nonchalantly, shaking his head slightly. "There's nothing to be sorry about. I was hungry anyway."

He paused. "Do you want to finish that movie?"

I smiled. He wanted to stay. "Let's go."

We strolled back into my bedroom and hopped back onto the small bed, the mattress creaking below us. We shifted in our seats, struggling to get comfortable, until our legs were pressed flush beside each other and our elbows were knocking. Isaac grabbed the laptop, hitting play and resting it on his lap.

We sat for a moment in silence, and I managed to actually pay attention for a few minutes before I found myself glancing at Isaac in the corner of my eye. His eyes weren't focused on the laptop, but rather my hand resting on my bare thigh beside his.

I blushed, heat creeping up my neck, and hitched my shorts down, trying to cover as much skin as my skimpy pyjamas would allow. My fingers brushed his leg, causing me to pull my hand away and my blush to spread up to my ears. This seemed to snap him out of his daze and his stare returned to the small laptop screen.

We sat in silence, scene after scene blurring together. My mind racing with thoughts of how close Isaac's hand is to mine, how his leg is touching mine, how he was staring at my legs.

Do I look fat? Do I—

Suddenly, Isaac shifted in his seat, snapping me from my thoughts.

"Aspen," he spoke lowly.

I turned to find him already looking at me, his jaw set. His eyes were dark, the screen glowing in their reflection as he stared at me. His voice turned serious, sending a shudder down my spine. I blinked, allowing a playful grin to tug at my lips.

"Isaac," I said back lightly.

"Did you end up asking anyone to the Halloween Dance yet?"

182

My eyes widened and I found myself blushing at the thought of asking Isaac to the dance. That was sudden. I definitely wasn't ready for that conversation. "No. Not yet."

There was a heavy pause as Isaac continued to stare at me, his eyes steely and dark, and I felt the need to fill the silence.

Maybe now was the time after all. Maybe this was my chance to ask him. I mean, it was my birthday. That had to be good luck or something, right?

I tapped my fingers against my thigh and tried my best not to think about Marcelina Pepper or the possibility of rejection. I took a deep breath, straightening my back. My fingers drifted to my necklace, tracing over the leaf—confidence. Eloquence.

"I mean I want to," I sputtered out, my eyes drifting to the laptop screen, unable to face Isaac. I blushed deeply and hoped it was at least partially masked by the darkness of the room. "I've been crushing on him since the start of high school."

I glanced at Isaac's reaction to catch him clench his jaw, his brow furrowed. His throat bobbled as he swallowed hard.

"Oh," he said. He paused as if in deep thought. His voice had turned low and raspy. "That long?"

My cheeks heated even further as I nodded. It was true.

I've had a bit of a crush on him since my first day of high school when I stopped by Café de Fleur for the first time and noticed him sketching in the corner. I mean, who wouldn't crush on the tall, handsome boy sitting in the corner, drawing quietly?

I never would have thought that years later he'd be sitting in my bedroom, actually aware of my existence.

No. I thought it was the type of crush where you notice the person's attractiveness from afar and never actually make a move— only send longing glances until they suddenly disappear from your life forever.

But now he sat beside me on my bed, his lips pursed—lips that I had kissed—and his legs pressed up against mine.

I didn't realise wewere silent for so long until Isaac shifted again, standing from the mattress and leaving my laptop discarded on the bed sheets.

"I'd better go."

I blinked, jumping from my seat. I didn't even get the chance to ask him yet. "Right now?"

"Yeah," he said, turning away from me. "Yeah, I just remembered. I have a thing on."

"Oh."

He rounded the bed and headed out my bedroom door. I followed, rushing after him.

"Thanks again for the present," I said, touching my fingers to the necklace sitting across my collarbone. We paused a step away from the front door and I shifted on my feet as he turned to meet my gaze. "It really means a lot."

He paused, his eyes moving to the necklace, then to my face, then to my lips. I shuddered under his gaze. He smiled gently, his eyes softening.

"I'm glad you like it."

His eyes glowed with his grin and I took in a deep breath before closing the distance between us with a few steps. I threw my arms around his neck, drawing him close.

Isaac reacted immediately, wrapping his own arms around my waist and resting his chin on my head. My stomach flipped at the feeling of his fingers gripping my waist through my pyjamas. I wondered if he could feel my heart racing against his skin. I could certainly hear it pumping in my ears.

"Really," I muttered into his chest, ignoring how hot I suddenly felt. "Thank you."

"Anytime, Aspirin," he replied quietly.

We pulled apart, remaining only inches from each other. His hand drifted down from my waist to my elbow before falling to a stop at my hand. His fingers held my fingertips for only a moment, skin barely touching skin, before he dropped his hand to his side, the heat of his body immediately leaving me.

"See you," he said curtly, nodding at me, before turning to grip the door handle and tugging it open.

And he was gone.

CHAPTER TWENTY-FIVE
Dark Roast

I was too late.

The weekend had passed, mostly uneventfully, after my birthday—after Isaac's surprise appearance at my house. I had spent Sunday night watching movies at William's, trying to understand the enigma that was Isaac Hensick with Riley while William sobbed over never receiving his letter to Hogwarts.

The Halloween Dance was this Friday, the night before Halloween; which meant, of course, that most students already had a date.

Except me.

I was sitting in my usual lunch spot, eating some grey sludge from the cafeteria labelled "Pumpkin Soup." Really, since when were pumpkins gray?

Riley and William sat in front of me, discussing a plan of attack for asking Isaac to the dance.

"All she needs to do is go up to him and ask." William shrugged.

Riley shot him a glare. "No, she needs to do something romantic. Right, Aspen?"

I stabbed the sludge in my bowl. "I don't know, I was thinking of just saying it."

"Ha!" William spat.

"No!" Riley cried. She turned to me, pouting. "Aspen, come on. He got you a necklace with your name on it! That's so cute! You need to do something back. This is the twenty-first century. Equality and . . . whatnot."

"What would she even do?" William raised a brow in challenge. "What does a guy like Isaac Hensick want?"

"I can think of a few things," Riley teased back, wiggling her brows at him. He blinked in confusion and I snorted.

"Guys, listen," I began, right when I was cut off by a loud screech coming from the grass quad.

My eyes widened and I quickly put my tray down. I stood, peering down at the oval to see Lacey hugging Isaac tightly, a bright smile across her face.

Of course, that demonic sound was Lacey, who else would it be? I could see Riley roll her eyes in my peripheral view.

"I'm dressing as an angel, so you have to be the devil, okay?" she squealed, effectively capturing the attention of the entire quadrangle. She smiled mischievously. She loved the attention.

This was her announcing that she and Isaac were still a thing—that Isaac was taken for the dance this week. I swallowed thickly, watching as Isaac rolled his eyes.

He groaned in response. "Why?"

"It's a Halloween Dance, silly." Lacey poked his nose with a long, manicured finger. "We have to be matching if we're going together."

My heart sank.

"Did I just hear my evil stepsister correctly?" Riley asked.

William spoke through a mouthful of sludge, "If by heard correctly you mean Lacey's going to the dance with Isaac, then yes."

"That little—"

"It's fine," I interrupted Riley. I sunk back into the grass, ignoring the way my chest panged. "It's fine. He probably would've said no to me anyway."

"He definitely would have said yes to you," Riley interjected, her eyes narrowed at Lacey's back.

"Whatever." I waved a hand, trying to act nonchalant. "It's not like we can do anything about it."

William and Riley exchanged a look, and I knew what they were thinking. They turned back to me, apprehensive expressions on their faces.

"Are you sure?" William asked carefully. "You don't look fine."

He was right.

I clenched my jaw, my fingers tightening into fists, nails digging into flesh.

It was stupid of me to think Isaac might want to go with me. And now he would be going with Lacey, because Lacey was pretty and confident, and their relationship wasn't serious. They'd be wearing matching costumes, and dancing together all night, and probably going back home together afterwards . . .

I shook my head, pursing my lips.

"It's fine," I said, my voice quieter than expected.

Riley opened her mouth to speak, when a bell sounded, saving me from any confrontation. I sighed, grateful that I had art, meaning I wouldn't have to try to convince William and Riley that I was okay for the next hour.

They meant well, but I wasn't in the mood for them to attempt to comfort me, carefully treading around the topic of Isaac Hensick.

I just wanted to be alone and not think about Isaac Hensick for once.

I stood before they could speak, heaving my backpack over my shoulder.

"Well, I'd better get to class."

I moved to walk to the classroom when Riley's voice interrupted me.

"Aspen!" she shouted before lowering her voice with a grin. "Why don't we all go together? To the dance. It sounds fun."

I furrowed my brow at her. "I thought you were going with Arthur Andrews?"

She shrugged. "Chicks before dicks."

I sputtered out a laugh, my chest vibrating at her sudden stupid statement. She cracked a smile at me, pleased with my reaction.

"Seriously," she said. "You can come with us. William too."

William's eyes widened. "I'm not going to the dance." Though his cheeks turned pink at her suggestion.

"Shut up, William," Riley scolded, oblivious to his sudden tomato face. She turned back to me. "Come on, Aspen. It'll be fun."

"I don't know, Riley. I want you to have fun." And the idea of third wheeling with Riley and Arthur Andrews was not the most appealing.

"Come on!" Riley whined. Her mind was set. "I'll have even more fun with you there. Please?"

She fluttered her lashes at me, pouting. I sighed. She wasn't going to give this up.

"I'll think about it," I finally said.

She smiled, happy with my answer, and I began making my way to class.

When I arrived, Ms. Laney had already written the class instructions on the board. We had all done terribly in the abstract art assignment, so we'd be spending the lesson practicing abstract portraits with a partner.

I groaned. Frankly, I was sick of all this partner work and drawing. I was here for the theory, not the practical work. I was halfway to my seat when a voice interrupted me.

"Aspirin."

I turned, surprised to see Isaac had actually shown up to class today.

"Isaac." I blinked. "Hey."

He smiled at me, his cheeks dimpling, and nodded towards the board. "You want to partner up?"

I opened my mouth to agree before pausing. Of course, I wanted to partner up with him. All I ever wanted to do these days was stick around Isaac. Spending an hour staring at Isaac's face was practically a past time for me.

But when I looked at him, I thought of Lacey.

I thought of him and Lacey going to the dance together. I thought of them wearing matching costumes, and dancing together, and leaving together, and my stomach grew queasy.

Instead, my gaze went over Isaac's shoulder to Sebastian Georges. He was already watching us, a brow raised in questioning. I pursed my lips, an idea forming in my mind.

Swallowing thickly, I carefully stepped around Isaac.

"Sorry," I said over my shoulder, acting as casual as possible. "I'm partnering with Sebastian today."

Before he could reply, I hurried over to the blond haired boy, pulling out the empty seat beside him.

Sebastian turned to me with a playful grin and muttered lowly so that no one could hear him but me.

"I didn't realise we had agreed to partner up today."

I said nothing, only pulling out my sketchpad to draw the outline of Sebastian's head, his blond curls sprouting out in all directions. His hair was especially messy today after he had spent all of lunchtime running across the quad dribbling a soccer ball.

Sebastian paused for a moment before a smirk tugged at his lips at my silence. He lifted a brow in curiosity and pulled out his own notepad. Slowly, he shaded the page with his pencil—a gesture which somehow only managed to make his drawing worse—when his eyes flickered behind me and he raised his brows.

I tried to ignore him, my gaze moving between his face and my paper as I drew, but he stopped now.

His pencil sat motionless in his hands, his eyes staring directly past my head.

"What?" I asked finally, following his stare to where Isaac had partnered up with Lacey.

Of course, they'd partnered up together. What did I expect, after the show they'd given us at lunch?

Lacey giggled nasally, twirling her blonde hair and posing for Isaac to draw her. Isaac laughed, his shoulders bouncing and his eyes crinkling in the corners. He said something that made her laugh louder, drawing the attention of the entire class to her.

I spun back around, my face beginning to heat, and met Sebastian's eyes.

He only smiled wider at my reaction; his expression annoyingly arrogant. He could see right through me.

"So," he began, his voice low and smug, his eyes twinkling with mischief. He narrowed them at me, staring at me with scrutiny. "Lacey and Isaac are going to the dance together, huh?"

I rolled my eyes, trying to focus on drawing an abstract portrait worthy of Ms. Laney's approval. "Yeah. So what? He can do whatever he wants. I don't care at all."

He quirked a brow at me, seeming on the verge of laughing aloud. "Yeah, it sure seems like you don't care."

I sighed. "I don't."

"Oh?" Sebastian was grinning, and I knew it was no use lying to him.

"It's just . . ." I trailed off, meeting his eyes, my face heating. "I was going to ask him."

Sebastian's eyes widened.

"Wow," he sputtered, genuinely shocked. "Aspen grew some balls. Who knew?"

"Shut up." I laughed, rolling my eyes at him.

He raised his hands in defence.

"Hey, I'm supporting you here." He paused to send a glare over my shoulder as another one of Lacey's high-pitched laughs rang out. "I would have loved it if he went with you instead. Now I'm going to have to suffer with Lacey at my table all night."

I paused, blinking slowly. An idea began to form in my mind.

"Sebastian," I started, lowering my sketchbook. "Do you have a date to the dance?"

"No," he said, still glowering. "We were supposed to go as a group, but then Arthur and Isaac both got dates. I'm going to be third wheeling all night."

"Right." I nodded in agreement. "I was planning to go with Isaac. Now, I'll be third wheeling all night with Riley and Arthur. So . . ."

His eyes snapped up to meet mine, at my pause. His brow furrowed as I tilted my head at him.

"Wait," he began slowly, his eyes widening in realisation. "Are you saying what I think you're saying?"

"We should go together," I said finally, releasing the words as a puff of air.

He paused, his eyes swimming with mischief. Behind him, another painful screech of laughter came from Lacey. He winced at the sound and I sent him a small smile, suddenly feeling invigorated by the idea.

"Well?"

He met my eyes and his lips stretched out into a cheeky smirk.

"I like where your head's at, Aspen."

CHAPTER TWENTY-SIX
Chai Latte

"Over there."

I turned, following Vivienne's gaze to find Isaac sitting in his usual corner, sketching in his notebook. He seemed completely unaware of anything but his sketchpad. I paused for a moment, watching as he sketched lazily, his head resting on his other hand, his eyes half-shut and his lips pulled in a gentle smile.

Beside his hand rested his usual black coffee, and another mug—my usual soy latte.

He had been waiting for me.

I spun back, my eyes wide, to see Vivienne smirking at me. She lifted a knowing brow at me, her eyes twinkling with mischief.

"Lover boy's waiting for you."

"Shut up," I said, a blush quickly creeping up my neck.

I spun, her laugh echoing behind me as I strode towards Isaac.

Why was he waiting for me? Did he want to talk to me about something? I ignored the way my heart hammered in my chest, and the way my mind was racing, imagining all kinds of scenarios I could be walking into.

Subconsciously, I reached up to trace over the necklace that rested over my collarbone, trying to gain some confidence as I approached him.

I pulled out the seat in front of him, grabbing his attention, before plopping down with an awkward smile.

"Hey," I said as casually as possible, though my cheeks still heated beneath his gaze.

"Hi." Isaac grinned, slamming his notebook shut. He slid the book closer to himself before pushing the mug towards me. "I got you your usual."

"Thanks."

I took the coffee from the saucer and had a sip, the warmth immediately enveloping me and alleviating my pounding headache. Isaac watched me in silence, taking a sip of his own coffee. I smiled, biting back the temptation to make awkward conversation.

As I took another gulp of coffee, scalding my tongue, my eyes drifted to his closed sketchpad.

Isaac's name was written on the top corner of the black notebook, and I found myself wondering if I had ever seen what was inside. After all these years of passing him in the café, watching him draw as I waited for my coffee, I've never seen a single drawing.

What did he spend all day drawing in there?

It must have been important, considering how he seemed to ignore the world around him when he was sitting in this corner, a pencil in hand.

I furrowed my brows, leaning towards it, when Isaac pulled me out of my daze.

"So," he began quickly. I snapped my eyes up to meet his. He slowed, his voice a nonchalant drawl. "Sebastian Georges, huh?"

I paused, blinking slowly, the blond boy appearing in my mind. I couldn't help but grin, remembering his idiocy and the cheerful air about him. "What about Sebastian?"

Isaac narrowed his eyes at my expression, sending me a steely gaze.

"He told me you were going to the dance together."

"Oh." I blushed, turning away. I thought of how I had told Sebastian that I was about to ask Isaac—the way he could easily see right through me. My cheeks burned. I hoped Sebastian hadn't mentioned any other part of our conversation to him.

"Yeah," I said eventually, trying to play it off as casual as possible. "I asked him yesterday during art class."

Isaac's brow furrowed. "I thought you said I didn't know the guy you wanted to ask?"

My eyes widened. I did say that, and completely forgot about it—*how did he remember?* I fumbled for an excuse.

"I just didn't want you getting suspicious." I shrugged casually, avoiding eye contact. Nice save. I cleared my throat. "That's all."

I mean, it was partially true. I had only said it in the first place because I didn't want him to realise that I was talking about him at the time. Of course, it just had to backfire on me, and I just had to end up asking Sebastian Georges to the dance.

And Isaac just had to go with Lacey. In matching costumes. I gagged mentally and almost physically.

Isaac nodded slowly. He took another sip of his coffee, narrowing his eyes at me over the rim of his mug. Flustered, I searched for something to move the topic away from me and Sebastian.

"What about you and Lacey?" I sputtered out. He locked eyes with me, and my cheeks heated further. "I thought you guys weren't dating."

"We're not," he said bluntly. I blinked.

"So, what's this about matching costumes?"

He smirked, tilting his head towards me. "You were eavesdropping on us?"

I blushed, turning away and crossing my arms. "It was hardly eavesdropping. Lacey was screeching loud enough for the entire school to hear."

He laughed, shook his head, and sent me a little shrug. "Well, I thought it might be fun."

"Oh," I said dumbly, trying my best not to sound bitter. Fun. "Right."

We paused and I took a large gulp of my coffee, an awkward silence falling over the table. A second passed when he stood suddenly, his chair scraping back.

"I'll go grab us some takeaway cups," he said, rubbing a hand over his neck. "Wouldn't want to be late for first period, right?"

I laughed, raising a brow at him in surprise. "Oh, so Isaac Hensick is an academic now, is he?"

"Hey, people change." He sent me a wink. He paused, meeting my eyes. The corner of his lips twitched up in a heart-lurching smirk. "Besides, I have a pretty good reason to go now."

I hated the way I blushed at his words. He was probably talking about Lacey, now that it looked like they were back together, but it didn't hurt to fantasize, right? He turned, walking towards Vivienne at the counter to grab some takeaway cups.

The café was almost completely empty aside from us, and Vivienne jumped at the opportunity to dig her claws into a long, drawn out conversation with Isaac—clearly bored at the lack of customers this morning.

I sighed, turning back to the table, my eyes falling to the closed sketchpad he had left behind.

He was always drawing in there, and yet I had never seen his drawings before. Ever since the first time I had seen him at the start of high school, he was always scribbling in that sketchpad.

And yet, after all this time, all I had seen were his drawings in art class—and they were brilliant.

196

I could only imagine the kind of drawings he could be hiding in there—the drawings he had been working on for hours.

I hummed, glancing over my shoulder at Isaac to see he was still talking enthusiastically with Vivienne. I would only take a second. Just a peek.

Before I could think otherwise, I reached forward and flipped the cover open.

The black cover fell aside, exposing a page with a gorgeous photo-realistic drawing of an Asian girl.

She sipped on a mug, the Café de Fleur logo bright and clear in the centre of it. Her face was sharp and angular, her cheekbones high and her sharp jaw coming to a pointed chin. Her eyes were shut, her lashes long and curled. Her hair was parted in the middle, falling in long, loose waves over her shoulders.

It was amazing.

I flipped the page only to see the same girl. This time, she was in colour. Isaac had drawn her laughing, her long black hair swaying as if in the wind. Her cheeks were bright with colour, her teeth exposed and straight.

My eyes widened, my breath getting caught in my throat.

She was beautiful.

It was almost as if Isaac had printed a photograph into his sketchpad, but the smooth lines of coloured pencil proved otherwise.

In a daze, I turned to the next page. This time, three smaller drawings covered the page—all the same girl. Her smiling in a pose, her candidly scrolling through her phone, her sticking her tongue out.

I blinked, realising that this wasn't a random girl, a stranger or a stock image. All of the drawings in here were of her. My heart pounded. I knew I had to stop. This was an invasion of privacy. But the drawings were so beautiful, and my curiosity already piqued. My hands moved on their own to turn to the next page, catching a glance of long dark hair when, suddenly, the notebook was slammed shut.

I jumped back, my chair scraping against the floor. Isaac towered over me, his eyes narrowed, and his jaw clenched.

"Isaac," I gasped. "I-I . . . I'm so sorry. I was-I just-I'm—"

"That's my notebook," he said, seething, dragging it closer towards him. "It's private. Who said you could look in there?"

I stood from my seat, my brow furrowing, my heart racing. "I'm sorry. You're right. I'm an idiot. I shouldn't have done that. I'm sorry."

My face heated, my stomach dropping. I was so stupid. *Why did I do that? How could I just invade his privacy like that?* Shame filled me.

Isaac sighed, shaking his head. His hand flew to his head and he rubbed it uneasily, turning away before glancing back at me.

"It's . . ." He took a deep breath and released it in an exaggerated sigh. "It's fine."

"No, it's not," I insisted, shaking my head. "I really shouldn't have done that. I'm sorry."

"It's fine," he repeated. He flipped the cover back open, revealing the laughing beauty. "They're just drawings. I drew them so long ago, I almost forgot they were there."

I blinked. His voice lowered, his eyes softening as he stared at the drawing. I didn't miss the way his lips twitched in a sad smile at the picture.

"Who is she?" I asked, my gaze trained on his face.

His eyes met mine, and I stilled.

"Her name is Marcelina."

It felt like the air had been sucked out of my lungs.

"Marcelina Pepper?"

"Yeah," he said, closing the sketchpad again. "I . . . sort of . . . used to go out with her."

"Oh." I had already known. Riley had told me. But hearing it from him, my stomach flipped. His voice had fallen so quiet, so different from how he normally acted.

I swallowed the lump forming in my throat. It was a painful mixture of guilt and embarrassment and rejection. My face burned in shame.

"Well," I said stupidly, unsure of what else to say. "I'd better go. Thanks for the coffee, Isaac."

I turned before he could reply, leaving my half-empty mug behind and dashing out the café door. I sped down the street towards the school.

The cool breeze immediately calmed my heating cheeks, but my heart continued to race, keeping time with my mind.

His sketchpad was filled with drawings of Marcelina. It wasn't just one or two drawings; it was pages and pages—and there was probably more where that came from.

His entire book was filled with just her. Just Marcelina. My heart pounded.

He still loved her.

CHAPTER TWENTY-SEVEN
Cortado

"Nice costume."

I tugged at my yellow and black striped tie, my long black wizarding robes draped over my shoulders and falling to my ankles. We stood in the school parking lot, the wind causing my dark robes to ripple.

"It was the only costume I had." I shrugged, adjusting my collar.

Sebastian laughed, his smile bright as he took my hand and placed it on his arm, leading me towards the school gym.

He had come dressed as a vampire, which for him meant wearing his usual t-shirt and jeans with some tacky fangs. Fake blood (my red lipstick he had borrowed minutes ago) stained the corners of his lips and trailed to his chin.

It was a terrible costume—and very Sebastian Georges.

"It's better than yours," I said pointedly, arching a brow at him.

He smiled, baring his oversized fangs. His words slurred as he spoke like he had a lisp, due to the fangs.

"You better watch yourself—" He paused to put on a stupid vampire voice, narrowing his eyes in a teasing threat. "Or I'll suck your blood!"

I rolled my eyes, turning to meet Riley's stare. She walked behind us with her arm linked with Arthur's. She had dressed as a cheerleader upon Arthur Andrews's request, matching his own football costume—though she'd spent the entire car ride complaining about how conceited Arthur was.

Something about Arthur chatting her ear off on the phone, planning their costumes, or more specifically—bragging about how good he looked in his costume. By the sound of it, I was glad Sebastian and I had a very casual, last minute arrangement.

Riley had driven me to the dance to meet with Arthur, Isaac, and Sebastian together. It was kind of funny. I never would have expected we'd be attending the dance with this strange array of a group a few months ago—but here we were.

At least, here most of us were.

I turned back to look at Sebastian.

"Where's Isaac?" I muttered, my gaze darting across the parking lot. He was nowhere to be found, and neither was Lacey's usual screeching voice.

Sebastian faux gasped, holding a hand to his chest. "My date is thinking about another boy? How could this be?"

"Shut up." I laughed, nudging his shoulder with my own. "I saw you eyeing out Jessica Jenson a few minutes ago."

"Touché." He grinned. "He's already inside with Lacey. She wouldn't shut up about how cold she was."

I nodded, releasing a breath. We walked into the gym, handing our tickets in at the front.

As we stepped into the dark gymnasium, my eyes immediately found Isaac and Lacey on the dance floor. They danced to the pounding music, Lacey's back to him as she grinded against him.

She'd come dressed, not as an angel, but as a slutty nun. At least it was creative. Isaac had come dressed as a sub-par devil. He wore his usual leather jacket and jeans, only tonight, he also wore some devil horns to go with it.

Sebastian's eyes followed mine and he groaned.

"Let's go get a seat," he said, his voice low beneath the music.

I nodded wordlessly, finding an empty table and falling into a chair beside Sebastian. Riley sat beside me, sighing as Arthur continued chattering on about some clothing sale he'd visited over the weekend.

I met her eyes and she sent me a sarcastic smile, waving her pom poms at me.

Beside me, Sebastian sat, his arms crossed over his chest as he watched the dance floor fill with students. I sighed, watching Lacey sway her hips against Isaac, when suddenly his stare shot up and locked on me.

I froze, my cheeks burning up. Isaac watched me from across the gym, his dark eyes narrowed at me, and I became keenly aware of Sebastian's arm gripped under my hand.

I swallowed thickly, turning to face Sebastian.

"Do you want a drink?" I asked, my face hot and red beneath my makeup.

"Sure," he said. "I'll grab us some."

He stood, striding directly towards the refreshments table. I watched on, noticing how girls seemed to flood to him immediately. He smiled, his tacky fangs poking over his lips as he laughed, and I could imagine him using his idiotic vampire accent—except unlike me, the girls giggled in response.

I sighed, turning back to the table with a frown. Beside me, I could hear Arthur's deep voice asking Riley to dance.

"I'm good, thanks," Riley muttered.

I raised my brows at Arthur's scoff.

"It wasn't exactly a question," Arthur retorted.

"You're not exactly a good date," Riley snapped back, tossing a pom-pom onto the table. "All you talk about is yourself. William would have at least told me I looked nice."

My breath got caught in my throat. *Maybe William did have a chance after all.*

Arthur paused, his eyes narrowing carefully. "You look nice."

Riley sneered, rolling her eyes and ignoring him. Instead, she turned to me. "I think I'm going to go. Will you be okay?"

"Yeah." I nodded, my eyes growing wide. "Will you?"

She shot Arthur a look. "I'll be better than okay." Standing, she tossed her hair over her shoulder. "Bye Arthur."

Before he could reply, she stormed past him, her ponytail and short skirt swaying as she strolled out of the gym.

Arthur glanced at me and I shrugged, biting back a smug grin. That was my best friend.

He scowled, turning to the dance floor, instantly being flooded by girls asking to dance. He grinned, taking the hand of one and leading her to the centre, already grinding against her in beat to the music. His hands drifted to her hips and I blushed, averting my gaze.

That didn't take long.

"What did I miss?"

I turned to see Sebastian, two cups of punch in his hands. I took one, taking a sip.

"Don't ask."

He laughed, falling into the seat beside me. We sat in silence, sipping our drinks and staring out at the dance floor. Random girls continued to grind onto Arthur, and Lacey swung her hips against Isaac, their backs turned to us. I sighed, distinctly remembering why I didn't go to school dances.

"Do you want to dance?" Sebastian asked eventually.

I glanced at him, noticing his careful smile. I shook my head, pursing my lips.

"I'm not really feeling up to it," I confessed, sending him a shrug.

203

"Oh." He paused, furrowing his brow. "Okay."

I looked at him. He sat leaning back in his seat, his arms crossed over his chest as he stared out onto the dance floor. I didn't miss the longing look he gave, his foot tapping in agitation.

"Sebastian," I said finally, my expression softening. I waved a hand at the dance floor. "You don't have to stay with me. Go and dance! Have fun!"

"I don't know . . ." he trailed off, glancing at the dance floor. He pursed his lips. "I don't want to just leave you."

"I'll be fine, Seb."

His brows drew together, and he looked at me in confusion. "Really?"

"Yes." I smiled, nodding. "Go."

His face broke into his iconic grin, his eyes immediately brightening. He stood, pulling me into a tight hug. I patted his back awkwardly until he released me.

"Thanks Aspen. You're the best."

I laughed, watching as he waltzed onto the dance floor, and fell back into my seat with a slump. Girls flocked to Sebastian and he smiled, swaying his hips against sparsely dressed girls. This was much more his scene than it was mine.

I watched on with a sigh. Girls dressed as bunny rabbits and skimpy witches rubbed against Sebastian. I lifted an arm, staring at the baggy Hogwarts robes that fell from my arm. I felt incredibly overdressed—quite literally.

My body was drowning in black robes.

I stood. Suddenly this dance didn't seem so fun after all. Maybe Riley had the right idea leaving early.

I sent one last glance to Isaac. He was in the corner, practically swamped by girls Lacey desperately tried to fight off with her ass shaking. I sputtered out a laugh, rolling my eyes and beginning to pace towards the exit.

At least he was enjoying himself.

I strode out of the gym towards the car park. Riley was my ride home, meaning I'd have to walk back from school. She probably expected me to get a ride back with Sebastian. It wasn't bad, I walked to school every day, after all.

Hitching my robes higher, I began walking.

It was a nice night. The stars were bright in the sky, not a cloud in sight. A slight breeze cooled my red face, and was refreshingly cold after leaving that stuffy, overcrowded gym.

I didn't know what I was thinking. A dance like that was nowhere near my kind of scene. I didn't even have a chance to speak to Isaac. The entire thing turned out to be a disaster.

I raised a hand, lifting the baggy black sleeve of my robes. I snorted at it, comparing it to all the other girls's costumes. Of course, Isaac wouldn't want to speak to me. Not when I was dressed like this.

Not in front of the entire school.

I continued walking, reaching the end of the parking lot, when a voice stopped me.

"Aspirin!"

I stopped in my tracks, turning to see Isaac sprinting across the school car park towards me. His red devil horns headband held his dark hair back from his forehead. His green eyes twinkled in the starlight. I blinked, narrowing my eyes at him.

"Isaac," I said.

"Hey." He came to a stop in front of me, panting. "Why are you leaving?"

I shrugged, my eyes looking over his shoulder to the school gym. "I told you, I'm not exactly the party type."

He raised a brow at me. "What about Sebastian?"

I spat out a laugh, shaking my head. "Sebastian?"

"Yeah." He quirked a brow at me like it was obvious. "You can't just leave your date like that in the middle of the dance."

"Why not?"

205

"He's your date," Isaac said pointedly. He wagged his brows at me with a teasing smirk. "Besides, I thought you had a huge crush on him."

I cut him a glare, my irritation beginning rise. "Not really."

"But you said—"

"I know what I said." I squeezed my eyes shut, shaking my head. I had a talent for shoving my foot into my own mouth. I had said a lot of stupid things to Isaac—I didn't need to relive my mistakes right now. I sighed, lowering my voice. "I know what I said. I . . . I was wrong."

He frowned. "Why would you ask Sebastian to go with you if you don't like him?"

I rolled my eyes, snorting. "Yeah, well, I wanted to go with you, dumbass."

Isaac blinked. A pause, then, "What?"

I sputtered out another laugh, shaking my head. My cheeks flamed with embarrassment, but adrenaline pumped through my body at the confession. I craned my neck, my gaze darting from the stars, to the empty roads—anywhere but Isaac's eyes.

"I never wanted to go with Sebastian," I spat out, my heart pounding at the words on my tongue. "I wanted to go with you."

He was silent. I could feel my face heating up, turning bright red to the ears. I glanced at his expression. His eyes were wide, his lips slightly ajar.

"I thought . . ." He paused. "You said you liked him since freshman year. We've only known each other for a few months."

"You've known me for a few months," I said, lifting a brow. "I've liked you since I first stepped into that stupid café."

His brow furrowed, his jaw clenching. The green of his eyes turned dark and my stomach flipped.

"You wanted to go with me?"

I nodded, the adrenaline beginning to wear off. I looked away, tilting my head to stare at the stars, unable to bear his green eyes drilling into me.

"I-I mean, I was going to ask you, but then that night you came to my room, and then . . . you know, you didn't remember the next day, and in the café, we were talking about it, and then Lacey, and—"

His lips pressed to mine.

My body shuddered to a stop, my eyes widening. His kiss was quick and breathless, pressing small pecks against my mouth. I was in so much shock, I forgot to kiss back.

Instead, I pulled back, my eyes wide and brows raised.

His arm had fallen to the small of my back, holding me close to him. His eyes flickered between my eyes and my lips, dark and wanting. His face was still close to mine, our foreheads were almost touching. His breath fanned over my face.

Even in the night, his breath smelled of coffee.

I blinked, dazed. "W-what?"

"I wanted to go with you too." His voice was low, his breaths heavy. "But you said you liked someone. I thought . . . I thought—" He shook his head with a laugh. "I didn't forget that night."

I furrowed my brow at him, my heart hammering away. He wanted to go with me. He didn't forget.

He took my silence as a sign to continue.

"You seemed so embarrassed. I didn't want to ruin anything. I thought you regretted it all. I thought . . ." He paused, his eyes drifting to my costume before he hollered out a laugh. "Of course, you're a Hufflepuff."

"What's that supposed to mean?" I scoffed, whacking his chest.

He laughed, leaning closer until our lips almost touched. His forehead rested on mine, his hands gripping my waist as if I was going to disappear. My own palms slid up, resting on his chest, my trembling fingers digging into his shirt.

"I really like you, Aspen," he muttered. His voice was low and raspy, and I shivered at my name on his tongue.

My breath hitched in my throat. I swallowed thickly, my eyes drifting to his lips.

"I like you too, Isaac."

My voice shook, but my shoulders sagged in relief at the words. How long had I wanted to tell him? How long had I been watching from afar? But now he was here, and I was in his arms. And he liked me—Isaac Hensick liked me.

His grip around my waist tightened, and I could feel his own heart hammering in his chest beneath my fingers. He tilted his head down, nudging my nose. His eyes dark, his usual smirk beginning to tug on his lips.

"Really?" he murmured, hovering an inch above my lips.

"Really," I whispered.

And he kissed me again.

CHAPTER TWENTY-EIGHT
Soy Latte and Black Coffee

I lied in my bed, my mind swimming.

After Isaac had kissed me, it felt like a dream. He had drawn me in again, his lips finding mine over and over until I was left breathless. He had walked me home, leaving me with a soft peck at my doorstep and nothing but my own thoughts as company.

I knew I wouldn't be getting any sleep tonight. Too much had happened. I was still trying to process my stupid costume, much less what had happened with Isaac.

I couldn't stop thinking of him.

I thought of how he pressed his fingers to my jaw as he kissed me. I thought of how his hand trailed down my arm when I pulled back. How he looked at me when I said goodbye, like he didn't want to leave.

My stomach flipped at the memory, and I wrapped my arms around myself.

I missed him.

I sighed, glancing at my phone. Midnight just passed, and I was still wide awake. There was no chance of me getting any sleep tonight, not with what just happened. Not with Isaac infiltrating my mind ten times more than usual.

You'd think I'd be used to it, after all this time, but no. My heart pounded in my ears every time those green eyes flashed through my mind. My body burned with the memory. I sank into the mattress, knowing I'd be up all night at this rate.

A rustle sounded from my window. Then a thud. Then, suddenly it was pushed open, Isaac tumbling into my bedroom.

My eyes widened and I bolted upright, instinctively pulling the blanket over myself.

"Isaac?"

He grinned, brushing himself off as he stood. He closed the window with a soft thud and turned back to me.

"I figured you wouldn't be able to sleep."

I laughed. He wasn't wrong.

He still wore his "costume"—his leather jacket and jeans—although he left his devil horns behind. I already changed hours ago, before diving into bed in my pyjamas to text Riley and William all the details.

I was still waiting for a reply from both of them.

I slid over in my sheets, making room for Isaac and patting the mattress beside me. He grinned, shrugging off his jacket and shoes before joining me beneath the blankets. I blushed at the way his arms flexed with the movement.

The bed dipped as he crawled onto it and immediately, I felt enveloped in warmth. He lied on the pillow beside me, his face inches from mine, and I was sure my face was glowing red even in the dark. His hand trailed up from my leg to my arm before finally resting on my waist and drawing me in.

I sighed in content, resting against his body. We laid silent in the dark for a moment, listening to our slow breathing and the occasional car speeding past. I lied my head against his chest, my mind falling quiet.

All felt right.

Our chests moved in sync as we breathed each other in. We didn't need words. We felt comfortable, just feeling skin against skin and sighing in each other's warmth. His fingers drummed against my waist, pushing my shirt up slightly to rub at my skin with his thumb.

I smiled at the feeling, electricity erupting from his touch and releasing a flurry of butterflies in my stomach. My own hand moved to wrap around his waist when I hit something sharp in his pocket. I drew back, a breath leaving my mouth and his eyes widened.

"Sorry," he said, reaching into his pocket and pulling out his mini sketchpad—about the size of his phone. "I forgot it was in there."

I blinked, my eyes moving from his face to the book in his hand. I remembered the drawings of Marcelina, the pages he had filled with her face. Suddenly, my happiness faded. I'd forgotten about her for a moment.

For a moment, it had been just the two of us, smiling like idiots, kissing beneath the stars.

But what did it matter when Marcelina was the one he loved in the end? Who cares if he kissed me? If he said he liked me? He told me himself, he doesn't date. What did I expect to happen?

This was a onetime thing. I was stupid to imagine otherwise.

He watched me carefully, his eyes narrowing, before sitting upright. The mattress shifted beneath his movement and I followed suit. He lifted the sketchpad and tilted his head to it.

"Look through it."

I furrowed my brow, glancing at the little black book. "What?"

"Come on," he said, taking my hand and placing the sketchpad in my palm. I warmed at the touch of his skin on mine. "I know you're curious."

He was right.

Ever since I had first opened that book in the middle of Café de Fleur, I've been thinking of it nonstop—thinking of his drawings of Marcelina, thinking of his perfect sketches and realistic artworks . . . wondering what else he had been drawing.

My hand hovered over the sketchpad. I held my breath, pulling the cover open to be greeted with the drawing of Marcelina and the mug in her hand. I chewed on my lip, turning to the next page, Marcelina's coloured eyes met mine through the drawing. Then the next, the smaller sketches of Marcelina covering every inch of the page.

"She's really pretty," I said finally. "I can see why you love her."

"Keep going," Isaac said.

I clenched my teeth turning page after page. My initial excitement had quickly disappeared, and my stomach lurched at the cruel reminder—the reminder that Isaac really loved Marcelina. She was the one he wanted.

And yet, I couldn't stop myself as I turned to the next page.

Marcelina laughing and smiling and running and dancing filled the pages. Drawings of her singing and scrolling through her phone. My stomach lurched at a sketch of her lying in pyjamas across a bed.

Smaller sketches filled pages in between. Sketches of Vivienne making a coffee, a bald man typing on a laptop or a random plant.

I flipped the page.

Another paper of smaller sketches flooded this spread—an empty coffee cup, a toddler giggling and a girl holding a coffee cup, the Café de Fleur logo printed over it.

I blinked, narrowing my eyes and looking at the sketch closer.

The girl had dark hair, pulled into a bun, her hands grasping the coffee cup as she sipped on it. He had captured her expression perfectly, her eyes crinkling in the corners with pleasure as the steam of the coffee curled around her face. Her face.

It was me.

It was me, my backpack slung over one shoulder as I sipped on my soy latte. He had drawn me at the café, sipping on my usual order.

My eyes drifted to the corner of the page. It was dated months before we had even spoken—almost a year.

I turned the page over. Between drawings of random objects and cats and one or two of Marcelina or Chloe—it was me. A small sketch of me digging through my backpack for my wallet, another half-page drawing of me eating a crumbling biscotti.

A full-page drawing of me laughing at something. A two-page spread of me at the library—the date a few months before we met.

He had been watching me too.

Slowly, the drawings of Marcelina and coffee cups vanished, replaced with drawings of me in Isaac's leather jacket the day he had lent it to me, me napping in the library, me sitting in art class beside Sebastian, me blowing out a candle stuck in a discounted cupcake.

"You're so pretty," Isaac muttered, his voice low and close. His breath fanned over my ear and down my neck. "I couldn't help myself."

I spun, my eyes meeting his. His gaze was dark and focused, sending a shudder down my spine.

"But Marcelina," I found myself stuttering out, blinking slowly.

His hand traced up my arm to cup my face. I leaned into his touch, my heart pounding so loudly in my chest I wondered if he could hear it.

"I love you, Aspen." My heart twinged at his words, a lump beginning to grow in my throat. "I've liked you since I first saw you in Café de Fleur. I've liked you since I found you napping in the library. I've liked you since I kissed you at Riley's birthday."

He paused, sending me a small smile. His ears had turned pink and his eyes darkened. "I've loved you since I climbed through your window at four in the morning and kissed you under the stars."

My chest swelled and I felt a burning sensation behind my cheekbones.

After years of watching him sketch in the corner of that café—months of him drawing me—and now he was in my bed telling me he loved me. I couldn't help the tears that sprung to my eyes, the pounding of blood in my ears.

"Really?" I asked, my nose stuffy from tears.

"Really."

"Really, really?"

He smirked, pressing his lips against mine in a soft, gentle kiss. We pulled apart, but I found myself leaning closer, wanting him as close to me as possible. His cheeks dimpled as he gazed down at me.

"Really, really."

I stared at him, speechless, and he laughed at me, his grip on my cheek tightening as he pulled me in for another kiss.

This time, it was full of need. His lips were hungry, nibbling on my bottom lip, our teeth clashing and our hands gripping each other tightly.

I pulled away suddenly, our chests heaving. His eyes searched mine, flickering between my eyes, and I smiled at him.

"I love you too, Isaac."

And I kissed him.

*   *   *

The next day, we walked to Café de Fleur together. Vivienne sent me a smirk and a knowing look as we entered, placing her hands firmly on her hips.

Isaac's arm was slung around my waist, his jacket hanging loosely over my shoulders, the sleeves rolled up delicately.

"Morning, Vivienne." I grinned. "One black coffee, three sugars, and a hot chocolate for me please."

She quirked a brow at me. "Coming right up."

Isaac's grip on my waist tightened and I turned to see him raising a brow with a smirk.

"What happened to your usual?" he asked.

"I don't need it anymore," I said as a matter-of-factly.

He narrowed his eyes at me. "You, the girl who naps in the library in her free time, don't need coffee anymore?"

I laughed, leaning against him with a smile. "I'm not tired today."

"You're not?"

"Nope." I grinned. It was true. He had fallen asleep beside me last night, his arms wound around my waist and his legs tangled with my own.

And I had slept all through the night—from the moment our heads touched the pillow, to the moment the sun rose, and he shifted beneath my grasp.

I felt more awake than ever. Even just standing beside him, I was buzzing with energy.

Because that's what caffeine did to me. It made my heart race, like when his eyes met mine. It made my skin tingle, like when his skin brushed against me. It sent jolts of electricity through my veins—sparks that echoed the feeling of his body pressed against me and our fingers laced together.

And if he could do that to me—all that and more—what did I need coffee for?

Where coffee burned a hole in my pocket and left my anxiety soaring, all for the feeling of wakefulness, Isaac left me refreshed and awake. He left me feeling comfortable. Calm, yet full of energy all at once.

And that was more than I could have ever asked for.

"I don't need it anymore." I smiled, meeting his eyes. My fingers drifted to the necklace resting over my collarbone, tracing the golden leaf. "I have you."

He chuckled, his hand gripping me tightly. He looked at me, his cheeks dimpling, his hair combed back, still dressed in the same clothes he had worn yesterday. The Isaac Hensick—but somehow, now, my Isaac Hensick.

His expression softened and I blushed beneath his gaze.

"You have me."

PART TWO

CHAPTER TWENTY-NINE
Chamomile Tea

I shuddered against the breeze, my hand tightening around Isaac's. He smiled at me, his green eyes twinkling, dimples digging holes into his tanned skin.

"What?" Isaac asked, glancing at me as I grinned up at his face.

"Nothing." I shrugged, knowing I was blushing.

"You're staring," he pointed out.

"It's just so weird," I said, shaking my head in disbelief. "Walking to school together."

He raised a brow at me, smirking in a way that made my heart lurch.

"Aspirin," he began, his voice low. "We've walked to school together before."

"I know, but not like this!" I exclaimed, raising our intertwined fingers.

His lips twitched in a lopsided grin and he released my hand. "You don't want to hold hands?"

"What?" I pouted, my hand falling to my side. He sent me a mischievous grin and I rolled my eyes, grabbing his hand. "No, you idiot. Of course, I want to."

As soon as the words left my mouth, I felt my face warm.

"Good," Isaac simply said. His grip on my hand tightened as we continued to walk, his gaze straight ahead. "Because I didn't want to let go either."

My ears turned red at his words and I stared forward, refusing to meet his eyes. Butterflies erupted in my stomach. Isaac really would be the death of me.

I sighed, my head pounding as I took a sip of my chamomile tea. My lack of coffee was giving me a constant migraine, but I was determined. My doctor had been pushing me to cut down on my caffeine intake anyway—it helps anxiety, he had insisted—and my insomnia had gotten a lot better since Isaac told me he liked me.

It was insane to think about. I had replayed that night in my mind a million times. Him running after me. me in my stupid Hogwarts robes, him looking as attractive as ever . . .

Him kissing me . . .

And every night, I'd be asleep in no time, grinning and dreaming of the green-eyed idiot that I couldn't seem to stop thinking about. Excited to wake up and see him again in the morning. It gave me something to look forward to.

"You're staring, again," Isaac remarked.

I blushed, pursing my lips at him. "And? I seem to remember you staring at me an awful lot. While I slept, too."

Isaac's grin widened. "And I remember you doing the same to me."

My face heated at the memory. I opened my mouth to retort when his grip on my hand tightened. I blinked, turning to realise we had already arrived at school.

And people were staring.

I froze, feeling students's eyes dig into me, their gazes dipping from Isaac's face, to my face, to our intertwined fingers.

And then the whispers started.

"Who is she?"

219

"Isn't that Isaac Hensick?"

"I heard he left the dance early on Friday."

"Wasn't she dressed as Harry Potter or something?"

"More like Snape."

"I bet they'll be history in a week."

"How did he go from Lacey to that?"

"Aspen," Isaac's voice was low. I turned to see him leaning down, his lips an inch from my ear. "Are you okay?"

I sucked in a shaky breath, feeling Isaac's fingers tighten around mine. His hand was warm, his thumb stroking gentle circles on the back of my hand. My heart is racing. At this point, I couldn't tell if it was from the stares or from Isaac Hensick holding my hand.

Either way, I steeled myself.

I wouldn't let them win. I was the one walking to school with Isaac. I was the one he had chosen.

I turned back to Isaac, nodding firmly. "I'm fine."

He raised a brow at me, studying my face, but I planted a firm smile on my lips, and he shrugged.

"I'm here," he simply said, and we began walking into the school.

If I thought the stares at the front gates were bad, they were worse inside the hallways. People craned their necks to watch us walk in, and instantly began to whisper with their friends. Some freshmen even had the gall to point at us and gawk.

I shook my head, trying to stop the unbearable pounding in my ears. I knew it was my anxiety, exaggerating everything and making it seem like the entire school was laughing at me.

I kept my stare straight ahead, my heart lodged firmly in my throat, until we reached my locker.

Riley and William were already waiting for me.

As I approached, William's eyes bulged, causing Riley to spin, her hair whipping the air. She paused, her eyes scanning me

220

and Isaac before she let out a loud gasp. Her hand gripped William's arm tightly, causing him to turn bright red.

"Hey guys," I said, pausing in front of them.

William's eyes moved from me to Isaac, then back to me. Riley seemed to regain her breath and she leapt forward, gesturing between us.

"When did this happen?" she squealed.

I blushed in embarrassment, feeling everyone's eyes on us.

"Oh yeah." I cleared my throat, shrugging nonchalantly. "By the way, we're dating now."

"Dating?" Riley echoed.

"Dating," Isaac confirmed.

"Oh, my God," William gasped.

"Why didn't you tell us!" Riley shouted, whacking my arm. Isaac stifled a laugh and I nudged him.

"I tried to tell you both, but none of you answered your phone all weekend," I pointed out, lifting a brow at her.

Riley paused. Slowly, she turned, exchanging a guilty look with William, before turning back to us.

"Oh, right," Riley began. She offered me a meek smile. "By the way, we're dating too."

"You're dating!" I shouted, my jaw falling.

Isaac's eyes widened.

Riley shrugged.

William turned bright red.

"When did this happen?" I continued, blinking in disbelief. I glanced at William, raising a brow. "You finally grew the balls to ask her out?"

"Hey!" William exclaimed, pouting. Then, his voice grew quiet in defeat. "No."

"I kissed him first," Riley replied haughtily, crossing her arms in triumph. She paused, narrowing her eyes at me. "What about you?"

221

"I kissed her," Isaac cut in, grinning down at me cheekily. His eyes narrowed at me and I grew hot.

"I confessed first," I shot back, whacking him on the chest.

"Really?" Riley raised a brow at me. "I'm impressed, Aspen. The student has become the master."

I laughed at her, rolling my eyes when the bell sounded.

"Ugh, history," Riley groaned loudly, stepping back to take William's hand. He blushed bright red and I stifled a laugh. She paused to look at me. "Are you coming?"

I glanced at Isaac. He wasn't in history with me. "I'll meet you there."

She nodded, turning to walk down the hall with William, already talking about how cute she thought Isaac and I were together. I blushed at their conversation. It was weird being talked about when normally I blended in with the walls.

"Will you be alright?" Isaac asked quietly. He leaned against the lockers, looking down at me, playing with my fingers in his hand.

"Yeah." I nodded, my voice soft. I looked up at him and he searched my eyes. He seemed worried, so I smiled widely, trying to comfort him. "I'll be fine. I'll meet you at lunch?"

"Definitely," he said. He let go of my hand, pushing off the locker, and I turned to leave. "Wait."

I stopped, spinning to look at him. He slid off his jacket and, in one swift move, wrapped it over my shoulders.

"What?" I blinked, tugging the leather jacket around myself. It was warm and I melted into it. It smelled of him; of coffee and his cologne, the smell of cigarettes long gone since the last time I had worn it.

"I know you were cold," he said curtly. "And maybe it'll get some of them to back off."

He tilted his head and I followed with my eyes to see half the hallway staring with wide eyes. I laughed, shaking my head.

222

"Thank you, Isaac," I said, pulling my arms through the sleeves.

He grinned, stepping back. "Anytime, Aspirin."

*   *   *

By lunchtime, my migraine had faded to a dull ache and I had become used to all the stares and whispers.

Riley and William walked beside me. William's arm awkwardly tossed around her shoulder as she chattered endlessly about how annoying Lacey had been since Isaac ditched her at the dance, but I wasn't listening. I watched them with wide eyes—it was hard to believe they were dating.

"Aspirin!"

I spun to see Isaac jogging up to me. His dark hair had been tousled and he grinned widely before coming to a stop before me.

"Isaac." I laughed, reaching up to smooth his hair out. He grinned leaning closer to tease me. I rolled my eyes, shoving him back, and he laughed. "What happened to your hair?"

"Had a nap," he replied with a shrug.

"You shouldn't skip class, Isaac," I scolded.

He pouted at me. "But it's no fun without you there."

A blush crept up my neck and I spun away from him, continuing to walk towards our usual lunch spot, when he stopped me.

"Do you want to sit with me today?" he asked. His eyes drifted to meet William's and Riley's. "All of you."

"What?" William sputtered. "Like . . . behind the old school building?"

Isaac nodded and William's eyes lit up. Riley narrowed her eyes at him.

"Arthur Andrews won't be there, right?"

223

"Nah, he plays soccer every lunch," Isaac said with a shrug, and Riley nodded with approval.

"Well, if you guys are okay with it," I said, smiling up at Isaac.

He grinned, his hand sliding down to grab mine before leading me through the grass oval and towards his usual spot. I blushed, watching as people parted to make way for us, greeting Isaac as we walked.

Girls glared at me; including Lacey, who stared daggers into the both of us as we passed.

A chill skittered down my spine and I turned to face the ground, avoiding her stare.

We continued walking, rounding the corner until the grass turned to gravel.

"Aspen!"

I raised my brows looking up to see Sebastian grinning widely at me. He stood, leaning against the brick wall as Chloe Pepper sat on the ground beside him.

"Sebastian." I smiled, stepping closer. "Hey, sorry for leaving you at the Halloween Dance."

A shadow fell over his face, but he shrugged, nonchalant. "It's fine. I get it."

"Seb," Isaac greeted, grinning. He let go of my hand, smacking it against Sebastian's before ruffling Chloe's hair. "Chlo."

"Piss off, Isaac." Chloe rolled her eyes. She dragged her gaze from Isaac to me. I froze.

Chloe had always been hard to approach. She was always glaring at people, sticking with her friends and not speaking to anyone else. Like Isaac, she was the kind of person who you watched from afar.

And to make it worse, she was Marcelina's sister. A shiver ran down my spine at the thought of Isaac's ex and I sucked in a breath, steeling my nerves.

If I had managed to become this close to Isaac, I was sure I could be friends with Chloe too.

Biting down my anxiety, I stepped forward, grinning at her and waving an awkward hand.

"Hey, I'm Aspen," I said. "Nice to properly meet you."

She turned, looking up at me. Slowly, her smile fell, her eyes turning into narrow slits. She looked me up and down, pursing her lips.

"Likewise."

This wasn't going to go well.

CHAPTER THIRTY
Peach Tea

Lunch with Isaac and his friends wasn't as fun as I had anticipated.

I sat on the ground, leaning against the brick wall, awkwardly eating my sandwich in silence. Riley and William sat to my left. William was trying to tell a story about his newest video game while Riley tried to fluster him. She rubbed a teasing hand over his arm before trailing down to intertwine their fingers together, a smirk on her face.

William continued pushing the story out, but his face had slowly turned a bright red and his stuttering was beginning to get out of hand.

On my other side, Isaac sat in silence, his arm pressed against mine. I ignored the way my heart hammered at the contact. We were dating now. He was my boyfriend.

This was too weird.

I couldn't even think about hugging him without feeling my face begin to heat. I could barely keep my head straight when he held my hand and stroked my skin with his thumb, or when he leaned in for a kiss and his breath fanned over my lips—my cheeks began to warm, and I released a shaky breath.

Ever since we had started dating, I' began to overthink it all again.

I shook my head, turning my attention back to the group around me. Sebastian sat across from me, uncharacteristically silent, with Chloe beside him.

She was glaring right at me.

My eyes widened and I immediately turned away, my head clashing clumsily with the wall behind me.

I yelped, wincing in pain.

"Aspirin!" Isaac's voice came. His hand moved, clutching the spot I'd hit with his large hand. "Are you alright?"

I blinked, melting into his touch. My head had been pounding all day from giving up coffee, and this had only added to the dull ache.

"I'm fine," I said finally, releasing a breath. I felt Chloe's eyes on me and warmed further out of embarrassment. I tried to play it off. "I just miss my soy lattes."

Isaac laughed, shaking his head. "Headache?"

"The worst," I sighed.

He smirked at me, opening his mouth to probably tease me about my caffeine addiction when he was interrupted.

"Soy lattes?"

I raised a brow, turning to see Chloe watching us. She narrowed her eyes, her long, dark hair falling to her waist. She hadn't spoken since we'd sat down.

"Yeah, Aspen used to drink like three lattes a day." Riley laughed, effortlessly easing the awkward tension. "It was an addiction."

"Hey, it had good taste!" I shot back. I levelled Isaac with a smug look. "Better than black coffee."

"I mean, she does have good taste," he agreed with a wink. I sent him a sharp glare and he only smirked wider.

"That's funny," Chloe said bluntly. The corner of her lip tilted up in a smile and she turned back to her lunch, acting nonchalant.

227

There was a pause and I exchanged a look with William and Riley. *What was that about?*

The banter and laughter had instantly been killed by her casual remark, and it didn't seem like she was going to elaborate anytime soon. No, she only continued eating, smirking down at her food like she was in on some hilarious inside joke. Isaac had stiffened beside me at her words, which only confused me further.

Riley clenched her jaw, narrowing her eyes at Chloe who pretended not to notice. She stabbed at her fries, her mouth tilted, eyes glinting mischievously—like she knew something we didn't. Like she was making fun of us.

My heart began to speed up and I gulped, swallowing my anxiety. *Had I done something embarrassing?*

"What's funny?" Riley asked finally, her voice sharp.

"Oh, nothing." Chloe shrugged. Her eyes shot back up to meet mine and she sent me an innocent smile. "Marcelina used to get those too."

My stomach lurched. It felt as if all the air in my lungs had been pushed out.

Marcelina.

I had been trying to forget about her all weekend.

Was that why Isaac remembered my order so easily when we first met? Because it was what Marcelina ordered? Just like that, doubt filled me. My heart raced, keeping time with my mind.

"Ah, I forgot about that," Isaac muttered awkwardly from beside me. He shifted in his seat and I turned to see him looking at me.

I blinked, speechless. *What was I supposed to say? What was the right thing to say in this situation?*

My heart raced so fast, I couldn't decide whether I was hurt or angry. All I felt was anxious. I clenched my fists, my nails digging into skin as I willed myself to calm down.

"I—uh," I sputtered. I spun, feeling Chloe's eyes still on me. She continued to watch me; her face expressionless but her eyes twinkling. "I didn't know."

"Oh, right, you never met her." Chloe shrugged, waving a hand in dismissal. "She's my sister. She's studying at Hunter College, actually. Maybe Isaac's mentioned her to you?"

"Um, yeah, I think . . ." I trailed off, suddenly feeling extremely unwelcome.

"She knows who Marcelina is, Chlo," Isaac cut in, suddenly sour. He glared at her, pursing his lips. "Can we not bring her up?"

"Yeah," Sebastian finally said. I turned to see him smiling at me, his curls flopping over his forehead as he grinned childishly. "I drink lattes too. It's not something special."

"Sorry, Seb. Marcy used to be one of us too, you know." She shrugged innocently. "I can't just pretend she doesn't exist."

Something flashed through Isaac's eyes and his lips pressed into a deep frown. Marcelina had broken his heart so badly he had sworn off love. *Why was Chloe bringing her up all of a sudden?*

I reached out to grab his hand, before hesitating.

We had only been dating for three days. What if he didn't want to be touched right now? Or comforted? Did he even need comforting?

I let out a tight breath. I was overthinking this.

I rested my hand over his and his eyes shot up to meet mine. Instantly, his sharp gaze softened. His fingers closed over mine and he tugged me closer.

My heart leapt in my chest and I leaned into his touch.

"She not here anymore, Chloe," Isaac said, his voice confident. He squeezed my hand, turning to smile at me. "Things change."

"Right!" Sebastian joined in, his voice bright. "And It's fun having you guys around."

He smiled at me, his eyes glimmering, and I felt a wave of relief wash over me. At least I wasn't completely unwanted here.

I smiled back at Sebastian, feeling Isaac's grip on my hand tighten.

"Are you okay?" he muttered, his lips close to my ear.

I spun, blushing hard as I met his eyes.

"Yeah," I whispered back. "You?"

He flashed me a smirk and sent me a cheeky wink. "I'm always fine around you."

My face heated up even more. I couldn't help the smile growing on my face, which only made Isaac grin wider.

"Anyway, as I was saying," William spoke up finally, sending a sharp look to Chloe. "After I left the house, Mitch—" He paused. "That's my mom's—"

"Dag of a boyfriend," Riley filled in, grinning.

"Right." William met her eyes and practically melted. He swallowed thickly, clearly battling between staring at Riley and continuing his story. "He told her that I was up until four in the morning!"

"Were you?" Sebastian asked.

William shifted. "Well, I was, but that's beside the point!"

I laughed, rolling my eyes at him. William's stories were entertaining—not because of the stories themselves, but because of how William told them. How he watched Riley for a reaction—waiting to see if she'd laugh. Grinning proudly if she did.

I wondered if Isaac looked at me like that.

I turned to see Isaac already staring down at me, the corners of his lips twitched up in a soft smile.

My heart started thumping hard.

"What?" I asked quietly, suddenly becoming insecure. *Was there something on my face?*

"Nothing," he replied, shrugging. He leaned closer so that he could speak in a whisper. "I just really want to kiss you right now."

I felt like I was on fire.

"Isaac!" I scolded in a harsh whisper.

He smiled, giving my hand a squeeze before letting go and leaning back.

"But I'll save it for later." He winked.

I spun, knowing my face was bright red, to see if anyone else had heard what he said.

William continued his story while Riley watched him with a loving grin. Sebastian also listened, but his usual smile was gone, replaced with a sort of half-frown and furrowed brow. And Chloe—my eyes widened.

She was glaring at me, her eyes narrowed and sharp, her jaw tight.

I met her eyes, but she refused to look away, only narrowing her eyes further at me.

I shifted beneath her gaze, turning back to listen to William, but still feeling her glare on me.

What was her problem?

First, she brought up Marcelina, and now this?

Isaac was oblivious, listening to William's story and laughing in all the right places, nudging me whenever he said something stupid or funny. But I had stopped listening a long time ago.

All I could think about now was Chloe.

Chloe was one of Isaac's closest friends. *Why would she hate me? I've barely even spoken to her! She didn't like Isaac that way, did she? I mean, he dated her sister before me. It wouldn't make sense.*

Slowly, I lifted my eyes to see her still watching me, her eyes still full of hatred and disgust.

A shiver ran down my spine. She didn't want me here. A lump rose in my throat.

I was overthinking it. I knew I was. She was probably just suspicious. It made sense, right? For her to be closed off. They had been friends for ages. I was a newcomer. It was normal.

Yet I couldn't help but feel her glare on me, and the hatred packed into it. I could feel her anger—her irritation radiating off of her, like I didn't deserve to be there. I clenched my jaw, trying to stop my mind from racing.

Suddenly, the bell sounded, and everyone let out a collective groan.

"Class," Isaac grumbled from beside me. He pouted, standing from his seat and grabbing my hand to pull me up with him. "I want to stay with you."

"Isaac, we have art together," I teased, dusting my jeans off.

"Oh." He raised a brow, his eyes widening. Slowly, his lips morphed into a smirk. "You're really organised, Aspen. I should keep you around more often."

"I should hope so," I shot back. I turned to Riley and William, sending them a smile. "See you after school?"

"Definitely." Riley smiled before the pair walked off to the opposite end of the school.

"You coming to art?" Sebastian asked, his eyes trained on both me and Isaac.

"You bet." Isaac grinned, bouncing forward to wrap an arm around Seb's shoulders, beginning to play fight him and ruffle his hair. I laughed, watching the two fight, laughing and shouting.

A chill ran through me and I pulled Isaac's jacket tighter around myself.

"Nice jacket."

I spun to see Chloe had moved to stand beside me. She flicked her long hair over her shoulder, sending me a snarky smile and I tugged Isaac's jacket tighter around me. She raised a condescending brow, muttering in my ear as she pushed past.

"He used to give his jacket to Marcelina too."

CHAPTER THIRTY-ONE
Green Tea

It felt strange going to art class with Isaac.

Just a week ago, I had partnered up with Sebastian and asked him to go to the Halloween Dance with me. But now, I was Isaac's girlfriend.

So much had changed—it was all happening too fast.

I stepped into the classroom, making a beeline for my usual corner seat as Isaac and Sebastian trailed along behind me. I slumped onto my seat with a sigh, immediately beginning to pull out my pens and paper.

My head was pounding, and after Chloe's attitude at lunch, I couldn't wait to go home and sleep this day off. Today had caused way too much anxiety—I felt as if my battery was drained. I needed to recharge.

"Aspen!"

I looked up to see Sebastian grinning at me.

"Want to partner up?" he asked, slinging his backpack off his shoulder. He sent me a mischievous smile. "Your terrible drawing will make mine look better in comparison."

"Terrible drawing?" I shot back, raising a brow. "I think you have my impeccable art skills confused with your own."

His eyes lit up and he opened his mouth to reply when Isaac appeared beside him.

"I think my girlfriend will be partnering with me," Isaac said curtly, rounding the table to take his seat beside me. He sent an annoyed look to Sebastian, who frowned in realisation.

"Oh," he said, letting out an awkward chuckle. He rubbed his neck uncomfortably. "Right. Obviously. Sorry."

Sebastian sent me a nod before turning, slowly making his way to the other end of the classroom in search of a partner; his usual bubbly personality smothered in seconds by Isaac's sharp attitude.

His smile had vanished, and he walked with a depressing slump. I frowned, turning to glare at Isaac and lightly whacking his shoulder.

"You didn't have to be so blunt," I scolded. "You should apologise."

Isaac arched a brow at me, rubbing the spot I'd hit. "Me? He wanted to partner with you!"

"He was just asking," I said, shrugging.

"He shouldn't be asking my girlfriend."

Butterflies erupted in my stomach at those words. His girlfriend. I blushed, turning to face the front of the classroom as our teacher entered and crossing my arms.

"Still," I muttered lowly. "You were mean."

"Why do you care so much?" Isaac shot back finally, spinning to glare at me. "He's a guy!"

My eyes widened at his outburst.

"He's my friend too!" I said, trying to keep my voice quiet. I sighed, shaking my head. "Sebastian was there for me during all those classes you ditched—when I had no one else. He's my friend."

Isaac's eyes searched mine, and I stood my ground, frowning at him. Slowly, his expression softened. He released a breath, his shoulders sagging.

"Right," he said. He shook his head at himself. "You're right, I'm sorry. I'm being an idiot, aren't I?"

"It's fine," I replied. I smiled, lightening the tense atmosphere that had settled between us. "I'm used to it."

He barked out a laugh, rolling his eyes and nudging my shoulder. He leaned onto the table, his face angled towards me. "If I'm such an idiot, why are you dating me?"

"Maybe that's my type," I teased, quirking a brow.

"Oh." Isaac raised a brow, smirking. "You have a type now?"

"Yes. It's boys who draw pictures of me in a café for months before ever actually speaking to me."

He groaned, burying his face in his hands. "You're never going to let that go, are you?"

"No chance." I grinned. I turned back to Miss Laney as she dismissed the class to begin working on their artworks. I read the whiteboard that she had scribbled our task on.

"Realism." I frowned. "I hate realism."

"You hate art in general," Isaac pointed out.

"You're not wrong," I agreed solemnly. "But realism is the worst."

I moved slowly, procrastinating on the artwork as I took out my sketchpad and pencils. Isaac, beside me had already begun drawing, his pencil gliding over his page with precision.

I sighed, flicking my book to the next page. *Why did I take art again?*

I narrowed my eyes at Isaac, beginning to sketch the outline of his face. I frowned. My drawing already looked wonky. *Why did his nose look like that?* I released a breath, my pencil dropping on the table. I really wasn't in the mood for drawing today.

My eyes lifted from the page to Isaac. He was staring at his paper intently with his brow furrowed and eyes low. It reminded me of him drawing in the café, absorbed in his own world. My heart fluttered at the idea that he looked like that while drawing me—and he had been for months.

Slowly, my gaze wandered from Isaac's face to over his shoulder, scanning the classroom until it eventually drifted to Sebastian.

He sat hunched over, smiling politely at the person he had ended up partnered with. It was one of his friends who I knew he had partnered with in the past. They both laughed at something he said, because Sebastian was like that. He was easy to get along with, always making jokes and trying to get people to smile.

Yet, even as he laughed, the smile didn't reach his eyes. He hunched back over, staring listlessly at his blank page.

I felt sorry for him.

In just a few days, everything changed for me—Isaac was my boyfriend, but it also changed for Sebastian. Now, he was without both me and Isaac.

It wasn't that I didn't want to be partnered with Isaac— that was all I've ever wanted for the past year of school.

I just wish it didn't mean leaving Sebastian out. He always cheered me up, and after that awful lunch with Chloe, I really needed some cheering up.

Chloe.

I sighed, remembering her words to me at lunch.

"He used to give his jacket to Marcelina too."

Those words had bothered me from the moment she said them. I knew I shouldn't be overthinking it. It was normal to give your girlfriend your jacket. But it reminded me Isaac used to be in love with Marcelina.

He wasn't anymore, and I knew that. But that meant he'd done everything with her already. Isaac was my first boyfriend, but I wasn't his first girlfriend.

He had given his jacket to Marcelina a million times, probably. He had known her coffee order too. He had filled pages upon pages of sketchbooks with her drawings.

He was experienced, and I wasn't. These were all firsts for me.

Hell, I was even anxious to hold his hand.

Suddenly, anxiety was bubbling in my chest about the idea of being Isaac's girlfriend. What did girlfriends even do? What if I wasn't as good as Marcelina at being a girlfriend?

I blinked, realising that Isaac had been staring at me the entire time I was zoned out.

Heat crept up my neck to my ears and Isaac sent me a mischievous smirk.

"Earth to Aspirin?" he teased, quirking a brow.

I swallowed thickly, turning back to my drawing. It was mostly blank, with just a misshapen head and a squiggle of a nose. I released a sigh, beginning to add eyes and a mouth to my scribble of a sketch.

"Sorry," I said as I worked. "Zoned out a bit."

"I could tell. Are you okay?"

I looked up, meeting his eyes. He watched me, his eyes slightly concerned, and I nodded.

"Yeah." I shrugged nonchalantly. "I'm fine. Just thinking."

"Are you sure?" he asked. He glanced at my hand which I was tapping unendingly against my pencil as I drew. I froze and he lifted a brow at me. "What were you thinking about?"

I hesitated, Chloe's words echoing in my ears again. My pencil halted and I met his stare.

"Did Chloe ever have a crush on you?"

Isaac's eyes immediately widened, and he began to laugh.

"Chloe?" he chuckled, shaking his head in disbelief. "No way. There's no chance."

"Really?" I asked, blinking in surprise. "Why not?"

It was hard to believe any girl wouldn't have a crush on Isaac—the Isaac Hensick. It felt like every girl in the school liked him at some point. Even Riley had liked him for a week, until Lacey wouldn't shut up about him, leaving a bad taste in her mouth whenever he was mentioned. I mean, I was pretty sure even William had a crush on him at some point.

I had just gotten lucky and somehow ended up dating him.

Isaac released a sigh, running a hand over his face. He shrugged, smiling awkwardly.

"Chloe's just . . ." he trailed off. "I'm not exactly her type."

"Oh?" I blinked, suddenly confused. "What's her type then?"

Isaac laughed. "Oh, you know. Tall. Cute. Women."

My eyes widened. "Oh."

"Yeah."

My face heated with embarrassment. "I didn't know. Sorry."

"It's okay, she came out years ago. Doesn't stop all the boys from trying, though," he chuckled, shrugging. He paused, raising a questioning brow. "Why do you ask?"

I sighed, chewing on my lip anxiously. "I don't know. I just kind of got the impression that she didn't like me. She was glaring at me all lunch."

"Glaring at you?" Isaac echoed, furrowing his brow. He shook his head. "No, she's just bad at making friends."

I hesitated. It really seemed like she was glaring at me. The entire time.

"Are you sure?" I pushed. "It sure seemed like she hated me."

"She doesn't hate you," Isaac said, his voice suddenly serious. "No one could hate you, Aspirin. Just give her some time. She'll come around."

I paused, watching him. His expression was stern. Chloe was one of his closest friends. I knew this meant a lot to him. And if Isaac was friends with her, I wanted to get along with her too.

With a sigh, I nodded. "Alright."

He broke out into a grin, releasing a breath of relief. Beneath the table, his hand moved to grab mine, squeezing my fingers encouragingly.

"Thanks, Aspirin. She'll come around," he said, smiling lopsidedly. "I swear. I'll speak to her."

I nodded again, sending him a small smile of reassurance.

I believed him. Isaac knew her better than me, after all.

And yet, her words echoed in my head. I could still feel her glare drilling into me for the entire lunch period. It really felt like she didn't want me there. It felt like she hated me.

I hoped I was wrong.

Chloe Pepper was an unpredictable storm, and I didn't want to get on her bad side.

CHAPTER THIRTY-TWO
Ginger Tea

I was getting used to the stares. It had definitely improved since Monday, but people still stared and whispered as I walked past, and I was at least ninety percent sure they were all directed at me.

It was even worse when Isaac was with me, so a part of me was relieved that I was alone for now. I dug my hands into my pockets, trying my best to ignore their stares as I walked down the hall. I'd get used to it eventually. I had to at some point.

So, I stuck my chin up, continuing my way towards my locker. Isaac would probably be waiting for me there. My heart skipped at the thought and I quickened my pace, suddenly excited to see him.

I was halfway to my locker when I saw her.

Chloe Pepper.

She passed me, her eyes drilling holes into me as she sent me a sharp glare.

I haven't spoken to her since we sat together at lunch, and ever since then, I've been doing my best to avoid her. Nevertheless, I pursed my lips into a polite smile, raising a hand to wave at her.

She ignored me, rolling her eyes and breezing past, sending a chill down my spine.

What was her problem?

Had she not seen me? Was I being too weird? Was my smile too small? Maybe I had done one of those weird, creepy smiles, or maybe there was something in my teeth.

Or maybe she just hated me.

"Aspirin!"

I blinked, looking up to realise I had made it to my locker. All thoughts of Chloe instantly vanished, taking my anxieties with them.

Isaac leaned against it, his face lighting up as he saw me. He reached out, revealing a steaming takeaway cup from Café de Fleur. I narrowed my eyes at him, quirking a brow.

"Did you skip class?"

He shrugged, smiling innocently. "It was important."

"More important than your grades?" I scolded. I shook my head at him, but took the cup from him, letting the steam curl around my nose.

"Yes." He nodded, stepping closer. He reached up, tucking my hair behind my ear. "Had to surprise my girlfriend after class."

I blushed, feeling my face warm at his touch. This boy would be the death of me. Avoiding his gaze, I lifted the cup to my mouth. "What is it?"

"Ginger tea," he replied. "It's supposed to be good for headaches."

I scrunched my nose. I hated ginger.

I peered up at Isaac to find him grinning down at me, bursting with excitement, and I let out a sigh. I guess I could suck it up for one cup of tea. He did skip class to get it for me after all.

Holding my breath, I took a sip of the cup. Instantly, woody bitterness filled my mouth, burning my throat as the tea slid down. I swallowed hard, immediately wishing I had a glass of water to wash the ginger taste out.

"Well?" Isaac asked. He watched me carefully, eyes glittering with hope.

God, he really wanted me to like it. And I didn't want to be a bad girlfriend and seem ungrateful.

I chewed on my lip, sending him a lopsided smile. "I think it's working."

He broke out in a wide grin and tossed an arm around my shoulder, beginning to walk with me out to the grass oval.

"Good, because I know those headaches have been killing you," he said, smiling.

I blushed at the fact that he noticed. I forced myself to have another sip. He noticed my headaches and researched remedies for me. The least I could do was drink it.

"So," he began as we stepped out of the hallway. A cold breeze hit us, and he pulled me closer to his side. I smiled, relishing in his warmth. "Are you sitting with us at lunch today?"

"Oh." My face fell. It wasn't that I didn't want to sit with Isaac—it was more to do with the fact that I didn't want to have Chloe glaring at me for the entire period. I hesitated, taking another scalding sip of the ginger tea. "I don't know. Chloe doesn't really like me."

"What?" Isaac exclaimed. He paused, spinning to face me. "Aspirin come on. She likes you, trust me! She even told me she thinks you're pretty. Just give her a chance."

I sighed. He pouted at me dramatically, batting his eyelashes and clasping his hands together. I laughed, rolling my eyes and shoving his chest.

"Fine," I gave in. "I hope you're right."

"Trust me," he repeated, wrapping his arm around my shoulders again and leading us straight through the grass, towards the old school building. "No one could ever dislike you."

"Tell that to Lacey," I muttered beneath my breath. I pulled out my phone, texting Riley and William that I'd be sitting with Isaac today, and letting them know that they could come if they wanted to.

I suspected that I wouldn't see them for the rest of lunch.

To be honest, it was kind of nice not third wheeling for once. As much as they tried to include me, they were obviously still getting used to dating. It was pretty entertaining watching Riley tease him and William turn bright red at the slightest wink. But it also got old pretty fast.

I was sure they'd be back to normal in a week. I wasn't sure what I'd do if they weren't.

We rounded the corner in seconds, revealing Chloe and Sebastian already sitting and joking together. Our shoes crushed the gravel beneath us, and their heads shot up to look at us.

Chloe's lip instantly curled, and her glare moved from Isaac's arm around my shoulder, to my eyes.

I was already regretting this.

"Hey guys," Isaac greeted, moving ahead of me to clasp hands with Sebastian. He moved, sitting against the school wall. He waved me over, gesturing for me to join him.

I sucked in a breath, steeling myself and steadying my nerves. I could do this. I wasn't going to let Chloe keep me from hanging out with my boyfriend at lunch.

I walked towards him, pausing as I realised the only spot beside Isaac was also next to Chloe. I hesitated, making a split-second decision to sit opposite Isaac instead, leaving me beside Sebastian.

Isaac watched me with raised brows, pursing his lips at me as I avoided his eyes.

Chloe turned, instantly launching into conversation with Isaac. "Isaac, are you going to the party this Friday?"

Isaac hesitated; his eyes still trained on me. He answered through clenched teeth. "Not sure."

"Do you remember what happened at last week's party?" Chloe continued, beginning to laugh. "When Samuel—" she couldn't finish her sentence, still laughing.

Isaac turned to her, his lip twitching up. "And then Jacob followed after him?"

Chloe snorted, beginning to laugh harder as Isaac started to chuckle with her. "That was classic! I was on the verge of calling the cops myself!"

I pursed my lips, sipping on my lukewarm tea. It tasted disgusting but it was better than watching Chloe share stories with my boyfriend. Why did I feel like the outsider here?

I shouldn't be bitter. It was my decision not to go to parties, they just weren't my scene. But, I missed out on so much because of it. Would it make me a bad girlfriend if I didn't go to parties with Isaac?

Did Marcelina go to parties with him?

"What are you drinking?"

I blinked, turning to see Sebastian nodding at my cup.

I shrugged, scrunching my nose at it. "Ginger tea. It's supposed to help with headaches."

"Ew." Sebastian stuck out a tongue playfully, shaking his head. "Ginger is the worst."

"Right?" I whispered, shooting a look to Isaac to make sure he couldn't hear me. "Don't tell Isaac though. It was really sweet of him to get it for me."

Isaac's eyes flickered from Chloe to me and Sebastian, and I noticed his jaw clench.

Sebastian laughed, miming as if he was zipping his lips up and throwing away the key. "Your secret's safe with me."

"Phew," I teased. I turned, glancing at Chloe who still chattered on with Isaac.

"Have you started college essays yet?" she asked him innocently.

Isaac shook his head, smirking at me. "No, but Aspirin's basically finished."

245

"No way, where are you applying?" Chloe asked, speaking to me for the first time all lunch. I raised my brows, surprised at the sudden change in conversation.

"Well, it definitely won't be an art school," Sebastian teased, nudging me.

I laughed, snapping out of my daze and rolling my eyes at him. "What do you mean? I had my art portfolio ready and everything."

"They might let you in if you include some drawings of me. Might charm them into forgetting you're the worst artist that ever lived," he shot back.

"I think that'd make it worse."

He laughed, his smile wide and curly locks flopping over his forehead. He opened his mouth to reply when Isaac cut in.

"She's going to college here," Isaac said quickly. I turned to him. He cut Sebastian a strange look.

"Really?" Chloe joined in. She hummed curiously. "Whereabouts?"

I sputtered, my eyes widening. "I—umm, I'm thinking Penn State."

"Nice," she replied, sending me a smile. I quirked a brow. Why was she suddenly being nice? "That's pretty close. What about you Isaac?"

He blinked, turning to face her. He paused, processing her question before shrugging.

"Probably Hunter College."

"Hunter College?" I spat, eyes wide. He'd never mentioned that. "That's like four hours away."

"I mean," Isaac hesitated, rubbing the back of his neck. "It's not one hundred percent."

"Isaac's been wanting to go there since we were kids," Chloe added knowingly. She turned to grin at him. "Remember, you and Marcy would spend hours touring the campus online? Hey

. . ." she paused, her eyes widening. "Marcy goes there now. Maybe she could give you a real tour."

My heart sank. Isaac wanted to go to Hunter College. He had always wanted to go there. I hated that Chloe knew him better than me. I hated that she shared all these memories with him.

I hated that she kept bringing up Marcelina.

I clenched my fists, anger beginning to rise in my stomach.

Isaac chuckled awkwardly, glancing at me. "Oh, uh. Nah, I don't know about that."

"Oh, come on," Chloe pushed. She smirked pointedly at me before looking back at him. "Marcy would love it. And you'd be seeing each other on campus anyway. Let me ask her."

"No, really. I don't . . ." he trailed off, his voice growing tight. "No thanks, Chlo."

"Come on, Isaac." Chloe glanced at me, her smile growing at my silence. "I'm going to call her as soon as I get home. I'm sure she'd love to see you."

"No, Chloe—"

"It'll be so much fun!"

"I don't think—"

"Marcy will definitely say yes."

"I—uh," he paused, looking at me with a frown. Something flashed in his eyes and his jaw clenched.

I warmed, turning away from him. I didn't want to have any part in this conversation.

A second passed, and I could feel Isaac's eyes trained on me. I kept my head turned down, my nails digging into my skin as I tried to control myself. He sighed.

"I guess." Chloe began to squeal, but he quickly cut her off. "But it's not definite. I need to think about it more. And my grades are pretty sh*t too."

"I'm sure Marcy could help you out with that."

247

I pursed my lips. My anger faded, a painful, sinking feeling replacing it. I knew I shouldn't have sat here today. Chloe hated me, no matter how much Isaac tried to convince me otherwise.

The bell rang and I jumped. Time had gone so quickly. My ginger tea was cold in its takeaway cup.

"Ah, sh*t, I've got algebra," Sebastian groaned.

"Aspirin, I'll walk you to class," Isaac said quickly, standing from his seat and offering me a hand. I took it, pulling myself up. I smiled, beginning to take him up on his offer when Chloe appeared beside him.

"Yeah, let's all go together." She smiled at me, mocking me, her eyes narrowed in a challenge.

I paused, swallowing thickly. "Actually, I'll just see you later."

"What?" Isaac began to say. He stepped forward, but I turned, beginning to race out to the school building.

Alone.

CHAPTER THIRTY-THREE
Milk Tea

Movie night was a weekly event with Riley and William. Almost every Friday night, we met up—normally at William's place—and binge watched some obscure genre of film.

This week was Barbie movies.

And Isaac would be watching it with us.

It wasn't his first choice. He wanted to go out to a diner in town that I had never been to before, and I wanted to say yes, but then I started overthinking.

Their menu wasn't available online. What if I didn't like any of the food there? What if there was an awkward pause? What if I said something stupid? What if he tried to take things too quickly?

What if he changed his mind and broke up with me?

My anxiety had kicked in and I used our weekly movie night as an excuse to bail, until Isaac asked to come too. We hadn't seen each other much at school—only briefly at Café de Fleur every morning and in class—so I jumped at the chance to spend some time with him without the added pressure.

A movie meant sitting in silence in each other's company without worrying about making small talk, it was perfect.

I sat on the couch, Isaac beside me, and Riley and William on the floor surrounded by cushions. His arm pressed into mine and my heart fluttered.

Was this a double date?

"I didn't even know Barbie had movies," Isaac said, leaning casually against the back of the couch. He rested an arm over my shoulder, and I was suddenly glad the room was dark, because I knew I was blushing like crazy. I leaned into his touch, his warmth enveloping me, and his grip tightening around me.

"What?" Riley exclaimed, her eyes shooting up from her laptop to stare at him, bewildered.

"That's heresy," William joined in.

"You've been missing out," I added, nodding sagely.

Isaac turned to me, raising a brow. "They're that good?"

"The Barbie universe is elite," I said wisely. I wasn't wrong.

Riley nodded. "Better than the Marvel Cinematic Universe."

William's eyes widened. "Well, I don't know about—" He paused, catching Riley's glare before clearing his throat. "They're better. Definitely better."

I snorted internally.

"Well, if they're that good." Isaac smirked, shrugging.

"Oh, trust me. Once you see *The Princess and The Pauper*, there's no turning back," I teased.

He laughed and Riley pressed play, the opening sequence beginning to stream onto the TV in front of us. I smiled, leaning back and beginning to hum to the music.

This was better.

I was comfortable here. If anything happened, Riley and William were here too. I didn't have to worry about what I say or do. There'd be no awkward silences.

I let out a breath, letting myself relax into Isaac's side. This was how it should be. Comfortable.

No glares from Chloe or mentions of Marcelina. Just me and Isaac sitting together, my heart steady and mind calm. This was why I fell for him in the first place. I smiled, sighing contentedly to myself, and I felt Isaac's arm tighten around me, tugging me closer.

He tapped along to the music against my arm and began quietly humming along with me, although he was extremely off-key considering he didn't know the songs in the first place. I smiled, craning my neck up to see if he was enjoying the movie, only to find him watching me instead.

I blinked, flustered, and he smirked at me, feeling smug after seeing my reaction.

"Isaac," I whispered. "Pay attention to the movie."

Hypocrite, I thought to myself. All I could think about was his leg pressed against mine and his chest rising and falling with each breath, and here I was, telling him to pay attention. He lifted a brow at me.

"I am," he replied quietly, smiling wider.

I rolled my eyes, nudging him and turning back to the screen. His laughter rumbled through his chest and he pulled me even closer until my head rested against his collarbone. His fingers reached up, pushing my hair out of my eyes, before relaxing back against the couch, our bodies pressed together.

I tried hard to fight my blush and pay attention to the screen.

We had reached my favourite song of the movie—when Anneliese, the princess, meets Erika and they sing together. Riley squealed, immediately belting the song out loud and falling dramatically into William's lap as she serenaded him.

Even in the dark, I could see William blushing madly, but unlike our usual movie nights, he was also grinning, running fingers through her hair as she sang. Suddenly, she leaned up, pressing a kiss to his mouth.

I turned back to the movie, suddenly feeling stiff beside Isaac.

This got awkward fast.

"I think I'm going to grab some water," I muttered, standing from my seat and trailing towards the kitchen. I

251

immediately felt the loss of his heat from my body and I wrapped my arms around myself.

I stepped onto the tiled floor, letting out a sigh, my shoulders sagging. It had been so easy the weekend after the Halloween Dance. When it was just the both of us.

But now all I could think about were the people staring at us, whispering as we walked down the hallways. Chloe's glares, the constant comparisons to Marcelina . . .

I had never been a girlfriend before. What was I supposed to do? What if I was doing all of this wrong and Isaac started to regret liking me?

I was thinking too much. I needed to stop.

My anxiety was getting out of hand.

I shuffled towards the fridge, pouring myself a cold cup of water. I sipped on it, willing myself to relax.

It was times like this when I hated my anxiety. It was like being chained to an always growing ball of thoughts. Thoughts that dragged me down and held me back—that settled painfully in my stomach or lodged in my throat until it eventually became too difficult to breathe and I burst in an explosion of trembling, and gasping, and crying.

"Aspirin."

I blinked, spinning to find Isaac walking into the kitchen. "Hey."

"You alright?" he asked, moving closer. He leaned against the counter across from me.

"Yeah," I nodded. I swallowed thickly, willing myself to shove my anxiety away and act natural.

Natural.

What was natural?

"I'm fine, just a little thirsty." I gestured to my glass of water and he nodded, pursing his lips.

"Headache?" he asked, quirking a brow.

252

I laughed, touched over the fact he was worrying about me. "It's fine. I took some painkillers."

"Aspirin?" he asked, smirking.

I nudged him but couldn't help the giggle that burst from my lips. "Tylenol, actually."

"Blasphemous." He smiled down at me, shaking his head and I grinned back cheerily. He paused for a beat, biting on his bottom lip as he thought.

"Can I ask you something?"

"You just did," I teased, raising a brow.

He rolled his eyes but smiled as he stepped closer. My heart skipped a beat as he tucked a strand of hair behind my ear, his eyes dropping from my eyes to my lips for a moment.

"Why don't you ever want to hang out at school with me?" he asked, his voice low.

My heart sank. He watched me carefully, his lips pressed into a line, his eyes searching mine. I let out a sigh, frowning back.

"It's not like I don't want to," I said slowly, looking for the right words. "Because I do. It's just that . . . you know, Chloe's always there and . . . I feel uncomfortable around her."

"Still?" Isaac asked, his brow furrowing. "Why?"

"I told you." I sighed, exasperated. "She just doesn't like me. I don't know. She glares at me and won't stop bringing up Marcelina. I just get anxious."

He paused, running a hand through his hair and stepping back. I watched as he clenched his jaw, shaking his head.

"Aspen, she doesn't hate you," he said, frustrated. "She's just—"

"Bad at making friends," I finished. I pursed my lips, setting my glass onto the counter. "I know, Isaac. But that doesn't change the fact that it makes me uncomfortable."

"But—"

"Why did you ask me if you didn't want my honest answer?" I interrupted, frowning.

He froze, scanning my face before releasing a tired sigh. He moved closer, his hands resting on my shoulders before drifting down my arms to grip my hands. His fingers played with mine, his eyes trained on our intertwined hands.

"You're right," he said finally, his voice quiet. "I'm sorry, Aspen. I-I'll talk to her, okay?"

"No." I sighed. "No, it's okay. I'll get used to it and—"

"No," he cut off. His green eyes dragged up to meet mine and I felt my throat go dry. "If she's making you uncomfortable then I'm going to speak to her. I'll get her to stop."

My lips twitched up into a small smile and, in a moment of bravery, I leaned onto my tiptoes, pressing a soft kiss to his lips.

He smiled instantly into the kiss, his hands moving from mine to wrap around my waist and press me against the counter. He took charge, tilting his head to deepen the kiss and lifting me so that I was sitting on top of the counter, him between my legs.

I tangled my fingers into his hair pulling him closer. He smiled against my lips at my reaction, his hand trailing from my waist to cup my face. He bit on my lip, kissing me deeply until we finally had to pull apart for air.

The anxiety in my stomach transformed into butterflies beneath his touch, taking all my overthinking with it.

I released a breath, my chest rising and falling as I blinked. He watched me, grinning and panting, his fingers tapping on my thigh. I knew my face was red without looking in a mirror. I was burning and my heart was racing, but it was nice. I wanted more.

"I've been wanting to do that all week," he muttered, his voice husky. His eyes were dark and flickered between my eyes and my lips.

I smiled gently at him. "Thank you, Isaac. For talking to Chloe."

"Of course," he said, shrugging. He grinned, his dimples appearing on his cheeks. "Anything for my girl."

God, those words sent my heart into a frenzy.

"Listen," he spoke, his hand going flat against my leg. He drummed two fingers on my skin, gazing up at me. "There's this party next Friday."

"Oh."

He must've sensed my hesitation because he quickly continued. "You don't have to come! But I think it'll be fun."

I blinked, processing his words. "You want me to go to a party?"

He shuffled, smiling up at me innocently. "Yes?"

"Isaac." I laughed, shaking my head in disbelief. "Do you remember what happened the last time I went to a party? I don't exactly fit in well there."

"I know, I know," he said, moving to grab my hands. "But it's going to be tiny. It'll just be us and a few friends. Not even a party—more like a hangout. I just . . ." He paused, his cheeks turning pink. "I want to introduce you to my friends. Show you off a bit."

My heart fluttered at the thought. He wanted me to meet his friends. He was proud of me. I considered it for a moment, but it was still a party, and parties were a bad idea.

I sighed. "I don't know . . ."

My anxiety had been acting up all week with all the stares and glares—this was new territory.

"It'll be fun. We can leave the second you ask."

"Really?" I asked, faltering.

He nodded eagerly, his dark hair flopping all over the place. "I swear."

I laughed, pushing my fingers through his hair, combing it off his forehead. "Alright, I'll go."

He broke out into a wide grin, leaning forward to catch me in a kiss. It was slow and passionate, his hands gripping my face before pulling away.

"You're the best, Aspirin," he smiled.

"I know." I shrugged. I leaned in with a grin, craving his lips again, when we were interrupted.

"Aspen!" Came Riley's voice shouting from the living room. "It's the princess scene!"

"That's the best part!" I shrieked, hopping off the counter and racing towards the door.

Behind me, Isaac chuckled, following suit. "Of course, it is."

CHAPTER THIRTY-FOUR
Jasmine Tea

"Today, we'll be working on art theory."

I sighed in relief, smiling as I left my sketchpad untouched and pulled out my notebook instead.

Oh, how I'd missed theory classes. It felt like we had spent months doing only drawing and sketching—I was glad to finally not make a fool of myself with my terrible drawing skills.

Placing my notebook onto my desk, I took my seat alone. Isaac would probably be here any minute now. He had a tendency to be late, now that he was getting used to actually attending classes.

"Hey."

I turned, seeing Sebastian take a seat beside me. He pulled out his notebook and a pencil—a blunt, short piece of wood he had probably been using since elementary school. He wasn't exactly the studious type.

"Where's Isaac?" he asked, looking around the classroom.

I shrugged. "I don't know."

He paused, raising a brow at me. "What?"

"I haven't seen him since before lunch. I sat with Riley and William today," I said nonchalantly.

Ms. Laney, our art teacher, began writing notes on the whiteboard and I hurried to copy them into my notebook. I flipped open to the next blank page, scribbling in a date and title.

Sebastian didn't care. He leaned closer, his brow furrowed, and voice hushed so that Ms. Laney wouldn't hear him.

"Isn't that weird?" he asked, whispering.

I paused and turned to him, confused. "What do you mean?"

"Well, you're his girlfriend, aren't you?"

I blinked. "Yeah . . ."

"So," he said directly. "Shouldn't you know where he is?"

I paused. He had a point. It hadn't even occurred to me. I was so used to him disappearing and reappearing when we were just friends. But now I was his girlfriend, and girlfriends knew where their boyfriends were, right?

"Right, obviously." My cheeks heated in embarrassment. "Did you—uh—see him? At lunch?"

He shook his head, sending me a half-shrug. "I was playing soccer all lunch."

"Oh." My voice wavered, and I tapped my pen. Suddenly, I couldn't concentrate on the lesson anymore. Where was Isaac? We were already ten minutes into class, he was never this late.

Sebastian's words kept replaying in my mind, building on my already existing anxieties. *You're his girlfriend, aren't you?*

He was right. I hadn't even considered it.

What if he was with someone and—I shook my head, stopping myself before my anxiety kicked in and I began imagining all sorts of scenarios. I should just message him, I determined, instead of jumping to conclusions.

Glancing at Ms. Laney to make sure she was busy writing up notes, I fished my phone out of my pocket. I shifted, hiding my phone beneath my desk as I shot Isaac a text.

To Isaac: Where are you?

I paused for a second, staring blankly at the screen, waiting for Isaac to read the message and reply. A minute passed. Nothing.

"Well?"

I turned to see Sebastian watching me.

"I'm sure he'll reply soon," I said, though my voice came out unsure.

When he used to skip class, I never asked him where he was. I wasn't being too clingy, was I? No, we were dating now. This was normal. Like Sebastian had said, I was his girlfriend, wasn't I? Yet, my heart still pounded in my chest as I stared at my phone.

I waited for the little tick to appear beside the text—to show that he had read it. But it remained on delivered. Why wasn't he opening my text?

I hesitated, wondering if I should send him another. Would that be overkill?

"Maybe he's just running late," Sebastian suggested, snapping me out of my thoughts. "Or he could have fallen asleep. I think he was at Arthur's until late last night."

"Oh," I said. I didn't even know about that. My mouth felt dry. "Yeah. Maybe."

I chewed on my bottom lip, suddenly feeling anxious. First, I didn't know all those things that Chloe and Marcelina knew about him, and now I didn't even know where he was? What kind of a girlfriend am I?

"Don't be so worried," Sebastian said quietly, sending me a calming look.

I paused in the middle of shaking my leg and wringing my fingers, releasing a haggard breath. "It's easier said than done."

"Just." He shrugged, thinking for a moment. "Think about something else. Forget about Isaac."

I furrowed my brow. The problem with my anxiety was that I thought about too many things, all at once. He sent me a small smile which I replicated, trying my best not to show my

259

anxiety; he was just trying to help. I didn't need to burden him with all my worries.

I grabbed my pen, trying to focus on copying notes about leading lines instead. I was one sentence in when I lost all concentration and paused to check my phone.

He still hadn't read my message.

"Have you started the assignment?"

I turned, raising a brow at Sebastian who watched me with a curious gaze.

"Nope," I whispered back, my thoughts moving from Isaac to our art assignment. "I haven't even decided what to draw yet. Maybe I should just get Isaac to do it for me."

"Hey, what good is a boyfriend if he doesn't do your projects for you?" Sebastian shrugged, grinning.

I stifled a laugh, shooting an anxious look at Ms. Laney who continued lecturing the class.

"Exactly," I murmured back, smiling.

"I might ask him too," Sebastian joked, wagging his brows at me. "We both could use all the help we can get."

"Oh, do not put me on the same level as you," I teased. "I'm practically Picasso compared to you."

"Yeah, if Picasso was blind and deaf," he shot back. "And also missing both arms."

I rolled my eyes, nudging his shoulder. "You're just upset that I'm a much better artist than you."

"You want to bet?" he asked, his brows raised. "Higher grade on the assignment wins."

I quirked a brow at him. "What do they win?"

"I don't know." Sebastian hummed in thought. He hesitated, meeting my eyes and sending me a coy smile. "Free dinner?"

Free food always sounded good to me. I paused, opening my mouth to reply when Ms. Laney interrupted.

"Isaac Hensick, you're late!"

I spun, meeting Isaac's eyes. He grinned at me, panting as if he were out of breath, his dark hair windblown and messy. He must've run a mile to get here.

He smiled widely before his eyes drifted to Sebastian beside me, his lips immediately dropping into a frown.

I watched as Ms. Laney lectured him on his tardiness, writing him a warning slip before sending him to sit down. He ignored her the entire time, his eyes trained on me and Sebastian. As soon as she waved him off, he marched towards me, taking a seat on my right side.

"Aspirin," he greeted curtly, his eyes focused on Sebastian. "Seb."

"Hey, man." Sebastian grinned, nodding at him. He paused, his brows drawing together. "Where were you?"

"I was talking to Chloe," he said, his eyes moving to meet mine. His expression softened and he lowered his voice. "I told her that she was making you uncomfortable. She said she'd back off from you from now on."

"Really?" I asked, suddenly feeling confused. She had given in so easily. *Was that really the end of it?*

Isaac nodded, proud that he'd successfully gotten Chloe to back off. "I told her off on practically the other end of the school. Had to run to get here."

"And she really said she'd stop?" I asked, doubtful.

He nodded again, grinning. "I told her she was being rude and making you uncomfortable." He paused, chuckling. "She really didn't like hearing that. Took ages to convince her. That's why I'm so late."

I sent him a small smile, feeling the pressure in my chest relieved immediately—he had gotten Chloe to back off. It was over.

Sebastian furrowed his brow at us.

"Oh, yeah, I noticed she was being pretty cold to Aspen the other day," he said, gesturing towards me.

I raised a brow, sending Isaac a smirk. "See?"

"Alright, I get it." Isaac waved off, sending a glare to Sebastian. "She's just not good with new people, okay?"

"Well, yeah." Sebastian shrugged. "But, I mean, wow. She was glaring at Aspen all lunch. I was getting chills myself, just from watching."

Isaac narrowed his eyes at Sebastian but said nothing. I resisted the urge to laugh and tell Isaac I told him so. I knew I wasn't imagining it.

Chloe hated me, and she wasn't afraid to show it.

Sure, maybe she was bad at making new friends; so was I. But that didn't mean that I glared at people or ignored them.

I felt my shoulders grow lighter, relieved at Sebastian's observation, before realising Isaac was still curling his lip as Sebastian. I glanced at Ms. Laney, making sure she was distracted before moving to block their view of each other.

"Anyway," I cut in, feeling the tense atmosphere settling over the two. "It's over now, right? So, let's move on."

Sebastian shrugged and Isaac nodded tightly, moving to pull out his notebook and pen. He flipped the front page open, tapping his pen against the paper, distracted, instead of taking notes.

Suddenly, he leaned towards me, speaking in a hushed tone. "So, that means we're good with the party this Friday?"

"Is Chloe going to be there?" I asked, looking up from my notes and raising a brow.

Isaac nodded sheepishly and I sighed. I should have known. Wherever Isaac was, Chloe seemed to follow. I was honestly surprised she wasn't in art with us.

Knowing her, she was probably going to transfer in within a week.

And she'd probably find some way to relate it to Marcelina too.

Isaac waited for my reply, watching me with hopeful eyes. If what he had said was true, then it'd be fine, right?

"Sure," I said as nonchalantly as possible.

Isaac grinned, releasing a relieved breath. "You'll have fun. I promise."

"I hope so," I muttered.

If I was going to have to see Chloe outside of school, it would have to be the best party that ever existed. It was bad enough seeing her at school. Hopefully Isaac was right, and she'd back down from now on.

"Oh, are you going to Chloe's party?" Sebastian cut in, his eyes wide.

"Chloe's party?" I blinked, furrowing my brow. "The one on Friday?"

"Yeah, it's at her house," he said, confused. "You didn't know?"

I turned, sending Isaac a look and he shrugged coyly. "I didn't think it was important."

I sighed, looking back at Sebastian and nodding. "Yeah, I'll be there. Apparently."

Instantly, he broke out into a grin, running a hand through his blond curls. "Cool, I'll see you there."

CHAPTER THIRTY-FIVE
Black Tea

"I can't believe you're going to a party."

I smiled at Riley in the reflection of the mirror, leaning closer as I applied a thick coat of gloss onto my lips.

"My baby's growing up so fast," she teased, wiping a fake tear from her eye.

She stood behind me, dressed in her pyjamas as she curled my hair. William was sitting on the bed, leaning against pillows as he chewed on a stale bag of Doritos. They were going to have a date night once I leave.

It was kind of weird—the fact that they'd be hanging out without me while I went out with Isaac. Everything had changed so fast.

"I mean, she's been to a party before," he said, raising a brow at us, deliberately not mentioning whose party it was.

Riley spun, shaking her head at him. "That doesn't count. It was a disaster."

I snorted, remembering my panic attack in a random bedroom. "Disaster is an understatement."

"Still," William pointed out, "that was the first night you spent with Isaac."

My face heated up. I avoided his eyes, turning back to touch up my makeup. "It wasn't like that."

Smirking at my reaction, Riley leaned closer. "Well, maybe it'll be like that tonight."

"Riley!" I squealed, blushing through my foundation. "Shut up, it's just a casual get together."

"Mhmm," she hummed, still smirking. "Sure."

"William," I groaned, rolling my eyes. "Tell her."

"Riley," William began. "You're absolutely right."

"Thanks babe." She winked. William turned bright red, his confidence fading.

"Anytime," he muttered, going back to eating his Doritos.

"When is he going to get used to you?" I asked, laughing as if William wasn't in the room with us.

Riley rolled her eyes, grinning and meeting his gaze in the mirror. "I don't know. It's kind of cute."

Somehow, William turned even redder. Riley giggled at his reaction, placing the hair curler onto her vanity and switching it off.

"Done," she grinned, fluffing my hair out with a proud smile. "You look hot."

I chuckled, standing from my seat and taking in my complete outfit. I was dressed casually—a pair of jeans and a crop top—something Riley spent all night pestering me about. She thought it was too casual, but I was stubborn, and she eventually let it go.

I had put on more makeup than I usually wore, following a YouTube tutorial until it came out somewhat passable. And Riley took it upon herself to do my hair. I had to admit, she was a magician with a curler.

As if on cue, her doorbell sounded.

"Riley, door!" Lacey screamed from her room down the hall.

Riley rolled her eyes. "I know, I heard it too!" she shouted back.

"Then answer it!" Lacey screamed.

"I AM!" Riley shouted.

I laughed. I had never seen the two of them like this before.

"You guys really are like sisters," I said, raising a brow at her.

"Stepsisters," she grunted in reply, pulling her bedroom door open. She sighed, sending me a gentle smile. "Have fun, okay? Stay safe. Text us when you get home."

"Or don't go home," William chimed in.

"Either way text us."

I set them both with an amused look, grinning. "Thanks guys. You have fun too."

"We will." Riley winked.

"Not too much," William added.

"We'll see," Riley finished.

I laughed at their idiocy, grabbed my purse, and headed for the front door. I had known Riley for so long, her house was like a second home to me. I swiftly unlocked it, revealing Isaac dressed in a leather jacket and ripped jeans. His hair was ruffled, and I leaned forward, smoothing it back.

"Hey," I smiled, running my fingers through his hair.

"Hey." He grinned widely, leaning closer to grab my lips in a quick kiss. I felt myself turn bright red. "You look beautiful."

"Thanks," I sputtered, caught in surprise. "Um, so do you."

That . . . was not the right thing to say.

He lifted a brow at me, showing a face that says how highly amused he is. "Thanks, I worked hard."

"Did you now?" I teased, giggling, my anxiety melting away.

He sent me a wink, taking my hand and leading me to his car. He walked me around to the passenger seat and pulled the door open for me before rounding the car and sliding into the driver's seat.

"Yeah, I raced home and had a nap. Then came here to pick you up," he said, starting the engine.

"Oh, yeah, that sounds like a lot of work."

"It was," he joked. "I'm exhausted."

"I guess we'd better stay at home then," I teased, pretending to open the door.

"Actually, I think I'm feeling a lot more energised now," he said quickly. I turned shooting him an amused look and he laughed. "But if you want, then I can."

"And put all this makeup to waste?" I asked, gesturing to my face. "No way. Start driving, Hensick."

He shot me an impressed look, smiling and stepping on the gas pedal. I grinned, feeling strangely confident with my cute hair and makeup.

As much as I dreaded this night earlier, I was suddenly looking forward to it. Maybe what Riley and William said was getting to me.

Only a few minutes had passed until we were coming to a stop outside a large house. It was quiet, but the lights were on and cars filled the driveway. At least he was right about it being casual.

"We're here," Isaac said, parking the car. He unbuckled his seat belt, turning to face me.

I sucked in a shaky breath, the nerves beginning to kick in. This was really happening. Suddenly, no amount of makeup or hair spray was helping me feel any better—I was going to a party.

Where I'd have to . . . socialise.

It was truly a nightmare come alive.

"Hey," he said softly, his hand finding mine. "One word and we'll leave. Promise."

I nodded and he squeezed my fingers, stepping out of the car. I sighed, swallowing thickly. It was casual. I'd be fine. Isaac was with me.

One word and we'd leave.

"After you." He appeared outside my window, pulling the door open for me.

I gave him an unsettled smile, stepping out. "What a gentleman."

He shrugged, smirking. "Hey, I try."

We walked to the door together, and Isaac raised a fist to knock before it was ripped open.

"Hensick!" a boy shouted, grabbing his jacket and tugging him in. They disappeared and his voice sounded from far in the house. "Hensick's here guys!"

I blinked, stunned for a moment. What just happened? The door was left open and I stepped in, slowly closing it behind me.

"Isaac!" someone shouted in the lounge room. Other voices hollered, the sounds of slapping hands following after. I trailed slowly after the shouts, until I reached the party.

It was a big house, and the living room opened into the kitchen, meaning small groups of people were scattered all across the place. Some sipped from their drinks, others bopped to the low music, but most gathered in the middle, each greeting Isaac one by one.

I had forgotten how insanely popular he was.

I watched for a moment in awe. It was like he knew everyone. There were people there that I've never seen before, hugging him and praising him. A chill shot up my spine—accompanied with the feeling of not belonging here.

I was a wallflower. What was I doing at a party on a Friday night with Isaac Hensick?

"Aspen."

I jumped, spinning to find Sebastian standing behind me. He grinned widely, his hair spiralling in wild, messy curls.

"Hey," I said, blinking.

268

"Hey." He took a sip from his cup and followed my gaze, watching Isaac chat with the others before turning back to me. "You want a drink?"

I opened my mouth to reply when Isaac shouted from the couch. "Aspirin! Come meet the guys!"

I sent Sebastian a timid smile before walking to join Isaac.

"Guys," Isaac said, tossing an arm around my shoulders. He grinned proudly. "This is Aspen, my girlfriend."

They all sent me nods and grins as Isaac went around the group, introducing each person to me. I caught a few names along the way—Lucas and his girlfriend Jasmine, Harry and his boyfriend, a boy whose name was either Ben or Tim, Arthur Andrews.

Weirdly enough, there was no Chloe in sight. *Wasn't this her house?*

I smiled awkwardly, waving at each of them.

"So, do you want anything?" Isaac asked finally, grinning comfortably. This was his scene. "A drink? Chips?"

I shrugged. "Maybe a drink?"

"And when you say drink . . ."

"Soda?"

He winked. "Got it."

He trailed off towards the kitchen, people greeting him along the way. I watched, awkwardly shifting on my feet, surrounded by his group of friends.

"So, Aspirin." I blinked at the use of my nickname. What was this guy's name again? Chris, maybe? He was cute—dark skin and a chiseled jaw. He smirked at me. "How long have you guys been dating?"

"Oh." I scrunched my brow. "Two weeks?"

"Two weeks." He raised a brow.

"That's like nothing," one of the other guys—Ben or Tim or something—said. He leaned closer, sending me a wink. "So, it wouldn't be cheating."

269

"What?" I sputtered.

"Stop teasing her, Tom," Harry said, pulling him back. "He's just joking."

"Oh."

"Unless you don't want it to be a joke," Tom cut in.

"That's a joke too," Harry added.

"Isaac hasn't shut up about you," Tom said, raising his brows at me.

I blinked, my face warming at the thought of Isaac talking about me to his friends. I wondered what he had told them.

"Except he called you Aspirin," Harry said with a grin. "I thought it was a bit unusual of a name. Aspen makes a lot more sense."

"Oh," I repeated, blushing. I swallowed thickly, realising I should probably say more than just oh. "It's an inside joke." Obviously.

"What did I miss?" Isaac asked, appearing by my side. I sighed in relief; glad he was back to save me from this awkward conversation.

He handed me a red cup, bubbling with what looked and smelled like Sprite. He slid an arm around my waist, tugging me away from the boys and closer to him.

"Just Tom being Tom," Harry said.

"Don't scare her off." Isaac shook his head at them, resting his chin on my head for a moment. "I really like her."

My face grew hot and I knew I was bright red beneath my foundation.

"I—umm," I stuttered out, struggling to find the right words. Isaac laughed, opening his mouth to probably tease me when he froze, his eyes growing wide. His arm tightened around me, and I noticed his expression grow dark—almost sad.

I furrowed my brow, following his gaze to see Chloe.

She walked down the stairs. Her long dark hair straightened over her shoulders. She was dressed in her usual dark clothes, but tonight she wore heels and smokey eyes to match.

Isaac grew stiff beside me and my eyes snapped to the person beside her as I realised why.

She was as beautiful as the drawings—long black hair and a glowing smile. She was a few inches taller than Chloe, but she had the same eyes and nose.

From her long dark hair and the way Isaac clung on to me, I immediately knew who she was.

Chloe had brought Marcelina to the party.

CHAPTER THIRTY-SIX
Oolong Tea

As soon as she reached the bottom of the staircase, everyone ran over to Marcelina. They pulled her into hugs and squealed and complimented her outfit. The entire room had flocked towards her, and I could see why.

She was gorgeous. She laughed at all the right times and her smile seemed to lighten the room. There were no awkward pauses or weird small talk. It was obvious why everyone was flocking towards her.

Except Isaac.

Isaac was frozen beside me, frowning with his eyes trained on Chloe and Marcelina.

For a moment, he seemed like a different person—like the person I had met months ago, when he told me he never wanted to fall in love again. His walls had flown back up, guarding any emotion from surfacing. His smirk vanished. His eyes hardened.

My heart had sunk into my stomach when I had seen them, but Isaac . . . I couldn't imagine how he was feeling.

This was the girl who had broken his heart.

I turned to him, squeezing his hand tightly.

"Isaac," I began quietly. His eyes moved to meet mine and my heart shattered. He looked so . . . sad. His brow was furrowed in confusion, but his eyes showed just how much she had hurt him in the past. I sent him a reassuring smile. "Is that . . ."

I didn't need to finish my sentence. He nodded.

"Oh, Isaac." I sighed, frowning. "Are you okay?"

He hesitated before nodding again, suddenly lost for words. He blinked slowly, his voice quiet and strained. "Can we just go—"

Before he could finish his question, Marcelina finally reached us.

She had crossed the room, following Chloe who made a beeline towards us.

"Isaac!" Marcelina called.

Isaac released a shaky breath, meeting my eyes and downing the last of his drink before turning to her. His grip around my waist tightened. "Hey, Marcy."

"I haven't seen you in so long." She smiled, ignoring the tense atmosphere.

"Yeah." He chuckled awkwardly. He glanced back down to me, his eyes pleading. I blinked, finally getting the message, when Marcelina interrupted.

"Did you get taller?" she asked, looking up at him. She pretended to measure him with her hand. I narrowed my eyes at her arm. "What, six feet wasn't enough?"

"I think you're just getting shorter." He managed a laugh, rubbing his neck.

I shuffled uncomfortably beside him. Marcelina was even more beautiful up close. Her skin was flawless, and she had applied her makeup perfectly. Even her hair had been curled better than mine. She was cuter than me, standing a head shorter despite wearing heels. I was glad I had worn sneakers.

I frowned, glancing at Isaac to gauge his reaction. He smiled uneasily, his eyes darting around the room. I squeezed his hand, hoping to ease his tension a little bit. The motion caught Chloe's attention and, sensing my discomfort, she leapt forward.

"Aspen," she started snidely. "I didn't realise you'd be here. Since when did you like parties?"

I caught the bite in her words. Swallowing thickly, I tried to shove my anxiety away. I hated confrontation, but I wasn't about to leave Isaac alone with them.

"Since my boyfriend started inviting me to them," I managed, though my voice wavered as I spoke.

Chloe raised a brow at me, simmering with annoyance. I warmed with embarrassment, trying hard not to look away.

"Marcy, this is Aspen." She smiled smugly, meeting my eyes. "Isaac's friend."

I didn't miss her glare.

"Girlfriend, actually," Isaac and I cut in simultaneously. We exchanged a look before I reached out a hand to shake Marcelina's.

She didn't even flinch.

"It's so nice to meet you." She smiled, her voice sweet and eyes kind. Chloe on the other hand glared at us, stepping forward to rest a hand on Marcelina's shoulders.

"Actually, speaking of heights," Chloe began, ignoring me completely. "Do you guys remember when we were kids—"

"Oh, my God," Marcelina interrupted, grinning. "On the wall?"

"Ugh," Isaac groaned, rolling his eyes, but grinning, nonetheless. "When we would write our heights?"

"Yes!" Chloe squealed.

"Chlo, you always got upset when I was taller than you," Marcelina teased. Isaac laughed heartily, nodding in agreement.

"Shut up." Chloe laughed. She paused, her eyes widening and turning bright. "We should do it again! As a last hurrah. I mean, this might be the last time we're all in this house together at the same time."

Marcelina immediately nodded eagerly, practically bouncing in her heels. Isaac paused, hesitating.

He turned to me, unsure. "No, I don't—"

"Oh, come on," Chloe rolled her eyes. "Aspen is totally cool with it. Right?"

I met Isaac's eyes, pursing my lips. I didn't want him to go. Not really. I didn't know anyone here and I didn't really want to leave him alone with Marcelina and Chloe. Reading my expression, Isaac spoke.

"No," he said quickly, shaking his head. "She—I mean, we were just about to leave anyway, and—"

Chloe narrowed her eyes, ignoring him and turning to me.

"Come on, Aspen. This is a tradition for us. Don't be such a buzzkill."

I blinked, surprised at suddenly being singled out.

"Chloe—"

"I was asking Aspen," Chloe interrupted Isaac, keeping her stare on me.

"I—well, I think . . ." I trailed off, feeling all their eyes on me, waiting for an answer that I didn't want to give. Isaac met my eyes and they narrowed slightly, trying to send me a message, though I couldn't tell what. I was busy overthinking everything. "Maybe . . ."

"It's okay, she clearly isn't comfortable with it," Marcelina said, smiling gently at me. *Why did it feel condescending?* "Don't worry about it."

"That sucks," Chloe muttered, frowning. "This was our last chance."

"It's fine," Marcelina replied, shrugging and sending me a small smile, though it didn't reach her eyes.

I furrowed my brow at her. *Why did I suddenly feel guilty?*

"I mean," I cut in quickly. I released a breath, clenching my teeth. *What was I doing?* "I mean, it should be fine. Right?"

I turned to look at Isaac. He watched me with a blank expression. This was the right decision—they have been friends with each other much longer than I've known Isaac. I couldn't hold him back from his friends. Right?

"Aspen," he started, shaking his head.

"Yay!" Marcelina squealed. She pulled me into an awkward half hug. "Thank you, Aspen! It was nice meeting you!"

I nodded, barely muttering out a, "You too," before Marcelina grabbed Isaac's arm and tugged him up the stairs. He sent me a look before disappearing around the corner.

I sighed, turning back to the room. He wouldn't take long, right? How long did it take to scribble their heights on a wall?

I scanned the room, searching for someone—anyone—I could hang out with. I spotted the boys Isaac had introduced me to earlier.

No. I didn't really fit in with them.

Taking a sip from my cup, I walked towards one of the sofas, plopping down on the corner and pulling my phone out. No texts. No notifications. I sighed.

Riley and William were probably having a great time on their date. I didn't want to interrupt. Instead, I opened up Instagram and scrolled through my feed for a few minutes. When that got old, I pulled up Snapchat, then Twitter, then TikTok.

Soon enough, five minutes had passed, then ten, then twenty, and there was still no sign of Isaac.

I frowned, taking a sip from my cup only to realise it was empty. Where was he?

I opened my texts, shooting one to Isaac.

To Isaac: Where are you?

I waited a moment for a reply but—nothing. I glanced at the staircase in the corner. Would it seem weird if I went upstairs looking for him?

I shook the thought out of my head—I was sure he'd reply soon. I locked my phone, looking around the room.

People were still hanging out in their little groups. I sat alone on the couch, my resting b*tch face probably keeping anyone from talking to me—just as I wanted it.

I didn't want to have another panic attack in a stranger's house, and I definitely didn't feel like making small talk with strangers when I was currently freaking out about Marcelina.

Suddenly, I noticed Sebastian standing in the kitchen, pouring a drink by himself. I smiled, trailing over to him.

"Hey again," I said, joining him behind the counter.

He looked up from his cup, raising a brow. "Hey. Where's Isaac?"

"Chloe dragged him off somewhere." I shrugged, not wanting to talk about it. I ignored the growing pressure in my chest. He still hadn't replied to my text. "You getting a drink?"

"It's Sprite." He shrugged, showing me his cup. "I'm driving."

"No way, I'm having Sprite too." I grinned, clinking my cup with his. "Cheers."

He laughed, taking a sip from his drink as I refilled my own.

"Are you having fun?" Sebastian asked me over the brim of his cup.

I shrugged, trying to muster up the best grin I could. "Yeah. I guess."

A laugh fell from his lips and he shook his head at me, seeing right through my lie. "Me neither. I think I'm going to blow this place."

"I wish I could." I sighed. "Isaac's my ride home."

I glanced at my phone—five minutes and still no reply. Quickly unlocking it, I shot him another text.

To Isaac: Are you okay?

"He's not replying?" he asked, furrowing his brow.

"Not yet," I said, frowning. I waited a minute, then another—still no response. I was starting to get anxious.

"Just forget about him," he said with a shrug. "It's probably nothing."

I nodded, a bit of hesitation still on my mind. Right. Forget about him. Simple.

"Hey," Sebastian started, grabbing my attention. "If you need a ride home, I can take you."

I blinked. "Really?"

"Yeah, it's no big deal."

It was a tempting offer, but I hesitated. I sent him a tight, close-lipped smile.

"Thanks, but I should probably wait for Isaac."

He shrugged, flashing a lazy, lopsided smile. "No worries. Just let me know if you change your mind."

I nodded, thanking him again before he grabbed his cup, crossing the room to rejoin his group of friends. I sighed, unlocking my phone again.

Still no reply from Isaac. At this point, I didn't care if I looked clingy.

To Isaac: Can you please reply?

I stared at the screen, counting down the minutes. He hadn't even read my messages. How long did it take to write their names on a stupid wall?

I drummed my fingers against the kitchen counter, scanning the room. Sebastian was in the corner, laughing with a group of boys I vaguely recognised from school—one of which

278

included Arthur Andrews. A few girls stood with them, flirting and dragging their nails through their hair.

I vaguely remembered the Halloween Dance when he had been happily grinding against a group of girls in skimpy costumes.

Suddenly, he looked up, met my eyes and sent me a schoolboy grin.

With a sigh, I opened my phone again.

To Isaac: Isaac, this is the word. I want to go home.

One minute passed.

Then two.

Then five.

He'd promised he'd take me home the second I asked.

It was a lie.

I frowned, clenching my jaw and crossing the room towards Sebastian. If Isaac wasn't going to reply to my messages, I'd find my own way home.

"Aspen." He grinned, pushing off the wall as I approached.

"Sebastian," I started, smiling hopefully at him. "Can you drive me home?"

He blinked slowly, then nodded, pushing past his circle of friends.

"I'll see you guys later," he said, patting them on the back as he passed. He reached me, pulling his keys out of his pocket. "Are you sure?"

I hesitated, glancing at the staircase—hoping Isaac would suddenly appear. But there was still no sign of him. My messages remained unread; my phone still silent in my pocket.

I nodded, ignoring the pang of hurt that rang through my chest and turning to face Sebastian.

"Let's go."

CHAPTER THIRTY-SEVEN
White Tea

We sat in silence, the car rumbling beneath us. My phone sat in my lap, opened to my messages with Isaac. I frowned, glaring down at the screen. Sebastian glanced at me, raising a brow.

"Still no reply?"

I sighed, turning the phone off in defeat. "Nothing. Not even read."

"Wow." He whistled lowly, drumming his fingers against the steering wheel. "I'm sure there's a reason."

"Hopefully," I muttered; my voice quiet. My mind was racing with a thousand thoughts of where he was, what he was doing, who he was with. I felt a lump growing in my throat.

"I mean, Isaac and Marcy have been friends for ages," he continued. "Since before I even met them. And, you know, Marcy broke up with him, so—" He paused, glancing at me. His eyes widened and he cleared his throat. "I mean, they're just friends. So, they're probably just . . . doing some . . . friendly bonding."

"Right," I said, my voice breaking.

Friendly bonding. That was definitely what was happening. That was the reason he wasn't replying to my texts.

"Hey," Sebastian said suddenly. "Did you start your art assignment?"

I blinked, looking up at him. He grinned cheekily, changing the subject as he glanced between me and the road.

"Were you even going to try, or do you want to just hand me my free dinner now?" he teased.

Grateful for the distraction, I remembered our little bet and laughed lightly. "Sebastian, I can beat you with my eyes closed. I'm just giving you a head start. Out of kindness."

"Oh, we'll see about that," he said, wagging a finger at me. "Wait until you see my masterpiece. I've been holding back."

"Oh?"

"Yep. Didn't want to embarrass you in front of Ms. Laney, you know?" he joked. He tried to settle his face into a serious expression but couldn't fight the grin tugging at his lips.

"Oh." I raised a brow at him, mirroring his smile. "Right. Of course not. Such a gentleman."

"What can I say?" He shrugged.

I laughed at him, rolling my eyes and nudging his shoulder. "You should really stick to soccer, Seb."

"Hey! I'm multitalented!" he shot back.

"Yeah?"

"Yes! As a matter of fact, I'm also incredibly talented at science."

I paused, blinking. I didn't take him for an academic type. "Wait, really?"

"Yeah." He sent me a cheesy grin. "Got a C- last semester without even trying."

I couldn't help the loud laugh that burst from my lips. I blushed, covering my mouth, still smiling widely. "Oh, we have a real Einstein over here."

"It's all hard work, baby," he teased, popping his collar. He was such a dork.

Silence settled around us and I searched for something to say—something to fill the pause with before my mind drifted back to Isaac and Marcelina. My phone still sat silent in my hands, Sebastian's words echoing in my mind.

Marcy broke up with him.

"I suck at soccer," I blurted suddenly. My eyes grew wide in embarrassment, but he quirked a brow at me, smirking.

"Oh, yeah?"

"The worst," I admitted solemnly. "Isaac tried to pass me a ball once and it hit me square in the face."

I snorted at the memory. We weren't even friends at that point, and now we were dating. Everything had changed so quickly.

"I could teach you," Sebastian suggested suddenly.

I lit up, grinning brightly. "Really?"

"Definitely," he said. He paused, humming. "You should play with me and the boys one lunch."

"You and the boys?" I arched a brow, shuddering at the idea. "In front of the entire school? No thanks."

He paused at that, turning to me with a confused expression. "Why not?"

I laughed, shaking my head. "With all those eyes staring at me? I could never."

"They're just people." He shrugged. "Who cares what they think?"

"I do," I said awkwardly. "I guess. I don't know, I can't really help it. It's just like . . . they stare, and whisper and all these thoughts just fill my head. You know?"

He furrowed his brow. "Not really. Why don't you just . . . ignore them?"

I laughed bitterly. If it was that easy, I would've done that a long time ago instead of taking antidepressants that kept me up at night and made me constantly nauseous. Sebastian continued to glance at me, completely oblivious. I sighed, smiling gently.

"I don't know, I guess it's harder than it sounds," I said slowly.

"Well, alright." He shrugged, letting it go. He sent me a smirk, narrowing his eyes. "You were probably beyond saving anyway."

"I'm not that bad!" I cried, whacking his shoulder.

He laughed, rubbing the spot I had hit him before he looked at me with a soft expression. There was a pause when he let out a short breath, quickly looking back to the road.

"I think we're here," he said, nodding towards the houses lining the street.

I looked out the window, nodding. "Yep, that's mine."

"Alright." He put the car into park and unlocked the doors, leaning back in his seat to meet my eyes. He smiled gently, his voice quiet. "I hope you're feeling a little better."

I paused. I had forgotten all about how upset I was. I glanced at my phone—I hadn't received any notifications the entire car ride. Pursing my lips, I looked back at Sebastian.

"Thank you, Seb," I said, smiling at him. "Really."

"Hey, anytime." He shrugged nonchalantly, though his cheeks tinted pink. "Call me whenever you need anything. Oh, right!" He paused, his eyes widening. He dug his hand into his pocket, pulling out his phone. "What's your number?"

I raised my brows at the realisation. "I can't believe you still don't have my number."

He handed me his phone and I quickly typed my number in, sending a text to myself before giving it back.

"Yeah, I realised when you disappeared during the Halloween Dance," he said, pocketing the phone.

"Oh." My face heated. "Sorry about that. I—"

"It's fine," he quickly interrupted, sending me a small smile. He rubbed the back of his neck. "You don't have to explain yourself."

"Still, it was a crappy thing for me to do," I said, frowning.

"Hey, it's in the past." He waved me off. "Besides, I was pretty preoccupied."

He blushed and I smiled at him. Sebastian really was the best.

"Thank you," I said genuinely. "I'll see you at school? You owe me soccer lessons. Maybe you can teach me to be the next Ronald."

He paused, furrowing his brow. "Ronald?"

"Yeah," I said, blinking. "The soccer player? Chris . . . Christian? Ronald?"

A beat passed and then he snorted, falling over the wheel in laughter.

"What?" I asked, my eyes growing wide. "Is that not his name?"

"Seriously Aspen? It's Ronaldo," he said while laughing and shaking his head. "Maybe you're more hopeless than I thought."

"Well, then I'll see you on Monday," I said, turning red in embarrassment. This was what I got for attempting humor. Why did I have to go and open my mouth? I knew that embarrassment would keep me awake at night for the next month.

"See you on Monday." He nodded, still chuckling, and I pushed the door open walking up to my house.

I paused at the door, glancing back to see him waiting in his car. I sent him a wave, entering the house and watching as he drove off before releasing a loud sigh.

What a night.

I trudged to my room, checking my phone as I walked— still no messages from Isaac.

I rolled my eyes, tossing the phone onto my bed. I wasn't going to check anymore. He was obviously too busy to reply.

Bonding with Marcy.

Pressure built in my chest, and I desperately shoved it down. Ignoring my phone, I beelined for the bathroom, removing my makeup and taking a long shower.

I couldn't help but wonder where Isaac was. Was he even still at the party? What could be taking so long that he couldn't even look at his phone and reply to my messages? How long would it take to type "yes" and hit send?

What could he be doing with Marcelina that was taking so long?

I felt my eyes watering, panic beginning to rise in my chest.

This was too much. This had been such a crazy week. Ever since I had begun dating Isaac, everything had changed too quickly.

People stared at me and whispered when I walked down the halls. Chloe glared at me and kept bringing up Marcelina. Riley and William were on a date, so I couldn't even call them and rant.

When had all of this happened?

What had happened to napping in the library, with Isaac watching beside me? What had happened to getting coffee together, and watching movies on my bed, and him sneaking through my window at night?

My hands trembled and I felt a painful pressure begin to grow in my chest.

I should've just sucked it up and told him not to go. I should've just stood up for myself for once.

Why were things so difficult now?

I was too in my head when the word girlfriend became part of the equation. My anxiety was getting in the way of everything— just like it always did.

By the time I was out of the shower, I could feel a mild panic attack coming. I was overthinking too much.

Sebastian's words echoed in my mind.

"Forget about Isaac. Think about something else."

How was I supposed to do that? My mind jumped from one thing to another, collecting thoughts before they sunk into my throat, suffocating me and ripping sobs out until I was sore and trembling.

If I wasn't thinking about Isaac, I was thinking about Chloe, Marcelina, Sebastian. I started thinking about my mother, and my sister. I thought about Riley and William, about something stupid I said a week ago, a month ago, a year ago. Something dumb I said to my teacher in eighth grade; falling down in front of the class in sixth; tripping on the bus in fifth.

I shuffled to my bed, desperate to crawl into my sheets and try to relax a little—try to lower my heart rate and slow my breathing. I picked up my phone to move it when I noticed the flashing light.

He had replied.

Twenty missed calls and voicemails flooded my notification screen.

He had sent me over thirty messages, all along the lines of "I'm so sorry, please let me explain," before ending with, "Where are you?" and "Aspirin, I'm worried. I can't find you anywhere." And, finally, "Aspen, please reply. I'm so sorry. Where are you?"

Beside them, I had messages from William, asking questions all along the same line—telling me to call Isaac and that he was worried.

I frowned, the lump in my throat growing bigger.

Another text popped up then, begging me to reply, and I sighed, finally tapping onto it.

I couldn't talk to him. Not right now.

To Isaac: Home.

Immediately, it began buzzing with notifications. Anxiety pulsed through my chest and I immediately turned the phone off, plugging it into the charger and burying my face into my pillow.

I couldn't talk to him. What would I even say? A million thoughts were burning through my mind. I couldn't make sense of

286

them all. I released a breath, sinking deeper into the mattress. Tears slipped from my eyes and I dug my nails into my palms.

Riley and William were right in a way. I wouldn't be getting any sleep tonight.

CHAPTER THIRTY-EIGHT
Raspberry Tea

I lay in bed, my mind racing. The silence of the room rang through my body and I struggled to relax in my bedsheets. I tugged at my necklace, running a thumb over the golden leaf that permanently rested against my collarbone

It was too quiet.

I sighed, turning my back and shutting my eyes. My whole body felt sore and tired. It had been such a long week; and an even longer day, somehow. And yet, I couldn't sleep.

All I could think about were the things I should've done differently—the things I should've said instead.

Frustration built up in me; frustration with myself, with my anxiety, with this entire situation. I hated that it affected me so much. If it was Riley, she'd probably tear Marcelina's hair off the second she tried to pull Isaac away.

Why couldn't I be more like her?

Why did confrontation have to send my heartrate spiking?

I groaned, covering my face with my hands when a knock came from the window.

I blinked, bolting upright. Did I hear that right? My heart pounded in my ears as I waited.

Another knock, then, "Aspirin?"

I paused. It was Isaac.

I glanced at my phone sitting on my bedside table. Maybe I shouldn't have turned it off—now I have to confront him.

"Aspen?" he whispered through the glass pane. "Are you awake?"

I frowned, trudging across the room and pulling the window open. He crouched outside my window, his hair tousled from the wind, and his brow furrowed. I fought the urge to run my fingers through it.

"Aspen, I'm so sorry," he said slowly. "I'm so, so sorry. Please let me explain."

I sighed at him, crossing my arms. "Isaac, I waited for you forever."

"I know," he groaned. "I know. And I'm so sorry." He paused, glancing past my shoulder into the room. "Can I come in?"

I hesitated. I didn't feel like talking, but I had to admit, I was extremely curious about what had happened. I conceded, stepping back. He sent me a timid smile, crawling through the window and joining me on the edge of the bed.

"I didn't see your texts," he started off immediately.

I rolled my eyes. "I know."

"No, no, listen," he begged, leaning closer. "Chloe took my phone. She said we didn't have phones when we were kids, so we couldn't have any distractions. I told her not to, but she didn't listen, and I thought it would only be, like, five minutes, so I let her, and—" He paused, releasing a tight breath. "I shouldn't have let her do that. I'm sorry."

I pursed my lips, crossing my arms over my chest. He looked at me, searching my eyes.

"So, why didn't it take five minutes?" I asked, raising a brow. "I was waiting for you."

"I know," he said, grabbing my hands. I hesitated and he frowned at my reaction, his grip wavering. "Marcelina started crying."

"What?" I asked, my chest growing tight at the mention of her name.

"She started crying, saying she missed being a kid, and doing things like that." He shook his head. "I . . . I think she's having a hard time at college."

"Oh."

"I didn't want to stay." He frowned at me, shaking his head. "I didn't want to stay, but I don't know. It was really awkward. I couldn't just leave with her crying there."

He paused and we sat in silence. I processed his words, narrowing my eyes. He was right, in a way. It would've been mean to leave her there, crying. But, still—I wished he had left her.

"I should've left her," he continued. He groaned, shaking his head and running his fingers through his hair. "I should've left her and taken my stupid f*cking phone back and come back to you. I'm so sorry. I shouldn't have gone in the first place. Even if it actually took five minutes, I shouldn't have f*cking left you."

There was a silence as I turned his words over in my mind. He sounded sorry, but the pressure in my chest was still building.

"Aspirin?" Isaac spoke finally, his voice quiet.

I looked up, meeting his eyes. He looked at me, his dimples long gone, his eyes sad and regretful.

I sighed. "And nothing happened?"

"Nothing," he said quickly, shaking his head. "Nothing at all. I swear. It was mostly Chloe comforting Marcy while I watched awkwardly."

He paused, leaning closer, his voice sincere. "Aspen, I don't like Marcy like that anymore. I promise."

I looked up at him and realised his eyes were watering. He frowned at me, shaking his head.

"She hurt me, Aspirin," he started, his voice quiet. "When we dated. Our relationship . . . it wasn't healthy. She broke my

290

heart. She ended things over text—like I didn't even matter. I wanted more than anything to leave the party and go back to you."

I frowned, pulling my hands out of his and sending him a sad look.

"You promised that if I gave you one word, we'd leave," I said, changing my expression to a sharp stare. "I really wanted to leave."

"I'm sorry," he repeated. "I'm so sorry. It'll never happen again."

I met his eyes, pausing for a moment. I needed to trust him. I had to believe what he was telling me. He is my boyfriend, after all. And he seemed sorry.

But all I could think about was my unread texts and Chloe's snide smirk, taunting me every time she brought Marcelina up.

Marcelina had broken his heart. When I had first met him, he was so clearly wounded by her, he didn't want anything to do with love again. But there was a small insecure part of me wondering, did he still have feelings for her?

"Aspen," he spoke, breaking the silence. "I'm so f*cking sorry."

I pursed my lips, searching for the right words, and he shook his head. His throat bobbed as he swallowed thickly.

"Please, Aspen," he said, his voice cracking. "Aspirin. I—I need you. Because you're my Aspirin. All you've ever done is make me happy. Just the thought of you makes me feel light."

"Isaac," I muttered, my voice quiet. He met my eyes then and I realised both of our expressions were watery and on the verge of breaking.

He refused to look away, his gaze steady and unwavering. I was grateful for the darkness of the night, already knowing my face was bright red from the heat of it. His jaw clenched and he released a quiet chuckle in disbelief.

"All I have to do is think about your brown eyes, or the way you smile when you smell coffee. The way your face glows at the smallest touch." He paused, his voice breaking, and rested a hand over his chest, clawing at his t-shirt. "And my heart—it hurts. You know? Like it's so full, it's going to burst. And-and I love you, Aspirin. I love you. I did something so f*cking stupid, and I'm so sorry."

He paused again, releasing a bitter chuckle. "I'm not making sense right now."

"Isaac," I repeated, unable to find my voice. My throat burned and I could feel the blood rushing in my ears. If I had doubted it a moment ago, it was clear now. He didn't love Marcelina.

He loved me.

Warmth flowed through me. I was still annoyed with him. Of course, I was—he left me for Marcelina. But seeing Isaac sit on my bed, his voice cracking and eyes watery as he rambled, it reminded me of the boy I fell in love with; of why I was doing all of this in the first place, no matter how my anxiety loved to torment me in unknown situations like dating.

Isaac frowned at my silence, his voice breaking and quiet. "Do you want to break up with me?"

My eyes widened. "No!"

"No?" he repeated, blinking.

"I—" I swallowed. "I don't. It's just . . ."

I wanted to tell him everything. Tell him how I felt about Chloe and Marcelina. That I hated Chloe. That I didn't want him to go with Marcelina tonight. That I was angry at him.

I wanted to tell him that I was insecure and overthinking everything.

But the words stuck in my throat and I choked on them, releasing a shaky breath. He watched me carefully, waiting for me to continue, and the words rested on my tongue, ready to be spoken.

But instead, I sighed, taking his hand. He squeezed my palm, staring at me with wide, hopeful eyes.

"Don't do it again."

"I won't," he said quickly. "I definitely won't. I will never piss you off again, for as long as I live."

"I doubt that." I chuckle, sending him an uncertain look, but still smiling at the idea.

"I swear it." He wavered, his eyes dropping to my lips. In a quiet, innocent voice, he asked, "Can I kiss you now?"

I laughed again, rolling my eyes and pressing my lips to his. It was a slow, gentle kiss and I sighed into his touch. He wrapped his arms around my waist, pulling me closer until I was sitting on his lap, straddling his hips.

I pulled away for a moment, smiling down at him. This was how it was supposed to be.

He paused, blinking at me through the darkness. "Have you been crying?"

I chuckled dryly. "A little."

He groaned, burying his face into my neck. "I'm such an assh*le."

"Yeah," I agreed, running my fingers through his hair. "You are."

He groaned again, and I laughed.

"But it's part of your charm," I said pulling back to look at his face.

"Don't say that," he groaned. He frowned at me, clenching his jaw. "I don't want that to be part of me. I want to be better for you."

"I know." I sighed. I leaned forward, moving to press my lips against his, but he pulled back and shook his head.

"Me and Marcelina," he started, his voice dying in his throat. "We weren't healthy. We fought a lot. We didn't . . . we never talked properly. You know? I—you deserve better than that."

"We're not like that," I said quietly. "We're different."

"I'm really sorry, Aspirin," he said slowly. His eyes drifted to my cheek and he reached up, taking my face into my palm. He brushed a finger over my tear stains, trailing over my lips. "Really, really."

"I know," I repeated. I reached up to run my fingers over his forehead, smoothing out the wrinkles in his furrowed brow. "I love you, Isaac."

"I love you too, Aspirin. My Aspirin." His lips tugged up in a small, uncertain smile. "What did I ever do to deserve you?"

"Oh, yes," I teased in a low drawl. "Because I'm way out of your league."

"You are," he said, grinning. His eyes darkened, lowering to my lips. "You're kind, and beautiful, and smart, and—"

I rolled my eyes, pulling on his collar until we were an inch apart. His words died in his throat at the sudden movement.

"Shut up and kiss me again."

His lips twitched up into a smirk, and he did as he was told.

CHAPTER THIRTY-NINE
Peppermint Tea

I stood at the counter of Café de Fleur, watching Isaac sit at his—*our* usual table. His sketchpad was open, and he was lost in his world again, his brow furrowed, and eyes focused on the paper in front of him.

His dark hair was pushed back—the result of me running my fingers through it too much—and his jacket loose over his shoulders.

"Earth to Aspen." I blinked, spinning to see Vivienne smirking at me. "I've been calling you for five minutes now. Your drinks are ready."

"Sorry," I muttered sheepishly, taking the two take away cups from her hand.

Today, I ordered peppermint tea. Isaac texted me a list of teas and their benefits last night, and I was determined to try them all. The headaches were getting better, but I was still desperate for them to disappear.

Who knew caffeine withdrawals were so painful?

"It's fine," Vivienne waved off. "I know how it is. Young love."

I raised a doubtful brow at her. "You do?"

"I was young once too," she shot back, rolling her eyes with a playful grin. "You've got to hold on tight. You never forget your first love, whether it's for the better or worse, they leave a mark on you."

I paused, glancing back at Isaac. I was hoping she was right.

"See, relationships are all about compromise and communication," she said, suddenly sounding sage. I widened my eyes at her, and she snorted at my reaction. "Hey, I can be all wise and serious every once in a while. I'm practically an old lady."

"Vivienne, you're not even thirty yet."

"Once you hit twenty-one, nothing's the same." She sighed solemnly, like a grandmother remembering better days. I sent her a funny look and she laughed, shaking her head. "I'm joking. Now go back to lover boy. Have a good day at school, you two."

I grinned, nodding and thanking her before trailing over to Isaac. I paused for a moment, watching him draw. It reminded me of the days before we had ever spoken—when I would watch him get lost in that sketchpad, a pencil gripped tightly in his hand, like his life depended on completing his drawing.

I wondered how many of those times he had been drawing me.

I set the cups onto the table, clearing my throat to grab his attention.

He blinked, looking up to meet my eyes. "Aspirin!"

"Hey." I smiled. Instantly, his face glowed.

"Look." He turned his sketchpad to show me his drawing. It was incomplete, but I could see what it was becoming.

"That's me," I said, raising my brows.

"Yeah," he said, watching me. "You looked so pretty when we went to Chloe's. I couldn't take my eyes off you."

I held back a retort—wanting to tell him he did take his eyes off me. For almost an hour. But instead, I laughed awkwardly, nodding towards the door.

"Let's go to school. I don't want to be late."

He smiled, shoving the tiny sketchpad into his pocket and scooping up his coffee cup. We walked out of the café, shouting a goodbye and thank you to Vivienne on the way.

"So," Isaac said as we stepped out onto the sidewalk. "I want to make it up to you."

"What?"

"For leaving you," he said, in a pretty direct manner. "For being a complete dick."

"If you insist," I teased.

"I do," he said quickly.

He turned to me and I released a warm breath, the cold air condensing in front of my mouth. He took my hand, intertwining our fingers and putting it into his jacket pocket.

"Are you free tonight?" he asked finally.

I almost snorted at the question. I was free every night.

"Hmm, let me think," I hummed sarcastically. I paused for dramatic effect and he rolled his eyes at me, a grin tugging at his lips. "Of course, I am, Isaac. Why?"

"Let me take you out," he offered, smiling boyishly. "Dinner. A movie. Whatever you want."

"Whatever I want?" I echoed. *What did I want?*

Dinner sounded like a perfect opportunity for awkward silences and for me to be anxious about the menu. A movie meant I would be overthinking how loud I chewed my popcorn and how close we sat.

I looked at him, smiling timidly. "Can we just stay inside?"

"Is that what you want?"

I nodded.

"Then that's what we'll do."

I smiled, leaning into his side and taking a sip of my tea. Things were becoming normal again. I hoped there wouldn't be any more drama at school today. And by that I meant I hoped there wouldn't be any Chloe.

We walked through the gates together, one hand still buried in Isaac's pocket, the other holding my half-empty cup of tea. People still stared, but it had been over two weeks now. They were getting used to it too.

We reached my locker and I sighed, pulling my hand out of his to start searching for my chemistry books.

"I wish we had class together," Isaac said as I searched. I turned to see him pouting playfully at me and I rolled my eyes.

"It's your fault for not doing chemistry with me," I said, quirking a brow.

He scrunched his nose at me. "Chemistry's the worst. You should transfer to my class."

"I think you can last one period."

"Can I?" he asked, smirking now. "Maybe we should just skip together."

"No," I scolded, pointing a finger at him. I knew he was just trying to tease me, but I still sent him a stern look. "No skipping."

"Yes, Miss Haste," he teased. He leaned against the lockers, tilting his head to look at me as the warning bell rang. "I'll see you in art, then?"

I nodded, shutting my locker and turning to face him properly. "See you in art."

I sent him a look that said go to class, but he wavered. He glanced around the hall for a moment before leaning forward to press a quick peck to my lips.

My heart jumped and just as I felt myself begin to melt beneath his touch. He was gone, spinning to sprint down the hall. He waved at me, grinning mischievously, and I knew my face was burning red. I could feel the blush creeping up from my neck, right to my ears.

I quickly scanned the hallway, hoping no one had seen that before a smile tugged at my lips, and butterflies erupted in my stomach.

*   *   *

Chemistry passed by quickly. All I could think about was Isaac teasing me and kissing me in the hallway, his green eyes glinting with mischief, and before I knew it, I was in the art room.

"Hurry up, take your seats," Ms. Laney said from the front of the room. "We're doing theory today."

A collective sound of groans came from the class, but I grinned secretly to myself. I hated practical classes. I made a beeline to my usual seat, Isaac already there, Sebastian beside him

They chatted loudly, used to drawing people's attention. It was kind of strange to see them laughing together. I had forgotten that they were best friends before I had met them. It reminded me of the days before I had spoken to Isaac. These days, Isaac paid more attention to me than to Sebastian.

I slid into my seat silently, but they noticed me, cutting their laughter short to greet me.

"Aspirin," Isaac said, grinning. Immediately, his hand shot out to intertwine our fingers. His smile was wide and boyish, and I felt my heart flutter. "You won't believe—"

"Mr. Hensick," Ms. Laney cut him off. She appeared in front of our desk, her expression stern. "Will you please come see me for a moment? It's about your portfolio."

Isaac paused, nodding and sending me a look before standing from his seat. He released my hand and I felt an instant loss of warmth.

"Be back," he muttered, his lips dangerously close to my ear as he passed.

299

"Carry on copying the notes," Ms. Laney called out, leading Isaac to her desk.

I watched with a sigh. Isaac was applying to study art at Hunter College, and Ms. Laney said a good portfolio would help his chances of being accepted, considering his average grades. I was still trying to come to terms with the fact that he wanted to go to college four hours away from me.

"You alright?" Sebastian asked suddenly.

I turned, realising that he was halfway through his notes and I hadn't even started. I blinked, shaking my head to snap myself out of my thoughts.

"Yeah," I said, chuckling. "Yeah, sorry."

"You don't normally zone out like that," Sebastian mumbled, glancing at Isaac and Ms. Laney.

"Yeah." I sighed, grabbing my pen and beginning to write. "Just thinking about college."

"Right. Isaac wants to go to Hunter's, huh?"

I nodded, frowning, and Sebastian shrugged.

"He's been wanting to go there since we were kids. One of our neighbors was an artist and he studied there too," Sebastian said slowly. "I think that's when he realised art could be an actual career."

I furrowed my brow, turning to him. "I didn't know."

He shrugged again, smiling lopsidedly before turning back to his work.

By the time Isaac had returned to his seat, he was strangely quiet. He began copying his notes, silently frowning at his page. I wanted to ask him what was wrong, but Ms. Laney had begun lecturing us on Romantic artworks and I didn't want to get into trouble.

Instead, I kept my mouth shut, waiting for the bell to ring.

"Isaac," I said, the second we were dismissed. "What happened with Ms. Laney?"

He shrugged, frowning and tugging his backpack on his shoulders. "Nothing really. Just have to improve some of my works."

"Oh," I said stupidly. I paused, searching for words of encouragement. "Well, I'm sure they'll turn out amazing. You're the best artist I know."

He looked up, meeting my eyes and let a smile tug at his lips. He reached out, taking my books for me. "Thanks Aspirin."

"Isaac!"

I blinked, spinning to find Chloe waiting for us—or rather, him—at the door. We stepped out and, much to my dismay, she invited herself to join our group.

"So," she began, completely ignoring me and Sebastian. "I hope you don't mind, but I gave Marcelina your new number."

We all froze. Isaac's eyes grew dark, his jaw clenching. There was something deadly in his expression and his fingers curled into fists, like he was struggling to hold it back.

"What?" he spat through clenched teeth, furrowing his brow.

Chloe shrugged. "Oh, come on Isaac. Can't we all just be friends?"

He swallowed thickly, pressing his eyes shut as he took a deep, shuddering breath. He shook his head and released the breath, tearing his eyes away from Chloe to send me a look that clearly said I had nothing to do with this.

I frowned, turning back to face Chloe. She smiled nonchalantly, though her eyes were dark and held a viciously mean stare. Fire bubbled in my stomach.

"You really shouldn't give out people's numbers without permission," I blurted out. Instantly, she turned, sending me a deathly glare over her shoulder.

"Did I ask for your opinion?" Chloe shot back, glaring at me.

Instantly, my anger was quashed, and I felt my heart pound at the sudden confrontation. My throat felt dry beneath her sharp glare and I struggled for words.

I felt it in my fingers first. That was where it always started. A tingling in my fingers like a lack of circulation—the kind that came with a cold winter's day. The kind that makes my hands tremble, keeping tempo with my racing heart.

My breath caught in my throat. I wanted to speak, but Chloe's eyes dug into me, and it suddenly felt very difficult to open my mouth. I forced my lips to move.

"Well, I—umm . . ."

At the sound of my wavering voice, Isaac turned to look at me, completely ignoring Chloe now. His dangerous glare was replaced with a new expression of worry. He studied me for a second, his brow deepening. "Aspen—"

"She's right," Sebastian piped up. He stepped forward, sending Chloe a stern look. "It's rude."

"Seriously, Seb?" Chloe spat, her voice in a loud shout now, sending a quake of anxiety through me.

I hated it when people yelled.

Sebastian stepped closer, raising his own voice into a shout. "Yes, Chloe. Just because you're sisters doesn't mean you can do whatever you want."

Around us, people began turning to look. They whispered, pausing on their way to their next class. I felt a pressure begin to build in my chest, my skin itching beneath everyone's eyes. Isaac moved towards me.

"Guys," I muttered, trying to stop the fight—to stop them from drawing attention to our small group. "Sebastian . . ."

But it was hopeless.

Sebastian was oblivious. He continued yelling, but his words had turned silent to my ears. Instead, all I could hear were the people around us, whispering, and muttering. Stopping to stare.

Suddenly, I felt aware of every insecurity, every possible judgement they were making.

"Is that Isaac Hensick and Sebastian Georges?"

"Why are they fighting?"

"Who's that girl with them?"

"That's Isaac's new girlfriend. It's probably about her."

"How annoying."

I dug my nails into my palms, trying to steady myself as the world spun around me—trying to ground myself. I tried to speak again, but my voice was lost to me. All I could hear was my heart pounding in my throat, too swollen to swallow.

Beside me, Isaac was still focused on me. He stiffened, wrapping an arm over my shoulders and drawing me close so that my face was shielded from everyone else.

"Aspen," he started, quietly, leaning close to my ear. "Breathe."

I nodded urgently, sucking in a deep breath before I could start to have a panic attack. I released it, trying to focus on Isaac—Isaac's hands on my arms, Isaac's cologne on his jacket, Isaac's voice in my ears, telling me to breathe. My heart slowed and my hands trembled a fraction less now, though fatigue was beginning to settle in.

I looked up, meeting Isaac's worried eyes.

"You good?" he asked.

I nodded, swallowing hard. "I'm good."

"Right," he said. A muscle twitched in his jaw and he turned his attention back to Chloe and Sebastian, who were still going at it. I watched him, my anxiety beginning to fade.

"—and I can't believe you're defending her—"

"It's fine," Isaac said curtly, interrupting Chloe mid-sentence. "Just stop. Can we not fight?"

It definitely didn't look like it was fine. Isaac was frowning, his jaw clenched as if he was holding everything in, but he had gotten them to shut up.

I reached out, taking his hand and watching him soften.

Chloe was an idiot. Marcelina had hurt him. When I had met Isaac, he had sheltered himself off; putting up walls to prevent himself from falling in love again. And now she was ripping those wounds back open again?

Some friend she was.

I had to bite my tongue to stop myself from saying something I'd regret.

Chloe and Sebastian had turned quiet, though the atmosphere was still tense.

"We need to go to our English class," Isaac said suddenly, sending Chloe an intense look. His grip on my hand tightened. She raised a brow at him, glancing at our joined hands before scowling and moving aside.

"I'll see you at lunch," Sebastian said quickly. He paused, sending me childish smile, his curls flopping over his forehead. "We need to get you to Ronald level."

I gave a half-hearted chuckle at the joke, feeling my face warm before whacking his arm. "Shut up."

He winked, giving me a half shrug and flashing a smile at Isaac. "See you guys."

And with that, he turned, grabbing Chloe's arm and dragging her to their next class.

"Ronald?" Isaac asked from beside me. I turned, still grinning to see him watching me, his eyes narrowed. I shrugged.

"It's a long story."

"Right," he trailed off. We walked in silence for a moment, his brow furrowed in thought, before he spoke again. "Actually, you never told me. How did you get home from Chloe's place?"

"Oh." My face warmed at the memory. I didn't want Isaac to take it the wrong way. After all, Sebastian and I were only friends. I tried to play it cool. "Seb drove me."

"Seb?" he echoed. His jaw clenched and he glanced in the direction Sebastian had left.

"It's not like you were available," I pointed out. We paused at the door to our English class. Mr. Greene still hadn't arrived, so we took a moment to ourselves.

Isaac stiffened as he processed my words. "Aspirin—"

"I know," I interrupted gently. "You're sorry. But it doesn't change the fact that it happened."

He hesitated for a moment, before releasing a breath. He nodded, his eyes hardening. He sent me a reassuring smile and turned to push the classroom door open. His voice was so quiet I almost didn't hear it.

"And it won't happen again."

CHAPTER FORTY
Earl Grey Tea

"That looks more like cardboard than pizza," Riley muttered over my shoulder, nodding towards the stale slices of pizza the lunch ladies were serving.

I nodded grimly. "I should've packed a sandwich."

"I don't know what you guys are talking about." William grinned, holding his tray out to receive his lunch. "This pizza is the best."

Riley rolled her eyes, but she couldn't fight the grin that stretched across her face. William was her weak spot. We collected our trays, making our way to one of the tables in the cafeteria.

The weather was getting colder as winter was fast approaching, making it much too cold to sit outside in our usual spot beneath the tree.

We clattered onto an uncomfortable metal bench and Riley instantly ignored her tray of stale food, leaning over it to whisper conspiratorially to me.

"So, Aspen," she began, sending me a mischievous look. "Are you sitting with lover boy today?"

A blush crept up my chest to my face. I swallowed nervously, shaking my head. "No, I don't think so."

At that, she paused, her eyes widening. The amused grin fell right off her face. "Wait, why not?"

I sighed, the words suddenly tumbling out of me like a waterfall. "We saw Marcelina at the party."

"WHAT?"

"Chloe brought her, and they wanted to do some tradition with Isaac, and Chloe was being so condescending to me! So, I let him go because I wanted to be the cool girlfriend, you know? Not the controlling girlfriend. But then he disappeared for, like, half an hour and Sebastian drove me home and—"

"Sebastian drove you?" Riley sputtered her eyes wide.

"Yes Riley, keep up," William said.

"And then Isaac came in through my window and he said Chloe took his phone—"

"Your window!" William repeated.

"Chloe took his phone?" Riley echoed.

"Yes," I said, nodding solemnly. "And he apologised and then everything was fine, but then Chloe gave his number to Marcelina and . . . and . . . I just don't know what to do anymore."

I finished, releasing a long breath and slumping over in defeat. William was frozen, his eyes wide as he processed my rambling words. Riley, on the other hand, had furrowed her brow, shaking her head.

She stood suddenly with her fists clenched.

"I'm going to kill that b*tch."

"Whoa," William said quickly, placing a hand on her shoulder. She was so tiny that he barely had to move to pull her back into her seat. "No killing." He turned to me, smiling politely. "Why don't you just tell Chloe to back off?"

"I don't know." I sighed finally. It felt good to get all of this off my chest. "I don't want to look like an annoying girlfriend."

"An annoying girlfriend?" William asked.

I shrugged, poking dejectedly at my food. "I've never had a boyfriend before. I don't know what the hell I'm doing. My brain wasn't wired for this kind of thing."

"Aspen." Riley sighed, relaxing. She sent me a small smile. "Don't overthink it. Just do whatever your gut tells you."

"My gut is telling me to stay in bed and never leave," I said, raising a brow.

"Okay, maybe don't do that."

"Yeah."

"I can't believe he spent an hour with Marcelina and Chloe," Riley spat, shaking her head. "I saw how Chloe was glaring at you last time. What a dick."

"I don't know." William shrugged. "I can kind of see where he's coming from. They're his childhood friends. They're like siblings."

Riley shot him a glare. "I'll let that slide, but only because I love you."

William let out an awkward chuckle, his face turning bright red. I groaned, my shoulders sagging.

"I just don't know what to do."

"Oh, my sweet, nonconfrontational baby." Riley sighed. She patted my shoulder, pouting. "Let's run away to a cabin in some faraway woods."

"No," William cut in, raising a brow. "No running away."

"Do you have any better advice, then, Mr. Know-It-All," Riley teased, sticking her tongue out at him. He ignored her teasing, turning to face me instead.

"Well," William began slowly. "Why don't you sit with Isaac today, and if Chloe says something, try stand up for yourself? You don't have to confront her on what she's done before, just stop her from doing it again."

"Huh." Riley hummed. "That's actually pretty good advice." She paused, giving me a deathly smile. "Or I can do it for you."

"No, no," I said quickly, shaking my head. I released a tight breath. They were right. I needed to stand up for myself. I couldn't let my anxiety control my life. I had to at least try.

I had already made so much progress. Just a year ago, I'd have a panic attack almost daily. Now, here I was, with a boyfriend, a new friend, going to parties and dates; if I could do all that, I could stand up to a condescending b*tch.

My phone buzzed in my pocket and I shifted my lunch tray to one hand, pulling it out to see a text from Isaac.

From Isaac: Where are you? You sitting with us today?

I sucked in a deep breath, steeling myself. I could do it.

To Isaac: Coming!

I put my tray down, taking the pizza slice off it.

"I'm going to sit with Isaac," I said determinedly. William's eyes widened, surprised at my newfound confidence, and Riley smiled proudly.

"That's my girl!" she whooped, patting my back in encouragement.

"Good luck," William said warmly, though I didn't miss the grim twist in his smile.

My grin wavered and I turned, marching out of the cafeteria and towards Isaac's usual lunch area while shoving the stale pizza down my throat.

I hoped Chloe wouldn't say anything today, but if she did—it would be the last time.

Giving Marcelina his phone number was the last straw. I was sick of her bullsh*t.

As usual, Sebastian, Isaac and Chloe sat together. Arthur Andrews stood a few feet away, speaking angrily into his phone— probably to his girl of the week. Sebastian was leaning against the ground, his curls pulled back at the front with a clip. He fanned out his t shirt, probably hot from a round of soccer.

Isaac was the first to spot me, pushing off from the wall to greet me halfway.

"Aspirin!" he exclaimed, grinning.

I smiled at him as he reached an arm out, wrapping it around my waist. Instantly, my heart seemed to calm slightly at the gesture.

"Hey guys." I waved awkwardly. Sebastian sat upright, smiling and greeting me, while Chloe simply nodded. I cleared my throat awkwardly, searching for a conversation starter, when Sebastian spoke.

"Where were you? I could've used a Ronald on my team," he teased, wiggling his eyebrows at me.

I sputtered out a laugh, shaking my head. "Sorry, I didn't feel like embarrassing myself in front of the entire school."

"She was with William and Riley," Isaac said. He looked at me, smiling proudly that he knew me well. "Right?"

"Yep," I said, popping the p. "I thought I'd come here instead of third wheeling all lunch."

Not a complete lie.

"Well, I'm glad you did," Isaac said as he smirked. His arm tightened around my waist, tugging me closer, and I felt my face heat. I didn't even have to look to know Chloe was glaring in my direction.

There was an awkward pause and I found myself quickly looking for something to fill it with. A breeze bit at my skin and I smiled uncomfortably. "It's getting cold, huh?"

Isaac looked down at me, raising an amused brow. "It is."

"Yeah," I nodded, shuffling awkwardly. Chloe already lost interest and turned to her phone while Sebastian grinned at me silently. "I think it's the, uh, wind." A pause. "It's getting windy."

"Aspirin," Isaac began, smirking. He leaned closer to lower his voice. "Do you want to keep talking about the wind?"

"Not really, no."

"Good." He chuckled, his eyes lighting up. "Because I was wondering if you're free after school today."

"After school?" I hummed, pretending to think over my schedule. We had practically hung out every day after school this week, and I was sure he already knew I was free today as well. "Maybe I can clear up an hour or two."

"Only an hour?" He pouted, and I shrugged.

"Hmm . . . I guess I could clear up a bit more time," I teased, drawing my words out as if in thought.

"Great." He flashed me a wide grin. "Because tonight's Percy Jackson night."

"Those movies are cursed," I said pointedly.

"Yes, but our 'nostalgic movies from the 2010s's marathon will be incomplete without them."

He had a point.

"Isaac," Chloe suddenly cut in. I turned, furrowing my brow at her sudden interruption. "Don't you have to work on that portfolio of yours?" She paused, settling me with a sharp look. "Marcy told me you still have a few more paintings to finish."

"What?" Isaac's brow furrowed in confusion. "How would Marcy know that?"

But Chloe wasn't listening to him. She was busy sending me a condescending smirk.

I felt like I had been lit on fire. I was so sick of her. I clenched my jaw, biting back my anger to send her an equally condescending look.

"Actually," I began, keeping my glare on Chloe. "Isaac, I'm free all night. You can work on it at mine. While we watch Percy Jackson, of course."

"Sweet, problem solved." Isaac grinned, tapping his fingers against my waist.

I smiled, raising my brows at Chloe and leaning into his side. Her eyes fell to my waist and I smirked at the reaction, tugging

311

Isaac's arm tighter around me. I kept my hand over his, lacing our fingers together.

Chloe's eyes snapped back up to meet mine, a new fire blazing through them.

"Well, Marcy's still home from college. She can give you some tips if you'd like."

She just wouldn't let it go, would she? Isaac opened his mouth to reply, but I cut in before he could speak.

"He's good, thanks." I smiled, trying my best to shove my anger down.

"I think he can speak for himself."

"Okay, let's ask him then," I shot back, the pressure in my chest beginning to rise. I spun to face Isaac. "Would you rather hang out with your b*tchy ex-girlfriend, or me?"

Isaac's eyes widened in surprise. "You."

"Nice, so that's settled then," I said, turning back to Chloe.

"What did you just call my sister?" she asked, her voice clipped by anger. She stood from her seat, clenching her fists, shaking her head in disbelief.

Adrenaline pumped through my body, and I felt as if I would burst in an explosion of pent-up emotions. I was practically vibrating from the sudden confrontation.

No. Not sudden. This confrontation had been waiting weeks to happen.

"Give it a rest, Chloe," I shot back, narrowing my eyes. "Marcelina broke up with him. Over text. It's over."

Chloe blinked, faltering. "What? She told me . . ."

I ignored her, rolling my eyes. "Whether you like it or not, I'm his girlfriend now."

Isaac nodded, squeezing my fingers in encouragement. "She's right, Chlo. Seriously. I let it go when you took my phone. I let it go when you gave her my number. I tried to settle it quietly— by speaking with you—but I'm losing patience, Chloe."

She recovered at that, though her eyes still held a certain flicker of confusion. She shook her head, her cheeks colouring. She turned to me, ignoring Isaac's words.

"Well, I'm his best friend!" Chloe shouted finally. She waved a hand at him, sending him a look. "Are you going to let her speak to me like this?"

"Come on, Chloe. Don't make me choose." His voice dropped, and he raised her brows at her in a silent message. "Because you know I'll choose Aspen. Please. Drop it before it's too late."

My face warmed at his words, but I managed to shoot her a smug look. Her expression faltered.

"What?" she scoffed. "I'm not doing anything. She started it."

"Oh, please," I interrupted, rolling my eyes. Adrenaline surged through my body, fuelled by anger. "You glare and condescend to me and keep trying to get Isaac to hang out with Marcelina, like, what's your deal?"

"I do not."

"You do," Isaac jumped in, his voice raw. He shrugged at her. "You do, Chlo. And I know we've been friends for ages, but Aspen's my girl. You need to stop. I thought we talked about this."

My heart swelled at him defending me. He leaned closer to me, our shoulders knocking, and sent me a small nod.

"I can't believe you." Chloe shook her head. "I can't believe you're going out with a girl like her."

"What the hell's that supposed to mean?" Isaac spat, beginning to grow defensive.

"Yeah, Chloe, what's that supposed to mean?" Sebastian shot up. I blinked turning to see him stand, towering over her. I had never seen him without a smile before—much less as angry as he looked now. "I noticed it too. You're always glaring at her and making jabs and mean comments. You keep bringing up Marcelina and ignoring the fact Aspen's literally right there!"

313

"Can you blame me?" Chloe asked, quirking a brow.

"Yes, Chloe, because that's a sh*tty thing to do!" Sebastian shouted.

My eyes widened, and I staggered back. Isaac looked down at me, his expression worried. He opened his mouth to speak, when Chloe interrupted.

"Just look at her!" she yelled. Her voice was so loud at this point, I was sure the entire school could hear her. "She's not one of us! She's nothing like Marcy! She's weird, and awkward, and antisocial and—and—"

She couldn't finish her sentence before the tears began to well up and I was gone.

CHAPTER FORTY-ONE
English Breakfast Tea

Somehow, I found myself in my usual corner of the library.

I sat on the floor, my arms wrapped around my knees and my face buried between them as I rocked back and forth. I hadn't had a full-blown panic attack in a while. My heart raced, my fingers were shaking, and my skin was clammy.

I felt like I was dying.

My breaths came out fast, combining with the silent sobs that wracked through my body. I clenched my jaw shut, keeping as silent as possible in the already still library.

I had become a master at keeping my anxiety quiet from a young age. I learned how to keep my sobs quiet and how to keep my hyperventilating to a light, barely-there pant.

It meant less questions. Less looks. Less worrying about others.

It was like a cycle. A silent sob ripped through my throat, and then I was gasping for air through trembling lips.

It felt as if all the air in my lungs had been sucked out. It was a vacuum—a void of air. My chest rose and fell quickly, so fast that my body ached, and I felt the overwhelming urge to gag and cough.

I vaguely heard the school bell, muffled by the sound of blood rushing in my ears. Normally I'd be worried about being late to class, but my mind was busy repeating Chloe's words.

She's weird, and awkward, and antisocial. I made a choking sound in my throat and another wave of sobs tore through me.

I squeezed my eyes shut, but my mind was already racing, replaying the stares I received in the hallways, asking question after question—was Chloe right? Did Isaac hate me? Was I a bad girlfriend? What was I doing wrong?

Why couldn't I be enough?

Why was this so hard for me?

It was a crowd of thoughts all playing at once. I wanted to scream. Instead, I desperately tried to control my breathing. I sucked in a shaky breath, counting in my head.

One, two, three. Out.

I released the breath in a weak sputter, beginning my count again.

One, two, three. In.

I continued over and over again until I realised the counting was no longer only my head.

"There you go," Isaac whispered.

He'd found me at some point. I couldn't remember when.

I couldn't hear him over the thoughts screaming in my mind. Those stupid thoughts that never left me alone, cramming themselves down my throat until I was suffocating. I couldn't hear him over the deep pain in my chest as I tried to catch my breath. The buzzing in my ears that drowned the world out.

He sat beside me with a light arm wrapped around my shoulders like a blanket of warmth. I whimpered, leaning into his touch as he whispered in my ear and stroked my hair.

"One, two, three. Out again."

I released a heavy breath, feeling my heart rate slow. Though my fingers still trembled, my breathing was mostly back to normal albeit the occasional hiccup.

His arms pulled tighter around me now and I let him tug me close until my head rested against his collarbone. His hand rubbed my back, his fingers soothing the tight muscles beneath my skin. I sighed into his touch, sniffling slightly.

Now, I just felt exhausted. My entire body ached like I had gone on a ten-mile run. My head pounded and my mouth felt dry. I was exhausted—and embarrassed.

I had run away in the middle of lunch.

Another thought hit me.

"I'm late for class!" I exclaimed, though it came out as more of a croaky hiccup.

I made to stand, but my legs trembled and gave way. Isaac reached out, catching me and lowering me back to the carpeted library floor.

"It's okay." He chuckled lowly, running his fingers gently through my hair. I melted under his touch; my crowded thoughts instantly quieting. "Sebastian's telling Mr. Lawson you're at the nurse."

"Oh," I muttered. I slumped against him, relief flooding through me, allowing me to relish in my exhaustion. "Thanks."

Isaac paused, his hands moving from my hair to cradle my face. He brushed his thumbs over my cheeks to sweep my tear stains away. I looked up to see him frowning at me, his brow furrowed in worry.

"Aspen," he murmured, his voice deathly serious and tense with worry. "Are you okay?"

I swallowed the lump in my throat. That was a loaded question.

"I'm fine," I said, nodding. "It was just—I guess it just all built up."

Isaac nodded, processing my words. "What Chloe said . . . if you want to talk about it . . ."

"No," I cut in quickly. "I'm fine. It was just, you know, I'm not very confrontational, and we had that argument a few days ago, and I just never really let it out so—" I paused, noticing the worried look he was sending me. I smiled softly, moving to take his hand. "I'm fine. Really."

A part of me wanted to tell him everything.

I wanted to tell him that I had no idea what I was doing. That Chloe and Marcelina got on my nerves. That I was sick of people staring at me and whispering about me. That I had been overthinking everything and all I wanted was validation that I wasn't doing this whole "girlfriend" thing wrong.

That a part of me believed Chloe was right, and he belonged with a girl like Marcelina or Lacey—someone who could socialise and dress cute and go to parties.

But I was scared.

And I was tired. All I wanted right now was a nap. I didn't have the energy to talk.

"I want to sleep," I groaned, leaning my head against his shoulder.

"Then sleep," he said, smiling.

I laughed weakly. "Why didn't I think of that?"

"That's what I'm here for," he teased quietly. "I'm full of good ideas."

I sighed, sinking into his side. He wrapped an arm around my waist, pulling me so that I sat in his lap. Warmth wrapped around me, lulling me, enticing me to sleep. He kept one arm secured around me, his other resting on my leg as his fingers traced patterns over my thighs and knees.

I could feel the thrum of Isaac's heart through his chest, racing almost as fast as mine.

He looked down at me, his eyes gentle.

"Aspen," he began, slowly. He pursed his lips, unsure. "I'm really sorry about Chloe."

"Ugh, don't bring her up," I whined, burying my face into his chest.

"I'm sorry I didn't listen to you," he continued. "I just . . . I wanted this all to work. I wanted everyone to be friends and be happy and . . . I really messed it up. I'm sorry. I'm so sorry."

His voice broke and my heart sank.

"Hey," I said, cutting him off. I pulled back, looking his square in the eyes. "This was not your fault. It was all Chloe. She's just—ugh! She's just so frustrating!"

"She can be sometimes." He sighed. "She can be cold and sheltered. Closed off. I just never thought she'd be . . . mean. I never would've introduced you two if I thought she'd . . ." he trailed off, shaking his head.

I mirrored his frown, Chloe's words echoing in my mind.

"Am I really awkward? And weird?" I asked, my voice coming out in a quiet squeak. I swallowed the lump in my throat. "Do you wish I was more like Marcelina?"

Isaac's eyes widened, his jaw falling slack. He paused for a moment before leaning forward, pressing a soft kiss to my mouth.

"Aspen," he said, an inch away from my face. He rested his forehead against mine. His skin was hot. His breath fanned over my lips and butterflies erupted in my stomach. "I don't want you to be anyone but yourself."

"Really?"

"Really, really," he said quietly. He shook his head, chuckling lightly. "I want you and your Hufflepuff robes and Elmo t-shirts. I want you and your bad taste in TV shows—"

"What's wrong with Riverdale?" I interrupted. He sent me an amused look and I sighed. "Okay, you're right."

He chuckled, brushing a strand of hair behind my ears.

"I want you and your library naps and cups of tea. I want you with or without insomnia. With or without anxiety. I'll take you anyway I can get you."

"Isaac," I muttered, pouting.

His hands rested on my waist and he tilted his head to press a soft kiss to my cheek before pulling away. He sent me a wide grin.

"I mean it Aspirin," he said. He paused, quirking a brow at me. "And for the record, you looked really hot when you stood up to Chloe like that."

A loud laugh burst from my lips and my hands shot up to cover my mouth. I paused, my eyes wide, before falling into a tumble of giggles.

"Isaac," I said in between laughs. "I love you."

He sent me a heart melting smile. "I love you too."

I chewed on my bottom lip, letting myself treasure this moment. Letting myself remember Isaac's hands on my waist and lips on mine and his words and smile and dimples and hair.

"So," I began, my mind wandering back to lunch. "What happened after I left?"

"Oh." Isaac chuckled. "Me and Sebastian told Chloe off."

"Seriously?" I asked, my brows raised.

He nodded. "She feels really guilty."

I doubted it.

"Actually," he continued slowly. He hesitated, his eyes darting like he was remembering whatever had happened after I left. "She wants to apologise."

"What?" My eyes widened in surprise. Apologising didn't seem like Chloe's forte.

"Yeah." He nodded. He paused, chewing on his bottom lip. "Aspen, listen. If Chloe apologises to you . . . would you hear her out?"

"What?" I echoed. I thought of Chloe's words. Her glares. Her constant mentions of Marcelina. I shook my head, furrowing my brow. "No way. I won't. She doesn't deserve it."

"Aspirin," Isaac sighed. He frowned at me, pleading. "Look, she told us some things after you left and—"

"What sort of things?"

320

"I . . . I can't tell you. It's for her to say," he said, frowning. He shook his head, swallowing thickly. "You don't have to, but would you at least think about it? It might explain some of her behavior . . . Make you feel better."

I felt my shoulders sag. He had been friends with Chloe for so long. I didn't want to get in the way of their friendship. Maybe we could start over.

Maybe we could actually be friends, and all get along.

I bit back a snort. Yeah, that wasn't going to happen anytime soon. But I could hear out her apology and leave all this behind us. I've learned my lesson—there was no being friendly with her.

I'd hear what she had to say and never speak to her again.

I released a breath, sending him a small smile.

"Alright, I'll think about it."

He broke out into a wide grin, squeezing me in a tight hug. "You are seriously the best, Aspirin."

"I know," I teased, my voice drowsy. He laughed, his chest vibrating with the laughter.

He held me close, his arms tight around me, and I sighed beneath his embrace. We sat together for a few minutes in silence, my head against his chest and his chin resting on top.

My eyes fluttered shut and I felt sleep tug at me, my entire body beginning to turn limp.

Before my dreams could pull me completely under, I felt his stare on my face and a smile tugged at my lips.

"Don't watch me while I sleep."

I didn't have to open my eyes to know he was smiling back.

CHAPTER FORTY-TWO
Honey and Lemon Tea

"Remind me why I took chemistry again?"

I laughed, slamming my locker shut and turning to face William. He scrunched his nose at me.

"None of it makes sense," he whined. "Make it make sense, Asp."

"Honestly," I said, sending him a half-shrug. "I don't know why I took it either."

"Shut up, you're literally so good at chem."

"My grades are a 70, that's pretty average."

"Exactly."

"William," I said, resting a hand on his shoulder. I sent him a look of pity. "I think chemistry might not be in your future."

"What am I going to do now?" William cried teasingly.

I laughed nudging him lightly. "Drop out and become a stripper?"

"I don't have the thighs." He frowned, shaking his head.

"We'll figure it out."

He laughed at me for a moment before his eyes drifted passed my shoulder, causing him to pause.

"Hey, Isaac," William said, grinning.

My eyes widened and I spun to meet Isaac's eyes. He looked handsome as ever, his dark hair messy and green eyes bright.

His cheeks dimpled with a wide smile and he moved to stand beside me, tossing an arm around my shoulder.

"Hey," I muttered, feeling my face grow hot.

"Hey guys." Isaac smiled. "How was chemistry?"

William's eyes widened at Isaac's mention of chemistry and he raised a brow at me, sending me a teasing smirk. I blushed further—he remembered my schedule.

"It was the worst. We were doing electron configuration and it was easy at first because we've done it before, you know? But then William moved to sit next to me, and he kept bothering me and talking so much—" I paused my rambling, feeling my face warm. "Kind of like how I'm doing now."

"But it's cuter when you do it." Isaac smirked, his eyes glittering with mischief.

"Hey!" William pouted.

I chuckled lightly. "Basically, it sucked." I turned to face Isaac, narrowing my eyes. "How was history?"

"I wanted to sleep the whole time," he said.

"Are you sure you didn't sleep?" I asked, quirking a brow at him. I reached up, smoothing his hair back as he grinned. He leaned closer and I froze.

"Maybe for a minute or two," he teased, his voice low as his breath fanned over my face. "It's not the same when you're not with me."

I blushed, stepping back suddenly and clearing my throat. He smirked at me, clearly amused by my flustered reaction.

William was looking away, his face tinted red to match my own, although his was probably more from embarrassment.

"Well, me and William are going to lunch. Are you coming?" I sputtered, eventually.

"Actually," Isaac began, his smile fading. He shuffled awkwardly, his dimples disappearing quickly. "Uh, would you sit with me today? Chloe wants to apologise about yesterday."

Chloe.

A shudder ran down my spine.

She had said such rude things to me yesterday to the point it caused a panic attack. Or, I guess more accurately, it triggered it. For the past few weeks, everything had been building up so quickly.

Chloe had sent me over the edge.

She called me so many things—awkward, antisocial, weird. She even said I didn't fit in with them, like I didn't already tell myself that every day I was with Isaac. Like I didn't doubt myself and compare myself to Marcelina every minute of every day.

"I mean, if you want," he quickly added.

I looked up, meeting his eyes, and despite his deadpan expression, his eyes swarmed with emotion. I knew he probably wanted us to get along. He wanted us all to be friends—like Marcelina had been.

So, I sighed and nodded.

"Alright," I said before turning to William. "You coming?"

"Actually," William said quickly, probably sensing how badly this was going to go. "Riley and I are going to the library. She needs help with an essay."

"Right." I smirked, raising my brows at him. "An essay."

"Shut up," William growled, though his face turned bright pink and he avoided my eyes.

I snickered at him, waving as he turned to make his way to the library. Isaac tugged me closer, sending me a comforting smile.

"Ready?"

I swallowed. No turning back.

"Ready."

He led me down the hallways and across the grass oval, chattering on about how boring history had been and cracking jokes, all while sending me worried glances out of the corner of his eye.

I knew he was trying to calm me down, but I fiddled my fingers anyway, picking at my nails and cuticles.

Was Chloe really going to apologise?

Was I going to accept?

Before I could figure out my answer, we turned the corner of the old school building. Chloe leaned against the wall, frowning with a furrowed brow. Great. She was already in a bad mood.

Was she ever in a good mood?

I've yet to see evidence of anything but a frown and a sour attitude on her face.

Across from her, Sebastian grinned widely, juggling a soccer ball on his knees. His blond curls flopped with each hop and his brows were drawn together in focus. He paused as we approached, catching the ball under his shoe.

"Hey guys!" Sebastian called, waving.

I sent a small wave back with a smile that didn't reach my eyes.

"Seb," Isaac greeted, grinning. He nodded curtly at Chloe. "Chlo."

"Hey," she said, not looking up.

"Chlo," Isaac repeated, sharply.

She sighed, rolling her eyes and turning to face us like it was an enormous waste of energy.

"Aspen," she began. "About yesterday . . ."

I raised a brow expectantly, meeting her eyes, when she froze. Her throat bobbed as she hesitated. "I . . ."

"Yes?" I said, slowly, waiting. I half expected her to start insulting me again. Instead, she wavered.

Something in her snapped, she spun to face the floor, pink creeping up her neck.

"I wanted to apologise," her voice came out cold and distant.

We paused and I honestly thought that was it until Isaac glared at her and she groaned.

"I shouldn't have said those things yesterday," she continued, pursing her lips. She refused to meet my eyes. Instead, her gaze darted around, from Isaac, to the floor, then to Seb—everywhere but me.

"Right," I said eventually, waiting for her to continue. I clenched my teeth—she obviously didn't mean her words if she wouldn't even meet my eye.

"It was mean," she said finally, dragging her words out. She clearly didn't mean them. "I am really, really sorry."

Why did she sound sarcastic?

Finally, she released a loud sigh and looked up to meet my eyes, sending me an exaggerated pout, her eyes narrowed. "Forgive me?"

I blinked, confused. Was she being serious? This was her apology?

A part of me wanted to scoff and leave. But then another part of me said do it for Isaac.

Sure, he'd just asked me to hear her out, but this meant a lot to him, right?

I glanced at Isaac to see him watching Chloe carefully. Surely, I could compromise to make him happy—forgive her and move on.

I swallowed, turning back to Chloe.

I could do this. Just leave it all in the past. Move on. I forced a smile onto my face.

"It's fine," I said through gritted teeth.

"Woohoo," Chloe cheered sarcastically. She slumped back against the wall. My chest swelled with anger, but I shoved it down, turning to face Isaac before I lashed out.

I sent him a half hearted smile, but he wasn't looking at me. He released an exasperated sigh.

"Chloe," he said, his voice stern.

She met his eyes, and her deadpan expression faltered for a moment. He quirked a brow at her in silent conversation and her cheeks tinted pink. She glanced away.

"Remember what you said yesterday?" Isaac started carefully. "You said you'd tell Aspen. Now's the time."

Chloe gave him an uncertain look, her eyes darting between me and him. She opened her mouth to speak, when Sebastian suddenly stormed forward.

"Are you serious?" he spat. His brow furrowed. He laughed, shaking his head in disbelief. "You're not seriously going to accept that, are you?"

"What?" I sputtered out; my eyes wide.

He waved a hand at Chloe. "That was the sh*ttiest apology I've ever heard."

"What's your problem?" Chloe asked, suddenly growing defensive.

"Seb," Isaac cut in, raising his hands. "Calm down. Give her a second. She needs to tell Aspen—"

"Oh, that's rich," Sebastian interrupted, shaking his head at Isaac. He stepped forward, narrowing his eyes. "First, she insults Aspen and then she makes this sh*t apology to her and expects us to all get over it? Aspen shouldn't have to forgive her. And Isaac, you're an idiot if you think that was an acceptable apology."

"What the hell, dude?" Isaac asked, stepping forward. "Who are you to tell Aspen what to do? If my girlfriend wants to forgive her, then that's her decision."

"Is it her decision?" Sebastian challenged, shoving a finger at Isaac's chest. "Or is it yours?"

"Oh, piss off, Seb."

"Sebastian," I cut in, finally finding my voice. "It's okay, really. Just let her finish."

"Aspen, you don't have to forgive her," Sebastian said suddenly, his eyes moving to meet mine. "Don't listen to whatever Isaac's been telling you. It's your choice."

I blinked, speechless.

"She knows that," Isaac cut in. He set his sharp eyes on Sebastian, frowning

327

"Does she?"

"She does!" he shouted finally. He shoved Sebastian back, shaking his head. "Why do you keep acting like she's not my girlfriend?"

"I—"

"You need to back off," he continued, his voice rising.

"Isaac," I sputtered eventually, moving forward to try stop him. "Sebastian. Both of you, stop it."

"No, Aspen," he said, still focused on Sebastian. He clenched his jaw, shaking his head. "Let's air it out. What's up Sebastian?"

Sebastian stayed silent, a muscle in his jaw twitching. I shook my head in disbelief at the sudden confrontation.

"Oh, so now you have nothing to say?" Isaac scoffed, stepping closer and squaring his shoulders. "Because it sure seems like you always have a lot to say when it comes to Aspen. When are you just going to admit it?"

"Admit what?" I asked, my voice coming out in a squeak.

"That he likes you, Aspen!" Isaac shouted.

Everything turned silent. My stomach flipped. "What?"

"Isaac," Sebastian said slowly, his voice low. "Stop."

"What?" I repeated, my throat turning dry. My head spun. "Seb, is that true?"

His eyes moved from Isaac to me, instantly softening. He grew very still, his brows drawing together. My heart sank.

Sebastian liked me.

They were all watching me now. Even Chloe. I felt like my throat was closing. What was I supposed to say to that? I thought we were friends. Hell, he had supported me when I was chasing after Isaac.

I staggered back, shaking my head.

"Aspen," Sebastian said finally, his voice croaking. "Please, wait."

328

"No," I said, swallowing thickly. I took another step back. "I-I just need a second."

"Aspen," he repeated, frowning, taking another step towards me.

I held my hands up to stop him, but he didn't, moving closer. Isaac stepped between us, placing a hand on Sebastian's chest. He faced me, his eyes showing a worried look.

"Aspirin," Isaac said, his voice pleading. He looked at me, his brow furrowed and expression soft. He stepped forward, reaching out to me, but I avoided his grasp.

I turned, my hands flying to my head. I needed a minute. This was all too much. *First Chloe, and now this?*

I began walking. I needed to be alone. I needed to wrap my mind around all of this.

"Aspirin, wait!" Isaac called out, jogging towards me.

I threw out my hand, stopping him in his tracks.

"Just leave me alone!" I shouted, shaking my head. "I don't want to see you right now. Either of you!"

I brushed them off, and I left.

CHAPTER FORTY-THREE
Cranberry Tea

"I just don't know what to do," I groaned, digging another spoon into the tub of ice-cream.

We sat on the floor together, digging into tubs of ice-cream and bags of chocolate while the screen flashed scenes of *Sixteen Candles*. Though, we weren't paying attention.

I had just spent the past hour unloading everything that had happened to Riley and William.

My shoulders sagged in relief at letting it all off my chest, but it had also reminded me of everything I had done wrong. All the things I had left unsaid. All the assumptions I had made.

Why was I so bad at this?

"Aspen," Riley began, pointing her spoon at me and speaking through a mouthful of vanilla. William sat beside her with his arm around her waist and her head on his shoulder. "Your life is a movie."

"Yeah, *'How to Lose a Guy in 10 Days'*," I whined.

"Shut up, you haven't lost anyone," she shot back, nudging me between the ribs.

I laughed, kicking out at her. "It's only a matter of time."

"You're just an idiot," William said wisely.

I frowned at him. "Gee, thanks Will."

"He's not wrong," Riley added, smiling.

"I didn't come here to be attacked," I complained, pouting at the two.

Riley laughed, throwing an arm around me. "You're all a bunch of idiots, but you can be cured."

"Please, Doctor Riley," I joked. "Cure me."

"All you have to do," she began, her voice deep and wise. She paused for dramatic effect, raising a brow at me. "Is talk to him."

"I do talk to him!"

"You don't, though," William cut in. "Out of everything you told us, how many times did you tell him what was actually on your mind?"

"I—" I paused. He was right. I let him go with Marcelina when I didn't want him to. I forgave Chloe when I didn't want to. I never even told him that I didn't want him to go to Hunter's College.

I groaned at the realisation. "I am an idiot."

"Boys are dumb, Aspen," Riley said, pointing a finger.

"Exactly." William nodded in agreement before pausing, his brow furrowing in confusion. "Wait."

"You can't expect them to know how you feel," she continued. "You have to tell them straight."

"But I don't want him to hate me."

"Aspen, if he hates you for speaking your mind, then he never really liked you."

"But he's so pretty." I pouted.

"Aspen."

"Fine!" I exclaimed, releasing a breath. "I'll talk to him."

"Right," Riley said, quirking a brow. "Like you tried talking to him the night of the party?"

"No, I'm doing it," I said pointedly. "I'm going to tell Isaac everything on my mind. And then after that, I'm going to talk to Sebastian and Chloe."

"Sure," Riley teased. "And then we'll ride my unicorn to Mars to hook up with some sexy aliens."

"What do sexy aliens have that I don't?" William asked.

"The point is," Riley said, ignoring his words but leaning closer into his side. "You said you'd talk to Chloe a million times. And Isaac. It's not going to happen."

I raised an arrogant brow at her, taunting her before I pulled out my phone.

"Look, I'm texting him right now."

Riley and William shared a look, but I ignored them.

To Isaac: We need to talk. Come over tonight?

I tried to pretend my heart wasn't pounding when he immediately read the message. Less than a second later, my phone buzzed with a reply.

From Isaac: Okay.

I released a breath, putting my phone beside me, face-down. My heart raced in my chest, yet I turned to send Riley a triumphant grin.

"See?"

She smiled at me, impressed, "When did you get so confident, Aspen?"

"It's a good look," William added, grinning, before returning his focus to the movie.

Normally, the words would've sent a warmth throughout me, but my smile wavered. I sure didn't feel confident.

I tried to follow, tried to concentrate on the sound of Molly Ringwald's voice. But my mind kept returning to Isaac—and the dreaded conversation we would have tonight.

*   *   *

I sat on my bed; my knees pulled to my chest as I picked at my blanket nervously. I didn't tell Isaac what time to come. I wished I did. Half of me hoped he'd forgotten and wouldn't turn up at all.

But when midnight came, so did a knock on my window.

I left it open and he came crawling through. He wore grey sweatpants and a loose white t-shirt, his leather jacket heavy over his shoulders. His hair was damp; he must have just showered.

"Hey," he said awkwardly, shuffling on his feet at the far end side of my room.

"Hey," I replied, my voice croaking.

For a moment, I felt the familiar urge to pull him into my arms and press a kiss against his frown, but I stopped myself. Riley's words echoed in my ears.

It's not going to happen.

I knew if I felt his skin against mine or looked into his stupid green eyes too long, I'd chicken out. I'd start overthinking everything, and it'd end up just like every other time.

So, I stayed sitting on my bed and he stayed nervously stood in the corner.

"I wasn't sure when to come," he said, shuffling awkwardly. "William said you were at his place."

I blinked. "You talk to William?"

His eyes widened slightly, like he had revealed a secret, and his face tinged pink. "Well, I thought I should be friends with my . . . with your friends." He paused, sending me a half-shrug. "Besides, William's pretty cool."

I was speechless.

How did I never notice? It felt so normal when Isaac would joke with William and Riley or invite them to sit with us at lunch. I almost forgot they weren't friends just weeks ago.

"You said you wanted to talk?" Isaac asked eventually, breaking the silence. His voice croaked as he spoke, and my heart cracked with it.

"I . . ." I trailed off, my throat swelling. I wasn't good at confrontation. I pressed my hands together, attempting to shove my anxiety down.

This was Isaac. He'd understand.

I reached up, my fingers drifting over the golden leaf that sat over my collarbone. I could do this.

"I have a lot to say."

"Okay."

"Alright, well . . ." I clenched my fists, steeling myself. "I hate it when people stare at us walking down the hallways."

I paused, meeting his eyes. He stood stiffly, nodding for me to continue. I sucked in a deep breath.

"I hate it when you fight with me about Chloe. She glares at me and says mean things and I shouldn't have to wait for her to 'come around'! I shouldn't have to accept her apology or listen to whatever she wanted to say to me."

He continued listening, nodding as I spoke.

My shoulders sagged slightly in relief. He wasn't defending himself or arguing with me.

"I didn't want you to go with Marcelina that day," I continued, frowning at the memory. "I hate that Chloe took your phone and you stayed there with them. I hate that you left me. I hate that you want to go to a school four hours away. And that Marcelina has your number and Chloe keeps comparing me to her and she's going to give you a tour of college and-and—

"I have no idea how to be a good girlfriend. I don't know what I'm supposed to say and do and I'm just—I'm so confused. I don't know how to be like Marcelina."

"Aspen," Isaac finally spoke. Within seconds, he was by my side. I didn't realise I was crying until he reached for my cheek, brushing a tear away. "I thought you were going to tell me I was a bad boyfriend. I thought you were going to break up with me."

"Break up with you?" I echoed, sputtering out a laugh through tears. "Me?"

"We need to talk," he said slowly. "That's what you texted me. When Marcelina . . . ended things . . . that's what she sent me. That's how she ended it."

"Oh." I blinked. It made sense now. The way he'd stood nervously in the corner, as if waiting for something horrible to happen. The way his eyes had glimmered in the light.

"I . . . Aspen, I had no idea you felt that way," he continued eventually. He released a tight breath. "You're the most amazing girlfriend. Don't doubt it for a second. I wouldn't replace you for anyone. Ever."

"Not even Marcelina?"

He scoffed, shaking his head. "The last thing I want is Marcelina. Aspen, she broke my heart, and not even in person. I never wanted to see her again."

"But I thought . . . I didn't say anything because I didn't want to seem controlling." I furrowed my brow, suddenly rethinking my actions. "I thought you still wanted to be friends with Marcelina. I didn't want to be clingy."

He sighed, running a hand over his brow.

"I'm sorry." His voice was suddenly quiet. "I'm bad at opening up. I should've told you how I felt. It's just . . . after Marcelina . . . you know, she was my first and only girlfriend. The only person I'd ever opened up to, and when she did that to me . . ."

"Isaac," I muttered, frowning.

"This is all new to me too. I dated Marcelina, but we had been friends for years before that," he continued. "We weren't healthy. Marcy hated when I called her at night. Now I realise it was because she was calling other guys. She hated when I did things

335

without her permission. She said it made her look bad." He paused, meeting my eye. "Honestly, I don't know what I'm doing either."

"So . . ." I trailed off, furrowing my brow in thought. "You didn't want to spend the party with Marcelina? You didn't want her to have your number or give you a college tour?"

"Honestly, she was making me really uncomfortable." He paused, chuckling lightly. He met my eyes and smiled shyly. "I just want to be with you."

My heart did a somersault.

"Really?"

"Really."

"Really, really?"

"Aspirin," he teased, raising a brow.

"Sorry." My face heated up and I smiled up at him cheekily. "Just making sure."

"Marcelina is history, Aspirin," he continued. His eyes flashed with sadness. "All I want is you. Even if that means I have to leave my friends behind. Even if that means I have to leave my college behind."

"No," I said quickly, shaking my head. "No, I don't want that. I just . . . I had to tell you how I felt. That's it."

"Okay," he said slowly. He paused, meeting my eyes and sent me a shy smile. "I really love you."

"Isaac." I sighed. I reached up, finally brushing his messy hair back. "We're so dumb."

He laughed, shaking his head. He tucked a strand of hair behind my ear, his palm flattening against my cheek and sending butterflies through my stomach.

"I thought . . ." I hesitated, chuckling awkwardly. "Maybe you weren't over her."

"Over her?" He laughed, shaking his head. "Aspirin, I want nothing to do with her."

"Oh, my God," I groaned, face palming. "I really am an idiot."

"I'm the idiot," he said, smiling widely. "I should've told you. I just thought it was obvious. I mean, she broke up with me through text. Who even does that?"

I hummed, frowning. "Yeah, but she's so pretty and social and—"

"Not you."

I met his eyes and he sent me a sad look. He smiled softly at me, his fingers lacing with mine, and gave my hand a gentle squeeze of encouragement.

"I'll be honest, Aspirin," he started, his voice quiet. "She broke up with me right before leaving for college, and that was it. A tiny part of me wanted closure, wanted to end it properly in person, but when I saw her at Chloe's party, I felt nothing. Actually, no. I felt like I didn't want to see her. All I could think about was you."

"What?" I furrowed my brow.

How could he possibly think of me when Marcelina was standing there, in her gorgeous, clear-skinned, social butterfly glory?

As if reading my mind, Isaac continued.

"Aspirin, I love it when you're awkward. I love your annoying punctuality at school. I love how my jacket looks on you. I love your smile and how you drool in your sleep. I don't care if you hate parties and my friends. I want you as you are."

"But Chloe said Marcelina had the same drink as me," I said, my voice quiet.

"Okay, so maybe I first noticed you because of the drink," he admitted, rubbing the back of his neck uncomfortably. "But everything after that—that was all you. You're not a stand-in for Marcelina. You're Aspirin."

He paused, brushing a strand of hair behind my ear and meeting my eyes.

"My Aspirin."

"I just—I keep overthinking it all and comparing myself to her all the time, Isaac. I don't—" My voice broke and I squeezed my eyes shut before they could water.

Isaac released a quiet breath and the mattress creaked as he shifted closer, taking my face into his hands. "Every time you compare yourself to her, tell me, and I'll remind you of every reason you're better."

I cautiously fluttered my eyelids open. He searched my eyes, his brows drawn together, and I frowned.

"She's prettier than me."

He laughed like the idea was absurd. "Definitely not true."

"She can hold a conversation."

"She doesn't have your cute ramblings about the weather and chemistry class."

"Her hair is perfectly straight."

"Your hair has cute curls that I love running my fingers through."

"She doesn't have anxiety."

He paused, shaking his head, his brow furrowed. It was like I'd slapped him. He sent me a deeply offended look, his jaw slack.

"Aspen," he said finally, his voice quiet. "Your anxiety isn't a flaw. It's part of you, and I love you as a whole. As you are."

My lips trembled. "Really?"

"Really."

A silence settled over us. I pursed my lips in thought. All this time, I was the only one comparing myself to Marcelina.

I had been worrying for nothing.

All I had to do was speak to him. All we had to do was speak to each other.

"I guess we're both just trying to figure out how to navigate a relationship," I muttered, thinking aloud.

Isaac nodded, intertwining our fingers together. "But we'll find our way together."

I smiled, liking the idea.

All this time, I had been struggling on my own—trying to be a good girlfriend, trying to be like Marcelina, doing what I thought Isaac would like, while he was doing all the same to me.

I squeezed his hand in mine. Now we were in this together.

"When you left," he said suddenly. "Yesterday, when you left. I thought about it and, God," he paused, releasing an embarrassed chuckle. "I feel like an idiot. Chloe was such a b*tch to you."

My eyes widened at his sudden language. "I told you!"

"You did, and I'm a huge idiot." He paused, smirking at me, his eyes twinkling with mischief. "I told her off again after you left."

I let out a loud giggle, quickly pressing my hand to my mouth to shut myself up.

"You did?" I asked, my voice a whisper.

He nodded. "I just wanted you to hear her out. I thought it'd make you feel better, knowing she had nothing against you personally."

"It sure feels personal."

"I know." He sighed. "I should've sided with you more. I think that's why I got so angry at Seb. That, and he interrupted before Chloe could tell you about . . ." he trailed off, frowning.

"Ugh, Sebastian," I groaned. I buried my face into his chest. "Don't remind me."

"You really never realised?" he asked, arching a brow. "He didn't exactly try to hide it. Didn't he ask you out to dinner?"

"I don't know!" I cried. "It's hard enough to believe you like me, much less someone else!"

"Oh, God." Isaac sighed, facepalming. "I'm a dickhead, aren't I? I thought you knew. I didn't think I outed him to you."

"Well, I guess I sort of suspected it," I said slowly, my face warming.

It was true. The way Sebastian teased me and turned pink around me. I'd be lying if I said I never thought about it. But I always brushed it off in the end. I mean, it was impossible. Two of the school's "It Boys" liking me?

Not likely.

At least, that's what I thought.

Riley would be screaming for joy in my position. Although, I guess after her experience with Arthur Andrews, she'd sworn off those types of boys.

"So," Isaac started, slowly. "What are you going to do?"

I blinked, pulling back to see him chew on his bottom lip nervously, his cheeks flushed in the dark.

"Are you jealous?" I teased, grinning.

"Shut up."

I laughed, shaking my head. "Well, I guess I'm going to have to talk to him."

"And?"

"Tell him that I dumped you for him, obviously."

"Aspirin," he whined.

"I'm joking!" I chuckled. "I'll tell him that I don't like him back. Not that way."

"Okay," Isaac said. He swallowed, leaning closer so that his breath fanned over my face. "Whatever you want."

"We really need to talk like this more," I teased.

"You're telling me everything on your mind from now on," he scolded, pointing a finger at me jokingly. "And you're going to have to put up with me telling you everything on mine."

"Good." I smiled, leaning forward to press a kiss against his mouth. His eyes instantly softened, turning darker. "In that case, I hate ginger."

"What!" Isaac exclaimed. "Ginger is so good!"

"It's really not," I replied, scrunching my nose.

"So, all those ginger teas I bought you?"

"Disgusting." I nodded. He pouted, and I quickly said, "But the thought was lovely. It helped my headaches!"

He laughed, shaking his head. "Aspirin, you're so . . . interesting."

"What's that supposed to mean?" I teased.

"That I love you," he said suddenly.

I paused, my heart dropping to my stomach. He grinned at my reaction, leaning forward to press a tender kiss against my lips. He leaned closer until I was leaning back against the bed, him on top.

My anxiety melted away, along with all my worries and stress. I felt like an idiot. All I had to do was speak to him. *Why was I so anxious about that?*

Isaac's hand drifted to my waist and he pressed me into the mattress.

We pulled away and I gasped for air as he moved lower, peppering my jaw and neck with kisses. I shivered under his touch, my fingers moving to grip at his messy hair.

"Isaac," I murmured, my heart pounding.

He moved back, sending me a wide grin. "Do you like that?"

"Shut up," I said, already knowing my face was bright red.

"I thought we were telling each other all of our thoughts from now on," he teased, wiggling his brows at me.

"I'm thinking you're an idiot."

"Ouch."

I rolled my eyes, but couldn't help the smile spreading on my lips. I grabbed his face, pulling him close for a deep, passionate kiss. His lips moved slowly against mine, his teeth nibbling at my bottom lip. His other hand drifted lower, fingers slowly dragging up my thigh.

My mind is racing with a million thoughts. I was only wearing my pyjamas—no bra. What if Isaac wanted to go further? What if I was bad?

His lips moved, pressing against the corner of my mouth, then my jaw, then my neck until he reached my collarbone. He sucked on my skin, his teeth brushing against it, his hair tickling my cheek.

His other hand reached up, fiddling with the edge of my shirt, his fingers sliding against my bare waist.

341

My heart leapt—this was happening too fast.

"Isaac," I said quickly, sitting up and almost knocking my head into his. He sat back, his eyes wide.

"Did I do something wrong?" he asked nervously. "I'm sorry."

"No," I said, shaking my head. I pressed my palms to my cheeks, trying to cool my burning face down. "I just—it's too fast. I'm sorry. I don't want to . . ."

I trailed off, too embarrassed to say the words. I was a senior in high school. We've already been dating for almost a month. What if he thought I was childish?

Instead, Isaac shook his head.

"Aspirin," he said carefully. "You don't have to be sorry. We'll take it slower. Whenever you're ready."

"Is that really okay?"

"Definitely," he said. He moved forward, wrapping an arm around my waist and pulling me onto his lap. He hugged me from behind, resting his chin on my shoulder and kissing my cheek gently.

"Whatever you want."

CHAPTER FORTY-FOUR
Blueberry Tea

I woke up to light streaming through my open window, a breeze brushing over my bare stomach. I groaned, tugging my shirt down and rubbing my eyes.

"Morning, sleeping beauty."

"Morning," I muttered back.

I blinked.

Suddenly, I shot up, my eyes widening to find Isaac sitting beside me in my bed.

"Isaac," I sputtered. The events of last night flooded back and I felt myself turning red in embarrassment. I swiped furiously at the corner of my mouth before running my fingers through my hair, attempting to flatten the bird's nest.

He grinned at me, quirking an amused brow. He held his sketchpad, a pencil gliding over the page. I narrowed my eyes at him.

"What are you doing?" I asked, leaning closer.

"Drawing," he said simply. He nodded towards my bedside table where a takeaway cup from Café de Fleur sat, still steaming. "I got you tea."

I raised my brows in surprise.

"Oh," I said, taking the cup.

Please don't be ginger, please don't be ginger.

I took a sip, sighing in relief at the taste.

"It's blueberry tea," he said, smiling proudly. "Now that I know you hate ginger."

"I should've told you weeks ago." I grinned, taking another heavenly sip of the tea.

He laughed, rolling his eyes. "You sure sleep heavily."

"What?" I blushed. "First of all, that's not true. I have insomnia." Though, I deliberately left out the part where I seemed to sleep a lot better around him.

"And second of all—" I narrowed my eyes, teasing him. "Were you watching me while I slept?"

"A little," he said, grinning widely without shame. "And you sleep like the dead. I woke up an hour ago and went home."

I blinked, scanning him. It was true. He was wearing a different outfit from yesterday, and that would explain where he got his sketchpad from.

"What? How did I not hear you leave? Why did you . . ." I asked, before my eyes widened. "Did my mom—"

"Yes," he chuckled. "But only because I rang the doorbell. She let me in."

"Did she know you were here last night?"

He shook his head. "Went out the window."

I released an audible breath before chuckling awkwardly. That would've been an uncomfortable conversation. "Wait, so why did you go?"

"Well, I have to look presentable for our date today."

My brows shot up. "Date?"

"Aren't you the one who agreed to going on a date with me?" He quirked a brow, his eyes mischievous. "Or should I ask one of my other girlfriends?"

"Shut up." I rolled my eyes, whacking his chest as he laughed.

"So, get ready, princess."

My face heated and I turned away, smiling. "Where are we going?"

344

"It's up to you," he said with a shrug. "But I was thinking I'd take you out to a café for breakfast." He paused, looking at my alarm clock. "Or lunch."

My eyes widened as I realised it was close to noon. I always slept the deepest when Isaac was beside me. I blushed, looking back to him. "At Café de Fleur?"

"Sure."

I smiled, liking the sound of that. "Alright, let me get ready."

He waved a hand, gesturing for me to go ahead as he turned back to his drawing. I stepped out of the bed, sipping on my tea and walking past Isaac towards my wardrobe.

As I passed, he reached out, grabbing my wrist and tugging me down to plant a kiss on my lips.

My eyes widened as we pulled apart. "What was that for?"

"Nothing in particular," he said, grinning cheekily.

I blushed, but leaned forward again, kissing him and catching him off guard. He blinked in surprise and I quickly pulled back.

"Payback," I teased.

His eyes darkened and he reached out, but I jumped out of his reach, speed walking to my wardrobe. He narrowed his eyes at me.

"Sorry," I said, pulling out a pair of leggings and cropped sweater. "I have a date to get ready for."

He groaned, flopping down on the bed. I laughed, striding past him towards the bathroom.

After a quick shower, I got ready and quickly took my usual pills before slowly making my way back to Isaac.

He was already waiting, sitting up against my bed head with an impressed grin as he watched me enter. My heart was pounding. I had gone on dates with Isaac before. We had gone to Café de Fleur for coffee and watched movies in bed—but this felt different.

We've been dating for about a month now, and it felt like a weight had been lifted off my shoulders after our talk last night. We were in this together for the long term now.

"Wow," he said, his voice low, a smirk on his lips. "You look gorgeous."

I blushed, crossing my arms. "Thanks."

"Let's go?" He offered me his hand and I took it, smiling. He laced out fingers together, burying our hands into his jacket pocket before leading the way out of my house.

It was a sunny day. The sky was blue, though the sun was weak, and combined with a chilly breeze, it was surprisingly cold. Perfect weather to walk together.

"Did you finish your drawing?" I asked as we made our way to the café.

He looked down at me, grinning. "Yeah, I'll show it to you when we're inside."

"Oh," I raised my brows. "Okay. What's it of?"

"It's a surprise."

I laughed, nudging him lightly. "It better not be of me sleeping."

"But it's basically tradition at this point," he teased back.

I bit back a grin. *We already had our own traditions and inside jokes.* Reading my mind, he squeezed my hand in his pocket, sending me a small smile.

Within minutes, we made it to Café de Fleur. Isaac pushed the door open with the sound of the bell. It was mostly empty, with only a few people in the corners of the café, typing on their laptops and sipping coffee.

Vivienne, as always, waited behind the counter.

"My favourite teenagers." Vivienne grinned as we approached.

"My favourite barista," Isaac shot back, sending her a charming smile.

346

"So," Vivienne began, wiggling her brows at him. "I heard you're dating now. Took you long enough. Aspen was always staring."

"Vivienne!" I exclaimed, feeling my face turn hot.

"And Isaac was always drawing you," she added.

Isaac only sent me a triumphant grin at that.

"It was only a matter of time before you both stopped being so damn oblivious," she said, shrugging. I felt myself blush further as Isaac sent me a wink. Vivienne laughed, leaning over the cash register. "So, what can I get you two lovebirds?"

I knew I was bright red at this point.

"Well, I'll get my usual with a Belgium waffle," Isaac started before turning to me, his eyes twinkling cheekily. "And you, lovebird?"

I rolled my eyes, whacking his shoulder. "I'll have a strawberry smoothie with a waffle too. Thanks, Viv."

"Alright, you two take a seat. I'll bring it over."

We smiled and thanked her before making our way to our usual corner. Isaac pulled my chair out for me before sitting in his own seat.

"So," I began, grinning mischievously. "Where's the drawing?"

"Ah, she remembered," he teased, his hand digging into his pocket to pull out a piece of paper. He straightened it out on the table, sliding it towards me.

It was me. That much was obvious. I sat at a table with a book open in front of me and a cup of steaming tea beside it. My hair was pulled into a messy bun as I focused entirely on the book. Opposite me was Isaac, hunched over in his chair as he drew into a sketchpad.

I furrowed my brow at the drawing. *When was this?*

"Well?" Isaac asked. He looked at me with wide, curious eyes. "What do you think?"

"It's incredible," I said honestly. His talent always blew me away. I paused, hesitating. "But when was this?"

"Excellent question, dear Aspirin." He grinned, pleased with himself, like he'd been waiting for me to ask that. "It hasn't happened yet."

"What?"

"This," he said, tapping on the paper. "Is a prediction of our future."

"Our future?" I echoed.

"It's us," he continued. "Studying at Penn State."

"I . . ." I trailed off; my brow wrinkled. "I don't . . ."

"I'm saying that I want to study at Penn State with you." He laughed.

My eyes widened in realisation as I shot up to meet his eyes. "Wait, really?"

"Yes, Aspirin," he chuckled, then gave a shrug. "I realised I don't want to study so far away from you."

"So, you're not going to Hunter's?"

"No," he said, shaking his head. He sent me a soft smile. "Penn State has art programs, and if I don't get in, I'll go somewhere else nearby. I want us to be together, Aspirin."

"But . . ." I trailed off, blinking in confusion. "Sebastian said that you wanted to go to Hunter's since you were a kid."

He shrugged, tapping on the table nonchalantly.

"I did. But it wasn't like my dream college or anything. It was just kind of the first one I discovered. And then, of course, Marcelina wanted to go there and she always talked about it." He paused, reaching across the table to play with my fingers. He sent me a small smile. "I thought about it and I realised there wasn't really anything Hunter had that I seriously cared about."

"Really?"

"I remember how it felt when Marcelina moved away for college, and I never want to go through that again." He paused to shrug. "Honestly, I'd rather just stay around you."

348

I felt my eyes water and I chewed on my bottom lip. "You mean it?"

"I mean it." He laughed, reaching over to wipe my eye. "Why are you crying?"

"I'm devastated, I'll have to see you every day now," I teased, laughing at my own dumb joke.

"Well, get used to it," he joked back. His hand drifted to cup my cheek and I leaned into his touch. "Because you're never going to get rid of me."

I laughed, rolling my eyes as he went back to his seat. My eyes drifted back to the drawing and I fidgeted with the edges of the paper, images of our future beginning to fill my mind.

Us at college together, us studying together, us in the library together . . .

Us together.

I could get used to that.

CHAPTER FORTY-FIVE
Iced Tea

I dreaded going back to school on Monday.

Even though everything between Isaac and I had been resolved over the weekend, I left Chloe on the wrong foot. And even worse, I had to face Sebastian.

I chewed nervously on my bottom lip as I made the dreaded trek up to school, my tea warm in my hands.

"Nervous?" Isaac asked from beside me.

I nodded, not meeting his eyes. There were so many thoughts going through my mind, imagining every possible scenario that could happen today. I was writing my own script in my mind.

It would start with me going up to Sebastian. I'd say hi, he'd say hi, then I'd say, how are you? He'd say good, and I'd say—

"I can go with you," Isaac interrupted my thoughts. I turned to face him, and he smiled gently at me. His hand moved to take mine, tangling my fingers through his. He squeezed my palm encouragingly. "If you're anxious. You know, for support."

"No." As much as I wanted it, I sighed, shaking my head. "I should tell him alone. It wouldn't seem right."

"Okay," Isaac said. He squeezed my hand again. "But if you need me, I'll be close by."

"Thanks." I grinned. I was already feeling less anxious. I decided to tease him, morphing my smile into a snide smirk. "Besides, you'd probably just get into a fight with him again."

"I wouldn't!" he argued. I arched a brow at him, and he sighed. "Okay, maybe I would, but only if he provoked me!"

"Isaac, you think everything is provoking you."

He sent me an exaggerated pout. "I'm just sensitive."

I laughed, shoving his shoulder with mine, but tightening my hand in his. I could see the school now, and just like that, the anxiety was back tenfold. Butterflies erupted in my stomach, so plentiful I thought I might be sick.

"You alright?" Isaac muttered. I swallowed nervously, nodding.

I had to face him. I had to get this over and done with.

Straightening my back, I marched forward, leading Isaac through the school gates and directly towards the grass oval. Every morning, Sebastian played soccer with his friends—something Riley used to love watching to start off her day, along with half the female population of the school.

It was easier than ever to ignore people's stares and whispers today. I only had one thing on my mind—Sebastian.

We walked through the halls, my heart racing, until we finally reached the edge of the oval. In the distance, I could see Sebastian juggling a soccer ball on his knees, laughing with some boys. Arthur Andrews was with him, trying to look good for the girls watching rather than actually playing.

I hesitated.

So many people. Suddenly, it wasn't just Sebastian I had to worry about, but his friends and the girls watching too.

"Hey," Isaac said suddenly. He released my hand, moving to grip my shoulders and force me to meet his eye, tearing my gaze from all the people on the field. He nodded, sending me a soft smile. "You got this."

I nodded with him, attempting to slow my breath and steel myself.

"I got this," I echoed. I paused, frowning. "But what if he hates me after this? What if he doesn't want to be friends?"

351

"If he doesn't want to be your friend, Aspirin," Isaac began, raising a brow. "Then he's an idiot."

I nodded; my stomach too twisted into knots to laugh. I've never rejected someone before. Especially not one of the hottest boys in school.

Lacey would probably murder me to be in my position. I glanced sideways to see her scraping her nails along Arthur Andrews's bicep.

Or maybe not. She sure moved on fast.

"Alright," I said suddenly. I clenched my fists, turning to look at Sebastian head-on. "I'm going in."

"You've got this, Aspirin," Isaac repeated. "I'll be here. If you need me, just send me a signal."

"A signal?"

"Yeah," he shrugged, grinning. "Like a bird call or something."

"You want me to caw at you?"

"Well, something like that," he said pointedly.

I laughed, feeling the pressure in my chest lighten. Rolling my eyes at him, I whacked his chest lightly, lacking the energy to do anything properly. "I'll give you a caw."

"Good," he said, smiling confidently.

Rolling my eyes again, I turned back to Sebastian, willing my legs to move. I inhaled a deep breath.

Any second now.

Slowly, I began walking towards the centre of the oval until I reached Sebastian and his friends. He didn't see me at first. His back was turned to me as he kicked the ball lazily back and forth.

I lifted my fingers up to touch them against my necklace, feeling the grooves of the golden leaf—here goes nothing.

"Sebastian," I said, my voice coming out in a strained squeak.

He stopped, catching the ball under a booted foot and glancing at me over his shoulder. His face turned pink, and he smiled shyly at me.

"Aspen," he said, surprised to see me. He kicked the ball to his friends, turning to face me properly. "What's up?"

"Well . . ." I hesitated.

He watched me carefully, his hands on his hips. His blond curls had been partially pulled back at the front and tied with a thin elastic band—an almost ponytail that threatened to flop over onto his face. He wiped at his forehead, nodding at me to continue speaking.

I could feel his friends's eyes on me, watching us curiously. A lump rose in my throat, and I forced it down. Before I could speak, Arthur Andrews stepped forward, grinning maliciously.

"Oh, it's the Harry Potter hoe."

I tensed, turning to meet his eyes. *Why was he suddenly speaking to me?* "That's not even creative."

"What are you even doing here?" he asked, smirking at me and glancing at his friends. "No one invited you."

I blinked, stepping back, feeling my anxiety rush back. Now, everyone's eyes were definitely on me. Over Arthur's shoulder, I could see Lacey smiling viciously and I instantly knew this was all her idea.

I guess she didn't move on as quickly as I had thought.

"Back off, Arthur," Sebastian cut in, rolling his eyes. "She's here with me."

"Dude, are you serious?" Arthur chuckled, shaking his head. "You're lowering your standards here."

"Chill, man," he replied, narrowing his eyes. "What does it matter?"

"We're playing soccer here, sweetheart," Arthur said, ignoring Sebastian now. He sent me a look that very clearly said I wasn't welcome here. "What do you want from us?"

Even Sebastian was watching me now, confused, probably asking himself the same question, waiting for me to answer.

I felt myself freeze under his stare, my heart beginning to race and my mouth turning dry. My cheekbones ached and I knew a flood of tears was building behind them.

Oh, great. Not now.

I sucked in a deep breath, trying to ignore the way everyone around me was staring at us. I clenched my hands into fists, my nails digging into skin.

"I—" I started, but my voice shook, and I stopped myself before it could crack into a sob.

"I-I-I—what?" Arthur mocked, narrowing his eyes.

"Arthur," Sebastian spat, spinning to face him. "Not cool. Stop it."

"Oh, come on," he replied, turning back to shoot me a smirk. "What happened to you, man?"

I felt incredibly hot all of a sudden, embarrassment flooding through me, only adding to my anxiety.

"Andrews!"

It was Isaac's voice. I turned just in time to see him sprinting towards us. He dashed forward; his fist clenched.

And then he punched Arthur, right in the jaw.

I gasped, staggering back. Arthur reeled backwards, not expecting the punch, but Isaac grabbed his collar before he could fall. People were whispering now, and I felt sick at all the attention.

Isaac pulled him close, his eyes dark and narrowed with an anger I had never seen on him before. Even Arthur whimpered under his glare.

"F*ck off," Isaac muttered, seething with anger, enunciating each word carefully.

He released his collar and shoved Arthur back. Now, he fell, landing on the grass. He sputtered, embarrassed, but Isaac ignored him, moving to meet me and Sebastian.

"You okay?" he asked, sending me a worried look.

354

I nodded, swallowing hard. I could still feel people's eyes on us.

"You guys should probably go somewhere more private," Isaac said quietly. He glanced over at Arthur who was currently being cradled in Lacey's arms as he stuttered out insults at us. He nodded towards the old school building. "Go."

Sebastian opened his mouth to ask questions, but Isaac set him with a hard look. He gave me a gentle pat on the back, and I found my legs, beginning to walk in a daze towards the old building.

What the hell just happened?

"Aspen?" Sebastian said. I blinked, looking up at him as I realised, we've been standing in silence for a while now. "You alright?"

"Yeah," I said, my voice wavering. Though I managed to fight my panic attack off thanks to Isaac, I still felt drained of energy. I ran a hand over my face and sent him a weary smile. "Yeah, sorry."

"So," he started slowly, sending me a curious look. "What did you want to talk about."

"Right." I cleared my throat, feeling my face begin to warm. "About the other day," I continued. He turned slightly redder and I knew I was blushing too. "When Isaac said you liked me. Was that true?"

He laughed awkwardly, rubbing the back of his neck with a hand and shuffling on his feet.

"About that," he began. He sighed, shaking his head momentarily before looking up to meet my eyes. Suddenly, he looked very serious. "It was true."

I froze. Everything seemed to turn silent as his words rang in my ears. So it was. He hadn't been lying. Now I felt even worse.

"Aspen," Sebastian continued, his voice low. "I like you. I think you're really funny and pretty and I-I know you're dating Isaac. I just . . . I guess I wanted you to hear it from me."

355

"Sebastian." I sighed, frowning. He smiled nervously at me, and my heart felt as if it might tear. "You're so sweet. You're insanely funny and kind, and you're always there for me, but . . ."

He pursed his lips, reading my thoughts. "I'm not Isaac."

I met his eyes, and I could see the sadness in his expression. His shoulders slumped, and he tried to run a hand casually over his face to hide his frown.

"I'm sorry," I said quickly, my heart panging with guilt. "It's just . . . with my anxiety . . . Isaac gets me, you know? He gets who I am as a whole. And I can't help it—I love him."

"It's okay," Sebastian said. He smiled at me, but it didn't reach his eyes. "I get it. We can't control who we like."

It felt more like he was referring to himself.

"Does this mean you don't want to be friends anymore?" he asked suddenly.

My eyes widened and I shook my head frantically. "No! No way! You can't get rid of me that easily."

He laughed, and finally he seemed to cheer up a little. "Good. I really thought I had ruined things for a minute."

"Are you kidding? We need to meet up during college!" I exclaimed, grinning. I narrowed my eyes at him. "You still need to teach me how to play soccer."

"Right," he raised a brow, playing along. "So, you can become the next Ronald."

"Exactly."

We both laughed, shaking our heads at our stupidity. I paused, raising a brow at him.

"Besides, you're going to owe me a free dinner when I beat you in the art assignment."

His eyes lit up and he sent me a wide grin, clearly surprised I remembered the bet we made all that time ago. "You wish."

"Better start saving up," I teased, humming. "I'm thinking . . . lobster. Some oysters. Maybe dessert too."

"Keep dreaming, because we all know who's the better artist."

"You're right," I said, grinning. "I think I will get dessert after all."

"I'll go easy on you." He shrugged. "You can buy me a steak and fries, and we'll call it even." He paused, glancing over my shoulder and rolling his eyes exaggeratedly. "I guess Isaac can come too."

I laughed and Sebastian released a heavy breath, smiling. There was a short pause and I sent Sebastian a soft grin. It was nice joking like this again—like we used to.

"Well, I'm glad that's over," he said, chuckling. "I spent the whole weekend freaking out."

"Oh God, me too," I agreed, my eyes widening.

His eyes drifted past my shoulder and he raised a brow.

"But if this whole Isaac thing doesn't work out," he said. He quickly met my eyes and sent me a smirk. He didn't have to finish his sentence. I laughed, rolling my eyes.

"I'll think about it."

"Good," Sebastian decided firmly. "And, will you sit with us at lunch again now?"

"Of course." I smiled. If I somehow resolved the whole Chloe thing.

The bell sounded then and I glanced over my shoulder to see Isaac standing at the edge of the oval, waiting, his brow furrowed with curiosity. He met my eyes and raised a brow. I laughed, turning back to Sebastian.

"I'd better go before Isaac starts cawing."

He shot me an amused look. "Cawing?"

"Don't ask," I said, smirking to myself. "See you at lunch?"

"Definitely."

With that, I turned, jogging back to Isaac. He smiled as I approached and easily slipped his arm around my shoulder, leading our way to class.

357

"So," he began slowly. "How'd it go?"

"Good," I said, smiling. I was glad that was settled. Even though things might be awkward with Sebastian for a while, we ended things on a good note.

We were still friends.

It felt like a weight had been lifted off my shoulders. I've been worried all weekend for nothing.

Isaac grinned, and I slipped my hand into his unconsciously. He squeezed my fingers, pulling me closer.

"I'm proud of you," he said quietly. I turned to him, my heart pounding at his words, and he sent me a wide smile. I felt my lips twitch, mirroring his grin.

I was proud of myself too. It felt like I had won against my anxiety. Sure, it wasn't a huge deal—all I had really done was spoken with Sebastian. But I've done it. I've done it and solved that one little problem that had been gnawing at me all weekend. And I felt great.

But I still had one more problem I needed to face, and I was sure it wouldn't go quite as well.

Chloe Pepper.

CHAPTER FORTY-SIX
Apple Tea

"If she doesn't apologise properly," Riley began, her voice low. "I will slaughter the b*tch."

I rolled my eyes at her, releasing a breath as I slammed my locker shut. It was lunchtime, which meant one thing—it was time to confront Chloe. I wrung my fingers together, trying to calm myself down.

I had no idea how she was going to react, but I couldn't even imagine her apologising to me. If anything, she was probably going to find another way to bring Marcelina into this. I sighed, a frown forming on my face. I really wasn't looking forward to this.

But a part of me wanted to do this—needed to do this. I've let Chloe push me around for so long. I needed to tie loose ends.

"There will be no slaughtering," I said, beginning to walk down the hall—as slowly as possible. "If she doesn't apologise, then that's it. There's nothing we can do to change who she is."

"I can think of a few things," she muttered.

"Will you be okay?" Isaac asked. He watched me carefully, his brow furrowed, and my heart did a little flip at his worried expression. I nodded, forcing a smile onto my face.

"Of course," I said, trying to convince myself more than him. "It's just Chloe. What's the worst that could happen?"

"She could beat the sh*t out of you," William suggested innocently.

"William!" Riley snapped, whacking his shoulder.

"What?" he asked, rubbing the spot she just hit. "Have you seen her? I'm pretty sure she beat up three freshmen last year for looking at her wrong."

"She did, actually," Isaac added.

"Guys!" Riley shouted, sending them both pointed looks. "She's literally tiny. Aspen could take her any day."

"I don't know." William frowned, narrowing his eyes and scanning me. "She's a bit scrawny."

"Thanks, Will."

"Look." Isaac sighed, wrapping an arm around my waist. "Don't stress. She won't do anything like that. I gave her a whole lecture on her attitude the other day. I'm sure she'll apologise properly this time."

"Yeah, you're always sure about her, aren't you?" I asked, raising a brow.

He blushed sheepishly and ran a hand through his hair, messing it up.

"Okay, so I was wrong every single other time," he said. I snorted in response. "But, this time I'm sure. Trust me, Aspen. She was just a bit nervous last time."

He paused, pulling me to a stop just before we reached the doors leading to the grass oval. Our eyes met. I raised a brow at his strangely serious expression.

"Trust me. She'll be serious."

I hesitated. His stare drilled into me and I wavered beneath his gaze. Sucking in a deep breath, I nodded.

"Okay," I said, and he visibly relaxed. "I'll listen to what she has to say. But this is the last time."

"Good." Isaac smiled. He reached for my hand, giving me a squeeze of encouragement. "You've got this. And if she ends up being rude—"

"We'll slaughter her," Riley jumped in.

"Yes," Isaac agreed solemnly.

"Well . . ." William trailed off. Riley sent him a sharp look and he turned red right up to his ears. "Yes. We'll slaughter her."

I laughed at my idiotic friends, rolling my eyes. At least I was feeling a little less nervous. The butterflies had subsided, and I straightened my back, willing myself to be confident.

We stepped through the hallway doors, reaching the oval field in seconds. William and Riley sent me goofy grins and thumbs-ups, wishing me luck before going to our usual lunch spot under the tree.

Isaac squeezed my hand again and I turned to meet his eyes. He sent me a small smile, nodding.

I inhaled a deep breath. Here goes nothing.

Sebastian was playing soccer today while Arthur Andrews was off with some girls. So, when we rounded the corner behind the old school building, Chloe was sitting alone, leaning against the wall.

Our shoes crunched on the gravel and she spun to look at us. Instantly, my heart began to race. I really hated confrontation. Her eyes narrowed into slits and a heavy tension fell over us.

The last time I saw her, I stormed off. She gave me a terrible apology after calling me all those horrible things. I swallowed nervously, beginning to imagine all the possible scenarios that could happen today.

I couldn't imagine this turning out well.

Isaac squeezed my hand again, bringing me back to reality, and I blinked.

"Take a deep breath," he whispered in my ear. I nodded, my mouth feeling dry, and sucked in a deep breath before releasing it through my nose.

"Chloe," I said, my voice surprisingly loud and confident and ringing in my ears like a foreign sound. Instantly, I shrunk into myself. "Um, can we talk?"

She paused, glancing at Isaac before nodding silently. I smiled nervously, releasing Isaac's hand and beginning to make my way towards her. I glanced back at him and he sent me an encouraging smile, his dimples drilling holes in his cheeks.

I nodded, trying to hype myself up—trying to believe in myself as much as Isaac did. I could do this.

"So?" Chloe asked as I reached her. She leaned against the wall, crossing her arms.

I hesitated at the gesture. "Well . . ."

She arched a brow at me, and I felt my face heat with embarrassment. This was a bad idea. I couldn't do this.

I craned my neck, looking back to Isaac with a frantic expression, and he met my eyes. He nodded slowly, his lips twitching in a small grin. I nodded, taking another deep breath.

It was about time I stood up for myself.

"Chloe," I began, meeting her eyes. "I think you owe me an apology."

We paused and she held my gaze, her eyes narrowed to scrutinise me. She didn't speak for a moment, so I continued.

"Honestly," I started, chuckling lightly to myself. "I can't believe I didn't say anything earlier, because it's so annoying how you constantly bring up Marcelina."

I shook my head as the words left my mouth and a long-awaited rant tumbled out before I could think.

"I might be weird, and awkward, and Isaac might be way out of my league in some ways—but guess what? I'm the one he chose, so you need to get over it. Marcelina broke his heart. They're done."

Chloe blinked, her eyes wide and jaw slack, the most emotion I've ever seen on her. She shook her head in the tense silence. Blood rushed in my ears; a mixture of adrenaline and embarrassment.

"I—" She hesitated, furrowing her brow. Her voice wavered and she cleared her throat, meeting my eyes. Her gaze faltered, like it was an enormous effort to maintain eye contact, and her face flushed.

"You're right. I'm sorry, Aspen."

I blinked. *Was I hallucinating?*

"What?"

"I'm sorry." She shrugged in a stiff way that she tried to play off as nonchalant. "You're right. What Isaac said to me on Friday made me realise—" She paused, laughing to herself in disbelief. "I haven't been the nicest."

"That's an understatement," I muttered, sending her a sharp look.

"Yeah, well." She sighed, shaking her head. "I just . . . I was scared of losing them. You know? Marcy's at college and Isaac's got you now. It was like . . . everyone was leaving me. Suddenly, I was home alone every day, and my parents—" She snorted. "Well, let's just say they're not very open-minded. And Isaac was always with you. I just . . ."

She frowned, her gaze turning to the floor and I shifted on my feet. I guess I could see her point. A part of me sympathised with her, but I shoved it away, trying to focus on the hurt she caused me.

"I didn't know," she continued, breaking the heavy pause.

I blinked. "What?"

"I didn't know that Marcy broke up with him. Over text, too." She released a laboured breath. "I thought . . . she always told me that it was mutual. That they both agreed to end things."

"Oh," I managed. I guessed that made sense. Why else would she have pushed Isaac onto Marcelina? But it didn't excuse her actions.

"I can't believe my sister would . . ." she trailed off, shaking her head. "Everything changed so fast."

My brows drew together at the familiar words; the words that kept me up at night. Everything changed so quickly for me as well, yet, I never stopped to consider what it was like for others.

Chloe's entire friend group was vanishing. Her sister wasn't who she thought she was. Isaac was slowly leaving her. I supposed

I could see where she was coming from—although she still didn't have to act the way she did.

I was torn.

"For the record," she continued, quietly. "It didn't work. Marcy preferred college boys. Isaac was too in love with you to even talk to her. When we hung out at my party, I took his phone thinking it'd force him to forget you, but he just sat in the corner the whole time pouting."

I furrowed my brow at her, confused, but before I could speak, she continued speaking.

"And then I confronted Marcy." She paused, her voice faltering. She shook her head in disbelief. "She confessed. She told me she dumped him over text. She told me she texted and flirted with other guys while dating him. I can't believe it. I just . . ."

She trailed off and I frowned, a tense silence settling over us. I reached for my necklace, brushing over the letters and leaf as I waited for her to continue.

"It's whatever," she said eventually. I realised her eyes were focused intently on the gravel floor and her face was an embarrassed pink. "Just—what I'm trying to say is—"

She sighed again, forcing herself to meet my eyes.

"I'm sorry," she said finally, her voice quiet. "I shouldn't have said those things. I just thought maybe if I could get Isaac to like Marcy again, we could all hang out like old times." She paused, her voice growing even quieter, red creeping up her neck. "And you'd be single."

My brows drew together as I tried to process her words. "What?"

"Oh, don't play dumb, Aspen," she shot back, suddenly cold. "You're not exactly ugly."

I was even more confused now. "Thanks? I guess?"

Her lips twitched and soon she was laughing, hunching over as bouts of giggles shook through her. I blinked—what was happening? *Was she laughing at me?*

364

"Aspen," she said finally through gasped breaths. "I'm saying you're cute."

I paused. And blinked. Then blinked again. She was saying I was cute? Slowly, I began to understand.

"Oh," I said dumbly. I felt my face heat and my eyes widened. "Oh!"

"Yeah, well." She shrugged, her voice harsh and distant. She avoided eye contact and despite her cold exterior, I noticed the blush spreading across her face and the wrinkle in her brow.

"But if you think I'm cute," I sputtered, my face getting warmer and warmer. "Why would you be so mean to me?"

"I don't know," she said quickly, and I realised that she too was blushing madly. "I'm not good at . . . I've never . . . Just—look, just forget it. Okay? I said sorry so can we stop now?"

I raised a brow at her. "Okay. Sure. Umm . . ."

"Cool."

"Great."

We paused and an awkward silence settled over us, both of us bright red and avoiding eye contact. I turned quickly to see Isaac practically bursting as he tried to hold in his laughter.

I realised at that second that Isaac knew.

He knew that Chloe liked me, and that she was mistaken about Marcelina. That was what she was trying to tell me before Sebastian interrupted. That was why he wanted me to speak to her so badly.

I thought it'd make you feel better.

He was right. Another weight had been lifted off my chest, and suddenly the air felt fresher and my lungs felt clearer. Knowing that Chloe didn't actually have anything against me; that her reasons for being mean were so much more complex than I had thought.

But right now, the awkwardness of standing in silence beside Chloe was stifling.

Especially with Isaac grinning with amusement at me.

I glared at him, trying to send him a message with my eyes—something that said, *'Please get over here and save me from this awkwardness'*. I narrowed my eyes further and he arched a brow at me, pausing.

Finally understanding the look I sent him, he collected himself and marched towards us, throwing an arm around my shoulders.

"Well, how did it go?" he asked, smirking down at Chloe. "Friends?"

I sent her a wary look. "Something like that, I guess."

I mean, I had forgiven her. But in reality, I probably wasn't going to be best buddies with her anytime soon. Chloe seemed to agree because she ignored Isaac's question, opting to glare at him instead, her cheeks still uncharacteristically pink.

"Great." He grinned boyishly. "You know, I'm really starting to regret my decision to introduce you to all my friends, Aspirin."

I rolled my eyes at him, nudging him. Hard.

"Alright, well—" he sent Chloe a teasing glare. "No stealing my girl, alright?"

"Shut up," she said dangerously, venom dripping from her tongue. Isaac nodded, his eyes widening and his grip tightening around my waist, like how a child clings to his mother.

"For once," I started, laughing and sending him a smug look, "I think I agree with Chloe."

CHAPTER FORTY-SEVEN
Hibiscus Tea

I lied bundled up in blankets and scarves on William's couch, Riley hugging me in her arms.

"William, fix your heater," I cried, shivering.

He glared at us from the opposite seat where he sat alone, trying to enjoy tonight's movie marathon: Disney Channel Original Movies.

The *Lizzie McGuire Movie* played on the screen, but I stopped paying attention ages ago. It was too cold.

"It'll kick in any minute now," William shot back, sending us an annoyed look, though I could see him tugging his hoodie tighter around himself. "Besides, it's not that cold."

"Stop lying to yourself," Riley said. She smirked at him, reaching an arm out. "You want to join us?"

Instantly, William's face turned bright red and he spun back to face the screen. "No. No. I'm not cold."

"What a dork," Riley mumbled to me, though she was grinning widely at the back of his head.

I was just about to give up and go sit in my own house where the central heating worked, when my phone buzzed.

"Oh sh*t, she's popular now," Riley teased.

I rolled my eyes, pulling my phone out. I knew it was Isaac before I even opened the message. Afterall, I was sitting with basically all my other friends—he was the only one not here.

From Isaac: Are you free?

I hesitated, glancing at William who was now openly shivering. I was about to leave anyway—and I was sure Riley and William would have zero arguments about being left alone together. They could probably think of a few ways to heat themselves up without me here.

To Isaac: Sure why?

A second passed before he replied.

From Isaac: You wanna come to mine?

I paused. I've never been to Isaac's house before. Whenever we hung out, we basically stuck to my house and Café de Fleur, occasionally going to William's place on movie nights. Isaac's house was a mystery.

I had barely wrapped my head around the fact that he was inviting me to his house, when my phone buzzed again.

From Isaac: My parents aren't home.

"Oooh, Aspen's getting a booty call."

I jumped at Riley's voice, whacking her shoulder and feeling my face warm. She chuckled as I angle my phone away from her eyes.

"Don't read my texts!" I scolded.

Her face lit up. "I was just guessing by the way you were blushing, but if you're agreeing . . ."

"No!" I sputtered, my eyes growing wide. "No, I'm not agreeing. It's just . . ."

"Isaac?" Riley filled in.

"Well . . . yes."

"And is he asking to come over?"

"He is actually asking me to come over."

"So," William cut in, grinning at Riley, "it's a booty call."

Before I could argue, my phone vibrated with another message.

"Aspen, you'd better answer. He's getting impatient," Riley teased.

I shot her a glare, ignoring their giggles as I read his message.

From Isaac: You don't have to if you don't want to!!!!

I smiled at that. I guess leaving him on read was making him worried.

To Isaac: Of course, I'll come

He replied immediately after, asking me where I was and offering to pick me up. I told him William's house and slid out from beneath the blanket, knowing he'd be here in a few minutes.

"Oh, she's actually going," William sputtered, his eyes wide.

"That's my girl." Riley winked.

"It's not a booty call," I said, rolling my eyes and grabbing my bag. "Not everything is about sex."

Riley and William exchanged a look that made me blush even further and made me glad I was getting out of here.

By the time I pulled my shoes on and said goodbye to Riley and William, Isaac had already pulled up to the house. I was out the door before he could get out of his car, racing for the passenger seat.

As soon as I opened the car door, hot air hit me and I sighed in relief, sliding into the seat and placing my hands over the air condition vents.

"Cold?" Isaac chuckled, arching a brow at me.

"William's house is a tiled mansion with no heater," I said, shivering.

"I see," he replied, smiling. "You look pretty."

I blushed, snapping my eyes up to meet his. He grinned at me, his eyes amused at my reaction.

"Thanks," I finally said. I paused, awkwardly glancing between him and the road. He started driving down the road while I watch the houses pass by. "So, um. How was your day?"

"Aspirin, you saw me at school."

"Right," I muttered. "So . . . how was your . . . evening?"

He laughed, shaking his head and smirking at me. "Better, now that you're here."

I rolled my eyes but couldn't help the grin that tugged at my lips and the blush creeping up my neck and tinting my ears.

We sat in silence for a moment and I stared out the window, listening to the quiet music playing through his speakers. It was nice. A silence that for once didn't feel awkward or strange. I wasn't overthinking anything anymore.

It reminded me of us, before Chloe and Marcelina—before we were 'boyfriend' and 'girlfriend' and I began overthinking every little thing even more than I already did.

Warmth enveloped my hand and I blinked, realising he had intertwined our fingers with his right hand, his other holding the wheel.

"You good?" he asked nonchalantly.

I nodded, smiling, warmth flowing through my body. "I'm great."

"Good," Isaac said, glancing at me to send me a gentle grin. "I know you've been stressed all week over college applications."

I groaned, leaning my head against the back of the car seat. "Don't remind me."

We've been working on our applications all week, putting the final touches on our personal essays and finishing off our forms. Penn State was notoriously difficult to get into. My grades were good, my GPA was high, but I haven't done much else. My anxiety held me back most of high school.

"I finally finished my portfolio," Isaac said quickly.

I spun to face him, my eyes widening. "Seriously?"

He nodded, his dimples drilling holes into his cheeks.

"Isaac!" I exclaimed. "That's great! We need to celebrate!"

"Why do you think I invited you over?" he teased. "I've been slaving over my desk for weeks. All I want to do is chill with my girl."

I felt a smile grow on my lips to replicate his own.

"Speaking of which," Isaac mumbled, the car slowing down. He turned into a driveway and pulled the car to a stop. "We're here."

I blinked, turning to face the house we had stopped in front of. It was surprisingly large. It was two stories tall with balconies and a perfectly trimmed lawn surrounded by hedges and a white picket fence.

Isaac rounded the car, pulling my door open and taking my hand as I stepped out.

"Isaac," I said slowly as we stepped up to his front door. He pushed it open to reveal a long-tiled hallway that lead into a huge living room. "You didn't tell me you were rich."

He laughed, his cheeks tinging pink. "I'm not."

"Right, that's something a rich person would say," I teased, walking in ahead of him. It was clear we were the only one's home. He switched the light on, and I looked around the room, my jaw slack.

It wasn't astonishing, but it was ten times better than my house. A part of me felt embarrassed that we had spent all this time hanging out in my tiny bedroom watching Netflix on my wheezing laptop when he lived in a place like this.

He had a massive flat screen TV on one wall with a fireplace beneath it and leather couches surrounding it. On one end

371

of the room, there was even a bar with shelves of alcohol lining the wall. It felt like something pulled out of a movie.

"My room's upstairs," Isaac said, snapping me out of my daze.

I blinked, following him wordlessly as he led me up a staircase and towards his bedroom. He pushed open the door, flicking the light on.

"I cleaned it up a bit," he said coyly, blushing and sending me a shrug. "Just don't look in the closet."

I laughed, slowly making my way around his room. It was a typical guy's room—at least, based on my extensive knowledge of William's room and Disney channel.

He had a double bed in the middle, a desk in front. He even had a bookshelf, which surprised me considering how much he skipped class.

On his desk, papers covered in sketches and scribbled out drawings were scattered. I was tempted to reach out and sift through them when a photo caught my eye.

It was framed and sat in the corner of the desk. Two faces smiled up at me, grinning widely.

It was me and Isaac.

I couldn't even remember taking it. It must've been right when we started dating, a simple selfie on one of our phones.

"Oh, that's my portfolio," Isaac muttered from over my shoulder. I blinked, glancing at him to find him staring down at the folder beside the framed photo. He must've thought I was looking at that instead. "You can look through if you like."

"Really?" I asked, narrowing my eyes.

He nodded, reaching around my waist and dragging it closer to the edge of the desk. He left it there, wrapping his arms around me and resting his chin on my shoulder.

"Go on," he said, his throat vibrating against my shoulder. I shuddered, suddenly feeling hot beneath his touch. "Look inside."

My fingers drifted over the portfolio and it reminded me of when I had flicked through his sketchpad a month ago after the Halloween Dance.

I opened it, instantly revealing the first artwork; a charcoal, life drawing. I flipped through the pages, passing half-completed progress sketches, a few portraits in pencil and oil, an acrylic stylised artwork and an oil painted portrait of a girl.

She lied on a bed, her brown hair strewn across white pillows and sheets. Below her, the bed blended into a blue sky, the mattress turning into clouds lined with gold, the bottom half of the page swirling in shades of blue and teal.

I narrowed my eyes at her face, realising it was me.

"That one's my favourite," he said, his arms tightening around my waist. His voice was quiet, his warm breath brushing my neck.

I leaned back, tilting my head up to meet his eyes. He smiled softly at me and I felt my face heat at how close we were.

"It's just a print," he said finally, shrugging and stepping back. "I submitted them all online and sent a few in, but—ugh. I don't know, I feel like it's not enough."

"Isaac," I said, turning away from the desk and stepping closer to him. He frowned, rubbing the back of his neck. I sighed, placing my hands on his arms and smiling up at him encouragingly. "They're amazing."

"You think?"

"If you don't get in, I'm going to sue," I said, completely serious.

He laughed, shaking his head. "I'm holding you to that."

"Good," I said, placing my hands on my hips. "Although, you might have to fund it."

He smirked at me, leaning closer until we were inches apart. "Is that all I am to you? A wallet?"

"No, you're more than that," I shot back. "Like, a chauffeur. You know?"

373

Chuckling, his hands moved to grab my waist, flipping me and pushing me to his bed.

"I'm glad I'm so useful to you," he joked, though his eyes were dark. He leaned close over me and I felt my heart thunder in my chest. "What else can I do for you?"

"Hmm," I hummed, pretending to think. "I guess I could go for some food." He arched a brow at me, smirking, and I laughed, reaching my hands up. "Just kiss me you idiot."

I didn't have to ask twice. He leaned down, capturing my lips in a hungry kiss. My fingers immediately found their way into his dark hair and he groaned against my mouth, tilting his head to deepen the kiss.

One of his hands cupped my face, his tongue entering my mouth and intertwining with my own. His other hand slipped down my waist, pausing at the hem of my shirt. His fingers slipped beneath the material, tapping against the skin of my hips, but not moving an inch higher.

My skin burned where he touched, and I knew my face was bright red. Adrenaline pumped through my body and I was about to move his hand higher when we heard the front door slam shut.

We both froze, Isaac jumping up to face the door, his eyes wide. I paused, my chest rising and falling as I tried to catch my breath. I leaned my elbows against his mattress.

Slowly, footsteps sped up the stairs.

"Isaac?" Came a woman's voice.

Isaac's brow furrowed. "Mom?"

Before we could react, his bedroom door was pushed open, revealing a brunette middle-aged woman in business attire. I bolted upright to a seated position, tugging my shirt down and smoothing my hair back.

Either way, I knew my red cheeks gave me away entirely.

The woman's eyes flickered to me and her lips twitched into an unamused frown before she turned back to face her son.

374

"I forgot my case," she said, holding up a stack of papers. She paused. "Who's this?"

"Uh, Mom," Isaac started, coughing awkwardly. He stood, gesturing vaguely towards me. "This is Aspirin—uh—Aspen Haste. She's my girlfriend."

"Oh," she said. She turned to me, scanning me with sharp eyes. "She's taller than Marcy."

The room fell silent and I blinked, trying to figure out if that was an insult or a compliment.

"She's the perfect height, Mom," Isaac said nervously, sending her a worried look.

She arched a brow, nodding thoughtfully. Finally, she sent me a barely-there smile. "Well, nice meeting you Aspirin. See you at dinner, Isaac."

And with that, she turned, closing the door and leaving. We were both stunned silent, listening as her footsteps trailed down the staircase before slamming the front door shut.

"Uh," I spoke first, breaking the awkward silence. "Did she just call me Aspirin?"

CHAPTER FORTY-EIGHT
Black Cherry Tea

Senioritis was really beginning to kick in.

With the majority of our college applications filled out and ready to send, classes began to blur together and feel really pointless—or at least, more pointless than usual.

I pulled Isaac's jacket tighter around me, making my way out of my chemistry lab towards my locker. I shoved my heavy chemistry textbooks into the locker, pulling out my art books and stuffing them into my bag with a sigh.

"Why the long face?"

I jumped, slamming the locker shut and turning to see Isaac smirking down at me.

"Chemistry," I said quickly.

He chuckled, throwing an arm around my shoulder and leading me down the hallway. "I told you to drop out and switch to my class."

"Right." I arched a brow at him. "And your class is?"

He paused, hesitating. "Like, English. Or something. We definitely write essays, so maybe . . . social studies?"

I laughed, knowing it was history, but deliberately keeping silent. It amazed me that he had all my classes memorised, but not his own.

"Yeah, I think I'll stick to chem," I teased.

"Your loss." He shrugged, shooting me a wink. I rolled my eyes, but leaned into his side, smiling to myself.

We made our way down the halls to the grassy oval where Sebastian juggled a soccer ball on his knees. He spotted us, his eyes widening and a bright smile pulling at his lips. I noticed as his eyes fell to Isaac's arm around me, his smile falling a fraction before he kicked the ball to Arthur Andrews and jogged to meet us halfway.

Isaac's arm tightened around me, but he lifted his other hand to wave at his friend.

"Hey guys," Sebastian greeted easily, his curls flopping all over his forehead. He shoved them back with a mischievous smile. "Did you get your art marks back?"

I narrowed my eyes, an equally mischievous smile appearing on my face. "Yes. Did you?"

"Yes, and I already know you're going to owe me a free dinner." He paused, noticing how Isaac quirked a brow at him. "Me and Isaac, I mean."

Isaac chuckled, slapping hands with Sebastian who shot him a wink.

"Isaac!" I gasped, whacking his chest.

He shrugged, "I can't say no to a free dinner, babe."

"On three, we say what we got," Sebastian cut in carefully. He narrowed his eyes at me. "One . . ."

"Two . . ."

"Three!"

"Eighty!" we shouted in sync.

I blinked, my brow furrowing. "Did you just say eighty?"

"Yes . . ." Sebastian trailed off. "Did you?"

"Oh, my God," I groaned, laughing. "We tied."

"No!" Sebastian whined. "I was looking forward to my free steak. That was the highest mark I've ever gotten! Isaac helped me shade it and everything!"

"Isaac!" I gasped again.

He sent me a shrug. "Bros before—" I shot him a sharp look and he cleared his throat, blushing. "I mean . . . he promised if he won, he'd share his winnings."

I arched a brow at him, and he pouted.

"Sorry love, but I swear I shaded yours better."

"What?" Sebastian sputtered. "You cheat!"

"He's my boyfriend." I shrugged, grinning at him. "What's his is mine, including his artistic talents. You, on the other hand—you're the cheat!"

"Well, now we tied," he said, pursing his lips. "So . . . Who gets the free food?"

Isaac's eyes glittered. "Well, I got a ninety-seven, so . . ."

"No," Sebastian and I said immediately.

Isaac pouted at me. "I'll share with you."

I grinned, facing Sebastian again. "Okay, Isaac wins."

"Hey!" Sebastian exclaimed.

I shrugged. "He got a ninety-seven."

"He wasn't part of the bet!"

"I vote that he becomes part of the bet."

"I do too," Isaac agreed.

"This isn't fair." Sebastian frowned.

"What do you mean? We all voted," I teased. He paused, as if in thought, before sighing.

"Fine," he conceded. "But the best you're getting is McDonald's."

Isaac whooped, high fiving me.

"But it's only because we're all going away to college soon," Sebastian added quickly. "And I'm going to miss you idiots."

"Aww, Seb," I said, pouting.

"You're getting all soft," Isaac teased. He paused, nodding towards the old school building. "You sitting with us today?"

"I'm not going to miss you that much," he shot back, glaring at Isaac. Isaac gasped, pretending to be offended. "I'm playing soccer today. See you later, though?"

We nodded and he flashed us a grin before jogging back to his friends. Isaac threw his arm over my shoulder again, leading me towards our lunch spot.

"He's still not over you," Isaac said. I craned my neck up to see him watching me carefully, his expression dark.

"What?" I sputtered, feeling my face heat at the sudden change in topic. "He definitely is. Are you kidding?"

"Alright, Aspirin," he laughed, shaking his head. He grinned at me, his green eyes glistening and dimples drilling deep into his cheeks. "Whatever you say."

We rounded the corner and I felt myself stiffen. Leaning against the wall, Chloe stood, a lit cigarette between her lips. Of course, she was here. She sat here every lunch. What was I expecting?

"Hey," Isaac said, filling the silence.

Chloe looked up at the sound of his voice. Her eyes fell on me and instantly her face tinged pink in an uncharacteristic blush. She sent us a curt nod, turning back to stare heatedly at the ground.

Isaac glanced at me, sensing my discomfort, but he pulled me closer and sent me an encouraging smile. He was right, I couldn't run away from Chloe forever.

"What's up?" I asked, my voice coming out in an awkward squeak. She glanced at me and I blushed in embarrassment, remembering how she'd called me cute. This was even more awkward than it used to be.

She turned to me, settling me with a glare that I was somewhat grateful for. At least I was used to her glares.

"Did you send your college applications off yet?" Isaac asked. I turned to him, sending him a small, grateful smile which he returned with a wink.

"Yep," Chloe drawled. She dropped her cigarette to the floor, stubbing it out with the heel of her boots. "Hunter College. Like Marcy."

It was mean, but a part of me felt relieved that Chloe would be four hours away at college with Marcelina.

"That's far," Isaac said eventually. He seemed a little sad, though, it was to be expected. We were all going to be graduating soon. We would all be off to college, far away from the people we grew up with.

We were becoming adults.

"Yeah." Chloe shrugged nonchalantly, though she wavered and sent him an unsure look. "You . . . you'll visit, right?"

Isaac opened his mouth to reply before hesitating. He met my eye and, reading his questioning expression, I smiled and stepped forward.

"We'll both visit." I say with a smile.

Chloe narrowed her eyes at me for a moment, searching my words for any edge. When she realised that I was being genuine, she turned away, her face turning a brighter red.

"Cool," she said curtly. She pushed off the wall, still refusing to meet my eye. "Well, see you."

"See you," Isaac replied, smiling at her. I mumbled a goodbye and she rushed past us, her boots crunching on the gravel.

The second she turned the corner, I released a breath of relief. Isaac then began to laugh.

"Well, I for one think that went pretty well," Isaac said, sending me a teasing grin.

"I think I preferred it when she hated me." I frowned. "I was already awkward enough."

"Hey, she never hated you," Isaac said pointedly. He quirked a brow at me, smirking. "More like the opposite, actually. She's just terrible at handling her emotions."

"You're telling me," I groaned, though I wasn't one to talk.

"Well," Isaac started, turning to me with a mischievous grin. He took a step closer. "Now that we're alone."

I caught his eye and a shiver ran down my spine. His cheeks dimpled as he smirked down at me, taking another step in my direction. I rolled my eyes, stepping back.

"We're at school, Isaac," I reprimanded.

He pouted. "No one can see us here."

I mean, he was right. I hesitated and he noticed. His smirk reappeared on his lips and he took another step to close the gap between us

"What if someone walks here?" I suggested, stepping back.

"No one will."

Another step.

"And if they do?"

Another step.

"I'll tell them to f*ck off," he said simply.

My back hit the wall.

"That's not very nice," I croaked, my throat suddenly very dry.

He smiled, leaning over me so that his arms trapped me against the wall—not that I had any plans to move. He hovered over my lips, his eyes dropping to my mouth, then back up.

"Well," he started slowly. He paused, dragging his tongue over his lips, wetting them. I swallowed nervously. "I can stop if you'd like."

He moved to take a step back, but I caught his mouth in a kiss before he could. He smiled into the kiss, completely expecting the reaction. Instantly, his hands moved from the wall to my face, cupping my cheeks and tangling in my hair.

My own arms wrapped around his neck, pulling him closer. He groaned, tilting his head and deepening the kiss further.

My mind was racing. We were in school, what the hell was I doing? I could get caught at any minute. But then, Isaac's teeth nibbled my bottom lip, and my mind fell blank.

Suddenly, his hands drifted down my body, sliding around my waist and tugging me closer. I moved in sync with him, pressing

381

my back against the wall and wrapping my legs around his waist. He lifted me easily and I felt the brick wall dig into my back.

"Aspen," he muttered against my lips.

The sound of my name on his voice sent another shiver down my spine. His hands dug into my waist, my shirt slightly riding up against the wall so that his fingers pressed against bare skin.

He pulled away briefly, meeting my eyes and sending me a teasing smirk. Our chests rose and fell in sync and his grip pushed roughly into my sides. I felt dizzy and hot, extremely conscious of everywhere we touched, but wanting more.

He noticed my distant look and narrowed his eyes, his smirk tugging higher.

"We're at school," he mocked, his voice imitating my own.

I rolled my eyes, though I knew my face was bright red. "Shut up."

"I don't know," he teased, pretending to hum in thought. "What if someone walks here?"

"I'll tell them to f*ck off," I shot back, the words tasting funny in my mouth.

Isaac gasped in exaggerated shock, his eyes widening. "Aspirin, did you just swear?"

"If you don't want to kiss me, then just say so," I said, sending him a pointed look.

He smirked, pleased with my reaction. "Well, in that case."

He leaned forward and caught my mouth in another kiss. I tangled my fingers in his hair, and the world melted away.

CHAPTER FORTY-NINE
New York Breakfast Tea

"You're getting married?"

The room fell silent.

I met my mother's eyes, and she sent me a bewildered look, her jaw slack. She shook her head in disbelief.

"But you're so young," she sputtered out.

My heart raced in my chest and I shifted uncomfortably. This announcement was turning out to be much more awkward than I had hoped.

"I know," my sister, Sabrina, said. She stood in the middle of the living room, her boyfriend's—no, fiancé's arm around her waist. He tugged her closer in a way of encouragement, and her back straightened a little at the gesture. "But we think it's a step in the right direction. We're already living together. I'm graduating in a few months, and I already work full-time."

"I promise to treat her with the utmost respect and love," Jason said solemnly. He met my mother's eyes, his gaze unmoving. "I love Sabrina, and I want to spend my life with her."

My mom ran a hand over her weary face. This was not the Christmas present she had been expecting.

Sabrina had arrived yesterday, flying in from UCLA where she attended college. She was my spitting image, with dark hair a few inches longer than mine. Freckles spotted her skin, the result of spending her weekends basking in the sun at Santa Monica.

She seemed older than when I last saw her. She lived far from home, so she could only really visit during special occasions and breaks. Her eyes had a hardy look in them that I haven't seen before, and the baby fat had melted away from her face, leaving sharp angles in their place.

You don't realise how quickly people change until you spend a long time away from them.

Jason, beside her, had been her boyfriend for a strong four years now. They had met on her first day at UCLA. He had deep, brown skin and a pointed face covered in stubble. His parents were from the south of India, and he was constantly introducing me to new foods whenever he visited.

"Well," my mom said finally after a tense pause. Her lips twitched up in a vague smile. "In that case, I can't wait."

Sabrina seemed to sag in relief, and a tumble of tears fell from her eyes. A mixture of relief and happiness and excitement all in one. Jason broke into a wide grin, leaning forward, to kiss my mom on the cheek before sending me a wink.

"Congratulations," I said, grinning. "Took you long enough."

"You're one to talk," Sabrina cut in, giving me that teasing smile all older sisters have. "When are you going to get a boyfriend?"

My mom sent me an amused look and I felt my face heat up.

"Right, about that," I started. Sabrina's eyes lit up in realisation and Jason began to laugh.

"No," Sabrina said in disbelief.

"Almost two months now," I said, shrugging as if it wasn't a big deal.

Sabrina squealed loudly in a way that was very Riley-reminiscent. She leapt forward, pulling me into a suffocating hug.

"My sister's all grown up!" she cried, the tears starting to flow again. "I've missed out on so much."

384

I rolled my eyes, shoving her away when the doorbell rang. The room fell silent. The pressure in my chest began to rise.

"Speaking of boyfriends," my mom teased, grinning.

"Is that him?" Sabrina gasped.

"Don't freak out," I groaned. She nodded tightly, fighting the smile that threatened to pull at her lips. Jason watched her, fully amused, his eyes swimming with love.

I wondered if Isaac looked at me like that.

I stood from my seat, stalking to the front door. My hand hovered over the doorknob and I tossed Sabrina a stern look over my shoulder before tugging it open.

Isaac stood with a shy smile dimpling his cheeks. He wore his usual leather jacket, though today he also had a beige sweater beneath, and a black beanie pulled over his head. He skipped his ripped jeans and sweatpants today, opting for a slightly nicer pair of black denim pants.

In his hand, he held a gift bag and my heart skipped a beat as I wondered if it was for me. My first Christmas with a boyfriend. I was excited, anxious, and scared all at once.

"Hey, Aspirin," he murmured.

Immediately, I heard Sabrina's voice in a not-so-subtle whisper behind me, "Did he just call her Aspirin?" Followed by my mom and Jason shushing her.

I felt uncomfortably warm.

Isaac's face tinged with pink and he lowered his voice to a whisper. "Is that your sister?"

I nodded and he turned even pinker. Immediately, he pulled his beanie off and patted his jacket down, adjusting the collar.

"Do I look okay?" he whispered coyly.

I fought a smirk that fought its way to the surface. I've never seen Isaac act so shy. I tiptoed to raise myself, running a hand through his hair to smooth it back. He relaxed slightly at the familiar gesture and before I could rethink it, I pressed a chaste kiss to his lips.

"You look perfect," I said quietly, still acutely aware of my family listening a few feet away.

His usual lopsided grin returned to his face at this. "Let's go, then."

I pulled the door wider and Isaac stepped in. My mom stood immediately, pulling Isaac into a hug.

"Merry Christmas, Isaac." She smiled.

"Merry Christmas," he replied, charm exuding from him. "Thank you for the invite. I brought you a gift."

She pulled away, blinking, and he reached into the gift bag, pulling out a box of chocolates.

"I didn't know what to get." He shrugged, colour returning to his face.

"It's lovely, thank you Isaac." My mom smiled. She took the box, leaving to put it into the kitchen.

"So," my sister started, taking this opportunity to speak to him. "You're Aspen's boyfriend?"

"And you're Aspirin's—" He cleared his throat. "Aspen's sister."

"Sabrina," she said bluntly, narrowing her eyes. He reached out a hand, but she didn't take it, instead scrutinizing him from head to toe. Jason chuckled, taking it instead.

"Jason," he said. "Sabrina's fiancé."

"Nice to meet you both," Isaac said, trying not to act flustered.

"Hmm," Sabrina hummed, still glaring at him. "So, Isaac. How long have you been dating?"

I sent her a questioning look. I already told her, what was she doing?"

"Two months next week," Isaac replied easily.

"Huh." Sabrina's lips twitched, but she quickly steadied them back into a deadpan. "And how did the two of you meet?"

I felt my face heat, remembering how I watched him in Café de Fleur for months before ever even speaking to him. Isaac shrugged.

"School," he said quickly. "We have art together."

"Ah, school. And how are your grades?"

He wavered now. "Decent."

Sabrina arched a brow at him. "And you're treating my baby sister well?"

"Brina," I groaned, rolling my eyes.

But Isaac's expression hardened, and he gave a sincere nod.

She hummed. "Okay. But I've got my eye on you."

"Brina." It was Jason who spoke this time, settling her with a stern look.

She sighed, giving Isaac a reassuring smile. "Hey, our dad isn't around anymore. I have to do enough grilling for the both of us."

"It's fine." Isaac shrugged it off. He sent her a charismatic smile. "How'd I do?"

"You passed," she said. Her grin morphed into something dangerous. "For now."

He laughed, but I noticed the edge in it. I stepped forward, taking his hand and tugging him away.

"If you're done, Brina," I started, cutting them off. "I'm taking my boyfriend back."

Before she could answer, I dragged Isaac to the furthest sofa, plopping down beside him. He leaned back, placing the gift bag between his feet. I glanced down, realising it was empty. Disappointment filled me, but I shoved it away.

I had gotten my hopes up and he didn't even get me a gift.

I swallowed, disappointed, suddenly feeling embarrassed for having so many expectations.

"That was interesting," Isaac said eventually.

I laughed, quirking a brow. "Interesting is an understatement. Sorry about her, she's just a bit protective."

He sent me a half-shrug. "It's fine, I get it. I'd probably do the same."

We both paused, glancing at Sabrina as she laughed loudly at something Jason said. She held her hand out, letting her engagement ring sparkle in the light. Jason grinned at the sight, sweeping her into his arms and pressing a kiss on her lips before she could push him away in embarrassment.

I turned away, feeling my face warm, only to realise Isaac was watching me now.

"They're cute," Isaac said. "When's the wedding?"

"In a few months," I replied wistfully. Sabrina wanted a spring wedding, and she had already begun planning it, texting me photos and sharing her Pinterest boards with me. It was almost impossible keeping it a secret from Mom for so long.

"Wow." Isaac whistled lowly. He paused for a moment, wringing his fingers together before meeting my eyes again. His ears were pink, and he looked down at me with usual mischievous smirk. "That'll be us one day."

The words took me by surprise.

I blinked. Then, laughter began to bubble out of my mouth. "Are you saying you want to marry me?"

His smirk grew wider and he arched a brow at me. "Would you say yes?"

He was joking, but I considered it for a moment.

We haven't been dating for long, but we've been through so much together. He helped me through panic attacks. He supported me whenever I tried to overcome my anxiety. Even my insomnia was getting better, now that I was drinking the teas Isaac had researched for me.

There'd been bumps along the way—Marcelina, Sebastian, Chloe and Lacey—but we managed to get past them all and learn from our mistakes.

I was sure there'd be a lot more to come, but right now, in this moment where Isaac is grinning at me in my living room, my mom preparing dinner in the kitchen, and my sister discussing her wedding with Jason—I didn't want anything else.

"I would," I said, the realisation hitting me as the words left my mouth.

Isaac's smirk fell, and his eyes softened. A blush crept up his neck and he released a long breath. My heart hammered in my chest.

"Good," he said slowly. He reached into his pocket, pulling out a small jewellery box. "Because . . ."

"Isaac," I started, my eyes wide.

"I'm joking."

"Isaac!" I exclaimed, whacking his arm as he doubled over in laughter.

"I'm sorry, I just couldn't let that opportunity pass."

"Honestly, I'm kind of relieved," I conceded, sending him an eye roll and a smile. "We've only been dating for two months."

"Which is why," he began. He flipped open the lid of the box, revealing a narrow silver bracelet, inlayed with white crystals on the front. "Merry Christmas, Aspirin."

I gasped, reaching forward to touch it delicately.

"Isaac!" I sputtered, looking up to meet his eyes. He sent me a proud smirk. "I thought you didn't get me anything!"

"Are you serious? I'm your boyfriend, Aspirin," he teased. He lifted it from its cushion, turning it over in his hands. "Read the inside."

I furrowed my brow, leaning forward to read the engraved words. There, on the inside of the cuff, it said 'Really, really.'

Instantly, I remembered the day we started dating—the Halloween Dance. I told him I liked him and the first word out of his mouth was 'Really?' And the next day, when he said he loved me.

Really, really.

I met Isaac's eyes again.

"Do you like it?" he asked coyly, his smile nervous. I laughed, nodding, and his eyes glittered. "Really?"

"Really, really," I teased. I leaned forward, kissing him quickly before any of my family could see us. He leaned into it, pouting when I pulled away.

"I have something for you too," I said quickly.

I stood, leading him out of the living room and to my bedroom where his present waited on my desk. It was a red and green hexagonal box, decorated very festively. On the top were the words 'Open Me.'

Isaac quirked a brow and I gestured to the box. "Go on."

Curiously, he stepped forward, gently pulling the lid off. As soon as he lifted it, the sides of the box fell open revealing photos I had stuck onto them. Words were scribbled beside each photo—short sentences describing when the photo had been taken and what I thought about them

Photos of me and Isaac at the Halloween Dance—his devil horns pushing his hair back, my Hufflepuff robes drowning me, photos of us at Café de Fleur, photos of me napping in the library as he snuck a selfie of us—before we had even started dating . . .

Beside that one, I scribbled on it, *"Don't watch me while I sleep!"*

In the centre, another slightly smaller box sat.

Isaac paused, taking his time to look at every single photo and read all the words, laughing occasionally. He then turned to me with soft eyes.

"Aspirin," he muttered, his voice raspy.

"Open the next one," I said, shooing him.

He did, pulling the lid off as more photos fell to fill the gaps between the other ones. Photos of us with Riley and William during our weekly movie nights that had quickly turned into double dates, photos of us in my room, binge watching Percy Jackson., photos of Isaac drawing as I posed for him . . .

A final box sat in the middle. Isaac looked at me and I nodded. He pulled the lid off, this time, revealing a small pile of art supplies.

I had spent weeks trying to figure it out, asking every artistic person I knew, including our art teacher. I bought him a new sketchpad to fill, new pencils and charcoals, Copic markers, and more.

He froze.

"Aspirin," he started slowly. "You didn't."

I shrugged. "I saved a lot of money after cutting coffee out of my diet."

"No," he said. He picked up the box, staring at it in disbelief. "You shouldn't have."

"Isaac," I said, stepping towards him. He immediately put the box down, his hands drifting to hold my waist. "You literally bought me a necklace and a bracelet. I can do this one thing for you. Besides," I paused, sending him a mischievous smirk, "you're going to need it for college, anyway."

He rolled his eyes but leaned in, nonetheless. "What did I do to deserve you?"

"Hmm, let me think," I started. "You creepily drew me for months before speaking to me, you stalked me to the library, you bribed me with coffee. Should I continue?"

Isaac answered by capturing my mouth in a slow kiss.

There was nothing fast about it. He took his time, cupping my face and moving gently against me. I sighed into his mouth, running my fingers through his hair.

He pulled away after a moment, his eyes reflecting the expression Jason had when he looked at Sabrina. My heart skipped a beat.

"I love you, Aspen," he said finally.

"Really?"

"Really, really."

I smiled, tracing my fingers through his hair and across his jaw. "I love you too."

And he kissed me again. This time, so quick I could barely breathe.

CHAPTER FIFTY
Bubble Tea

I sat on my bed in shorts and a t-shirt, the sun warming my skin. Spring had come quickly and chased the cold bite of winter away. And with spring, came anxiety.

College acceptance letters were been floating around all month, and I still haven't received a single one.

I pulled my knees up to my chin. YouTube blasted from my laptop as I tried desperately to ignore the one thing that had been stuck on my mind since I clicked "submit" months ago. I was just about to click onto a new video when a loud knock came from my window.

I didn't even have to look up to know it was Isaac.

"Aspirin!" he exclaimed as he crawled through the window. He bounded over to me in a flurry of limbs and smiles. "Aspirin!"

"Isaac?" I blinked. He reached me, pausing beside the bed, and I rolled onto my knees to smooth his hair back, tousled by the wind. I furrowed my brow at him. "Did you run here?"

He panted, nodding frantically, gasping for breath.

"What's wrong?" I asked, suddenly feeling anxious.

His cheeks dimpled as he grinned widely at me. He sucked in a deep breath before saying, "Penn State results are out."

My heart sank.

"No."

"Yes!"

"Holy crap!" I scrambled back onto my bed, closing my tab and opening up the admissions page where I would discover if I had been accepted or not. "Holy crap, holy crap, holy crap. Did you get in?"

"I haven't checked yet," he said, flashing his phone at me. He was on the page—he just had to log in.

"Oh, my God," I started, my chest pounding like crazy. "I'm so nervous."

"You? Nervous?" He snorted, reaching out to run a hand over my head in a comforting gesture. "You have, like, a 5.0 GPA."

"3.8." I pouted, leaning my head against his stomach as I continued navigating the Penn State website.

"Same sh*t." He shrugged, and I couldn't help but laugh a little. He watched as I opened the page, the words flashing up at me—LOG IN.

"You ready?" he asked gently.

"Never," I replied.

"Well—" He moved me over, the mattress dipping as he took a seat behind me so that I sat between his legs and leaned against his chest. "It's now or never."

"Can we do never?"

"That wasn't actually an option," he teased, gently.

I released an anxious breath. "I know, it's just . . ."

"Aspen," he said. I turned to face him, and he cradled my face in his hands, cold from the wind outside. "You have nothing to worry about."

"But what if I don't get in?" I pouted, my mind beginning to race. "What if . . .what if you get in and I don't? Or I get in and you don't? Or neither of us gets in? And then I never get accepted into college and no one will hire me. Then I can't get a job, or pay the bills, or feed the kids—"

"You want kids?" he interrupted, smirking.

My face warmed. "Well, at some point."

"Well then—" He leaned forward, taking me hand and placing it onto the mouse pad of my laptop. "It all starts here. Whatever happens, we'll figure it out. Together."

"Okay." I breathed, the pressure in my chest building as I hovered my cursor over the button.

"Ready?" Isaac asked.

I nodded, unable to speak.

"Three . . ." he began slowly, shifting to hold his phone in his hand. "Two . . ."

"One."

I clicked.

Dear Aspen Haste,

Congratulations! I am pleased to offer you . . .

The words blurred together as my eyes grew watery. All the breath from within me escaped and I felt the world around me slow.

"Aspirin?" Isaac's voice came. He pushed my hair back, his voice frantic. "What's wrong? Did you . . ."

"I got accepted," I said, my voice so quiet it sounded like a whisper. My eyes met his and the reality of the situation hit me. A wide grin broke out across my face. "I got in!"

"Really!" Isaac exclaimed.

I nodded, my voice rising. "I got in!"

"That's great!" He pulled me in for a tight hug, his arms squeezing me, and his face buried in my neck. His mouth moved against my skin as he spoke. "That's so great, Aspen."

My smile fell and I pulled away. "Wait, what about you?"

He pursed his lips, pulling his phone up to show me the page. My heart immediately sank at his reaction and I leaned forward to read his letter.

Dear Isaac Hensick,

Congratulations!

I blinked, reading the rest of the page before pulling back to meet his eyes. He sent me a wide, lopsided grin, mischief dancing in his green eyes.

"Isaac!" I scolded, whacking his chest.

He caught my hand, holding it over his heart. "We got in."

"We got in," I echoed quietly. Suddenly, I was grinning all over again. I grabbed his arms. "Isaac! We got in!"

He laughed, leaning forward to catch my lips with his in a slow kiss. He grinned against my mouth, his hands moving to cup my face.

"Oh, my God," I muttered as we pulled away. "What are we going to do? Where are we going to live?"

"On campus?" He shrugged. He moved forward to kiss me again, but I cut it short.

"Do you think we'll have classes together?"

"Maybe," he said. He kissed the corner of my mouth before moving to my jaw, peppering kisses down my neck.

I hummed absentmindedly. "We can go to the library to study together. You're going to have to actually try, you know. College is different from high school."

"Aspen," he murmured against my skin. "Let's talk later."

I reeled back to meet his dark eyes. He pushed a strand of hair behind my ear and I felt my skin light on fire at the soft brush of his fingers.

"Okay," I said finally. I grabbed the collar of his jacket, pulling him close to meet his lips in a frenzied kiss.

There was nothing slow about it this time. We kissed fast and hard—lips against lips, tongues wrapping each other. He flipped us, pushing my back into the mattress as he hovered over me, smirking.

"Can't wait to do this at college," he teased.

396

"If we have time," I chastised. "Between all the studying we'll be doing."

"Right," he said, rolling his eyes with a grin. "Between all of our studying."

*   *   *

Packing for college was tough.

I had so many things I wanted to bring, how was I supposed to choose?

"You're not bringing that, are you?" Riley asked, scrunching her nose at the t-shirt I held. It was a Sesame Street shirt—the one I accidentally wore to school all those months ago when Isaac had first lent me his jacket.

"It has sentimental value," I simply said, folding it and placing it into a box.

"It's ugly," Riley replied.

"Hey!"

"I'm just saying," she said, raising a brow and plucking a lacey red bra from the pile. "You should be packing things like this." She wiggled her brows at me, pulling out the matching lacey underwear. "Isaac won't be complaining."

"Riley!" William shouted, blushing in the corner of the room.

"She's right," Isaac said.

I jumped, turning to see him in the doorway.

"Isaac!" I exclaimed. I leapt across the room, ripping the lingerie from Riley's hands and hiding them behind my back. "When did you get here?"

"Just now," he said. His eyes glimmered, warming my face. "Packing?"

"Yeah, I wanted Riley's opinion before she leaves forever."

"I'll just be a few hours away!" Riley scolded.

"Two hours is forever in friendship time." I pouted.

397

"What's friendship time?" William asked innocently.

"It's not a real thing," Riley said softly, patting his head.

"It's the time friendship runs on. One hour in real time is five in friendship hours, so really, you'll be ten hours away." I blurted out at the same time, in a tone that betrays how fake that explanation was.

"Oh," William blinked, clearly not understanding that I was making all of this up. "Right."

"Well." Isaac smiled, wrapping an arm around my waist. "We only have a week left here, so do you mind if I steal Aspirin for a minute?"

"Sure." Riley shrugged, standing from my bed. "We weren't getting anywhere anyway. I'll see you tonight, Asp."

Riley and William smiled goodbye, leaving my room and exiting my house. Even though I knew we'd be seeing each other again in a few hours, a part of my heart went with them.

We were all growing up, moving out, going to college. Nothing would be the same again.

"So," I said, turning to Isaac, "what are you stealing me for?"

"Well, we have five days left here," he began slowly. "I thought we could go for a walk together. Like a last goodbye."

I nodded, liking the sound of that, although my heart ached at the idea of saying goodbye to the neighbourhood that I grew up in.

"Okay, let me grab a sweater. I'll meet you outside," I said.

Isaac nodded, glancing at the lingerie in my hands with an amused smirk before turning and leaving. I blushed, looking down at the bra. I bought it weeks ago on a whim, but I've never actually worn it.

Maybe Riley was on to something.

Shoving the bra and underwear into a box before I could change my mind, I grabbed my sweater and jogged out to meet Isaac.

He took my hand into his as we walked. We passed the houses that I used to walk by every day to and from school. We smiled at neighbours I grew up with.

I sighed, leaning into Isaac's side.

"I can't believe we're going to college."

"Things are changing." He nodded, squeezing my hand. "But some things will always be the same."

"Like?" I asked, raising a brow.

"Like us," he simply said. He paused, glancing past me. "And our spot."

I turned, realising we reached Café de Fleur.

Vivienne worked the counter, greeting customers and making coffee. Cakes lined the glass display, including the biscotti I usually ordered. Our table sat in our usual corner—empty, like it was waiting for us.

He was right, in a way.

Café de Fleur hadn't really changed since the day I'd first set my eyes on him. Sure, the paint had been refreshed, and the tables rearranged, the cup designs had been replaced, and the plastic straws were gone.

But it was still our café.

I thought of all the memories we shared in there. Secretly learning each other's orders—his, black coffee with three sugars. Mine, soy latte with no sugar.

I thought of watching him draw, absorbed in his own world. I thought of him giving me his jacket, and him ordering me a coffee. I thought of sneaking a peek at his drawings and seeing Marcelina smiling back at me, before he had shown me the ones that came after—the ones of me.

I turned, realising Isaac had been watching me with soft eyes.

"I love you, Aspen," he said suddenly.

I blinked, surprised at the sudden words. He sent me a small smile and I realised he must have been remembering the same things as me. I smiled back, squeezing his hand in mine.

"I love you too, Isaac," I said, grinning cheekily. "Really, really."

THE END

EPILOGUE
Isaac

Before

I slammed the bottle onto the bar, the clink of glass against granite echoing through the empty tiled house. My head spun—swimming with foggy thoughts and images of her at Reb . . . Rachel . . . Rose—what was her friend's name?

It didn't matter.

All I could think of was her in the kitchen, her back pressed against the counter as I kissed her.

Aspen.

Her dark hair through my fingers. My name from her voice, the way she whispered it like it was a prayer. The thrum of her heartbeat under my touch.

I took another gulp, letting the alcohol burn a path down my throat.

Aspen.

Her lips on mine. I kissed her; I asked to kiss her. Even though she came with a painful pressure in my chest. Even though she made my brain work overtime, trying to figure out how she saw me, trying to win her approval, I went ahead and kissed her, ruining everything.

And I loved it.

401

I loved how she tugged on my hair, so lightly. I loved how she tasted of popcorn. I loved how her body felt pressed against mine.

I was close to finishing the bottle now, alcohol turning my mind to static and my throat raw.

I ruined everything.

We were friends, almost. And I destroyed that for my own selfish desires—my own greediness. I wanted to kiss her, so I did.

She probably hates me now. And if she didn't, she would soon. That's what always happens.

A flash of black hair and a dimpled smile ripped through my memory and I tensed, letting the last scraps of alcohol wash down my throat. I was friends with Marcy. And then I had gotten selfish.

I wanted too much of her, and I got it for a while.

But then she was gone completely, and I was left with nothing but a broken heart.

I didn't want Aspen to go.

Aspen.

Aspirin.

My Aspirin.

I didn't want her to leave me too.

Friends. Being friends was enough. It was. Being able to make her laugh; buying her coffee;drawing her; talking to her; smiling with her; watching her blush from embarrassment.

It was enough until it wasn't anymore, and suddenly she was in my arms, pressed against my chest, her fingers in my hair— and I ruined everything.

Marcelina appeared in my memories, her face and Aspirin's overlapping each other, and I could feel my heart pounding in my ears.

And then, she came to school and avoided me. I tried to take it back. I told her to forget about it. But, our relationship didn't go back to the way it was before. The damage had already been done.

Being friends was enough, but I went and ruined that too.

She partnered with Sebastian. I've seen the way he looked at her. Even if he hadn't realised it yet, he liked her. Everyone did.

She was everything.

She was Aspirin.

And I f*cked it all up.

Aspen.

Aspen.

Aspen.

The bottle was empty now. My parents weren't home, leaving me with their entire bar unattended. Not that they'd care anyway.

Aspen.

Before I knew what I was doing, the cold air was already hitting my face. How long have I been walking? My feet were sore. I tripped too many times, stumbling over my own steps. The buzz was beginning to wear off, and I wished I took another bottle with me.

I was becoming too sober.

A house appeared in front of me and I blinked before narrowing my eyes.

Aspen's house.

Without thinking, I rounded it, making my way to what was clearly her bedroom. The light was still on, and it was well past midnight. I could even hear the hum of a YouTube video playing— probably those conspiracy videos she loved so much. The ones she watched when her insomnia kept her up.

I reached forward, tapping a knuckle against the window.

Aspirin.

Aspirin.

"Aspirin!"

I knocked again, and the muffled video fell silent. And then her footsteps approached. She shoved the curtains away and her face came into view—her tousled hair, her slack jaw, her wide eyes. My heart panged and I could hear blood rush in my ears.

Aspirin.

I smiled, leaning my forehead against the window. I wanted to hold her. I wanted to kiss her. My head was pounding, and my chest was aching. My painful thoughts were quickly returning with sobriety, and I knew I'd regret this in the morning.

But for now, a tight pressure swelled in my chest and I wanted her to smooth it out, take my thoughts away.

I wanted to kiss her until I couldn't breathe.

*   *   *

Now

My pencil glided across the page, shading the waves of her hair and the dip of her collarbones. She peered up at me from beneath her lashes and let out a huff, shooting me a glare.

"Isaac," Aspen said, sternly. "You're supposed to be drawing your assignment, not me."

"But you're so much prettier." I pouted.

Her glare remained steady, but I noticed the tug at the corner of her lips. I sighed, reaching across the library desk to tangle our fingers together. The library would close in thirty minutes, and it was almost the midsemester break, so it was deserted.

She let me take her hand into mine, dropping her pen to the side.

"Isaac." She sighed. "I need to study."

"You don't even have any exams until after the break."

"Yeah, but I want to do good. It's our first year," she said pointedly.

404

I raised a brow at her. "Exactly, it's our first year. So, relax. Let's mess around a little."

I wiggled my brows at her, and she sputtered a small laugh. I shot her a wink and she rolled her eyes, a frown beginning to pull at her lips.

"I'm anxious," she admitted.

I blinked. Her other hand fiddled with the paper she was scribbling notes on, and she chewed on her bottom lip; a bad habit she did when she was nervous or overthinking something.

I released her hand and she frowned, but I stood, rounding the table to sit beside her.

"Aspirin." I sighed, reaching forward and taking her into my arms. She relaxed into the hug, resting her head against my chest. I wrapped my arms around her, pulling her close, and I knew without looking that she shut her eyes to listen to my heartbeat.

I lifted a hand, stroking her hair back.

"You've been studying like crazy all semester," I started, my voice quiet. "You'll do amazing. What's the worst that could happen?"

"I could forget everything and fail," she said, her voice muffled against my chest.

I shrugged. "So, we'll just do another semester together."

She pulled away to meet my eyes and blinked. "But that's such a waste of time."

"So, you're saying the worst that can happen is that we waste a bit of time?" I asked, lifting a brow. She seemed to mull it over in her mind, her brows slightly scrunching together in the middle. I leaned forward to kiss it, smoothing the wrinkles out. "That hardly seems like something to stress about. You'll do amazing, Aspen."

She paused, nodding.

"Right," she said, her voice growing stronger. "You're right. I've been studying all semester. And we're still freshmen." She paused again, meeting my eyes. "We should go out."

"Aspirin, I'm already your boyfriend."

"You know what I mean." She rolled her eyes, shoving me. I laughed, tightening my arms around her to hold her still. She tilted her head up to look at me properly.

"Where should we go?" I asked.

She hummed, thinking. Her brows furrowed in thought and I felt tempted to press my lips to hers, even if she'd whack me on the shoulder for doing it so publicly. She was adorable when she made that face.

"What about—" She paused, her face tingeing pink. "My room?"

I smirked, feeling my heart begin to pound beneath her palms, flat on my chest.

"Miss Aspen Haste," I gasped, feigning shock. "Are you inviting me to—"

"Shut up!" she quickly cut me off, slapping a hand over my mouth. She was blushing like mad now, her eyes darting around the library as if her mother might be sitting right behind us.

I chuckled, pressing a chaste kiss on her palm to grab her attention again. "Let's go."

*   *   *

After

"Aspen Haste," I began, her name like velvet on my tongue. "My Aspirin. I have loved you since the day I saw you in this very café, with your hair messy in a bun and your backpack slung over your chest. You have always been by my side, from helping me pass my senior year of high school, to helping me pass my senior year of college.

"You make my life complete. Will you marry me?"

Aspen stared at me, her jaw slack.

"Aspirin?" I whispered. "This is the part you answer."

She blinked, and I watched her throat bob as she swallowed thickly. Her eyes watered and her hands trembled against the hem of her dress.

I took her to Café de Fleur for a date—to celebrate four years together. Vivienne managed to close the café, and, despite her adamant objections to payment, I hired her to serve us dinner.

We had the candles set up. I got her flowers. Riley told me what Aspen's dream ring was.

Everything was perfect—except for the fact that Aspen wasn't responding.

"What?" she sputtered eventually.

"Will you marry me?" I repeated.

She blinked.

"Really?"

"Really, really."

"Really, really, really?" her voice croaked, and I laughed, the ring still untouched in its box.

"Aspirin," I started, sending her a warm look. "Really, really, really, really."

"Oh, my God," she whispered, more to herself, before flinging herself into my arms.

I staggered backwards, her grip like steel around me. She squeezed me and I realised too late that she was crying into my chest.

"Yes!" she squealed, finally.

I released a heavy breath, all weight off my shoulders going with it.

She really scared me there.

"Yes, yes, yes!" she repeated. She pulled back, her eyes wide and watery. "I love you! I love you so much!"

"I love you too," I said, feeling my own eyes beginning to water. I moved to take the ring out of the box, but she ignored it, grabbing my face and pulling me forward in a fast kiss.

Her lips moved quickly against mine, tilting my face to angle it perfectly. My eyes widened, shocked at her sudden boldness, but I soon relaxed into the kiss. It turned slow and passionate, and I forced myself to pull away, knowing Vivienne was probably watching with my camera somewhere behind the counter.

I chuckled, finally taking the ring and placing it on her finger.

She smiled at the sight, the tears flowing freely now.

"Isaac," she managed through her sniffles. She clutched her ring like it would disappear at any second. "Isaac. I love you."

I smiled, taking her hand into mine. Her ring pressed against my finger and a pang shot through my heart—she is my fiancée. She is my future wife.

Standing in the café where it all began. A woman who had conquered every obstacle the universe threw at her. A woman who had struggled with insomnia and anxiety—who had come so close to giving up a million times.

My future wife, wearing the ring I bought her. Living in our house.

We had changed. We had grown. We made mistakes along the way, but we managed to work through it in the end. We managed to always be there for each other when it mattered. We patched each other up countless times.

This was the woman I loved. The woman I wanted to marry. Really, really.

"Aspirin," I said, finally. "I love you too."

This was the start of everything.

EPILOGUE
William

Before

I sat in my living room alone.

It was the night of the Halloween Dance. Riley and Aspen were both at school, dancing their nights away, so I had no one to binge watch *The Office* with tonight. The TV glowed in the dark and I rested my head against a pillow with a sigh.

It wasn't that I didn't want to go. In fact, I planned to go— I had gotten dressed and everything. I wasn't staying home because I wanted to. It was more to do with the fact that Riley was going with Arthur Andrews of all people, and I didn't want to spend my night watching them.

She was probably making out in the dark with him right now.

I shoved my face into the pillow, letting out another dramatic sigh.

Why couldn't I be like him? Look like him? He was tall. He had biceps the size of my head. All the girls in school practically fawned over him. Maybe I should start going to the gym with Mitch.

I snorted at the idea. I didn't even want to be in a ten-foot radius of him, much less pumping iron together.

The TV flickered, moving to the next episode when a knock sounded on the door.

I grumbled, standing from my seat. *How could my mother and Mitch—her dag of a boyfriend—have forgotten their keys on their date night?* I must have reminded them ten times.

Another knock echoed from the door and I rolled my eyes.

"I'm coming!" I shouted, deliberately slowing down. They could wait. This was their punishment for not listening to my advice.

I walked through the hallways until I reached the front door. My fingers wrapped around the brass handle and I ripped it open with a hard tug.

"Mom, I told you—"

I paused. It wasn't my mother.

Riley stood on my doorstep, her blonde hair tied back in a tight ponytail, topped with a neat blue and white ribbon. My eyes roamed over her body, donned in a short cheerleader costume. My eyes snapped back up to her face, already beginning to feel my cheeks heating up.

"Riley!" I stammered out stupidly. "What are you doing here?"

"I . . ." She paused, sighing. She turned away, shaking her head. "I don't know."

I blinked in confusion. Riley was never speechless. She was always rambling on, ranting about one thing or another. I loved listening to her talk. She was so passionate.

But tonight, her usual bright smile was missing from her face. Her fire was gone. Instead, her forehead creased with worry, her lips pulled in a tight frown. Her eyes stared unmoving from the ground.

"Are you okay?" I asked, finally, my voice quiet.

Her eyes snapped up to meet mine and I grew hotter.

"Yes," she said. She paused, turning away. "No. Maybe. I don't know."

"What's wrong? What happened with Aspen? And Arthur Andrews?" My voice grew low at the mention of Arthur's name. I swallowed nervously. I didn't want to hear about anything to do with Arthur, but if she needed to talk about it, I would listen.

I would always listen. No matter the topic. No matter how much it hurt each time she squealed over him, I would listen.

I was happy for Riley—all I've ever wanted was for my best friends to be happy—but it unsettled me that Arthur Andrews liked Riley so much, and that Riley liked him back. And out of all people—it had to be him? Arthur Andrews? The douche of the school?

He had a new girl every other week. I had to bite my lip from trash talking him in front of Riley. If she really liked him, I'd force myself to support her. To be a good friend.

"Aspen," she began, shaking her head. "I left her. I'm an idiot, I should go back."

She turned, her skirt flaring as she spun. On a whim, I reached out, gripping her arm. She whipped her head back to face me, her hair slicing through the air, and I froze.

"Don't," I began, my face warming. There was clearly something wrong. I didn't want her to leave. Not so soon. I cleared my throat, releasing her arm, my fingers burning at the touch of her skin. "I mean, Sebastian will look after her."

"Right," Riley said slowly, thinking. She nodded. "Right. I should leave them."

She was silent and I hesitated, pushing the door open further. "Do you want to come in?"

She raised her brows and sent me a small smile. "Can I?"

"Of course."

She stepped inside, brushing past me as I shut the door behind her. Suddenly I was hoping my mom and Mitch took their time together.

My heart raced and I could feel the panic beginning to settle in. I had hung out with Riley a million times over the years, but we rarely met up without Aspen. Especially not in my house. When it was empty.

Just the both of us.

I sucked in a deep breath, following behind her as we made our way to the living room. I flicked the light on, my eyes straining against the sudden brightness in the room. Riley spun, her eyes dropping to scan my body and I flushed.

"What are you wearing?" she said, arching a brow.

I looked down at myself and felt embarrassment flood through me.

I wore a striped blue and white shirt with a red sailor's tie around the neck. Slowly, I looked back up to meet Riley's eyes which were now twinkling with amusement.

"It was a costume," I said eventually, rubbing my neck awkwardly. "Steve from Stranger Things."

Her eyes widened and her jaw fell slack with realisation.

"I should have guessed!" she exclaimed, snapping her fingers. "I love Steve!"

She paused her smile falling. "Wait, why are you dressed as Steve from Stranger Things?"

I sighed. I felt like I had been caught red-handed. I tugged at the hem of my costume, my mouth turning dry as I worked up the courage to speak.

"The Halloween Dance is tonight," I started.

Riley nodded, her brows furrowed. "Yeah, but you said you weren't going. Unless—"

"I wanted to go," I cut in. My heart raced with adrenaline and I stepped forward. "I wanted to go. I bought this costume on a stupid whim because I wanted to go the dance tonight."

Riley paused, blinking. "So," she said slowly, "why didn't you?"

"Because, Riley, I wanted to go with you."

Her eyes grew wide. It felt like slow-motion, the words tumbling out of my mouth before I could stop them.

412

"What?" she muttered; her voice quiet.

I felt the air escape from my lungs.

"I mean," I began frantically, "with you and Aspen, obviously. I—"

"No," Riley interrupted. "That's not what you said. You didn't mention Aspen."

"Well, the Aspen was implied," I attempted to redirect her. I shook my head, quickly searching for something, some kind of change in topic. "Speaking of the dance, what happened? Why'd you leave?"

Immediately, her face grew dark. "I don't want to talk about it."

I frowned, my brows drawing together in confusion. "Was it . . ." I paused, hesitating. "Was it Arthur?"

"Ugh," she groaned. She wiped at her eyes frantically and a pressure grew in my chest. Was she crying? "I-I don't know. It just wasn't what I expected."

"Riley." I breathed, stepping closer and pulling her into my arms.

She fit perfectly, resting her head against my chest with a pout. I wrapped my arms around her, squeezing her tightly in my grasp. Instantly, she relaxed and released a haggard breath. I wondered if she could hear my heart pounding. At least she couldn't see me blushing.

"See," Riley said, her voice muffled as she spoke, "It' different with Arthur. When he hugs me—" She paused to swallow, and I frowned at the idea of Arthur Andrews with his arms around her. "When he hugs me, it's awkward. It's like—I don't know, hugging a stranger. You know? And every time he hugged me or got me a drink or spoke to me . . . I was comparing him to you."

My breath hitched in my throat and I tried not to tense beneath her touch. *What did that mean? As a friend?* She leaned back then, craning her neck up to meet my stare.

413

"William," she said, narrowing her eyes. "Did you . . . Did you want to go as a couple?"

I swallowed nervously. There was no going back now. I messed up and gave myself away. She'd hate me now. She would probably never want to speak to me again. I ruined our friendship.

Slowly, I nodded, my eyes trailing up to meet hers.

All at once, she reached forward, grabbing my face and pressing her lips to mine.

My eyes widened as I leaned down to catch her mouth. My hands flew up, tentatively holding her waist.

It was fast and crazy and completely unexpected. Our teeth knocked and I bit her lip, but slowly, my eyes drifted shut and everything felt right. Her fingers dug into my jaw, holding me as if I would disappear. My hands moved from hovering over her waist to snaking around her back as I pulled her to me.

What was happening?

We pulled apart, breathless and panting for air. Her eyes searched mine, wide and frantic, and I knew mine mirrored them.

"What—" I began, but she quickly interrupted.

"I hated it with Arthur," she said, the words escaping in a flurry. "I hated it with him. He was rude and annoying and I just— the whole time I was thinking, William wouldn't have said that. William would have laughed at that. William wouldn't have asked me to dress up as a stupid cheerleader."

"I really wouldn't have," I agreed.

"Right!" Riley shouted, waving her arms. She paused, settling down. "I just—I couldn't stop comparing him to you, and . . . I ended up here."

My heart pounded in my chest at her words and I found myself gently gripping her hand, playing with her fingertips. Her eyes moved, drifting from her hand in mine, to my eyes, then to my lips.

My heart swelled.

"Riley," I started, my voice croaking. "I've loved you for years."

She exhaled loudly and her hand tightened around mine.

"Really?"

"Yes. Since the day you crashed into my life and dragged me into our little friend group."

"I never—how could I not—" she cut herself off, meeting my eyes. "Kiss me again you idiot."

I smiled, pressing my mouth on hers in a slow, gentle kiss. I moved to pull away when she pulled me back.

"No, not yet," she said quietly, muttering against my lips. "We need to make up for all those years of missed kisses."

I grinned, my hand moving to tilt her chin and deepen the kiss. She sighed in my lips and I moved my fingers to tangle in her hair, ripping the hair tie out of her ponytail. She laughed, pulling away and tousling her hair out into long waves around her shoulders.

"For the record," she began, grinning. "I would have loved to dress as Robin with you."

I smiled, tightening my grip around her waist. "I know."

And I pulled her in for another kiss.

Do you like YA stories?
Here are samples of other stories
you might enjoy!

Tyler's Gem

Rua Hasan

PROLOGUE

I looked at my reflection with dull eyes while drops of water were dripping from my hair. The steam from the shower was fogging the mirror, but I could still see myself through it. I sometimes thought that maybe, just maybe, one day I would see a different person with happiness and confidence.

I looked in the mirror to see my flaws that I have grown to accept. The flaws everyone used against me, but why should I care?

Yes, I could be a better person. I could walk to school every day with so much confidence that would bring everyone to their knees.

But why haven't I done that yet? Why did I keep on staring at myself every morning as if it would make things better or make a difference for everyone to like me?

My chubby cheeks and fat belly were one of the reasons why nobody liked me. I was the chipmunk of the whole middle school. I would walk around while everyone called me names, emphasizing why I stood out so much.

It had been like this since elementary school. Probably because I was not much of an active person. I would usually stay home all day and watch TV. I didn't like most things except eating. I mean, who wouldn't? It helped ease the stress. My dad owned a pizza shop that was quite known in our little town of Strawberry Forest in California.

Yes, I knew it was a weird name. Our town was known for growing strawberries in the old days that covered our land like a forest.

I used to go to his pizza place every Friday just to have a bite of heaven, which was probably another reason why I became chubby.

I wrapped the towel tighter around my body as I let my short, straight hair fall down to my shoulders.

I really needed to let it grow.

Walking out of the bathroom, I then headed to my closet. I grabbed a pair of baggy jeans and my favorite sweatshirt that my mom bought me on my twelfth birthday. My fashion sense was another thing I needed to fix.

But should I really care about what everyone would think of how I dress?

I put the clothes on, let my wet hair fall down naturally, and climbed down the stairs to smell the scent of my mom's amazing pancakes. I inhaled it happily and skipped towards the kitchen to see my dad sitting down, reading a book while my mom works at the stove.

My dad was the first to notice me and gave me a smile as he put his book down. He then motioned me to come over.

"Good morning, pumpkin," my dad said, catching my mom's attention. She put the pancake she had on the pan into a plate and turned the stove off. She wiped her hands on the towel next to her and turned to look at me.

"Good morning, mom and dad," I said as I kissed each of them on the cheek. I then grabbed the chair next to my dad and sat down, licking my lips as I stared at the plate in front of me with hungry eyes.

"Is my little girl excited to finish school today?" my mom asked.

Who wouldn't be? School was a living hell because of the constant bullying from none other than Tyl—

No! I promised myself I would never bring up his name as long as I'm alive!

Okay, maybe I was exaggerating a bit. Could you blame me when everyone constantly picked on me just because of how I looked, especially if it was only because one person started it?

"Mom, I'm not a little girl anymore." I groaned playfully as I cut a little piece of my pancake and shoved it in my mouth. The delicious taste in my mouth made me want to moan.

My mom took a seat in front of me and smiled as she pinched my cheek.

"Oh, but you'll always be my little girl," she said, attracting my father's attention. He put his book down again and glared at my mom.

"Hey, that's my line," he said.

I rolled my eyes at them, knowing what they were about to start.

My mom leaned against the table as she put her fist under her chin and smiled teasingly.

"Well, I stole it. *Whatcha* going to do about it?" She teased.

"Why, you!" my dad said.

That was my cue to look away. I ate my breakfast quickly before it got cold. It was obvious that I preferred to watch the pancakes over my parents smooching.

I ignored my parents' little playful argument which would lead to a make out season right here in front of me because trust me, it would always make me want to gag. I finished my plate and placed it in the sink. I turned around and found my parents eating each other's faces.

Ew, couldn't they get a room?

"Mom." I whined.

"Dad!" I said a bit louder and heard a knock at the front door.

"I'll get it," I muttered and headed to the door. I looked through the peephole and smiled when I saw who it was. I opened it and jumped into my best friend's arms as I ruffled his hair and messed it up.

I pulled away and smiled seeing Matt's annoyed face. He was probably the only reason I wake up every morning to go to school. He was practically my rock who was always there for me when I needed a shoulder to cry on, and defended me from all the bullying.

It wasn't like he could stop it in general, but his presence would help me cope with it.

We met somewhere in elementary school and clicked instantly. Matt was like the big brother I never had, supporting me through both the ups and the downs.

"What?" I asked with a smirk. He glared at me and pointed at his hair.

"Really? It takes me forever to fix this." He whined as he tried to fix his hair. Sometimes, I thought he cared about his looks more than I cared about mine.

I grinned and shrugged my shoulders.

"Oh, don't be such a grouch! It's the last day of school, lighten up," I said, punching his shoulder. He gave me a small smile and nodded his head.

"Are you ready?" he asked.

"Yeah, just give me a second," I said and ran back into the kitchen. "Mom, dad, I'm leaving." They smiled and engulfed me a big hug and wished me good luck.

My parents knew that I was being picked on, but they didn't really know that I was being bullied every single day by Ty—

No! Not again.

As I was saying, I thought it was best that they didn't know for them not to worry. Besides, they have already reported it to the principal countless times, but nothing happened. It just wouldn't stop.

I went to the front door where Matt was waiting and closed it behind me. The chill of the morning hit my face as the breeze quickened. It was still early, about seven something, but classes wouldn't start until eight.

I was actually excited to finish this day without problems. Matt and I walked to the school which wasn't too far away and talked about summer. Time went by quickly and the next thing I knew, I was in front of the place I hated the most. I started walking down the hall with Matt at my side as I tried to ignore everyone including the snickers made by some girls hanging by their lockers. As long as I wouldn't bump into him today, I would be fine.

When the bell rang, I sprinted out of my seventh period class and down the hall to head to the school gates at the edge of the school's parking lot. I would usually head towards that direction to meet Matt and walk home together afterwards. Surprisingly, this day just went by simply. I mean, I got called with names a few times, but there was nothing new. I guess everyone was too busy to go home from school and begin their summer vacation, so I wasn't their priority today.

Matt and I usually took our lunch together, and as I went between my classes, I would hide in the mass of children who were bumping into each other to avoid being spotted by my enemy.

Luck was on my side for not seeing him today. I stepped out of the door at the end of the hallway, walked to the parking lot, and looked around for Matt but couldn't see him. I assumed that I was early so I waited under a tree that was planted on the side of the gate. After all, it wasn't the first time he was late.

Suddenly, my vision blurred as something cold hit my head. I squealed in surprise and wrapped my arms around me. When I opened my eyes, I heard laughter echoing through the air and found myself soaking wet.

I wiped the water blurring my vision and looked up in the branches to see two boys, holding empty buckets and laughing their butts off. I was embarrassed, and I felt tears run through my cheeks, but I held them back.

Why would they do this to me? All I wanted was to go home and forget about the worst seven hours of my life that I had to repeat five times a week. All I wanted was to have a normal life like everyone else.

I pushed those thoughts away and was about to shout at the boys when someone else called my name. Shivers ran down my spine as I feared what I was about to face.

Taking a deep breath, I looked upon the face that I hated the most—the one who made my life a living hell.

Tyler Grey was holding something in his hand which I thought a water balloon.

"Just a little reminder of me throughout your summer," he said with a smirk, and threw the balloon at me before I could even move.

Paint. It was paint.

The boys up in the tree climbed down and walked over to Tyler. They were barely able to contain themselves from laughing and gave him a pat on the back. It was then that I could no longer control the tears in my eyes from running down my cheeks. I saw Tyler's eyes glaring at me, and clenched my fists as I watched them walk away with taunting smiles as if they had just won the lottery.

I took a shaky breath as the tears blurred my vision. My day spiraled from ten all the way to a zero because of him. I was freaking wet and my favorite grey sweatshirt now turned pink. I fell to the ground as I sobbed with my knees on my chest and hid my head.

I heard Matt call out from a distance, but I didn't pay attention. My mind was clogged and overflowing with hateful thoughts toward Tyler Grey.

My eyes were blinded from any light that I could have seen. My ears were plugged with his words. He got what he wanted; I was never going to forget him this summer. His face would forever haunt my mind.

CHAPTER 1

I stepped out of the taxi and paid the driver his tip. My long, tan legs resembled like hotdogs that were being heated under the bright, shining sun. I pulled the sunglasses away from my eyes and rested them on my head, looking around the place I used to call home where I lived many years ago.

Once I was completely alone in the quiet, familiar streets, I made my way to the house, and could instantly tell that not much had changed. The grass was as green as ever, and the birds were flying from branch to branch. It was as if I had never left. Although, it did look like it needed some dusting and a few plants in the front yard. But other than that, everything was fine.

I had argued with myself countless times about whether to buy a new house or just come back to this place. My childhood wasn't quite the best, but I would always choose my heart's desire. It wanted to go back home—to the place where I was raised.

I decided to come back to this small town everyone called Strawberry Forest. Was going back to the same house that hold good yet disturbing memories a good idea? Would I enjoy my life here? Or would I just end up regretting my decision?

I walked to the front door and stared at it for what seemed to be hours but were only seconds. Was I ready to face the past? Coming back here after so many years could be a good thing. I may had been away for so long, but it wasn't enough to help me erase and forget the dreadful memories of what this house and town gave me. Nevertheless, I couldn't exactly stop now. I was here for a reason, and that was to stop running away. I had to face reality.

I looked around to see that the house next to us was a bit different than I remembered. Its paint was in a different color and had a different vibe radiating from it. The decorations were of a different taste than that of the previous owner.

New neighbors perhaps?

I finally gathered all the courage that I had and grabbed the keys in my pocket. I opened the door and it creaked as I opened it slowly. Dust flew in the air as the house had not been touched for years. I took a step into the house, and looked around to see memories of the past flood my mind.

The interior and furniture were untouched. I didn't want anything removed when I moved away. I didn't even let my grandma sell it, knowing that I would be back one day.

I closed the door and realized that I would need help in cleaning this place; I didn't think I could do it alone. I grabbed my phone from my bag to send my best friend a text message on my arrival, telling him that I would be expecting his presence in a couple of minutes. I rubbed my eyes to prevent the tears from falling. I was done running away and was going to start a new life now that I had returned. A life that would make my parents proud.

*   *   *

Three years ago

I walked up to the front door as I wiped the water off my face with the napkin Matt gave me. Matt had been furious throughout the entire walk. He was ranting about how people could be so cruel, especially on the last day of school. Well, we were talking about Tyler Grey so I wasn't surprised.

He also blamed himself for being late. In his mind, if he was there sooner then maybe he could have prevented it. I disagreed and told him that it was fine. My life had been like this for years so I was pretty used to it.

After saying our 'goodbyes' a couple of blocks away, I stood right outside the front door, too afraid to face my parents. What would they say if they saw me like this? They would definitely freak out.

What would I tell them?

I could just lie and say that it was a goodbye prank from a couple of friends. Or, that there was this activity in school where we fought with water balloons. But of course, that would be such a lame lie, and they would not believe me. They knew me too well, and would be suspicious of the pink paint that stained all over my sweatshirt.

I decided to just tell them the truth and get it over with.

I rang the doorbell, waiting for the door to open. Moments passed as I stared at the door and rang the doorbell again, assuming they may have just not heard the first attempt. I waited another minute or two until I figured out no one was going to open the door. I rolled my eyes and guessed that my parents were probably up in their room making out because this wasn't the first time they've been getting it on while I waited outside.

Sighing, I grabbed the pot that had a plant in it and dug for the emergency key to open the door. I walked in to see no one. I took the risk of going upstairs to my parents' room and was surprised to hear nothing and thought that maybe they have fallen asleep.

Pft, come on. Who sleeps at this time?

I knocked on the door and waited for an answer, but nothing happened. I knocked again but this time, I opened the door to stare at nothing. There was no one in the room. It was completely empty as if it haven't been touched since I had left for school.

I ran down stairs to the kitchen and saw that my mom haven't made dinner at all. Well, that was strange. My parents used to leave something for me to eat before going somewhere else. It wasn't that I was always hungry; I just found it strange.

I walked into the living room and grabbed the house phone. I dialed my mom's number, but no one answered. I dialed dad's number, but he didn't answer either.

I was just about to go upstairs to my room when the doorbell rang. I skipped toward the front door thinking it might be them. When I peeped *through the peephole, it wasn't my parents standing outside but two men wearing police uniforms.*

I opened the door and stared up at the strangers who were standing in front of me, both of whom gave me sympathetic looks for some unknown reason. I lifted an eyebrow in confusion.

"Can I help you officers?"

They both glanced at each other then looked at me.

"You must be Crystal Clare," one of them said.

I nodded my head slowly, wondering why and how they knew my name.

"Yes, that's me. Is there something wrong?" I asked nervously.

"Yes. Unfortunately, your parents were in an accident, and we need to take you to the police station for some information."

My eyes widened, and my heart started to beat so fast that I could feel it hitting my chest. I felt a lump form in my throat as his words sunk into my brain and my world started to spin.

"An accident?" I gasped softly.

I felt tears form in my eyes, and my palms began to sweat.

"Are they okay?" I asked.

I couldn't imagine living without my parents. They were one of the reasons I stayed positive in life. They were amazingly supportive and always gave me warm hugs when I needed them.

If something were to happen to them, then I would be in this life all on my own. I didn't have anyone else here in this small town to take care of me. My life would become way worse than it already was.

One of the policemen took off the cap he was wearing and looked down at me with tender eyes, shaking his head.

"I'm sorry for your loss," he said.

After hearing those words, I couldn't stop the tears from flowing. My parents were dead.

*　　　*　　　*

I snapped out of my thoughts when I heard the doorbell rang. I took the sunglasses off my head, placed them on the counter, walked over to the front door, and took my shoes off. I looked through the peephole and smiled.

I quickly yanked the door open only to face the sight of Matt holding a broom.

"Matt!"

I jumped into his arms, causing him to drop the broom as he wrapped his arms around my waist. He picked me up off the ground, and our laughter filled the air.

He put me down on my feet and smiled, showing me his straight white teeth. He then looked at me from head to toe and whistled as he gave me a wolf grin.

I laughed as I punched his shoulder playfully.

"Oh my god! It's been ages," I said, letting him in before closing the door behind me.

"Yeah, I know, right? How have you been?" he asked.

"I've been good. What about you?"

It's been a very long time since I've seen Matt. But ever since I've moved to my grandparents' house in New York four years ago, we have been keeping in touch by using *Facebook* and *FaceTime*. Later on, I bought my own phone, and we called each other every day.

"Better now that you're here," he answered, as we walked toward the living room.

"You look the same like I never left," I said.

He still looked and felt like the Matt I knew many years ago, except that he had grown much taller and broader with facial hair.

"You…well, you look—"

"Different?" I asked.

He shook his head and gave me a smile wrapping his arm around my shoulders.

"Beautifuler," he said.

"That's not even a word, idiot." I chuckled, punching his shoulder again.

"It is for me," he said.

I smiled at his compliment.

Now, don't get me wrong. It wasn't like in the past four years I've been trying to change myself and get skinnier so that everyone would like me. No, that's not what happened.

I got depressed when my parents died and lived in a place I'm not familiar with. I had to meet new people which I wasn't a big fan of, but I found a solution to deal with it.

No, it wasn't drugs or alcohol. It was exercise. I would go out for a run and feel free. I wouldn't stop until I was panting for air and soaked all my clothes with my own sweat.

Doing the same routine every day, running became a hobby and made me into how I looked today.

"I hope you're ready because this place needs some cleaning," I said, as I grabbed his broom and threw it at him.

"Some?" he asked, as he grabbed the broom. "You mean, a lot. This place hasn't been touched in ages."

I cleaned the kitchen while Matt got to work in the living room. My house didn't seem huge when I lived here with my parents. We had two bedrooms upstairs and a bathroom. But now that I was going to live here all alone, it seemed so big and lonely.

I thought about it a lot and came to a conclusion that I wouldn't be moving out anytime soon. This place was sentimental, and I couldn't just let it go. I was pretty sure this was what my parents would have wanted, and I booked the nearest flight ticket to return home, the minute I turned eighteen. I've been planning that ever since I've left.

I was never close to my grandparents. I appreciated them for taking me in though, but I knew that once I turn eighteen, I'd be on my own.

After an hour and a half later, Matt and I were done cleaning the first floor. I walked out of the bathroom after cleaning myself up and saw Matt in the kitchen drinking some water.

"Let's take a break and have something to eat. I'm pretty sure you're hungry," he said.

I watched as Matt took his phone out and ordered pizza. I took two cups and a bottle of *Pepsi* to the living room and placed them on the coffee table in front of the couch. I sat down and grabbed my phone out since the TV wasn't working, and it needed some fixing with the wires and stuff.

Matt walked into the room and sat next to me. We spent time talking about everything that happened in the past four years and how the people at school were sorry for me and my loss. I wasn't planning on holding grudges against anyone, but I could never forget what they have done to me.

I told him about New York and how awesome it was. But I guess I was just a Californian girl who could never trade California for any city. I was born here after all.

Twenty minutes later, a knock was heard on the door. Matt got up to open it while I sipped on the Pepsi I had in my hand. I wasn't such a big fan of soda and preferred juice more, but there wasn't any in the fridge at the moment. I needed to buy groceries.

Matt came back with a box of pizza in his hand. I licked my lips as my stomach grumbled in hunger. When the box was opened, we dug in and ate until we were full. We pretty much finished the box, but you can't blame us. It's been a long day.

We sat in silence, gathering our thoughts until Matt spoke.

"You ready for school on Monday?" he asked.

I sighed. I knew this topic was going to be brought up. Besides, I still had to go to school.

I wished I could delay the time of me having to go to school sooner.

"Yeah," I said, nodding my head. Let's just hope that some things have changed while I was gone.

If you enjoyed this sample, look for
Tyler's Gem
on Amazon.

CHAPTER ONE

The worst part about losing someone is losing them when you least expect it. It's not every day you have your parents break the news to you that your best friend has committed suicide. It's one of those days where I just have that gut feeling that something is bound to go wrong—and trust me, I've had more than one of those days—but never in my life could I have imagined something going this wrong.

The memory of hearing of my best friend's death is as fresh in my mind as ink on a sheet of paper. The days after hearing of her death are a blur of tears and locking myself in my room all day, convincing myself that this is all just some cruel joke. I soon learned this to be the first stage of grieving—denial. I'm not ready to move on, but I know I have to try because even if she isn't here to live her life with me, I know that she will want me to live mine for the both of us. Even if I'm still angry and confused about why hers ended.

*   *   *

I sit in my car and stare up at my high school. The lawn is littered with teens conversing about what they did over break, going on as if absolutely nothing has changed when it feels like my whole world has changed. Taking a deep breath, I grab my things before opening the car door and stepping out. Putting my head down, I try to walk briskly into the building without having to run into anyone.

"Alexa!" *Just my luck.*

"Paige, hi." I force some enthusiasm into my voice, but it just ends up falling flat. "I heard what happened, and the girls and I just wanted to say sorry for your loss. If you ever need anything, I will be happy to help," she says with what I can obviously tell is fake sincerity. I look at her and the rest of the girls sitting at a table a few feet away.

"Thanks for your concern, Paige," I say, forcing down any hint of anger. "But I'm fine." I abruptly turn around and walk away before she can get a chance to reply.

Walking through the crowded hallway, I glance at the place where my best friend's locker used to be. The place where I would meet with her every day to complain about how awful our mornings were as we headed to our first class together. The place I will no longer be going to every morning. I trudge through the halls with memories surging my mind as I try hard not to break down right here and now. It's hard enough waking up this morning and driving past her house on my way here, but this . . . this just adds salt to the wound. The shrill ringing of the bell breaks me out of my trance, and I hurry to my locker before heading off to my first class of the day.

I can't seem to focus as Ms. Anderson promptly starts the lesson. I can't stop hearing her voice at the back of my head or picturing her next to me, not paying attention to the lesson at all as she makes snarky comments about how awful Ms. Anderson's outfit choice is that day.

"Alexa? Ms. Parker, are you with us?" The sound of Ms. Anderson's saccharine voice interrupts any further thoughts, and I try to clear my head.

"Yes. Sorry," I say quickly. She gives me a sympathetic look before continuing with the lesson, a lump forming in my throat. Time seems to be moving agonizingly slow as my next few classes go by; it doesn't help that every few minutes, I am approached by people saying how sorry they are for my loss and how she was such an amazing person. Half of them don't even know her. It infuriates me that these people didn't give her a second thought when she was alive, but now that she's dead, she suddenly matters to them.

When lunch finally comes around, I sit at a table towards the back. I'm relieved to get a break and a chance to sort my thoughts. My break is short-lived as I'm joined by company.

"Hi, Alexa. How are you?" Alison greets timidly as she and Madison sit down with their lunch trays. Alison and Madison are twins and probably the sweetest girls you will ever meet, but right now, I just wish they will get up and leave. I'm tired of people coming up to me with their pity and condolences, which only reminds me more of my loss.

"I'm fine," I reply half-heartedly, not having it in me to ask them to leave. "What brings you guys here?"

"Can't we have lunch with our captain?" Madison says with that bright smile that can light up any room.

"We just want to check on you, and the team wants to know if you'll be at cheer practice today." *Right. There's practice.*

"Yeah, totally." I flash them a smile. I can't let them see my weakness, and if moving on means that I have to resume the role of the girl I was before that day, then so be it. As lunch progresses and they make no move to leave, I struggle to stay focused. Everything reminds me of her.

The table near the center of the room used to be our table. The table we would sit at every day and talk about boys while also discussing our future. She would always talk about how we would attend the same college and become roommates and then rent an apartment together in a different city after graduation. It all just keeps leading me back to the question of 'why?'. I can feel my eyes start to blur with tears, and I stand up suddenly. The twins look up at me with concern-filled eyes.

"I-I'm going to go. I just remembered I have to go to the library and check out a book for my next class," I say while grabbing my things.

"Oh okay. I guess we'll see you at practice?" Alison asks.

"I'll be there," I promise her.

I emerge from the cafeteria and make my way to the bathroom with my eyes locked on the ground so no one can see the tears ready to fall.

"Sorry," I say after accidentally bumping into someone, not even bothering to look at them as I start to sprint to the bathroom in my frantic state. After making sure it's empty, I slide against the wall and do the one thing I promised myself I wouldn't do today— I cry. The tears pour out like a waterfall, the confusion and anger and pain with them. I cry until my vision is blurry and my eyes are red. I cry until I know that I can't be in here any longer because someone is bound to walk in, and I'm not sure I can handle confrontation in this state. It's been a month since she's been gone, and instead of things getting easier with time, everything seems to be getting harder. I wish that I can just go back in time and stop any of this from happening.

It's taking me some time to compose myself. I missed the remainder of my classes for the day, and I can't even bring myself to care. I end up leaving cheer practice early at the suggestion of the team. I can't focus on the routine, and I was messing everything up. Pushing through the double doors of the gym, I let out a frustrated sigh as I lean against the wall and pinch the bridge of my nose. I eventually head to the school's parking lot, which is mostly empty with the exception of a few cars.

"Alexa?" I hear my name being called and I go rigid. *Why can't I be left alone?*

"Hey, Matt." I turn to look at him and his friends surrounding his truck with sweat and dirt running down their faces. Matt Carpenter is the quarterback of our school's football team. I don't really recall having any real interactions with him other than at football games.

"It's been awhile since I've seen you," he says.

"I have a lot going on at the moment." I unlock my car door, not caring to continue this conversation after the crap day I've had.

"Wait," he says as I'm about to make my escape. I look at him expectantly, feeling annoyed that I'm being delayed from leaving.

"I'm sorry but I need to go." I shut my car door and leave, not allowing myself to feel bad for how harsh that probably sounded. When I finally enter my house, I'm greeted by the smell of my mother's cooking.

Before, I would be rushing into the kitchen, anxious to get a bite of whatever was on the stove. Now, I barely have an appetite.

"How was school?" she inquires with a smile as I throw my keys down on to the table.

"It was okay." Sighing, I watch as she dumps some pasta into the pot of boiling water.

"You know you can talk to me, Alexa. What happened isn't something you can easily recover from," she starts with a soft gaze in her eyes as she looks at me. "I know you both were close but—" I clench my hands into fists at her words.

We weren't *just* close; she was all I had. She's the only person that understood me, and now, she's gone. No explanation, no warning, and no apology.

"Mom, I know you're trying to help me and I appreciate it; I really do, but I just need time and space. She's my best friend and I don't want to think about the fact that she's gone." She looks taken aback by my words but she nods anyway.

"Okay. Well, I'm here if you need anything. I just want you to know that you're not alone," she replies with a sad smile, and I give her a quick hug before heading upstairs to my room. I lock the door and collapse on to my bed as I stare up at the ceiling. I grab my journal from the nightstand and open it up to a clean page but I freeze as a picture falls out.

It's of her and I at a party. We were holding red solo cups—which were filled with ginger ale—and smiling like there was no tomorrow.

"I can't believe you did that!" I exclaim as we both stumble into my room, hunched over in fits of laughter. "The look on her face was priceless!"

"It was definitely an accident," Cam says with a smirk.

"I think Paige knows you spilling that drink on her wasn't an accident."

I shut the journal and hold it tightly to my chest. It isn't fair. It isn't fair that Cam is gone, and I'm expected to just move on. How can I when most of my happiest memories are with her? How can I when all I can think about is her day in and day out? The tears fall down my cheeks for what feels like the thousandth time today. I curl into a ball with the picture clenched against my chest. I don't know how long I stayed like that, but before I know it, I'm asleep.

If you enjoyed this sample, look for
Say You Won't Let Go
on Amazon.

SWEET REVENGE

FLORA MCCONNELL

ONE

"Move, fat ass!" A loud voice echoes as I am pushed face first into the grimy blue lockers. My fat cheeks slam against the cold blue surface and splay out like an ice cream dropped on the ground. I wince and let out a groan of pain.

Nothing out of the ordinary though, being bullied is an everyday occurrence for people like me. By that, I mean people who are overweight.

Fat.

I push myself away from the lockers and shrug my hoodie back onto my shoulders, turning around to see the retreating figure of my tormenter. A mop of blond hair turns around to look at me, a smile etched on his face. It's Lucas Keith, one of the most attractive boys on this earth whose mission is to make my world a living hell.

Sometimes, I convince myself that he must have some reasoning for tormenting me the way he does. But then realization sinks in. He's just a bad person.

Edging on 280 pounds, I am obese. So much for inheriting my mother's slim figure. The apple doesn't fall far from the tree? Seems like a web of lies to me.

Somehow, my brother is the most praised boy in school—athletic, clever and nice—who doesn't like him? I was unfortunately not blessed with such good genes.

Unlike your typical high school drama, the popular kids at this school don't mix well. My brother forms his own clique and everyone wants to be them or be with them. On the flip side of the coin is Lucas' posse who seem to think that beauty is the only way to a successful life.

I fall into neither clique. I fall into you're-a-loser-and-Lucas-Keith-hates-you-so-if-I'm-nice-to-you-he-will-hate-me group. It's a sad life.

Fortunately, I have one thing going for me—my brains.

When Lucas works at McDonald's and finally realizes what it's like to be fat, I'd be working as a scientist finding a cure for cancer or being the best friend of some royalty. That would serve him right. Ha!

But at the moment, he's at the top of the food chain and I'm right at the bottom. He's the predator and I'm the prey. Brilliant. If I just hold on one more year, I'll be out of this hell hole and into real life where people don't treat fat girls like animals, a life where your weight doesn't matter. A life where the size you are in doesn't dictate the magnitude of your success.

Thankfully, I only have one more day of hell until summer starts. After that, I am a senior, reigning above the squirmy, acne-covered freshmen. But who am I kidding? I will still be below the freshmen, especially in Lucas Keith's eyes.

The books I dropped lay scattered on the floor, looking up at me in misery. *Grow a pair of balls!* They scream at me. I woefully shake my head and tell them that once again, Lucas Keith has won this battle. I slowly pick up the books and realize that I'm late for my class. Cursing under my breath, I run as fast as my legs can take me towards the door.

Heads turn one by one as I make my entrance. Sniggers to the right. Whispers to my left. I block them out and head to the last seat available. I close my eyes and sigh, falling into my seat.

"Great. Now, I can't see the board," says a low voice behind me, followed by a couple of sniggers from his faithful posse. I turn around to see the smirking face of my bully. In an attempt to take the high road, I ignore his comment, unpack my stuff, scribble down the task Mrs. Fatimiah wrote for us on the board, and immediately start.

"Mrs. Fatto!" Lucas shouts out, using the nickname he created for our fattest teacher in the school.

"My name is Mrs. Fatimiah, Lucas. Do you have a question about the task?" She sighs, sitting on the edge of her desk. More sniggers come from the corner as the desk creaks. Her cheeks blush and I can't help but feel for her. She stands up again.

"I think something may be obstructing my view. I can't see the task." He whines. I ignore him once more. I won't let him get to me. "Oh wow! It's a person! Sorry Grace, I didn't know you were so big that you could cover the whole board."

"Lucas, we've spoken about this. Verbal abuse in the classroom gets reported to the principal," she says, trying to hold her ground. Lucas just laughs.

"I'm not scared of him. He is my uncle after all." Lucas points out, using the my-uncle-is-the-principal-so-if-you-lay-a-finger-on-me-I-will-get-you-fired card once again. Mrs. Fatimiah sighs at a loss.

"Lucas, if you really can't see, then move seats." She proposes. *Really, ma'am?* I want to ask her. *Is that really the only solution you can come up with?*

"There's no other seat in the classroom. Why don't I swap seats with you, Grace?" he asks. *Best not to get on his bad side.* I think to myself as I pull myself out of the chair. I gather up my stuff before exchanging seats wordlessly.

"Wow, this seat is warm. Also, bigger than the other one. What did you do, stretch it?" Lucas teases. I restrain from snapping back. *No, wood can't stretch you dumbass!* But again, I take the high road and ignore him for the hundredth time today.

Crack.

I suddenly hear from the small chair underneath me.

Before I know it, I'm lying sprawled on the ground, breaking the small wooden chair.

The realization hits me like a tidal wave. I broke the chair. Embarrassment overwhelms me and I feel my face heat up. Why couldn't I just last one more day? That's all it is, one day.

I'm a stranded whale on the shore—hopeless, huge, and unable to get up or get away from the public eye. My arms and legs flap around and I try to roll over. But I am hopeless. I am stuck.

Laughter roars around me, especially from a certain Lucas Keith. I thought I couldn't redden any more than I already have, but I feel another surge of heat hit my face.

I am completely and utterly stuck.

"Need a little help?" says a low voice. I look up to see Lucas hovering above me. I give him a puzzled expression. Why is he offering to help?

"Yes!" I exclaim. Lucas bends down before jerking straight back up, glory etched all over that arrogant face of his.

"I'm sorry Grace, there is no way I can lift you up. You are probably three times my weight." He laughs and his posse joins in. I should have known.

"Don't apologize," I hiss sarcastically. "I'm fine getting up by myself." I roll around some more before giving up.

"She looks like a beached whale!"

"She's so fat. You can barely see her face!"

Comments soar around me and Lucas looks much too pleased with himself. I close my eyes and before I know it, tears form around them. I can't help it as they quietly fall down. With one surge of power, I roll over and pull myself up.

"Being attractive and having every girl beg on their knees for your attention don't mean you can treat me like a piece of dirt. I happen to be the only girl in this school who hates your guts and I'm proud of it. You can make fun of my weight but at the end of the day, you'll be the one with the guilty conscience and I'll be the one who ends up with an actual life. So, screw you, Lucas!" I scream in his face before storming out of the room.

I'm done with this.

I wipe the tears off my face with the back of my hand and jog down the corridor, heading outside. The air is cool and I take a deep breath in to calm myself down.

I unfortunately see my brother, Will, coming through the doors with his friends. He instantly recognizes me and hurries over with a worried expression on his face.

"Grace! What happened?" he says, taking my fat face in his hands. I try to push him off me but his grip remains firm.

"Nothing!" I shout and push his muscly arms off me and carry on jogging into the car park. He is a lot fitter than me so he catches up in an instant.

"Was it Lucas again?" he asks. I shake my head. The last thing I want is for my brother to get involved. It'll only make Lucas realize his power over me.

"It's nothing. I feel ill so I'm going home," I mumble, finally reaching my car.

"Do you want me to drive you home?" he asks sincerely. I shake my head, before carefully climbing into the car.

"I'm fine. See you later Will," I tell him, before starting the engine and driving away. I allow a tear down my cheek as my surroundings rush past me. How can Lucas treat me that way? There are plenty of other overweight students at Jistie High. Why me?

I park my car in my driveway and look up at our beautiful family home. Thank goodness. Wandering into the warmth of the house, I place my jacket on the coat rack.

"Mom?" I call out, hoping she isn't home. Nobody answers and I settle myself down into the kitchen. I need some comfort food. Reaching to the cupboard I retrieve a full tube of Oreos. *Twist, lick, dunk.* I think to myself after pouring a cup of milk. Why does Lucas have to be so horrible? I may be fat but I can't help it. My eyes look down to the Oreos in my hand. *Yes, you can.*

No, I can't! I reply to the small voice in my head. I was born with more meat on my bones than most girls. Even if I stopped eating all together, I would be fat still.

No, you wouldn't. You were born with your mother's figure but you ruined it.

I hit the side of my head with the tube of Oreos. *Gah!* Stupid voices. I stick my hand down the tube and take another Oreo out.

I suddenly stop, my mouth watering and my hand hovering by my open lips.

Do you really need to?

Once you've eaten that, it'll go to your stomach and make you fatter than you already are.

Why would you do that to yourself?

You're already fat.

Instead of casting the voices in my head away, I let them win the battle and place the cookie back into the tube.

That's it. You've realized, haven't you? It's your fault Lucas bullies you. You don't have to be fat.

"No, I don't."

If you enjoyed this sample, look for
Sweet Revenge
on Amazon.

ACKNOWLEDGEMENTS

Thank you to everyone who supported me during this long journey!

Thank you to BLVNP for giving my fifteen-year old self a chance. She never would have imagined this book leaving the confines of her laptop.

Thank you to my family, to my parents and my sister Holly. Without you guys, I never would have pursued this dream.

Thank you to my wonderful friends Gabriella and Francesca, who always managed to distract me from the stress of uni with laughs and Zoom calls. Thanks especially to Angela Yarad for being one of my first readers and for always supporting me!

And thank you to my readers. Without you, I wouldn't be anywhere. Thank you for reading my words, and following Aspen along her journey. I love you all. Really, really.

AUTHOR'S NOTE

Thank you so much for reading *Caffeine*! I can't express how grateful I am for reading something that was once just a thought inside my head.

I'd love to hear your thoughts on the book. Please leave a review on Amazon or Goodreads because I just love reading your comments and getting to know you!

Can't wait to hear from you!

Livia Halteh

ABOUT THE AUTHOR

Livia Halteh grew up in Sydney, Australia, reading fantasy books and rollerblading with her sister. Her love for writing started at a young age, when she'd write stories about her and her friends in primary school. Today, she writes YA books in her free time, when she's not studying neuroscience or French at the University of New South Wales.

Printed in Great Britain
by Amazon

72958696R00261